Dear
ENEMY

Dear ENEMY

KRISTEN CALLIHAN

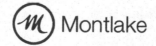

Text copyright © 2020 by Kristen Callihan

Published by Montlake, Seattle
www.apub.com

Amazon, the Amazon logo, and Montlake are trademarks of Amazon.com, Inc., or its affiliates.

ISBN-13: 9781542016773
ISBN-10: 1542016770

Cover design by Caroline Teagle Johnson

Printed in the United States of America

I could easily forgive *his* pride, if he had not mortified *mine*.

—Jane Austen, *Pride and Prejudice*

PROLOGUE

Ten Years Ago
> Shermont High School, Shermont, North Carolina
> Senior Class Yearbook Exit Interview
> **Question 1: If you had to do high school all over again, would you?**
> **Macon Saint:** You're kidding me, right? No.
> **Delilah Baker:** Is this a trick question? No.

> **Question 2: Who is most likely to succeed from our class?**
> **Delilah Baker:** Oh, come on. Everyone knows it will be Macon. Not that he'll deserve it.
> **Macon Saint:** Me. And Delilah Baker. She's like a barnacle; she'll cling until she gets where she wants to go.

> **Question 3: Who do you want with you if there's a hostile alien invasion?**
> **Macon Saint:** Delilah Baker. She'd yap so much and so loudly the aliens would turn around and flee.
> **Delilah Baker:** Macon Saint. I'd toss him in their path and gain valuable seconds running for my life.

Question 4: Most memorable moment in high school, and did you enjoy it?
Delilah Baker: Graduating. Yes.
Macon Saint: Prom. Not one f*cking bit.

Macon Saint was the devil. Anyone with a lick of sense knew it. Unfortunately, when it came to Macon, none of my fellow classmates at Shermont High School seemed to possess the sense that God gave them. No, they'd all fawn over him as though he were a god. I suspected that was the true mark of the devil: turning people into starry-eyed fools when they ought to know better.

Not that I could blame them. Beauty made fools of us all. Macon had the face of an angel—so beautiful you wondered if it truly had been sculpted by the hand of God, black hair so thick and glossy it might well have had a halo floating over it. Yes, he was that pretty. The only one who could rival him for sheer physical perfection was my sister, Samantha.

While the rest of us were entering adolescence with all the awkward grace of molting swans, struggling with our too-big puppy feet, crooked teeth, and certain features that grew faster than others, only Macon and Sam remained immune.

What a pair they were, pimple-free and perfectly proportioned. Luminous against the normal tarnish of puberty. It wasn't any surprise that they became an on-again, off-again couple throughout middle school and high school. The beautiful ones.

The ones destined to make my life hell.

Cold and often silent, Macon would usually stare at me as if he couldn't quite understand why we were sharing the same air. It was one thing we agreed on. Otherwise, we got along like snow and salt.

The first time I saw Macon, he was standing on the great expanse of lawn that stretched toward the manor house that had been in his mama's family for generations. Clutching a baseball, he watched me as I rode my bike up and down the road. He was skinny as a rail and two inches shorter than me. I'd felt oddly protective of him, believing the look in his eyes was one of vulnerability. I found out quickly how wrong I was.

"Hey," I said to him, after stopping in front of his house on my bike. "I moved into the house down the way. Maybe you'd like a friend?"

He turned his eyes on me then. Those dark, dark eyes, so brown they were almost black, surrounded by thick, long lashes. Eyes that girls would call pretty and sigh over throughout all our days of school. Cold and calculating eyes, if you asked me. Those eyes narrowed on my face. "You stupid or something?"

His words hit me like a slap. "What?"

He shrugged. "Guess so."

I didn't understand this boy. I'd been polite, just as my mother had taught me. "Why would you call me stupid?"

"I've lived here my whole life. You think I wouldn't notice if someone new moved in on my street? You think I *need* more friends?"

"I was just being sociable. My mistake."

"Sociable? You talk like an old lady."

Politeness was clearly for chumps. "You're a jerk."

He lifted his chin then, revealing a bruising scratch along the edge of his jaw. "And you're annoying."

Whatever I might have said was lost to time, because Sam decided to show up then. Younger than me by a mere ten months, Sam and I were what people sometimes snidely referred to as Irish twins. That had a darker component when they were referring to us, since it was clear to anyone with eyes that I bore little resemblance to the rest of my family.

Blonde hair french braided and gleaming, she smiled. Her missing front teeth made her look like an impish pixie. "Don't pay any mind to Delilah. Our grandma Belle calls her ornery."

Which is why I liked Grandma Maeve better.

Sam's cute nose wrinkled then. "I think that just means grumpy."

The nasty boy looked at me from under the inky fringe of his bangs when he answered her. "It does."

I blew a raspberry. "Stating an opinion contrary to others isn't being ornery; it's called having a working brain. Sorry you two don't know anything about that."

At that Sam laughed loud and exaggerated, slapping her hand on my shoulder, hard. "She's such a kidder." A warning squeeze came while she gave the boy her wide, sunny smile. "I'm Samantha Baker. What's your name?"

"Macon Saint."

"Macon? Rhymes with bacon. I love bacon. Oh, but Saint is so cool. You look kind of like an angel. Not a pretty girl one, of course. A boy angel. Can I call you Saint? You live in that big ol' house? It's so pretty. Do you like peanut butter cookies? My mama just made some."

Macon blinked under her verbal barrage, and I waited for him to lay into Sam the way he had to me, because even I was tempted after all of that spew. But he simply smiled in that lopsided way I'd soon come to know and hate. "Guess you're never ornery, huh?"

The way he said it, with that smarmy drawl, I knew he was imply-ing Sam was basically brainless and that he approved. But she didn't notice.

"Nope." She beamed. "I'm a happy girl."

I rolled my eyes, but neither of them cared, and that had been that. Macon had gone off with Sam to eat cookies, and I'd officially become the third, unwanted wheel. I'd lost my sometime ally of a sister and gained a pain-in-the-butt, sneering boy.

Two years later, Macon shot up several inches and became the most sighed-over boy in school. And Sam became his girlfriend. That pretty much sealed it. Macon Saint was at my house more than he wasn't. Hanging out on my couch, stealing the remote to watch sports, sitting at the dinner table, and pinging bits of food my way when my parents weren't looking. The worst was it hurt being around him. Around *them*. Because I always felt lesser.

I never dated or had a boyfriend. No one asked me out, and I didn't know how to ask anyone. I was simply Delilah, party of one. The friends I made were intimidated by Sam and Macon and did not want to hang out at my house for fear of running into them. Which meant I either went to other people's houses or braved facing the beautiful pair on my own.

By high school, Macon and I actively bickered whenever we got within sight of each other. But it wasn't until the end of our senior year that my dislike turned to acute loathing.

"Saint and I are going to the prom." Sam smiled triumphantly as she opened her locker door next to mine.

I barely glanced up from shoving my violin case into my locker. "Sammy, that is a 'well, duh' statement if I ever heard one. Prom is over a month away; why are you even telling me this now?"

Sam rolled her eyes. "Can you at least be happy for me?"

"For what? Dating the devil? Setting the bar so low the rest of your romantic life will seem like a victory?" I shrugged. "I suppose that is good planning."

"You're just jealous because you don't have a date."

"Date," I scoffed. "Your date is a life-size Ken doll, with less personality. I'd rather go to prom alone than have to deal with that."

"Liar. I bet if Matty Hayes asked, you'd go with him." Damn Sam for seeing what I didn't want her to. I had a *slight* crush on Matty. Sam grinned, reading me like a cheap tabloid. "He probably would if you put a little effort into your appearance."

5

"Like hell he would." The declaration was deep and confident and not mine.

My shoulders stiffened, and a cold wave of dread went over me at the sound of *his* distinctive voice rumbling from somewhere over my head.

Macon leaned a shoulder against the edge of my locker, his eyes mocking me from under the mop of his stupid Zac Efron–style hair. Every time I set eyes on Macon Saint, the reaction was visceral, a punch to the solar plexus. He was gorgeous, sure, but it was his eyes that did it. They burned as if he could strip the skin from my bones and rip right into the heart of me.

Mama always said I was fanciful with my words, but that was the truth of it: locking gazes with Macon was like forging into an angry storm. You'd come out of it weak, breathless, and a little bruised.

"I don't recall asking you to join the conversation," I said.

He snorted. "I don't need an invitation. And you don't stand a chance with Hayes. He likes his women stupid and thin. You know, like a *Barbie*."

The thin comment cut into me. Clearly, he'd heard my Ken-doll comment as well. I didn't give a shit and was about to say as much. But Macon wasn't done. Standing toe to toe with me in the hall before lunch, he let that dark, wild gaze of his slide over me as his nostrils flared in disapproval. "You look like a tater tot in that dress, Baker."

I hated that I suddenly regretted wearing my camel-colored sweater-dress with matching knee-high suede boots and the fact that I instantly felt like a potato under his assessing eye.

But I didn't let Macon Saint see that. "Some of us know that looks aren't everything, Con Man." Because that's what he was—a perfect con, tricking others into believing he should be adored. "Beauty fades, and the ugliness inside you will eventually show."

He straightened then, looming over me with a sneer. "I suppose you're one of those people who sees past beauty and only loves someone for their personality?"

I felt the setup. I just didn't know where it was going or how to avoid it. I thrust my chin high and played it cool. "I am."

He nodded as if confirming something only he knew before leaning in close. When most boys back then smelled of an overabundance of supermarket body spray, Macon smelled of cedar soap and do-me pheromones. "Tell me, Tater Tot, is it a beautiful soul you're looking at when you moon over the half-naked-firefighters calendar you have pinned in your room?"

All the blood rushed from my face, leaving painful prickles in its wake.

Macon's smile was cutting. "I don't believe for a second that you like Hayes for his riveting personality. You act all high and mighty while you're as susceptible to good looks as the rest of us. At least I have the guts to admit it."

The worst thing? He was right. I slammed my locker shut and fled.

"It's been fun, Tater Tot," he called after me in a laughing voice. *A loud-ass voice.* And when Macon Saint spoke, people listened.

By lunchtime, snickers of "Tater Tot" could be heard all over the cafeteria. The horror only grew when grilled cheese and taters were on the lunch menu the next day. Dozens of those tiny brown pellets of potato sailed my way. I'd been labeled by the king of Shermont High, and everyone acted accordingly.

Misery followed to the point I almost refused to go to prom. It was Sam who finally stepped in, hunting me down in my bedroom to have a talk.

"Don't let Saint get to you. He's only having fun." Her blue-gray eyes were guileless as she grabbed my hand. "And, really, it's cool that he gave you a nickname. No one else has one from him. Not even me."

She frowned at that as if the thought had just occurred to her, and she didn't much like it.

"Tater Tot is not a nickname," I snapped. "It's an insult, and you're welcome to have it."

"No." She shook her head, sending her straight hair over her shoulders in a glinting wave. "I'd need something else. Something to signify our deep connection."

I held in my gag admirably, but I found myself speaking without forethought. "How about 'Mirror'? Since you both love gazing into them."

As soon as I said it, I knew it was unkind. Sam's pretty face flushed bright pink, and she launched herself from the foot of my bed.

"Sam, I didn't mean—"

"No," she cut in sharply. "You said what you said. You know, Saint is right; you can't help but pick people apart."

"Excuse me while I choke on the irony," I shot back.

"Always with a joke," Sam said, even though I hadn't been joking. She crossed her arms over her chest. "Your problem is that you don't know how to play the game."

"The game? Life isn't a game."

"Bullshit. It always has been and always will be. Smile whether you want to or not; compliment the people in position to help you or have your back." She counted her points off on her fingers. "When everyone assumes you're the sweetest, most helpful, or honest person in their world, they'll let you get away with anything."

"This is what you think I should be?" I cut in. "A fake schemer?"

Sam shrugged then. "Fake or not, it's how the most successful people get ahead. They plot, forge alliances, and they execute their plans."

"If that's success, then I want no part of it. I'd rather fail and have a conscience."

Sam huffed out a breath. "Be a bitch if you want, but I know you're just scared to go to prom. Alone." She flounced out then.

That decided it; I went with Mama to buy a dress. Because I wasn't going to be called a coward. I chose a classic floor-length sheath dress with little cap sleeves in kelly-green satin. I felt ridiculous and overexposed, but Mama swore I was beautiful.

I went alone. Logically, I knew I wasn't the only person without a date; that didn't stop the flutter of nerves when I walked down the main corridor to the hotel ballroom where our prom was being held.

Then I saw him.

Macon stood just beyond his group of friends, his expression bored as Sam held center court. I didn't know what alerted him to my presence, but he turned his head just as I walked into view. Our eyes locked, and I found my steps slowing.

Dressed in a tux that fit him to perfection, he looked . . . frankly, like he didn't belong there. He belonged with the beautiful people, partying on a yacht or walking down a Parisian runway, perhaps. I didn't know why I hadn't realized it before: he didn't fit in our town any more than I did. The difference was, when it came to Macon, no one cared that he was an outsider—they were simply happy to have him around.

I didn't remember moving, but we ended up face to face, his dark eyes sliding over me, a frown pulling at his mouth. "You came."

Okay . . . "Was I not supposed to?"

His frown turned into an outright scowl, his gaze roving as if he was unnerved by my appearance. "I didn't think you would."

I shrugged, all too aware of my fancy dress, the makeup I wore, my hair styled in loose curls; I didn't feel like me, but I felt pretty. "Sorry to disappoint."

When he finally answered, his voice was low, almost a mutter. "I'm not disappointed."

We both paused, equally shocked and confused. He might not have been disappointed, but he didn't seem pleased. And neither was I; I didn't trust Macon Saint. As if by silent agreement, we both turned and walked in the opposite direction.

Insides jittery and my heart beating too fast, I went to the ballroom. Most of the senior class was either dancing or milling around in small groups. A long buffet had been set up along the side of the room, and the line for food had already started.

I didn't pay it much mind since I was too unsettled to eat, but a ripple started running through the room, an undercurrent of startled laughter. As if feeding on itself, the noise grew, turning less shocked and more malicious.

The source was the buffet table, and when I looked that way, I found dozens of eyes staring back at me. Heat bloomed on my cheeks, and I glanced around. *Everyone* was looking at me.

Panic clawed at my throat as I found myself slowly walking toward the table. The laughter bubbled up, whispers of "Tater" flowing over the air. And then I knew: the food.

Tater tots in every damn tray. All of it, tater tots.

I couldn't breathe. Hurt locked my muscles. Someone whistled; a few tater tots were lobbed, one of them hitting my skirt, leaving a streak of grease along the satin. I flinched, my skin burning. Across the way, my sister gaped at me, her eyes wide and panicked, but she didn't move to stand by me. She seemed frozen.

Somehow I knew Macon had entered the room. He stood a few feet away, staring at the table. His friend Emmet called out to him, "Excellent prank, Saint!"

Everyone laughed. I sucked in a pained breath.

Macon didn't answer. His gaze flicked to mine. Something unsettling blazed in his eyes, a weird mix of emotions I couldn't decipher. For one tight second, I thought maybe it was regret, but then he set his shoulders back as if expecting a showdown.

Rage roared in my ears and gave me strength.

The room fell silent as I stalked over to an immobile Macon.

"You . . . asshole," I hissed. "You might have them all fooled, but I know the truth. You are ugly on the inside. A worthless soul who will *never* find redemption."

An answering rage flared over his perfect face, but he didn't say a word, just bared his teeth as if he was working to keep from lashing back. But it didn't matter; I was done.

"I truly hate you," I whispered before I fled the room.

That night, I clung to my mother, unable to cry but shivering with humiliation and anger. An hour later, Sam came home, crying, her makeup running in dark rivers over her cheeks. Macon had dumped her.

"He said he was finished with the Baker sisters," she sobbed, huddled by my side. "That I wasn't worth this hassle."

I wanted to show sympathy, but I couldn't. I gave her a half-hearted hug. "You're better off without him." Truer words I'd never spoken.

Sam had turned to me then, her hug fierce. "I'm so sorry, Delilah. I'm so sorry I chose him over you. I'm sorry for everything."

Macon Saint might have hurt me, but he'd brought the Baker sisters together once more. Our family moved away shortly after that, and I never saw Macon again. But the scars he left on my psyche lingered for far too long.

CHAPTER ONE

Delilah

Grandma Maeve used to say hate will toughen your dough; a good bake is made with love. I don't know about hate, but my stress seems to be leaking out all over my brioche. The dough has become tacky and warm when it should be smooth and cool. I've overkneaded it in my distraction.

Mama's birthday brunch is tomorrow, and I haven't heard from Sam in days. Sam, who was supposed to get Mama's present while I do the cooking. Sam, who promised that she would find Mama something "ah-mazing!" and not to worry about paying her back. Well, I do. Especially since Sam is almost always short on cash. When she's flush with money, it usually means trouble.

The surface of the dough clings to my palm, and I utter a sound of disgust. Scooping the mass up, I dump it in the garbage and start arranging my *mise en place* all over again. I'm a professional chef, not a baker, and it shows. But I'm determined to up my game.

My phone dings with a text just as I'm opening a packet of yeast.

Unknown number: Sam, if you don't get your ass back here in
30 min, I'm calling the police.

It's such an odd text I can only stare at the phone and frown. I don't
recognize the number, but "Sam" has me hesitating. Weird how I was
just thinking of my sister, Sam. Then again, Sam is a common name.
This "Sam" might be a dude, for all I know.

Another text lights up my phone.

I mean it. I'm not falling for your "I'm just a sweet little ol'
southern belle" shit anymore. I know you took the watch. You
WILL return it.

Now this gives me pause. Many times has Sam accused me of complaining about her sweet little ol' southern belle act. A glance at the
phone also reminds me that it's April 1.

Rolling my eyes, I dust off my hands and pick up the phone.

This has got to be the lamest April Fools' joke yet, Sam. At least
pretend to be someone other than yourself.

Immediately, I get a response.

Are you shitting me? Mistaken identity? That's what you're
going with? Cut the crap. Get. Over. Here. Now.

Annoyed, I type back harder than usual.

This isn't even "Sam's" number so I'm the one calling bullshit on
YOU. Stop with the funny business. I'm busy making Mama's
surprise brunch.

Please. I've tasted your cooking. I'd be safer eating canned food.

Oh, that's just low and uncalled for. I fire back a response.

You know, Sam, you're kind of acting like . . . an asshole.

There's a pause, and I can almost feel Sam wondering if she should drop the charade. When she finally answers, it isn't what I expect.

Did you just quote Sixteen Candles to me?

Well, duh. It's my favorite film, despite the fact "you" get to star in it.

I have to smile a little. It always stuck in my craw that the main character has the same name as my sister and not me. Something Sam used to needle me with all the time.
Another text makes my phone ping.

That was Delilah's favorite. You, OTOH, can't sit still long enough to finish a movie. Stop diverting. Bring me my watch.

I frown. Her response is just weird. Sam never insults herself. Especially with something that's true; Sam never can sit still for a movie. Something only a few people know. Sam is great at hiding what she perceives as flaws. A short attention span isn't a flaw in my book, but it certainly is in Sam's. Tension snakes down my neck and over my shoulders. I don't like these texts. They aren't funny, and there's something off about them.

Enough already. I'm baking. Come up with a better joke.

There's no response, and I assume that's the end of that. I grab some flour and begin to measure it out when Sam replies.

Delilah cooks and bakes. Not you.

I don't want to believe anything other than this is Sam trying to annoy me. She's an excellent liar—a professional where I am but an amateur. But there's something about the text, the tone that conveys genuine trepidation, and it has my hackles rising.

My hands are not as steady when I type my response.

That's because I AM Delilah. (The "der" is implied here.)

There's another protracted pause. One that I feel in my bones. My stomach clenches as I wait. It doesn't feel like a prank anymore. But it has to be. Sam is just that evil.

A ding from my phone fills the silent kitchen.

Tater Tot?

I suck in a sharp, pained breath, my fingers tingling. All the oxygen in the room disappears. For a long moment, all I can do is stand in my kitchen, my ears ringing, my body clenched.

Other than Sam, only one person knows *Sixteen Candles* is my favorite teen film. The only person who would boldly call me that name.

No, I will not think about Macon Saint. Lord knows I've tried my best to eradicate him from my brain entirely. But he is like a cold sore, popping up now and then, a painful irritation whether I want him there or not.

It grew worse when he won a starring role on *Dark Castle*, the series everyone on the planet but me seems to be obsessed with. I didn't know he was into acting until then. And damn it, I wanted to watch that show. Now, it is all I can do to keep clear of it, what with every person I know talking about it on social media each Sunday night.

Sam was beside herself about the news. *"Just think, we both know someone famous, Dee."*

"Hold my hand while I try not to faint from excitement."

"Sarcasm makes your face pinch in unattractive ways."

"How about when I stick my tongue out? Don't give me that look. I'm a caterer in LA, Sam. I've met loads of famous people. Most of them haven't been very impressive."

"But you don't know *them* know them. *We knew Saint before he was famous. People are more likely to show you their true selves when they're not worried about fame."*

"Yeah, well, Macon's true self is an arrogant asshat."

"Pish. You hold grudges for too long."

"Too long? He was a monumental dickhead to me for years!"

"Water under the bridge. You should let it go too."

Too. As if she'd been called Tater Tot by a mob of sycophantic Macon worshipers. As if she'd had those little potato bits pelted at her when she was the most vulnerable. To this day, I can't stand tater tots.

"They show his ass in two episodes," she went on blithely. *"And I'm here to tell you, it is hot. I mean, we're talking grade A bubble-butt perfection. He's definitely built that thing up since high school."*

Not wanting to talk about Macon's butt or the fact that my sister may or may not have seen said butt long ago, I had changed the subject. She knows how much I hate Macon. The fact that she's using him as a practical joke now is too much. Anger flows through me in a rush of heat. I'm all thumbs as I reply.

How dare you bring that ass canal into this?

Ass canal? Only one person I know uses that term. Jesus, this really is Delilah, isn't it?

I want to scream. I want to chuck the phone to the devil and run out of the kitchen. But mainly, I want to punch my sister.

Fuck you, Sam. Consider yourself uninvited to brunch.

It's Macon. And you really hate me that much, Tot? After all this time?

No, no, no. It is not Macon Saint texting. Sam hasn't talked to him since he dumped her the night of the prom. It's a matter of pride with her. Never mind the fact that he's famous; he probably has people to text for him, for Pete's sake.

It has to be a bad dream. A nightmare.

Stupefied, I stare at the phone in my hand while it lights up.

Tater?

Tot?

Delilah? You there?

Pick up the phone, Delilah.

Wait. What?

I nearly jump out of my skin when the phone starts ringing.

Oh. My. God. No. Just no. It cannot be Macon.

The call goes to voice mail, but the phone simply rings again.

He won't stop; Macon is like a tick that way. He'll keep at this until I lose my mind. I've got to nip this in the bud now. Taking a deep breath, I answer. "What!"

"Still all the grace, Delilah." His voice is deeper now, a rumble of smoke and ashes.

I ignore his sarcasm. "How did you get my number, and why are you bothering me?"

Laughter comes through the phone. "What, no 'It's been so long. How have you been?' At least confess how much you missed me."

Oh, how I remember that irritating smugness. The fact that I'm actually talking to Macon after all this time unsettles me so much my legs tremble, and I have to lean against the counter.

It's a surprise my voice is anywhere near normal. "Answer the question, or I'm hanging up."

"I'll just call you again."

"Macon . . ."

He makes a noise, almost a laugh but something drier. "No one calls me Macon like that. As if it's a curse or a bad taste in your mouth. Only you."

Back when we were kids, his mama called him Little Saint, which was just weird in my book. His daddy called him "boy." Everyone else simply called him Saint. A less deserved title, I cannot recall. But it isn't a surprise people still refer to him as Saint; he spent enough time cultivating that image.

"Why are you harassing me, Macon?"

He huffs out a breath. "Firstly, I called Samantha's number." He rattles off her number, and I'm left frowning—not that he can see that. He continues on in an officious tone. "Secondly, I addressed my messages to Sam, not you. Why you seemed to think I was pretending to be Sam makes absolutely no sense."

"It's April Fools' Day," I mutter. "I thought it was a poorly executed joke on Sam's part."

He laughs without humor. "I wish."

Yeah, me too.

If I am to believe he was texting Sam—and why would he bother texting me?—then I have to believe the rest. Unfortunately, I'm remembering the time Sam forwarded her messages to me when she dumped a particularly clingy guy named Dave. I had to deal with an alternately crying and raging Dave for a week before he finally stopped calling me.

Which means Macon isn't lying.

Shit on a platter.

"Well," I say, desperately reaching for calm. "Clearly, I am not Sam. Nor is this her number. I suspect she forwarded her messages to me, for which she and I will have words. However—"

"You're talking like your grandma again, Tot."

"Do not call me that."

A slow chuckle rumbles in my ear. "But you don't object to sounding like your grandma?"

I shift my feet and scowl. I *was* talking like Grandma Maeve, damn it. I tend to get wordy and overly formal when nervous. The fact that *he* knows I do chafes. "You're veering off course. The fact remains that I am not Sam."

"Do you know where she is?" He's harder now, the anger back.

"I wouldn't tell you if I did."

I can almost hear him grinding his teeth. Which is satisfying.

"Then I guess I'll have to call the police," he says.

All at once, I remember his first texts. He demanded she bring back a watch. Gripping the phone, I pace the length of my kitchen. "What did she do?"

I could have phrased it differently, but having dealt with Sam's shenanigans over the years, I'm not going to waste time making excuses until I hear Macon's side of the story. I'll talk to Sam afterward.

"She took my mother's watch."

I suck in a sharp breath. Holy shit.

Though I didn't know much about Mrs. Saint as a person, everyone knew about her watch. It was the envy of the entire town. It wasn't so much a watch but a piece of jewelry, rose gold and covered in glittering diamonds. It was beautiful, though not one I'd wear every day as Mrs. Saint did.

I remember it well on her slender wrist, the elegant piece glinting in the light. A knot of dread rises up within. Sam coveted that watch. Oh, how she loved it. The worst of it is, Macon's mother passed away years ago, which means the watch would be both an heirloom and a treasured memento.

Weakly, I press a cold hand to my hot cheek. "She . . . ah . . . when could she have possibly done this?"

Macon makes a noise of annoyance. "She really doesn't tell you anything, does she?"

The truth stings.

"Why would she tell me about a watch that she may or may not have stolen?"

"I thought Sam had been renting a room from you."

I blink in surprise.

Three years ago, I was given the opportunity to partner in a high-end catering business. Angela, my partner, eventually sold the other half to me, and it became so successful I was finally able to buy a small bungalow in Los Feliz. A few months later, Sam moved into the loft over my garage because money was tight for her.

Truth is, I never know how she gets her money since she never mentions any jobs. It's hit or miss if I receive the small amount of rent she insisted on paying, and since I don't actually need money from her, I've learned not to rely on it.

But I thought we were close enough that Sam would tell me she'd been seeing Macon. I hadn't a clue they were even in contact.

"That doesn't mean I know everything that goes on in her life," I finally say.

Macon makes a noise that sounds far too pitying before answering with an overly patient tone. "Sam has been my assistant for the past month. Though it soon became clear that she greatly oversold her qualifications."

I don't know what to feel. I'm glad they aren't dating; if Sam and Macon took up again, inevitably, he'd be back in my life as well. But he is in *her* life, isn't he? They've been working together for a *month*. And Sam never told me a thing. Hurt is a numb throb in my temples.

"I've been away for a week," he goes on. "I returned home yesterday, found Sam gone and a couple things missing, including the watch."

"What was she doing in your house?" I wince at the question. I don't want to know. I don't.

But I do.

"Being my assistant is a twenty-four-seven job," he says as if this is obvious. "I have a guesthouse. Sam was staying there."

I don't miss the way his tone implies that he thinks it's odd I hadn't noticed Sam was living elsewhere for weeks. I had. But I'm used to her coming and going. My place is more of a base camp for her than anything.

"You might have had a break-in," I offer weakly.

"Bullshit. The damn woman asked to see the watch for 'old times' sake,' and I was fool enough to show her."

Closing my eyes, I run my hand over my face. "Well . . ."

Shit. I have nothing.

His voice turns weary and resigned. "Just tell me where she is, and I'll leave you to your baking."

"I don't know where she is. But I'll find her. Talk to her."

"Not good enough. I could almost let the rest go, but that watch means something to me. She's gone too far this time. I'm asking the police for help."

"Please." The word rips out of me and burns on my tongue. I hate that I've said it. But I can't take it back. "I'll get your watch."

I can't let Sam go to jail. For better or worse, she's my sister. And it would kill Mama. Figuratively, but I have a horrible fear that it might be literal as well. We lost our father last year, and our mother's health is fragile at best. One day, I turned around to look at her and was stunned by how much she'd aged, as if my father had taken her spark of life with him. Sam and I are all she has left. Sadly, she's always been overly protective of Sam.

"You have twenty-four hours; then I'm calling the police," Macon says with a rough voice that speaks of impatience.

"Twenty-four? Are you funning me?"

"Do I sound like I'm having fun?" he shoots back.

"Well, I had to ask, what with the ridiculous time frame you're proposing."

I can't possibly hear him grinding his molars, but I imagine he is. "That wasn't a proposition," he grinds out. "It's a deadline."

"This is LA, Macon. It takes at least twenty minutes to travel five miles in any direction. On a good day." I let out a noise of pure annoyance. "Not to mention that if Sam is hiding out, she might not even be in the city. She could have hopped on over to Vegas, gone up to San Francisco, or even down to Cabo."

All of them are favorite escapes for Sam. Not that I've been able to figure out how she can afford it. Hell, maybe she's been a professional thief all this time.

"Point being," I say tightly. "If you truly want to find her, you've got to give me more time than twenty-four hours. I'm not some female Jack Bauer, damn it."

A strangled noise, like a protracted laugh, comes through the phone. "It almost would be worth the hassle to imagine you scurrying around the city with a countdown clock dinging over your head."

A haze of red fills my vision. I swear, if he were in front of me, he'd be wearing a bowlful of flour. "Still an asshat, I see."

"Still insulting me, I see."

"You always were quick, Macon." Shit, I need to stop taunting him. "Give me a week."

"Two days."

I snort. "Five."

"Three," he counters. "That's the best I can do for you, Tot."

My back teeth meet at the name. It isn't much time, given the task. But hell, I don't blame him for his anger or wanting this done. "Sold."

"Three days," he repeats. I relax a little until he finishes with, "I expect you and Sam at my house with the watch in hand."

"What?" I practically hiss. "Why me? I don't need to be there. I'm not—"

"Yes, you do. I don't trust Sam to show up without you."

"She'll show." If I have to threaten death and dismemberment. "I want no part of this reunion." No way am I coming face to face with Macon. I can't do it.

"Then you shouldn't have stuck your nose into it."

Ass. Hole.

Macon's tone is hard and cold. "Those are the terms. Take it or leave it."

I have to believe he's serious; the Macon I knew never said what he didn't mean. I would have admired that if he hadn't been such a prick to me every time we got in each other's orbit. The thought of facing him, meeting that cool, smug gaze once more, makes my insides flip sickly.

Just once, I'd like to bring that man to his knees, see him desperate and panting for me the way so many women are for him. There is little chance of that looking like I do at the moment, covered in flour, sticky with sweat, and my hair in desperate need of a cut.

"Delilah? We have a deal?"

I hate the way he says my name, all clipped and imperious, as if he's my superior. I grip my phone hard enough to hurt my hand. I picture throwing the thing at his big head. Lord, grant me the strength not to do just that. "I'll see you in three days."

He sounds entirely too pleased. "I'll text you my address. I'm looking forward to it, Tot."

I'm looking forward to strangling my sister.

First, I'll have to find her.

CHAPTER TWO

Macon

My hand shakes when I set down the phone. I've been in constant pain for the past two weeks, so I could blame it on that, but it would be a lie. Delilah Ann Baker is the source of my current weakness.

"Damn," I mutter under my breath.

"You look like you've seen a ghost," North says from the doorway of my office.

"I think I just conjured one." I turn to face the window and the sea beyond, but I don't see the view. I see Delilah. Big eyes the color of gingersnaps, surrounded by thick dark lashes, a round face with a blunt nose, and plush pink lips. That mouth was always moving, always spewing out verbal acid aimed in my direction.

No one on earth has ever annoyed me as much as Delilah Baker.

No one put me on the defensive faster than Delilah Baker.

Christ, she sounded exactly the same. No, that isn't right; she gave me the same amount of shit as always, but her voice has changed. It is a little different now, holding an undertone of a soft, sweet rasp as if she just finished a bout of hot, sweaty . . .

Where the hell did that thought come from?

I run a hand over my face and snort.

North moves farther into the room. "I take it this ghost isn't Samantha?"

The way his voice catches on Sam's name has my hackles rising. At some point, she clearly sank her claws into North, and he's feeling the effects. It pisses me off. Everywhere Sam goes, destruction follows. I learned that lesson long ago, but like a fool, I ignored it when she came begging for a job.

Everybody grows up, I reasoned. Sam included. Only she hadn't. Not one day into the job, she tried to get into my bed. Awkward as all hell considering I can barely stand being in the same room with her. I knew I had to fire her. But there wasn't time. When I finally got the opportunity, she was gone.

I think of my mother's watch, and pure, scorching rage sears through my belly. The watch is gaudy and not to my taste, but when I see it, hold it, I am instantly with her.

My mother was a fairly distant figure in my life; she had her own problems. But there were good memories as well—her holding me as a child, stroking my hair, reading to me. Every memory I have of her features that watch on her slim wrist. Now it's gone, and I feel the loss of my mother all over again, and a deep, wide pain spreads through my chest.

Fucking Samantha. She has burned me in many ways, but the worst of it is that I let her. She is the last of a long line of people I've allowed into my trust only to be betrayed.

"No," I grit out, remembering North is waiting for an answer. "I can't find her."

He flinches, his jaw bunching tight. "It's my fault."

"Yours? How do you figure?"

Crossing his arms over his chest, he faces me with grim determination. "I'm your bodyguard. Something happens to you on my watch, it's my fault."

Kristen Callihan

Tired and far too jittery for my liking, I rest my hands on my lower abs. Just about every inch of me hurts in some fashion, but it's as comfortable as I can get for now. "Not if I don't let you do your job properly. Besides, I'm the one who was foolish enough to trust Sam to be alone here."

A moment of pure nostalgia weakened my judgment. I saw Sam and remembered . . . everything.

North tenses as if he's going to protest, but he doesn't say a word. Instead, he glares out the window much like I'd done. "So if you didn't find Samantha, who is this ghost?"

My lips curl, but it isn't a smile. I'm too . . . unsettled for that. "Delilah."

Just saying her name out loud has power, as if by uttering it, I risk conjuring her in the flesh. I give myself a mental slap; the pain meds I'm on are clearly messing with my moods. Even so, I can't shake the feeling that part of her is right next to me, looking over my shoulder with her disapproving frown.

For one choking second, I see her clear as day, just as she was on the night of our prom, standing in front of me in a green satin dress clinging to curves I had no business noticing, golden-brown eyes snapping with hate fire, her skin dusky with anger.

Even at seventeen, I appreciated that she was stunning in her rage. I was struck dumb, not able to say a word as she tore me to shreds with hers.

The last thing she said to me was that I was worthless, and she hated me. She clearly meant it with every fiber of her being.

I lick my dry lips. "She's Sam's sister."

North's brows kick up. "Samantha has a sister?" He sounds vaguely horrified.

"Don't worry. They are nothing alike." I roll my tight shoulders, and the pain feels almost good. "Delilah is . . ." Hell, even now my

28

teenage self collides with my current self, both of us struggling to find a way to explain her. "Forthright."

North looks at me as if I'm nuts. I feel nuts.

Shrugging, I try again. "What you see is what you get with Delilah. She gives it to you straight." No matter how deep it cuts. "She doesn't care if you're impressed with her or not."

"Sounds like you know her well."

Do I know Delilah? Yeah, I do, though she'd hate that. And she knows me. A weird twist goes through my chest—part excitement, part revulsion—as if I'm being unwillingly stripped bare and am not sure whether I like it or not.

"We grew up together. Sam, Delilah, and me."

The three fucked-up musketeers. Because even though Sam and I were shits and tried to exclude Delilah, she was always part of the equation. Always.

"Does Delilah know where Sam is?"

"She says she doesn't." Shit, my neck is tight. I lift my arm to squeeze it, and my ribs scream in protest.

North's eyes narrow. He knows I'm in pain but thankfully doesn't point it out. "You just said Delilah was a straight shooter. So you believe her?"

"Yes. Unfortunately." I stare out at the sea once more. Everything is on its head now. "And if Delilah can't find her, no one can." Which means my mother's watch is truly gone. I wouldn't be surprised if Sam has already pawned it.

The rage grows so thick it chokes me. Sam has taken one too many things from me—my memories, my freaking safety—and I'm past forgiveness. I need to call the police. I need to hunt down the watch, not think about a certain sassy woman with a honey-and-arsenic voice.

Delilah.

Her name swirls in my mind without warning, pushing its way in and settling there. She's coming here—with or without Sam. My money is on her showing up alone. Whether she wants to admit it or not, Delilah knows as well as I do that when Sam makes an escape, nothing is going to bring her back until she is good and ready.

Either way, I'll be dealing with Delilah. My old enemy. The one person I have never been able to ignore. Somehow, she's always been able to slip past any defense I've tried.

And now she's going to be on my home turf. Which sounds juvenile as hell, but I find myself fixating on it—on her: Will she look the same? Hate me as much as before?

Without meaning to, I pull my wallet from my pocket and take out the battered card I have tucked into it.

Dear Delilah Catering Co. is printed in bold, bright orange across a deep-pink background. The colors are too flashy for the brooding girl I knew, but the old-fashioned business card is pure Delilah, who tended to slip into talking all formal and stodgy when she got flustered.

I feel a smile tugging at my lips, and it pisses me off. I have no business getting nostalgic again. I've been robbed and taken advantage of by one sister. And now the other sister, the one who told me I was a worthless, hateful soul, is coming to see me. Doubtless she'll be pleading Sam's case, willing to take the fall for her little scam-artist sister yet again.

That pisses me off too. But the clench of anticipation in my gut cannot be denied. I text Delilah my address and tell her to be here by five on the day of the deadline. I can't help adding "or else," knowing it will piss her off. When she replies with an eye-roll emoji and tells me to piss off so she can bake, my smile is wide.

Like it or not, I still enjoy pushing her buttons, and I can't wait for her to show.

Chapter Three

Delilah

DeeLight to SammyBaker: Since you're not checking texts, I'm hunting you via Instagram and FB messages. Don't make me start publicly Snap-chatting you. I know what you did to Macon. If you had any honor you'd get your butt home.

> DeeLight to SammyBaker: You'll have to do it eventually. And I have knives, Sam. Sharp as shit knives.

> DeeLight to SammyBaker: Did I mention I can debone a chicken in under a minute with those knives?

> DeeLight to SammyBaker: CHICKEN!

———

Honestly, I thought I knew what desperation felt like. But it is abundantly clear that I've been woefully ignorant on that matter. Desperation, I have come to learn, causes a humiliating amount of roiling insides and shaking hands. I am sick—*sick*—with it. I want to do as Sam has done and disappear. Good Lord, disappearing sounds like the answer to all my prayers right about now.

When I gave my promise to hunt down Sam, it hadn't occurred to me that since she'd forwarded her calls to my phone, I wouldn't be able to call her either. I blame this oversight on being flustered by having to talk to Macon Saint for the first time in ten years. So I've been left to search for her by driving to all her regular haunts and calling her friends.

I searched all night. Sam is still MIA, gone as if she never existed. It's a talent, truly, her ability to simply drop out of life. I'd like to say this is something new or surprising. But it isn't. My sister lives in a world in which she is the sun, and everyone around her is simply orbiting. She often leaves me to either clean up her messes or take the blame.

I've been covering for her for as long as I can remember. Even when we were kids, my parents simply accepted it as fact that I'd be the prevailing head and keep her out of mischief. It's a hard habit to shake.

Now, I'm pacing my sunny kitchen, my fingers cold and clammy, my stomach so sour even the bright, fluffy lemon scones I made an hour ago in a sad attempt to ease my agitation don't tempt me. And I know they'll be delicious.

But no, instead of eating, I clutch my phone, willing myself not to dial but doing it anyway. I have always had this need to make my parents—especially my mama—happy, make them proud to have me as their daughter. It isn't logical as much as a bone-deep compulsion. I hate disappointing her.

A cold sweat breaks out along my back as the call rings through.

Don't pick up. Don't pick up. Don't pick—

"Hello, dear." My mother is far too cheery this early in the morning. "I was just thinking about you."

"That is not the comfort you believe it to be, Mama."

Slightly offended amusement lilts through her voice. "My thinking about you isn't comforting?"

"No. Because I immediately wonder if it's about something bad."

"You are a horrible pessimist, darling. I assure you it is always good things."

Snorting, I pace the length of my kitchen. "I'm pragmatic, not pessimistic."

"Really," Mama drawls. "And what makes you believe that? In your professional opinion?"

She is the only person who can manage to tease me yet make me feel a little bit lighter in my soul while doing so. I smile despite my disquiet. "Because my dire predictions almost always come true. I'm merely planning ahead of time." At that, all my happy fades.

Clearing my throat, I lean against the counter and dive in. "Mama, have you heard from Sam today?"

"No, baby. I haven't heard from Samantha for over a week." She laughs lightly. "Which is just about regular for her. Why?"

Because I want to strangle her with my bare hands, but I need her here to get a good grip on her neck. "No reason. Just . . . sister stuff." I clear my throat again. "Mama, I'm really sorry, but I'm going to have to cancel lunch today. I . . . ah . . . one of my work colleagues is in a tight spot and has no one else to help her out."

It is the worst of excuses, and even saying the words makes me cringe deep within myself.

"It's all right, baby," Mama rushes to assure. "We can plan for the weekend. Easier all around. Don't you worry over it another second. JoJo is in town for my birthday. She can keep me company."

JoJo is my mother's best friend and partner in crime. I'm almost afraid when those two go off alone together. Mayhem usually ensues.

"We'll drive up to Santa Barbara," Mama goes on. "She's been asking to go."

And this is why I love her. I suppose most people love their mothers on some level. But not everyone likes their parents. I *like* my mother. I like talking to her, sitting in her kitchen, and letting the soothing sound of her voice slide over me with all the warm comfort of a beloved childhood blanket.

My phone's case creaks under my grip. "Thank you, Mama. I'll make it wonderful, I swear. But if Sam happens to show up today, please let me know. And . . . well, please don't let her leave before I get there."

There's a protracted pause before my mother answers. "You're canceling because of her, aren't you?"

I suppose my request to keep Sam on lockdown was a bit much. Still, I play stupid. "What? No . . . of course not. Don't be ridiculous."

"Delilah . . . do not lie to me."

"I swear, Mama." I cross my fingers behind my back in a reflexive move I've never been able to quell. "I really do have to help out a friend." The term *friend* is a joke when it comes to Macon, but I can equivocate with the best of them. "Though, as it happens, it is true that I cannot find Sam to let her know, and she . . . well, she forwarded her calls to me, so I can't exactly hunt her down."

She makes a sound of exasperation. "That girl will be the death of me."

Not the words I want to hear. "Does it truly bother you when Sam gets in trouble?" Because I have to know how far to go. If only for my own peace of mind.

Mama sighs. "Of course it does. She's my baby girl. Just as you are."

"True. But, Mama, there might be a time when she can't wiggle her way out of a fix."

Say, like when Macon Saint throws her little ass in jail. If I didn't hate Macon so much, I might find it in me to applaud him on that one.

"Maybe it's for the best," I continue cautiously, "if you resign yourself to that inevitability."

I close my eyes against the surge of anger and disappointment I feel for my sister.

"I am a mother, Delilah," Mama says in a tired voice. "I will never give up on my children. And it will always cut to the bone when either

34

of you are hurting. You two girls are all I have left. After your daddy . . . when I lost him . . ." Her voice breaks on a weak breath.

"I know," I rush to tell her.

We fall silent. Then my mother speaks in a halting voice. "I miss him. When you give your heart to someone, they become a part of you. And when they're gone, you feel the hole they left behind."

"Mama . . ." She's killing me.

"I'm all right," she says softly. "I'm only trying to explain that I am comprised of parts. Your father was a big piece of me. But there is also you and Sam. I could never give up on either of you; it would be like giving up on myself, losing another piece of myself. You understand?"

The last of my strength leaves me, and I sink to the floor to lean against the cabinets. The sick twist in my insides hurts so badly that I press a hand to my middle. "Yes, Mama, I understand you perfectly."

This is going to suck.

My hands are downright clammy as I drive along the Pacific Coast Highway toward Malibu. Normally, I love this road with the endless glittering ocean on one side and sloping wild mountains on the other. Now, it's simply the route taking me to misery.

For three days I've searched. I've made calls to all the best resorts within reasonable driving distance—Sam hates to fly, but she also loves her comfort. I've even tried to look under her aliases. It hit me like a brick to realize that for years, I've known my sister *uses* aliases, and I never thought twice about it. Talk about willful ignorance.

Fuming over that uncomfortable nugget of truth, I even went as far as to break into my sister's old laptop she left behind in the guesthouse in the hopes there'd be some clue to what she'd been doing with her life. All that I came away with is that she has a thing for lumberjack porn and has amassed an impressive collection of hot bearded man gifs.

By one o'clock, I conceded defeat, and—God help me for this—I called my hairstylist to book an emergency cut and color. Okay, maybe it's vain, but if I have to drive all the way out to Macon's place by myself and somehow convince him not to press charges, I need to look as good as possible.

So here I am, hair beautifully styled and angled just so around my face with pretty caramel and golden highlights designed to make my nut-brown hair look sun kissed. I went full out at the salon and had my brows shaped and a mani-pedi as well.

Yes, I am guilty of primping, but it's not vanity; it's war paint. One does not go into battle without armor. To that end, I put on my favorite short-sleeve cream knit top that clings in all the good places but flows around my less desirable spots and an ink-blue skirt that hugs my hips and gently flares around my knees.

Maybe it's overkill, but at least I look put together yet no nonsense. Unflappable. Professional.

"Who the hell am I kidding?" I yell at the road before me. "It won't make a lick of difference. I'm so screwed."

Perspiration tickles my spine as I drive onto a smaller road, heading closer to the shore. Despite all my years living in LA, I haven't visited this part of Malibu. The narrow coastal road is utterly unfamiliar, but the car navigation informs me that the address Macon texted me is six hundred feet to my left. Of course Macon would live right on the beach.

With a lot of work and a dash of luck, one day I might become a famous chef and be able to afford to live out here. Right now, I couldn't even rent a guesthouse in this neighborhood.

My lips pinch as I finally turn into a driveway blocked by a big wooden gate. The thing about the Malibu coast is that curb appeal means little more than having a nice garage or a big gate. The true beauty of the houses is saved for the owners. And while most of Malibu is an ever-shrinking strip of space squeezed between the mountains and the ocean, Macon's property is on a rare bluff of flat land that juts out and curves back toward Los Angeles.

Taking a shaky breath, I edge up to the intercom, noting the cameras placed all around, and press the call button.

Fuck, fuck, fuck a duck.

"Yes?" a man answers. He doesn't sound like Macon.

Even so, I find myself stuck, lips parted, mouth dry, and not a sound escaping me.

Answer him, dimwit.

No, turn the car around, and run away while you still can.

"Hello?" he asks again. I swear I catch a hint of humor in the question as if the man on the other end is holding in a laugh.

Buoyed by sheer annoyance, I find my voice. "Delilah Baker to see Macon Saint."

My hands are so sweaty one slips off the steering wheel. I surreptitiously wipe my hand on my skirt and stare into the dark little eye of the camera. It feels like forever but is probably only a few seconds before the gate slides open.

A long driveway lined with lacy old olive trees beckons me inside. Slowly, I drive along, my heart pounding a steady tattoo against my ribs. A small one-story white house comes into view. I begin to brake but then quickly realize it's a guesthouse. In the distance looms a far bigger white house that faces the ocean.

"Jesus wept, what a setup." A laugh escapes me even though I'm not finding anything particularly funny at the moment. But I can't help myself. If I had to point to my perfect dream house, this would be it.

There are four main styles of houses favored by the wealthy in Southern California. The classic twenties Spanish style, the ornate wannabe French or English manor, the ultramodern, and the craftsman on steroids. Macon's house is a mix of craftsman and modern, which shouldn't make sense. But it does.

I roll up before the warm, inviting doors of weathered wood, and my breakfast threatens to make itself known once more.

"You can do this," I whisper to myself, pressing a hand against my roiling belly.

Outside, the air is fragrant with wild chamomile, sweet lemons, and the salty sea air. The gentle lull of the ocean just beyond seems mocking in the face of my wildly pounding heart. I take a long, easy breath and let it out slowly.

Running a hand through my hair, I prepare to meet my childhood nemesis. God help me.

Macon Saint does not answer the door.

I shouldn't be surprised. However, I can't help but stare at the guy who stands before me.

He looks like James Bond, to be honest. Roughly handsome with dark-blond hair, a pouty sneer, and a body that borders on brutish, he's fairly intimidating. His sky-blue eyes rake me over, but I sense he's curious, not antagonistic.

"I'm North," he says by way of greeting.

I put on my visiting smile and hold out a hand. "Delilah."

He shakes my hand briefly. "I know."

Of course; he was the one who answered at the gate. And I'm expected. Neither of us mentions that Sam isn't with me. Maybe he expected that too.

For the thousandth time this morning, I swallow down my irritation with Sam. It won't help me now.

"Come on in." North inclines his head in invitation.

I don't want to. I want to run. The corners of his eyes crinkle as if he knows this well and empathizes. I'm led into a sun-filled front hall, and I'm hard pressed not to gape and sigh.

The interior of Macon's house is even nicer than the exterior. Perfection. It is space and light and peace. It somehow manages to be grand without feeling empty.

"You find the place okay?" North asks me as we walk past a great room.

"Navigation aids are a lifesaver."

"True."

I catch glimpses of a living area with wide weathered plank floorboards, coffered ceilings, creamy-white paneled walls, and beyond, the blue, blue ocean. It's perfect. A dream.

A nightmare.

I hate that Macon Saint, a.k.a. the devil, gets to live here, that he gets to look out these floor-to-ceiling windows every day. I hate that I'm jealous.

The house is extremely quiet and smells faintly of timber and citrus. Every few feet, an ocean breeze drifts through the open windows and teases the ends of my hair. We pass a dining room and a glass-walled wine room filled with bottles.

I imagine a drunk Macon sprawled on the floor, deliberating which wine to try next, and suppress the urge to snicker.

"Are you a friend of Macon's?" I ask, partly to fill the silence that's getting to me and partly because I'm genuinely curious.

"Friend?" North seems to ponder the question, then glances my way. "Yes. But I'm also his temporary bodyguard and personal trainer." His expression turns devious. "So he's not allowed to play the friend card when I'm busting his butt."

"Tough love, eh?"

"Something like that." He moves with crisp strides, and it's not difficult to imagine him taking out bad guys.

I hadn't thought of Macon needing security. I can't seem to get my head around the fact that he is famous. As it is, I can barely think about how I'm about to see him for the first time in ten years. I'll vomit if I do.

"You're nothing like your sister," North says suddenly, his eyes on me.

My steps falter. Of course I'm not; anyone with functioning eyes would be able to tell that in one glance. Still, I'm surprised he mentioned it. My estimation of North sinks a bit, and I find myself disappointed.

He grimaces, obviously reading my expression well. "That wasn't meant as an insult. It just struck me that you're very different in temperament."

It becomes clear that Sam has had her hooks in North at some point. Over the years, I've learned to recognize the signs—the slight strain in a man's voice when he speaks of her, the unfortunate mix of disappointment and wistfulness in his eyes.

"And in looks," I say before I can stop myself. Then I'm the one grimacing. I sound bitter. I'm not, really. I'm simply used to that comparison too.

North's expression turns solemn. "Yes." His gaze flicks to my breasts so quickly I might have missed it if I wasn't looking at his face. Then his eyes meet mine, and he smiles faintly. "Again, that's not an insult."

Warmth washes over my cheeks. North is capable of turning on the charm when he wants to. I almost pity any woman who gets a full dose of it.

He appears to remember why I'm here and starts walking again, his back straight and tight, his pace quicker now.

Unfortunately. I'd rather dally here. God, Macon's going to be pissed. And he isn't going to go easy on me.

Why am I here? I shouldn't be here.

I think about Mama's voice this morning. *"I could never give up on either of you; it would be like giving up on myself, losing another piece of myself."*

Yeah. That.

The sound of my heels clicking against the floorboards bolsters my spirits. Grandma Belle used to say that a woman wearing her best red heels and favorite red lipstick can accomplish anything. There is some truth to her words. When Grandma Belle donned her red pumps and a glossy coat of Dior Rouge, she fairly glowed with an inner confidence that reduced men to obedient puppies.

While I do not possess the classic beauty of Grandma Belle, nor do I think Macon Saint will ever act anything close to an obedient puppy, I do admit to feeling a bit more powerful in my red suede Jimmy Choos and Ruby Woo lipstick.

At least that's what I tell myself as North stops by a closed door and knocks.

I'm so worked up at this point that I'm sure my pulse is visibly beating at the base of my neck.

I nearly jump out of my skin when a deep masculine voice bids, "Come in."

North opens the door and then steps back to give me room to enter. For a brief and shining second I envision myself turning tail and running for the nearest window like the Cowardly Lion. But I step into the wizard's lair instead.

Chapter Four

Delilah

There are times in life when everything sort of slows down, all your senses go on high alert, and you see everything from a distance.

This is one of them. I'm taking in the whole of the room at a glance—the retractable glass wall that's open to the ocean view; the built-ins with a gold Emmy sitting among various books and decorative items; the massive desk cluttered with books, papers, and dishes; and *him*.

His presence rubs over me like a pervasive itch that won't go away.

Sitting behind his desk, he's turned my way, staring at me as I stare at him. I take him in as a whole: his big muscled body—the sheer physicality of him. And I see the details. The details are what throw me.

"You look like hell," I blurt out.

His eyes lock onto me, and I'm momentarily hurtled back to being seventeen again. Those eyes, deep set and carob brown under black brows that are straight, angry slashes. When he was a kid, those eyes somehow managed to appear angelic and sweet with their long curling lashes and shining depths. Now he resembles an Old Testament archangel, all fierce judgment and wrath—the type who smites wrongdoers with one look.

"Well, hello, Ms. Delilah Baker," he drawls. "So nice to see you too."

"Sorry." I force a smile, though it feels strained on my face. "That was rude of me."

He waves an idle hand. "No, no, do go on. It's been years since anyone has insulted me to my face. I'd say about ten years."

"Surely I haven't been the only one to insult you in all this time."

Macon's lush wide mouth, surrounded now by stubble so thick it's nearly a beard, pulls in a half smile. "Perhaps. Perhaps not." He shrugs one shoulder. "And I do look like shit, so . . ."

He doesn't really. He's still Macon, brutally handsome and possessing far too much charisma for one man. He's just beat up as all hell and in a wheelchair. A cast encases his left leg from the knee to his foot. Another soft cast is on his right wrist. He wears his hair cropped so short it borders on militaristic, but it also highlights the clean bone structure of his face and the fact that his right eye is black and blue and slightly swollen. Various scrapes mar his tan skin, and a line of surgeon's tape bisects his right brow.

"What happened to you?" I step farther into the room.

"Car accident. Broken fibula, sprained wrist, two bruised ribs, and a gash over my eye, if we're being exact." He appears to find his list of injuries amusing, but I don't.

"I'm sorry." And I am. Whatever animosity has passed between myself and Macon, the idea of him bloody and broken sends a chill through me.

He simply looks me over, his gaze leisurely and irritating. His attention stalls on my lips, and that slanted smile of his reappears. "A lady friend once told me that when a woman wears red lipstick to meet a man, it's for two possible reasons. Either she wants him to fuck her, or she wants to tell him to fuck off."

My body seizes on the word *fuck* and the way it sounds coming out of Macon's mouth—all carnal and hard. Normally, if a man I was meeting for business used that word in front of me, I'd have turned and left. But this is Macon. We've cursed each other out on multiple occasions—although never quite with this undertone.

Heat flushes over my cheeks, and I find myself glaring. "We both know when it comes to you it's the latter."

"Considering you've arrived alone, I'd rethink that tone, Tot."

I'm so tempted to snap back that my lips twitch. But he's pointed out the dreaded truth of the situation. Sam isn't here. And I'm screwed. But I can't show weakness.

"The day I offer to have sex with someone to get out of a sticky situation is the day I swim out to sea."

"I wasn't asking. Perhaps you should start explaining why you're here without Sam." He gestures to the chair in front of the desk. "Have a seat."

Part of me is still stuck on the fact that I thought he had teased me with the idea of prostituting myself. Unfortunately, to my horror, I picture it anyway—rounding the desk, hiking my skirt up to straddle his thickly muscled thighs. What would he do? Push me off, or pull me close? Would he grip me tight? His hands are wide, his fingers long. My sex clenches with the thought of being penetrated by those fingers, being used by him.

Jesus, Dee. Get a grip. You hate this man.

But I've never had hate sex. Hot, sweaty, angry sex. Hate sex with Macon. Hmm . . . I could leave him weak and panting for more, then stride out of the room.

Beneath my top, my breasts grow tender, and I grit my teeth. Thinking about Macon in conjunction with sex is just asking for a drop into the deep end of the swamp. As is falling for his mind games. He always used crude innuendos to get under my skin. He'd laugh his ass off if I made a pass at him. And I'd have to throw myself off a cliff somewhere.

Setting my shoulders back, I cross the room, aware of my clicking heels and swaying hips, aware of Macon watching me. I'm being overtly sexual, but there is power in that. A woman can choose to embrace it when it suits. And it definitely suits me now. If my lipstick is stating, "Fuck off," my body is saying, "This is what you missed out on, and you haven't cowed me one bit."

Petty? Maybe.

Enjoyable? Definitely.

But not advisable. I give myself another mental slap to stop messing around.

His expression gives nothing away as I sit down and cross my legs. "I couldn't find her," I say without preamble.

"Clearly."

"I know it looks bad—"

"Because it is bad."

"But she's never . . ." Hell. Never what? Stolen something before? I can't say that for certain. Never skipped town? I know for a fact she's done that before. Many times. I feel sick. "It'll kill my mother if Sam gets arrested."

Macon's lips flatten, going white at the edges. "My mother is dead. All I had left of her was that watch."

Empathy softens my tone. "I know."

It happened the summer my family moved to California. By the time we received word that Mrs. Saint had died of an aneurism, she'd already been buried. It was the one time I felt truly sorry for Macon, and I willingly signed the card my parents sent.

Faced with Macon's tight expression, I feel the urge to offer some words of comfort. But he talks before I can open my mouth. "Sam knew that too. It didn't stop her from stealing it."

The hole just keeps getting deeper. And here I am without a shovel. "I know. I'm sorry. I really am. But if you could give me more time to—"

"No." The word is as flat as his stare.

"I'm certain I can eventually—"

"No, Tot. Not even for you."

I blink. Even for me? When has he ever given me any sort of concession?

Macon gives me a knowing look. "We may have hated each other, but our interactions were always interesting. That has to count for something, considering how boring our town was."

If he says so. I'd rather kick his good shin every time he calls me "Tot."

Don't kick the guy holding your sister's freedom in his hands, Dee.

"Look, Sam was a total shit for what she did. And I know I can't replace a sentimental heirloom."

His brow lifts as if to say, "No shit, Sherlock," but he stays silent.

"All I can do is attempt to cover the loss." My hand shakes as I fumble with the catch on my purse. "I have a check for fifty thousand dollars that I'm—"

"Hold up." He lifts a hand to forestall me. "I can't take that check."

"But you can," I insist. "I know it isn't the same thing, but I can try to make amends by reimbursing you."

His lips twitch with clear irritation. "Delilah."

God, it's almost worse when he says my real name. At least with "Tot" my immediate reaction is rage and annoyance. When he says Delilah, his voice works over my skin like hot prickles. It can't be helped. The man has a whiskey voice, deep, raspy, and slumberous. It makes a woman think of rumpled sheets and sweat-slicked skin. And I really don't know what is the matter with me; I must be ovulating or something. Because I cannot be sexually attracted to Macon Asshole Saint.

"I can't take the check," he repeats firmly. "Because the watch is worth two hundred and eighty thousand dollars."

"Fuck. Me."

His eyes crinkle, an unholy gleam lighting them. "I thought we weren't doing that."

I'm going to be sick. Legitimately ill. I'm going to throw up all over Macon's pristine desk. I swallow against the greasy feeling crawling up my throat. "Don't joke."

All vestiges of humor leave him. "You're right. It's not a joking matter."

"Two hundred and eighty—" I wipe my damp brow. "How the hell can a watch be that expensive?"

Macon gives me a pitying look. "It's a rose-gold Patek Philippe with a diamond-pavé face."

I slump back in my chair. "I know Patek Philippe watches are expensive. I've seen enough people around LA wearing one. But I never thought the damn thing was the price of a condo." Macon raises a brow because real estate prices here are no joke, and I wrinkle my nose. "Okay, the down payment on a condo. Good Lord . . ." I make a weak gesture. "Your mother wore it every day. Like it was a Seiko."

He gazes out toward the sea, giving me the clean lines of his profile. "I think she liked to taunt my father with it."

"Didn't he buy her the watch?"

His mouth twists. "Despite the airs my father put on, my mother's family was the one with money. The house, the cars, the watch—they were all hers. And she made him feel it."

Oddly, it sounds like Macon approves. Then again, he never did get along with his father. Not many people did. George Saint was a beast, and I learned early on to avoid him.

"Well . . ." I drift off, unable to think of a thing to say.

"Well," Macon repeats as if agreeing.

"Macon . . ."

"Delilah." My name is a singsong taunt.

I bite my lip to keep from shouting.

"You really didn't know a thing about Sam working for me, did you?" he asks quietly.

Yep, still hurts that Sam kept me in the dark. "The only time we've spoken of you since high school was when Sam said you were on *Dark Castle*. I had no clue you two had been in contact."

Macon's expression remains blank, but something stirs in his eyes. It looks a lot like rage. "I was surprised as hell when Sam applied to be my assistant. Didn't really want to hire her, if I'm honest, but she said she was in desperate straits."

"Feeling sorry for Sam is always a recipe for disaster," I mutter.

"Yet here you are."

A fire lights in my belly, and I lean forward with clenched fists. "I'm not here for Sam. I'm here for my mother. Daddy died last year, and we're all she has. Personally, I could kill Sam for this. It would give me great satisfaction to punch her in the tit right now . . ."

Macon huffs a laugh. A perverse part of me wants to laugh, too, but the situation is too horrible.

"But she isn't here, and I'm doing what I can. I just . . . I already lost my dad; I can't lose Mama, Macon. I can't."

"She knows what Sam is like," he says almost gently. But it isn't for me; I know it's out of respect for my mother. Just as I know that respect still won't soften his stance.

"There's a difference between knowing and experiencing. Twice already, Mama has been taken to the hospital for panic attacks. She's on meds for hypertension, with orders from her doctor to take it easy. She puts up a brave front, but her nerves are shot."

Macon's jaw bunches, the tendons along his thick neck standing out in sharp relief. He swallows hard, then visibly releases his tension. "I don't want to hurt your mom. But Sam is a thief. She stole documents from me, personal information." His dark eyes flash with rage. "People got hurt."

"Who?" I choke out.

"Does it matter?" he snaps, then blows out a breath. "Point is, she causes destruction everywhere she goes. And I'll be damned if she weasels out of it this time."

Sam's deeds aren't mine, but I'm so ashamed of her right now I feel covered in dirt. "Perhaps a payment plan?"

"Hmm . . ." His index finger rasps along his jaw. The stubble on his face only serves to draw attention to his lips and the soft curve of them. I can't tell if the near beard is intentional or if he hasn't been able to shave since his accident. "You owned a popular catering business."

It's not a question but a statement. One that skitters along my spine. "How do you know that?"

There's a hint of censure in his expression as if I ought to know the answer already. "I looked you up. Stanford University, majoring in art history, until you dropped out junior year and transferred to the Culinary Institute of America. Internships in Paris for a year, then in Catalonia the next. Worked at Verve and Roses in New York City before moving back to Los Angeles three years ago to open up your own business."

"Jesus." My skin feels too tight for my face. "It's just creepy you dug up that much. You realize this?"

Macon shakes his head in reproach. "It's on your website, Tot."

And now I'm cringing. "Right. Forgot about that. Still invasive, though."

He simply hums in that irritating, supercilious way of his. "You think I wouldn't look into your life when I was trusting you to bring back my mother's watch?"

"Technically, I was supposed to bring back Sam, not the watch."

"Bang-up job on that."

"Ass."

He allows a ghost of a smile before it fades. "Why did you close your business last week?"

"It's really none of your business."

Unfazed, he continues to assess my whole life. "By all accounts, it was extremely successful. Hell, over the past year, I had at least three people suggest you for events."

God. He knew about me being here for that long? And obviously didn't want to employ my services. That stings. Though it shouldn't. We parted as enemies, after all.

"Yes, it was successful," I snap. Until I closed shop, I had a dozen employees and a full client list. I made good money, though with the crazy high-priced cost of living in LA, making payments on my house and on the little industrial kitchen I leased for business, I still lived on a budget. That's all right. Everything is forward movement, inching up bit by bit. I'll get to the top eventually. "My decision to close wasn't financial."

Macon doesn't appear to believe me. "Were you short on overhead to keep it open?"

His tone implies all sorts of things that have my gut prickling.

"If you're suggesting that I somehow worked with Sam to rip you off for the price of a watch—"

"Funny how your mind goes right to that."

"Oh, don't play coy. Of course it does when you're sitting there giving me that raised brow and playing Mr. Detective."

He simply stares. With that damn raised brow.

I roll my eyes. "I don't need money. I offered you fifty thousand dollars, didn't I?"

"Why did you close it, Delilah?"

"Because I'm moving on," I blurt out.

Both his brows go sky high with that one.

Damn it, I sound like I'm skipping town. I stifle the urge to squirm. "I'm going on a tour of Asia to learn new techniques and recipes." Unless he takes the money. Then I'm shit out of luck and going back to catering.

Macon sits back in his chair and continues to run the tip of his finger along his jaw. There are too many things going on behind those dark eyes. "How are you going to fund your trip?"

No way am I explaining that. Not a chance.

But he knows. It's there in his expression, the way it softens just a bit before twisting as though he's disappointed in me.

With a sigh, he rests his hands over his flat belly. "You don't have a job, so you can't pay me back." Right. Damn it. I open my mouth to say . . . something, anything, but he continues. "Save your money, and take the trip."

Despite knowing his refusal was coming, my insides plummet with dread. "Sam will return eventually. She always does. Just give her a little more time."

A long-suffering sigh escapes him. "No."

"Why this urgency?"

"Because I don't believe she'll return," he snaps.

"There has to be a way."

"There is—you just don't like it."

At an impasse, we both fall silent. The chair beneath him creaks as he shifts his considerable weight. Not that he's hefty; the man is pure muscle and decidedly bigger than he was in high school. At seventeen, Macon had the physique of a model, lean and lithe. He's still lean, but now he looks like he could play tight end in the NFL. I wonder idly if he built his body up to fit his character, Arasmus, the sword-wielding Warrior King.

The silence stretches out between us until the only sound in the room is the distant crash of the waves and the pounding of my heart. I've exposed my underbelly, and the knowledge twists me up. But the truth is I'm all out of ideas.

When he does speak, the sound is so abrupt I almost flinch. "Look, Delilah, I understand your situation. But that doesn't change what Sam did. I'm going to have to sort it out with the police now."

The room tilts beneath me, and panic sets in. I can't breathe. It can't end like this. Macon Saint cannot tear apart my family any further. I cannot let him win.

"Take me."

———

Take me.

I said that. Hadn't I? I can't think. My face feels numb. My mind is blank.

There's an awkward pause. Macon's brows pinch together. "I'm sorry—what?"

Okay, that came out wrong. But I will steel into my spine. The Macon I knew never backed down from a chance to prove me wrong. I have to take a chance and believe he's still the same. "I am betting that Sam will return in less than three months and make up for her theft. As a show of faith, I offer myself as collateral. You need an assistant. I'll work off Sam's debt."

He's outright gaping now. "Let me get this straight. You want to be my assistant?"

"I don't *want* to be," I say, calmly pretending sweat isn't running down my back. "But I will, if you—"

"That isn't enough." His body might as well be carved out of granite for all he moves now. But his eyes, they are alive with irritation. "We are talking about a three-hundred-thousand-dollar loss. Of something highly sentimental."

I get it. He wants blood. I would, too, if I'm honest.

I lick my dry lips. "I'll be your personal chef as well." When he tries to speak, I hurry on. "Top assistants make around one hundred to a hundred and fifty thousand a year. Personal executive chefs can earn up to a hundred and fifty thousand as well."

"One year of work would equate to three hundred thousand dollars. You're saying she'll return in under three months."

Damn, he is correct.

"If she doesn't return, I'll stay on for one year."

It sure as hell will spill my proverbial blood to work for Macon. But if it keeps my fragile family safe, I can do it. I can survive a year with Macon. Besides, I know Sam will come back before then. Whether she'll have the watch is another matter. I push that fear aside and hold his gaze.

For a moment he says nothing. But then a snarl rumbles in his chest. And he flops back in his seat as if trying to put as much physical distance between us as possible.

Macon rubs a hand roughly over his stubble, and for once, I see some true emotion color his cheeks. "What the hell, Delilah? We have a history of tearing into each other given the slightest provocation, and yet you jump right into indentured servitude. Have you lost your mind? Or do you simply enjoy playing the martyr when it comes to Sam?"

"Playing the martyr?" I sound screechy. I know I do. I just can't seem to stop it.

He winces like I'm hurting his ears. "You seem hell bent to take on Sam's sins yet again."

My hands curl into fists. "I've never defended Sam."

"Don't give me that offended-innocence act. You were always stepping in and covering for Sam. Or turning a blind eye to her antics."

Despite my best effort, my nostrils flare with a huff of breath. "I never turned a blind eye—"

"Oh, yes you did." His lip curls in a sneer. "She's much worse than you give her credit for."

"Then aren't you the fool to have hired her?"

"Touché, Tot." He smiles thinly. "It was foolish. And it's the last time I feel sorry for Sam. You, however, I trusted to know better than this."

"Well, lucky me."

He glares. "You're still annoying, though."

"And you're still an ass canal."

With a blink, he bursts out laughing. The sound of his laughter is so jovial my lips quirk in response. I bite down on them hard.

Macon's laugh dies as quickly as it was born. "This is a shit deal for you, Tot. I don't understand why you'd offer."

Because I have lost my mind. Because I can't think of anything else to offer. But I can't tell him any of that. "Sam is my sister. Family takes care of family."

"Try telling Sam that."

Keep it together, Dee. "Look, I can either pay you back slowly, or you accept my offer."

"Neither option is really appealing."

"But you're considering it." I can tell that much. It's in the way his expression has shifted from irritated to thoughtful. Oh, butter still won't melt in his mouth, but he isn't throwing me out.

Macon turns his head to stare out the window. "I am." He snorts under his breath. "I must be insane."

"Join the club," I mutter.

His head snaps back around. Dark eyes pin me to my seat. "I could make your life hell."

"You don't even sound ashamed of the prospect."

"I'm not. You're the one who is here pleading I take you on instead of holding Sam accountable."

My back teeth meet with a click. I haven't spoken to this man in ten years, and already I'm arguing with him more than I have with anyone else since. Even my fights with Sam don't have this back-and-forth. She doesn't call me out as much as attack. Macon makes me own every word.

Arguing with him is like trying on the skinny jeans you've pulled out of the closet after a number of years and finding they still fit, albeit tightly. It might not be exactly comfortable, but there is definitely an empowering kick to the experience.

"Three years ago," I say. "Sam disappeared for a week. The police found her car abandoned on the highway. Mama had to be admitted to the hospital when they came to tell her. It turned out to be high blood pressure, exacerbated by a panic attack. And that was when Daddy was alive to soothe her. So when I say her heart cannot take it, it isn't hyperbole."

Macon's expression turns grim. "And Sam? Where was she that time?"

I force myself to hold his knowing gaze. "Off with some guy. She claims her car broke down, and she was going to deal with it later."

Macon's lips twist on a half-repressed smirk. "When I first moved to LA, Sam came to see me." Shock ripples through my body; Sam had never let on she knew where Macon was all these years or that she even cared to know.

He keeps talking. "Somehow she found out I had acquired an agent. Sam wanted to get into acting as well. She begged me to set up a meeting, for old time's sake." His smile is tight and unamused. "Little brat showed up drunk and insulted my agent within the first two minutes. Because that is what Sam does. She takes advantage over and over, and the rest of us are left to fix the damage."

"Then why did you bother to hire her again?" I ask, truly stunned.

The smirk turns bitter. "Clearly I have a weak spot when it comes to the Baker sisters."

"You don't expect me to believe that crap, do you?"

Macon shrugs one massive shoulder. "All right, don't. Maybe it was simple arrogance to assume I could control the outcome if Sam was working for me. I don't know." He sits forward, pinning me with a look. "What I do know is that I'm done letting it slide."

"I understand, Macon. I truly do." When he simply lifts a brow in disbelief, I forge on. "But you'll be getting something out of this arrangement too."

"So you keep saying," he murmurs. But a calculating glint enters his dark eyes. Control. Macon loves control.

"Come on," I taunt—whether I'm taunting him or myself is another matter. "Think of it; I'll be your servant for a year. It's the ultimate one-up between us. Isn't that what you always wanted? Me under your thumb?"

There's a weird sort of beat between us, a heavy pause in which he freezes, his muscles bunching. A current runs between us, humming over my skin. Then Macon barks out a short, hard laugh. "Holy shit, you're good."

A frown pulls at my brows. "I don't know what you're—"

"Oh, yes, you damn well do." He shakes his head. His smile is not amused. "This offer of yours, it's a mind trip. You want me to feel guilty, feel so dirty about the situation that I drop the whole thing."

I shift in my seat, the urge to look away so strong that my neck aches. Shit.

Macon's lips press together in a hard line. "Typical Delilah Baker move—manipulate everyone into place with your earnest self-sacrifice while turning me into the villain."

"You're being melodramatic." But I can't stop the hot itchy feeling that crawls over my skin. That is exactly what I've been doing. Part of me had hoped he'd be so appalled he'd drop it.

"I've a mind to agree, just to see you eat your words." He leans back and links his hands together over his abs. "I bet you'd run out of this room so damn fast you'd make the curtains sway."

That itchy heat turns into a rush of annoyance. "I'm not running. Whatever my motives may be, my offer is real. Sam might be a lost cause, but I owe my mother more than you can understand. I'll do whatever it takes to keep her peace of mind intact."

I don't know what he sees in my expression—I'm not even sure what I'm feeling right now: fear, anger, determination, even a weird sense of anticipation.

When he finally answers, his tone is all-business. "If I accept the bet, you'll live here. Your room and board will be included."

It is surprisingly generous of him to offer room and board.

"And if Sam returns with the watch before the year is up, I keep whatever salary I've earned for the duration."

His eyes narrow. "Fair enough. But when you work for me, you do as I say—no questions asked, no holding this little agreement over my head. You own it."

This is real. A cold sweat breaks over me, my lips going numb. I concentrate on breathing through my nose and trying not to be sick.

"It's killing you, isn't it?" he says, way too pleased. "The thought of being subservient to me."

"What was your first clue, Detective?"

His grin is all teeth and anticipation. "I'll own you, Delilah. For one year, your ass will be mine."

Good Lord, he says it like he relishes the idea. Like he has plans for me. The little hairs along the back of my neck stand up and quiver. My fingers curl into a fist. "I'll work for you. You won't own shit."

"Good as," he counters.

"If you're trying to run me off, it won't work."

"Better you do it now than three weeks into it."

Like Sam.

I wish I knew how to read Macon better. He barely gives anything away that he clearly doesn't want me to see. But there are things I have to know. "Anything happen between you and Sam?"

Right now, he might as well be a wall of granite. "You think I was fucking her? I don't know why you'd care either way."

"I don't. But if this is some sick game of revenge between the two of you, I want to know about it now."

Leaning forward, he rests his good arm on the desk. The movement isn't exactly slow, but it lacks his usual grace, and I wonder how much his injuries pain him. "I wouldn't touch your sister while wearing a hazmat suit. She's her own level of toxic. I learned that long ago."

He isn't wrong, but I'm surprised that he is aware of Sam's faults and that he has actually voiced them to me. "That's an unkind thing to say about your childhood sweetheart."

He blinks at that as though I've surprised him too. But the stoic expression remains. "I never considered her my sweetheart." The ice in Macon's eyes thaws just a bit as he studies me. "Last chance, Delilah. Call it off, and we'll both pretend it never happened."

"I can't." It comes out a sad little husk of sound.

He blinks, and his expression goes oddly blank. "I can't either."

God. I can't believe I'm doing this. That I'm pushing it. "Then what else is there to talk about?"

He shakes his head with a tired sound. "I'll give you a couple of hours to come to your senses. Say, until midnight?"

It's a kindness I don't expect. It's also fairly cruel, as it would be easier to jump without thinking.

"Fine." I push to my feet. I need to get out of this beautiful house and away from this man. I need my bed and a good sleep before I can pull myself back together.

CHAPTER FIVE

Delilah

I'm searching for a silver lining. On my ceiling. Not the best plan, of course, but it's all I got. I can't do this. I can't.

Yes, you can.

I try to think about laying down my pride and being under Macon's thumb. And . . . can't.

MamaBear: Delilah, this is your mother.

DeeLight: I know. I have your number programmed.

I have no idea what she wants, but since I'm not getting any sleep and have been staring at my ceiling for the past few hours, any distraction is welcome.

Yes, well. I tried to call Samantha. She isn't answering her phone.

Under the cocoon of my covers, I flinch. This wasn't the distraction I had in mind. With a sinking gut, I try to think of what to say that won't cause my mother to panic.

Mama, it's the middle of the night. Maybe she's asleep. Why aren't you?

I'm in my sixties and live alone. I never sleep. I watch HGTV and plot my girls' weddings.

Maybe that's why she isn't answering.

Delilah Ann, stop trying to distract me. That's why you called before, wasn't it? You were looking for her because Sam has run off again, hasn't she?

Well, hell. It's one thing to gently query my mother about Sam. It's another when my mother actually starts to worry. I had hoped she wouldn't put two and two together.

It would seem so.

The phone rings in my hand. I'd been expecting it but still dread answering. "Hey, Mama."

"Oh, that girl," she says with exasperation. "Why is she always doing this?"

"I don't know. I only know that she'll eventually slink back." And if she doesn't, I'll be completely screwed.

She sighs. "There are nights when I wake up terrified I'll get a call telling me Sam has been arrested or has met a bad end."

Pinching the bridge of my nose. "I know."

"Do you know what she's gotten herself into this time?"

Nothing much. Just a little grand larceny. "No."

I hate lying to my mother. Hate it.

My mother makes a sound that's suspiciously close to a sniffle; I hate her tears worse. "My heart can't take it, Delilah. If something happened . . . I couldn't . . . I just lost your daddy."

Shit sticks. "I know."

Licking my lips, I glance at the bedside clock. I've blown the deadline Macon gave me. Panic floods my system and makes my words brusque. "She'll come back, Mama. Everything will be okay. I promise."

My mother expels a shaky laugh. "What would we ever do without you, Dee? My sensible, steady child. I'm fairly certain what's left of our little family would fall right apart."

And like that, my course is set in stone.

———

Macon

SweetTot: Do we still have a deal?

It's the middle of the night, way past the deadline I have given Delilah. And yet I'd practically lunged at the phone when it buzzed. Now I'm staring at the words as if they don't make sense. But they do. She wants this. Damn it all, she was supposed to back out.

The deadline was midnight, Tot.

She doesn't respond, and a pang of something I don't want to call regret hits me straight through the chest. But then small dots appear.

It's midnight somewhere. I'm in. Are you?

Such cheek. Fuck. Why does it have to be her? Why is she the only one who's made me feel truly awake in months, hell, *years*? Why am I so damn relieved she's pushing for this?

My heart is doing its best to pound its way right out of my chest. My mind is racing, trying to figure out what the hell to do. Rubbing my hand over my tired face, I reply the only way I can, then toss the phone down as though it were a snake.

My house, 9am. Instructions to follow.

I've done it.

What the hell have I done?

Lying in my bed, I stare up at the ceiling and ask myself the same question I've been asking since Delilah went all *Godfather*, making me an offer she knew I couldn't refuse. Somehow she knew I'd jump at the chance to have her under my thumb.

When I first became famous, I felt like a king. Everyone wanted to please me, and I let them try. Having people fawn over me was a familiar comfort, as arrogant as that sounds. But after growing up in the house I had, positive attention was like stepping out into the warm sun after years of ice-cold darkness.

I'd underestimated Hollywood and the way everyone uses everyone else. I shouldn't have; I know far too much about manipulation. But I was so starved for something good, something mine, that I let my guard slide. I soon lost count of the amount of times my trust had been betrayed. I thought I could at least see Samantha's lies and manipulations a mile away. Look where that got me. Now, I'm actually letting Delilah into my life? Delilah, who openly hates me?

But her blatant disdain and attitude is such a relief. It is fresh air. I need to breathe it in deep or suffocate. Or maybe it's just the devil you know.

Whatever the case, apparently I do not possess a lick of sense when it comes to this girl—this woman. She is all woman now. Her baby softness has melted away, leaving lush curves and elegant lines. Delilah Baker is a ripe peach, with pouty red "fuck me" lips.

"Don't go there, man," I groan in the dark. But I am there and can't escape.

Seeing her walk into my office was a kick to the chest and a hard tug to the balls. She was all jiggle and sway in the best of ways—curvy hips, bouncing breasts, glossy hair floating around her shoulders.

And those red lips, like an exclamation point on the "go to hell, Macon" statement she made with each look my way. I have zero doubt Delilah wanted to nut me the entire time we talked. She never could hide her irritation. But what irritated me, what irritates me still, is her willingness to pay for Samantha's sins.

I've always hated that about Delilah. She would fight me tooth and nail, but with Sam, she would roll over and play doormat.

I can't exactly blame her in this case. Delilah believes she's protecting her mother from pain. It's noble as hell. I'm the asshole taking advantage of it, because I don't believe for one second that Sam will come back and make amends.

I shocked myself accepting Delilah's crazy offer, part of my mind screaming to shut the hell up and let the poor woman leave. Let the whole thing with Sam go. But I didn't. I can't. I don't want to examine too closely *why* I can't because I'm no longer certain if this is about the watch, Sam, or Delilah.

Delilah. We react to each other like the vinegar-and-baking-soda experiments we used to do in science class as kids. Even now she brings out the immature ass in me. But the second she walked back into my life, I became aware of two uncomfortable but undeniable facts: I am lonely as hell, and Delilah Baker feels like home.

And now she will be living in mine. It's both a victory and a calamity waiting to happen.

"Damn." This is a terrible idea. The woman hates my guts, and rightly so; I was an asshole to her in my youth. I hurt her in ways that make me cringe. She has hurt me in ways she doesn't even know. We could end up tearing each other apart.

Sharp pain shoots down my leg as I reach over and grab my phone, determined to halt this madness. Her last text looms bright in the darkness: It's midnight somewhere. I'm in. Are you?

She might as well have said, "I double-dog dare you, Con Man."

I find myself smiling, my thumb rubbing over the edge of the phone. I should text her back, call it off. I know this. But my fingers don't move.

I have been on my own for the last ten years. Since becoming Arasmus and inheriting all the bullshit that comes with fame, I locked myself away from all but the most essential contacts. I thought I liked my solitude. There is safety in not having anyone around who really knows me. I can be anyone, as glossy as a well-polished mirror.

And there's the rub. People see what they want to see, like what they want to like: my money, my fame, my looks. In the end, they see nothing. Delilah won't be fooled by the exterior shine. She never has been. If that's a good thing or bad, I'm not certain.

A voice whispers in my head that I'll regret it for the rest of my life if I step away now. For all I know, it could be the devil urging me on. But my gut has gotten me this far, and so I set the phone down.

CHAPTER SIX

Delilah

DeeLight to SammyBaker: I'm cleaning up your mess as usual. If you have any love for me or Mama, you'll come home.

———

I should hate the sight of Macon's house. But I can't. It's just too damn beautiful. That I love the house makes me want to kick something—preferably Macon's tight butt.

Once again, North answers the door. "Good morning, Ms. Baker."

"Delilah, please." I step inside and draw in a breath of that lovely lavender-and-lemon scent. Damn it.

"Delilah."

"Is North your first name or last?" I ask as he shuts the door behind me.

His nose wrinkles, and he seems to hesitate. "First." He visibly winces before bracing himself. "My full name is North West."

There are many things I can say, but I'm figuring he's heard them all.

"*North by Northwest* is one of my favorite movies."

North stares at me as if I'm off my rocker before breaking into a wry smile. "Are you messing with me? Did Saint tell you my name?"

"No. Why?"

North shakes his head. "That's my mother's favorite movie."

"Ah. Hence the name?"

"Yep. Unfortunately."

"Well, I'm named after my great-aunt Delilah, who drowned in a pie."

North chokes out a laugh. "I'm sorry, what?"

"She was packing up one of her blue-ribbon-winning Strawberry Delights to take to a Monday-night social when she fainted—the doctor thinks she had a problem with low blood sugar—and ended facedown in the pie."

North blinks. "I . . ."

"Don't get sucked into one of Delilah's yarns, North," Macon suddenly says from the entrance to the hall. "That's one rabbit hole you don't want to go down."

He's in a wheelchair, which is an unnerving sight. I might think of Macon in terms of ass and hat, but somehow, in my mind, he was always invincible and immune to injury. He's still an asshat, though.

"It's not a yarn," I snap. "It's the truth."

He rolls his eyes. "The woman asphyxiated on rhubarb. She didn't drown in a pie."

"Poh-tay-toe. Poh-tah-toe."

"Let's call the whole thing off," North finishes with a wink.

I smile.

Macon makes a sound of annoyance. "Don't you have work to do, North?"

North doesn't bother looking his way. "No, *boss*." His tone isn't exactly sarcastic, but it's clear he's not worried about his job security.

"Then find some," Macon says blandly. He isn't even looking at North, but at me. "I told you to bring your things."

In his instructions, Macon said I needed to pack enough for at least a week. After that, I'd be given an opportunity to return home and gather what I thought I'd need for the year and make arrangements to put my house up for rent if I so chose. I'd wanted to fling my phone.

"My bags are in the car."

"North can bring them in for you."

"Aren't they going to the guesthouse?"

"Sorry, Tot. You're not getting the guesthouse. North lives there."

Frustration blooms like a hot rash. "So? Didn't Sam live there as well?"

Macon's dark eyes narrow to slits. "You're not Sam. You're staying here."

I can't let it go. "Why?"

Red washes over his cheeks. "Because I said so."

The words ring through the house, startling us both, I think. He blinks as if coming out of a fog. I, on the other hand, huff out a humorless laugh. "You sound like my mother."

"Be careful I don't spank you."

Unwelcome heat touches my thighs, and I shift my weight to keep from clenching them. "Try. It."

We glare at each other from across the way. I'm fairly certain we're both playing a game of chicken with this arrangement, seeing who will cave first.

North claps his hands together. "Okay, children. I'm going to bring Delilah's bags in. I want to see happy faces when I return. Happy. Faces."

Macon doesn't take his eyes from me. "Piss off, North."

North shakes his head. "Your funeral, man."

He leaves us alone.

Macon's gaze darts over my face. "You gonna be a pain in the butt the whole time?"

"Only when you act like an ass."

His lips quirk. "Kind of feeling the urge to pull one of your pigtails right now."

I won't smile. Nope. No way. "I'm not wearing pigtails."

A husky note enters his voice. "Maybe tomorrow, then."

"Don't hold your breath."

He snorts lightly. "Come on. I'll show you around." He touches a knob on his armrest, and the wheelchair turns around.

I catch up and walk alongside him. Macon glances up at me and frowns. "Don't know if I like you looming over me."

"Now you know how I felt all those years," I say happily. In high school, Macon was always at least five to six inches taller than me. He looks larger now, and I'm guessing he probably tops me by a foot when he's standing.

He grunts and stops at a set of doors. "Hit the button, will you?"

I do as asked. "An elevator? That's convenient."

"It's ridiculous in a two-story house," he admits with a touch of self-deprecation. "But the previous owner was an artist. She painted massive canvases and didn't trust them to be taken down the stairs. Her one request of the house was that it had an extrawide elevator."

Ah, the whims of the rich. Want an elevator in your seaside mansion? No problem.

A small click and a light on the panel announces the car. I open the doors and slide back an inner door. Macon rolls in, and we're soon riding upward.

"How long are you in the chair?" I ask.

"Another week; then we go to the doctor, and they're fitting me with a walking boot."

"We?"

He glances my way as the car stops. "Yes, 'we.' You're my assistant now, Tot. You go where I go."

He might as well have said, "Welcome to hell."

Pinching the bridge of my nose to ward off a headache, I peek at him from under the curve of my hand. "So what does the assistant part of the job entail?"

"You're asking that now, after you've offered yourself up on a platter?"

"Just answer the question, Macon."

The edges of his lips curl. It's not a smile. It looks more like victory. "Get shit done for me, no questions asked. And obviously help me out while I heal."

I'm surprised at this. Macon never likes conceding weakness. The mere fact that he expects me to aid him is not only surprising; it's shocking.

"Okay," I draw out, feeling not relief exactly but as if there's a tiny spot of light at the end of the tunnel. It doesn't sound so bad.

It's going to feel like a yearlong dental visit, and you know it.

"As for cooking," he says as we move down the hall, "I expect healthy meals. No heavy southern shit."

I don't bother telling him that not all southern cooking is heavy. And it certainly isn't shit. He knows all of this well. He's just being . . . Macon, trying to get my goat.

"We start shooting again in June," he goes on, either ignoring or not noticing my side-eye, "and they'll have a fit if I gain an ounce."

"Have to keep your ass in tip-top shape for all those screen flashes?"

He pauses, and the air becomes too close as his gaze glides over me, a smile oozing out—smug and heated. "Why, Delilah, have you been watching my ass on screen?"

"No. But Sam has. Can't say it was enough to keep her around, though, eh?"

His gaze narrows.

What. Are. You. Doing? You can't antagonize him!

But if I roll over for him completely, I'm as good as dead. It's a delicate balance, dealing with Macon Saint. So I merely keep my bland smile in place and wait him out, pretend that my chest isn't tight and that uncomfortable heat isn't burning my skin.

Thankfully, I'm given a reprieve.

"My room is at the end," he says. "Your room is here."

We stop at a door one down from his. I'd been hoping for the other end of the house.

Reading me well, Macon gives an amused look. "You need to be near in case I need something in the night."

"Seriously? Is this some form of extra punishment?"

Macon's nose wrinkles in affront. "Jesus, Delilah. I've been in a car accident. I need someone nearby. End of story."

He looks so put out and offended that my shoulders slump. "I'm sorry. I'm a little tense."

"You think?" But his scowl eases as he reaches out for the door. He rolls into the room and then moves back so I can enter.

The room is incredible. It's as big as my living room back home, with a sitting area on one side and a bed with a cream-colored linen headboard on the other end. But it's the view that grips me, all glittering ocean and sunlit skies. A set of french doors that open up to a wide veranda beckons me closer.

"Still want to live in the guesthouse?" Macon says behind me.

I take another look around, tempted to either fling myself onto the soft white bedspread or race out onto the balcony, where a set of cane chairs waits for me. "I suppose this will do."

"While we're waiting for North, I'll show you around, and then you can make me breakfast."

I'd almost forgotten why I was here.

He leads me past other guest rooms, an upstairs gym, an office, and then down we go to the main level, where there is a home movie theater, a glass-walled wine room, a cozy den, and an open great room. It's all gorgeous, but I head for the kitchen, itching to look around.

I try to contain myself, but it's difficult. No expense has been spared, from the marble countertops that will be perfect for baking to the Sub-Zero catering fridge.

I let out a small gasp at the sight of the massive black-enamel-and-brass stove. "A *La Cornue*."

"A what?" Macon asks, frowning as if I'm off my rocker.

"Your stove." I stroke the sleek edge of it just because I can. "It's exceptional for cooking." And about forty thousand dollars retail. I swear, my eyes water a little.

Macon moves farther into the kitchen. "I have fans who look at me the way you're looking at that stove."

"Their priorities are out of whack." I bend over to inspect the oven. Flawless. "Have you ever even used this thing?"

"I believe I burned some eggs while attempting an omelet. Mostly, I use the microwave."

I place my hand on my chest. "You are killing me here."

He gives me a rare genuine smile, and it transforms his face from stern and bitter to something almost boyish. It makes him breathtaking. I'm so stunned by the sight, I almost miss his reply. "I have a kick-ass blender, if you're interested. I make a mean kelp smoothie."

"Getting excited over a kelp smoothie? I almost pity you, Saint."

All at once, his affable expression dims. "Don't call me Saint. I don't like the way it sounds coming from you."

Stung, I turn away and inspect the fridge. I'd almost forgotten that Macon and I don't rub well together. It's easy to do, and that has always been part of my frustration when dealing with him. Because when Macon wants to, he is utterly charming, fun, and engaging. He draws people in like moths to a bright flame. Only I'm the one who constantly gets burned. Everyone else walks away happy and wanting to know him better.

"You'll need to tell me how you want to take your meals," I say, keeping my attention on looking over what I have to work with. "Do you want them delivered on a tray? Set up in a certain room?"

His presence is a weight against my back, and I know he's watching me. Tough shit.

"Also any food allergies you might have," I go on when he doesn't answer. "I read over the dietary restrictions the studio's nutritionists have placed you on. I'm going to have to get creative because there isn't much to work with. I'll go shopping later."

The kitchen clock ticks softly.

"You pouting now?" Macon finally asks in a flat voice.

Sharp pricks dance along my skin, and my jaw begins to ache from clamping it shut. When I know I won't shout, I answer in measured tones. "I'm maintaining a professional manner with my employer."

"Then why won't you look at me?"

Because I might grab one of the lovely heirloom tomatoes you have displayed in this fruit basket and chuck it at your fat head.

"I wasn't aware that you needed constant attention," I grit out.

"Now you know better," he says equably.

Of all the . . . a breath hisses out between my clenched teeth. Slowly I turn to find him smirking as if he knows perfectly well he's working my last nerve.

"There is an old saying," I tell him pleasantly. "Never bite the hand that feeds you."

Far from being cowed, he seems to be enjoying himself. "I'm kind of partial to 'Don't look a gift horse in the mouth.'"

Those heirlooms are growing more tempting. He catches the direction of my gaze, and he appears delighted.

"Try it," he says, all silk and promise. "See what happens."

Oh, but I want to. I can picture little squishy bits of red sliding down his cheeks, tiny seeds clinging to his stubble. But that's what he wants. Macon loves fighting with me. I have to remember that. I have to ignore that I love fighting him too.

Well, *love* isn't the right word. "Derive some sort of weird satisfaction from it" is closer to the truth.

Sucking in a breath, I turn and pull a carton of eggs from the refrigerator, then grab one of the tomatoes. "I'm making you eggs in a cloud with roasted tomatoes, smashed avocado, and herbs." I flick on the oven before searching for bowls and a frying pan. Oh, Lord, all copper. All French. I'm in love.

Behind, Macon makes one of those expansive noises men draw out when they think women are being unreasonable. "Sounds . . . fluffy."

"They are." Everything in his kitchen is in the perfect place, and I easily locate a few bowls and a whisk.

"Delilah."

My back tightens. I crack an egg and separate the yolk from the whites.

He sighs again. "Countless people call me Saint. Only you call me Macon with that bitter honey voice."

Bitter honey? The description does something to me that I don't like, that sets me off-center. Resting my hands on the cool counter, I remain quiet, but I'm no longer actively ignoring him. There is no softness in his tone, but it is thicker now as if the confession wants to stick in his throat before he forces it out. "I like it."

The words take the starch out of my spine. But I don't know what to say.

He isn't done, at any rate. "How about this? You promise not to call me Saint, and I'll knock three months off the deal."

I whirl around. "What? Are you crazy? You are. You knocked a damn screw loose in that accident, didn't you?"

Macon's grin is wide and devious. "Got you."

For a second I just stare. Got me? Got me! Blood rushes to my face. "You . . . you . . ." I don't think. I let the tomato fly.

He isn't so quick in the chair, and despite me zinging it to the left, the heirloom smashes apart on his shoulder. Doesn't stop him from laughing his ass off, though.

"Get out of my kitchen, you rat," I yell, waving my whisk at him.

"I'm going, I'm going," he says, still laughing as he spins around and starts wheeling away. He's almost out of sight when he calls over his shoulder. "Missed you too, Tater Tot."

Lucky for him, he's out of range. I grab another egg and get on with my work. But I find myself fighting a smile as I make breakfast.

CHAPTER SEVEN

Delilah

Between creating a menu for the week, shopping, unpacking, and getting my new kitchen in order, I barely hear from Macon the next day. He sends a note to skip breakfast, then has his lunch—a roast-chicken-and-avocado salad with a lemon vinaigrette—in the upstairs den. North comes to collect it, and I go about my business. So far, I've been told via text that I'll start all the administrative duties later. I take the opportunity to drive out to my favorite seafood monger and come home with succulent and glossy shrimps and scallops.

My catering kitchen was a sterile industrial space with stainless counters, concrete floors covered with dull-gray epoxy, harsh fluorescent lights, and rows of overhead steel vent fans that left a constant hum. It was hot when cooking and cool during early-morning prep. Nothing meant for comfort, but everything I needed to feed mass numbers of people.

Macon's kitchen is warm and inviting. The wide-plank hardwood floors are silky smooth underfoot. Sunlight streams in through the windows and tracks a path across the honed marble counters as the time passes.

There is a cozy wood booth tucked into a corner nook that overlooks the ocean. I sit there, drinking a latte made with the commercial-grade espresso maker, and flick through magazines I've neglected for months—never finding the time to relax while running my business.

Surrounded by the sun and the sea and the thoughtful beauty of the house, the long-held tension that has settled deep into my flesh over the past few years starts to lose its grip.

With a slower rhythm than I used in my catering kitchen, I start dinner. There is a different kind of pleasure cooking here. I'm not in a rush. Instead, I sink into the essence of the food, the crisp sound of my knife slicing through red peppers, the fresh clean scent the vegetable gives off as its flesh yields to the blade.

My breathing becomes slow and deep, almost as if I'm meditating.

I'd stopped cooking like this—for an individual, for myself. Somehow cooking had become a race, a need to prove my talent, but in doing so, I'd distanced myself from the very thing I love.

"You thinking deep thoughts, Tot?"

Macon's voice pulls me out of my zone with a jolt. He's by the kitchen booth, sitting in a patch of amber sunlight that colors his skin deep bronze. It also emphasizes the bruising around his eye and the lines of strain along his mouth. He's leaning back in the wheelchair with a casual air, but there is a deliberate stillness about him that makes his pose a lie. He is in pain.

"I was actually thinking about how much I love to cook," I tell him, moving to the fridge.

"Just as long as you're not contemplating another tomato launch," he says lightly.

I cut him a glance, and he widens his eyes as if entirely innocent. Snorting, I pull out some milk. "Alas, the tomatoes are all used up. But I do have an extra head of cauliflower, so I wouldn't tempt me."

"Ouch." He holds a hand up in surrender. "I'll be good now. Cross my heart." Biting back a smile, he draws an *X* over his broad chest, then tracks my movements as I collect honey and spices. "You always did flow around a kitchen like you were dancing to music only you could hear."

My brows lift, a beat skipping in my heart. "Did I?"

"You never noticed?" He runs the edge of his thumb along the armrest of his chair, eyes on the movement. "I used to envy that ease. How you found a place to fit in perfectly."

"One place," I correct thickly. "Whereas you fit in everywhere else."

He takes that in with a short exhale, and his lips press together, caught between a smile and a grimace. "Looks can be deceiving." He nods toward me. "What are you doing now?"

"Making some turmeric lattes." I put the spiced milk under the foaming nozzle on the espresso machine and let it froth and heat. The scent of cinnamon, cloves, cardamom, and turmeric fills the air.

"It smells like Thanksgiving," he says as I pour the lattes into two cups.

"Here." I offer him one and then take a seat on the booth.

Macon moves up to the end of the table, then takes a sip. "Delicious."

"Mmm . . . turmeric is an anti-inflammatory, which can help with pain."

He pauses, eyes meeting mine over the rim of his porcelain cup. "It isn't that bad."

"Why do men pretend that they're not in pain when they clearly are?"

"Because we don't like being fussed over," he answers with a small smile.

"See, that's the strange part about it," I say, cupping my latte. "Men love being fussed over. I've never heard so much whining as when a man is sick."

A gleam of challenge lights his eyes. "You're missing the key factor." Macon sets his cup on the table. A bit of creamy foam clings to the corner of his lip, and he licks it away with the tip of his tongue. "We only do that when we expect our women to kiss and cuddle us, then tuck us into bed."

I blame the steam from my latte for the hot tightness over my cheeks.

Macon's gaze zeroes in on them, and his lip curls upward. "So unless you're offering?"

"Remember the cauliflower, Macon. My aim is stellar."

He huffs out a laugh. "Didn't think so." Then a speculative look enters his eyes. "You got a boyfriend who might give you a hard time over this arrangement?"

I smirk into the well of my cup. "A little late to be asking that, don't you think?"

"Wouldn't be my problem," he says with a shrug. "I'm simply curious."

"My last relationship ended a few months ago." Ah, Parker. He'd been perfect on paper: cute without being intimidating, nice without being challenging, a successful marketing exec with his own condo. He liked giving oral and didn't fall asleep directly after sex. Always a plus. It also had been too easy to let him go, which means it had been the right thing to do.

Macon sits back in his chair and rests his hands on his abs. "What happened?"

"We didn't suit."

"Didn't suit." He sounds skeptical as if he assumes I'd been dumped and was embarrassed to admit it.

I set my cup down with a sigh. "He snored."

Macon barks out a laugh. "You dumped a guy because he snored? Jesus, Delilah, everyone snores now and then."

"I know. I'm not a total jerk." I glare at him when he raises a brow. "I'm not. You weren't there. This was not normal. He snored so badly his dog would run out of the freaking room and cower. The neighbor would pound on the walls, for pity's sake."

Macon chortles, grinning wide. "And he didn't know?"

"The man slept like he was in a snore-induced coma. Meanwhile, I couldn't sleep a wink with him around." A shudder passes through me at the memory—like a chain saw meeting a boulder. "Maybe if I'd been in love with him, it would have been different. The sex was great, I'll say that. He was very good with his—"

"You really don't have to elaborate," Macon deadpans.

I fail at hiding my smile. "Anyway, if I couldn't even spend an actual night with him, how could I maintain a relationship that was doomed to never move forward? And you?" I counter, wanting the spotlight off my romantic failures.

"I can safely report that no woman has accused me of snoring."

"Har. Har. You know what I meant. You have some girlfriend who's going to look at me funny when she finds out I'm living here?"

His tone becomes droll. "I'd hope any girlfriend I'd have would trust me enough to hire a female live-in chef, but no, I haven't had a girlfriend since . . . well, your sister." His mouth twists as if tasting something off.

"Truly," I squeak, not believing it. Ten years, and no other close relationship with a woman? It's both a crime and slightly horrifying to learn that Sam has been his only girlfriend. Did she break the mold for him? God, I don't want to be here knowing that.

Thoughts of Sam have my insides coiling tight. I wonder where she is and if she can feel my ire like a chill on her back.

He pulls a face. "I'm not cut out for long term. It's no fun for me. I'd rather go for casual dating, frankly."

Now that I can believe. But Sam fills the space between us like a ghost. All right, more like a poltergeist; Sam would never be the type to quietly haunt.

"I am truly sorry about Sam, you know," I say to Macon. "I'm so ashamed of what she did."

His eyes dart between mine, a small frown forming. "She doesn't deserve you, Delilah. She never did."

My answering smile is tight and bittersweet. "And yet I still love her. Go figure."

We finish our lattes in pensive silence, and then I wash out the cups while he studies me.

"Dinner will be ready in about twenty minutes," I tell him.

"Okay." He doesn't make a move to go.

"You want me to serve it here?"

Warm brown eyes move over me. "I want you to eat with me."

I go still. "That wasn't part of the deal."

Macon tilts his head as if trying to view me from a new angle. Whatever he sees has his features smoothing out, wry humor filling his gaze. "You afraid to eat with me?"

"I'm not afraid." But I am. Less than twenty-four hours I've been in his orbit, and already I'm in over my head. As a teen, I knew exactly how to handle Macon: aim for head-on collision; sort out the collateral damage later. This Macon keeps disarming me with moments of rare honesty and sly humor. This Macon *flirts*. He cajoles. He can probably charm a thief into turning themselves in.

I take too long to say anything else, and Macon's expression darkens. "You haven't changed, have you? Still looking at me as if I'm the devil."

"Macon," I say with a voice gone dry. "To me you were the devil."

Silence settles between us as we stare at each other. The intensity in his gaze is a living thing that I try not to quail under. Finally he blinks, and it's as if a shade has been drawn over him. "I'll have dinner in the den. Text me when it's ready."

He leaves me to my work, and I try not to feel guilty. And fail miserably.

———

DeeLight to SammyBaker: Sometimes I really hate you.

Most of us will pretend away the shit we're dealing with in life; if we don't think about it, it isn't happening. Just like I can pretend that I am merely a cook for a famous actor. Little details such as the actor is Macon Saint are best pushed to the far corners of my mind.

Macon makes it impossible to ignore him.

According to the detailed list of instructions he has provided me, Macon likes to rise with the sun every day. Which is just plain deranged in my book; if humans were meant to get up with the sun, we wouldn't have invented blackout curtains.

Upon rising, Macon *must* have his smoothie.

Said drink is a superfoods green smoothie with a list of ingredients as long as my arm, including spinach, kale, apples, and algae. I add coconut water and a half a banana for a touch of sweetness since the concoction tastes like funky socks without it.

He sends a text for his drink just as I'm pouring the goop into a large glass and cursing the early hour.

ConMan: Why am I waiting?

Rolling my eyes, I text back.

DeeLight: Is this like one of those "What's the sound of one hand clapping" riddles?

Riddle me this, what's the sound of Macon dialing 911 to report
a robbery?

Asshat. Seriously, he could convey a little sense of hesitation or
meekness today.

You only get three chances to hold that threat over my head.
After that, I'm making a jerk-off gesture.

I don't know if Macon takes his drink with a straw or not, but
earlier I found a massive silly straw in a drawer. I plunk it in the glass
as his text comes in.

Am suddenly dying to see you make this gesture. Get up here
so I can use up my threat quota.

"Here" being an upstairs den at the far corner of the house with
a killer view and a small corner cupola that boasts a wall of windows.
Within a nearly 360-degree viewing area, Macon sits behind a desk. He
waves me in and keeps talking to someone.
"I'm fine, Karen. The bruising around my face is nearly gone." He
takes his smoothie without a glance but then pauses when the red silly
straw bops him on the nose.
Attempting to be the picture of innocence, I bite the inside of
my lip when he glares up at me. He holds that glare as his tongue
snakes out and snares the end of the straw. It should look ridiculous,
Macon sucking hard on a twisty, loopy kid's straw, his lean cheeks
hollowing out from the force he needs to get to his smoothie. But
it doesn't.
I feel each tug along with the straw.
Craziness. Utter insanity.

I move to go, but he holds up a hand and points to a leather-and-chrome armchair by the window. Apparently I am to sit and stay. Bah. I cross my legs and lightly bounce my top leg with impatience.

"I have a new assistant," he says to Karen, giving me a withering glance as he tosses the straw into a trash can. "Yes, another new one." His lips curve just slightly.

My leg swings with more vigor. Macon's gaze zeroes in on it, and his lids lower a fraction. I find myself rethinking my decision to wear jean shorts that draw attention to my bare legs and go still.

It doesn't stop him from staring. His gaze turns slumberous as he leans back in his chair. "Hmm?" he murmurs into the phone.

The muscles along my inner thigh draw tight, and I uncross my legs, switching to the other leg. It's too hot in this damn room without curtains to mute the morning sun beating down on my shoulders and the tops of my breasts. I fight the urge to fan myself.

A slow smile unfurls over Macon's lips, and he raises his head until our eyes meet. "Oh, I won't be having any problems with her."

On pain of death, his expression implies.

With deliberation, I lift my middle finger and pretend to put lipstick on with it. His smile turns positively gleeful, his teeth catching on his lower lip as if to rein it in. "Call it instinct," he says to Karen. And then he faces the ocean, taking another long drink of his smoothie.

Karen says something that makes his nostrils flare in clear irritation. "For fuck's sake, no." Another pause. "Because she's my employee and just . . . no."

He sounds so offended that my insides pinch. Because it doesn't take a genius to know Karen is asking if we're screwing each other. Macon rubs his forehead. "She's not an actress." He huffs out a truly entertained laugh. "Believe me, she wants no part of this life. You'll understand when you meet her."

The smug assurance in his tone rubs over my skin like grit.

"No more questions," he says with an impatient wave of his hand. "I'm going now."

Cool quiet falls over the room, and I content myself with listening to the waves crash into the beach. I'm not going to give him the satisfaction of asking why he wanted me to listen in on his conversation. We haven't faced each other since the awkward way we ended things last night. Which is fine—employers aren't supposed to hang out with the help.

But now Macon sits in his chair like the lord of the manor, his gaze boring into me so hard it prods at my breastbone like a pesky finger, daring me to look back at him. I don't give in to the urge.

He finishes his drink before speaking. "You put something different in this."

"It's arsenic. I'd have gone the powdered-cookie route, but you're on a diet."

Amusement gleams darkly in his eyes.

"That mouth." From under the fringe of his lashes, he assesses me, the tip of his long finger idly stroking his lower lip. "I'd thought my memory exaggerated the sass that mouth is capable of. Clearly not."

Irritation catches at the back of my throat. "My memory is crystal clear, Con Man. Don't pretend as though you weren't every bit as bad."

We glare at each other from opposite sides of his desk while visions of me dumping the green smoothie on his lap dance through my head. Those severe brows of his lower, and I wonder if he knows exactly what I'm thinking.

His voice is a soft thread cutting through the silence. "I remember everything, Delilah."

Maybe he intends that to be a threat—a promise, perhaps, that one day there will be a reckoning—but it sounds like something else, almost as if he's kept those memories close all this time, pulling them out every now and then to examine them like some sort of kitsch bauble you keep for nostalgia.

Without waiting for a reply, he sets a new phone on the desk. "Yours." He pushes it toward me. "My calendar and list of contacts are synced to it. All calls for me will go to you."

"All calls?"

"On that list, yeah." He nods to the phone, which I've left lying on the desk. "Only calls from you, Karen, and North will ring to my phone."

I take the phone and scroll through the contacts. There are about forty names on it, both men and women. "Who are these people? Your friends?"

"Some of them. Mostly business contacts. Whenever a call comes in, take a message. I'll call them back if I want to."

"Every time? That sounds kind of cold."

"Why? Because I won't answer?" His expression is somewhere between *you poor deluded thing* and *aren't you precious?* "No one is going to be offended. They're used to it."

"All right, then."

"Don't answer unknown calls. If a preprogrammed name pops up, it's okay. But no one else, Tot. Ever."

"Jesus, you make it sound like life and death," I say with a little laugh.

He doesn't blink. "I'm completely serious about this. The world is full of unhinged people. If one of them happens to get through, you'll only encourage them by answering." He rests his hands on the flat of his stomach. "Which brings me to another point. At the moment, no one knows who you are, but if, at any time, someone approaches you and asks about me, pretend you don't know what they're talking about, disengage, and call either me or North immediately."

My fingers curl around the hard edges of the phone. "Are you trying to scare me?"

"I'm trying to keep you safe. Promise me you'll listen, Delilah."

He's so intently serious that I can't find it in myself to tease, even though I want to. Because the whole thing makes me uncomfortable. I don't like the idea of having to watch my back. Some of this must show on my face because his tense shoulders relax, and his expression eases. "It's just safety protocol, Tot."

My back grows cold as if unseeing eyes are staring at me. I shake off the fanciful image; it will do me no good to become paranoid. "All right. I got it."

Satisfied, Macon wheels away from the desk. "I've sent you a list of tasks for the week. Things may be added at will."

I find the email in question and read through it. Dry cleaning to be fetched, dress shoes and a couple of suits to be picked up from various shops on Rodeo Drive. He has a mountain of emails he wants me to answer, a calendar to reschedule, calls to return. I have a script I must follow when talking to people, nice little ways to evade giving away any solid details about Macon's injuries. I'm also expected to purchase a long list of birthday presents for various people and see them personally delivered. None of these things can be purchased online—they're all from specialty stores around LA. Make that from all ends of LA.

"Seriously," I say when I'm finished.

The space between his brows wrinkles. "What's the problem, Tot?"

"I never knew you to be a shopper, Con Man. This reads like a list made by a diva."

He snorts. "You should be thankful I'm not a diva."

"And when am I going to find time to cook your meals?"

"You'll figure it out."

Tucking the phone away, I stand. "Is that all, sir? I've got a few menus to plan."

He grins wide. "Sir. I like that."

My finger is itching to flip up and say hello again.

He knows it. His dark eyes gleam with anticipation. I won't give him the satisfaction, though. I turn to leave when he speaks up again.

"Oh, and I expect a snack at ten. Stop glaring, and get to work, slow coach."

Yep. Definitely in hell.

CHAPTER EIGHT

Macon

The steering wheel presses hard against my cheekbone, airbag clumped up under my neck, hot metal on my leg. Rain falls through the shattered window, blurring the lines, making the blood run faster into my eyes. I hurt. I hurt all over.

The tiny voice of my car service drifts from somewhere overhead. "Mr. Saint? Are you injured? Mr. Saint?"

My mouth fills with the metallic taste of blood.

"Mr. Saint?"

I'm here. Don't leave me.

"Macon?" A voice of hot, sticky honey. I want to taste it, let it drizzle over my skin. "Macon?"

The camera flash pops in my eyes.

God, look at him. He's really hurt. Shouldn't we get help?

We will just take one more picture. Feel the muscle on his arm. It's so hard.

They're taking pictures of me stuck in this car. They're fucking feeling me up. While I'm twisted up in this fucking car. A hand grabs my arm. Shouting, I swing wide, connecting with something hard. A tremendous crash rings out.

"Macon! What the great hell?"

It's her voice—no longer honey sweet but sharp and irate, a voice I can never fully get out of my mind—that pulls me out of my fog. My surroundings come into focus with a breath. Delilah kneels on the floor, gathering up the ruins of what looks to be my dinner.

"Shit, I'm sorry," I say, honestly horrified I took a swing at her.

"What the hell is wrong with you?" she huffs. "I called your name several times, and you were just sitting there, staring out the window."

"I was asleep." I run a hand over my face and find it damp with sweat. "Did I hurt you?"

"I'm fine. But the tray might take exception to being whacked." She shoots me a glare, and I brace for another rebuke, but her stiff expression eases. "You were having a nightmare, weren't you?"

"Just got disoriented. The painkillers make me loopy."

Delilah's hard stance softens. "I shouldn't have grabbed you without checking to see if you were awake. Daddy always said it was dangerous to jar people out of a nightmare."

"It wasn't a nightmare." The lie comes out snappish. Probably because I'm lying. But damn if I want to see that pity in her eyes. "Although I agree, you shouldn't go around grabbing people while they're sleeping. Kind of rude, regardless." *God, shut up, Macon. You're the rude ass.* But I can't seem to help myself around this girl.

Her nose wrinkles. "I guess that bug up your butt is a permanent condition."

"Bringing up my butt again." I force a smile. "You think about it a lot, do you?"

Her answering smile is all sharp edges and bite. "I think about kicking it nearly every time we're in the same room together."

A laugh breaks free, pushing at my aching ribs. "That I can believe. Here, let me help you." Without thinking, I bend forward to help her and immediately regret the action when a shard of pain punches into my side. She hears me hiss and sees the way I shoot back into my seat.

"Macon, when are you going to admit you're in pain?" She rises to help.

A shudder runs down my back. The thought of her touching me in pity turns my skin cold. "Don't," I snap. My mind yells that I'm making things worse, but my mouth can't keep closed. "Don't touch me."

She halts, her hand still stretched toward me. She has slim fingers, short-trimmed nails with numerous scars and calluses marring her skin. Chef's hands. Her capable, abused fingers curl into a fist. "Don't touch you?" she repeats dully, but the hurt and outrage is still there. "Seriously?"

Heat swarms around my neck. I don't know how to explain to her why I cannot have her touching me right now. "I don't need help."

For a second, she stares. Shame washes over me. I haven't felt that particular emotion in so long I'm choking on it.

This is what she does; she exposes me—lays bare all the parts I want to hide, need to hide.

Hot in the face, I try to back up. My wheels run over the fallen tray with a crunch. "Shit."

"Here, let me—" She reaches up, but I back away.

And hit the corner of the desk with my bad side. "Shit!"

Delilah stands and attempts to help. "You're going the wrong way."

"I'm not . . ."

Suddenly we're stuck in this farce of a dance, me smashing at the controls of my chair and whacking into everything, Delilah hopping around so she won't get her toes crushed while yelling at me to let her help.

"I've got it," I snap. "If you'd just back off."

Her cheeks flush dark red. "You're zooming around like an angry bee! Calm down."

"Don't tell me to—" The lamp falls off the desk with a crash. "God damn it," I finally shout. "Leave it be, Delilah!"

The force behind my order lashes out with the efficiency of a whip, and Delilah flinches. It's enough to make us both pause. Breath coming out in hard pants, I stare at her for one awful second. Her eyes are round, lips parted with her agitated breathing. Then a glint, a rage I'm familiar with but haven't seen in ten years, forms.

"What the actual hell is wrong with you?" she cries, her arms akimbo.

She stands over me like a teacher ready to give a lecture. The band around my chest won't abate. "Nothing a good dose of privacy wouldn't fix."

Delilah snorts long and loud. "That's not what you need a dose of. For crying out loud, Macon. You hire me in part to help you while you're convalescing, but the second I try to offer a hand, you have a temper tantrum."

Temper tantrum? My back teeth click together.

"I didn't hire you. You came to me." My thumb hits my chest for emphasis. "And part of that bargain was that you obeyed my orders without question."

I can see her struggling to keep her cool. She takes a deep breath, her breasts lifting high. I don't want to notice. I don't want her here.

"Look," she starts. "I was simply trying to help you get out from under the desk."

Everything feels too tight now: my skin, my flesh, my insides. I am exposed. "I said I didn't need your help."

"All evidence to the contrary."

"Get out."

She simply raises her brow, crossing her arms under those ample tits.

Undirected rage, helplessness, and frustration rise up. The ugly hot mix surges through my body, and without thought or care, I set it free. "Get out! Get out!"

My shout rings in my ears, crashes over the room. It's so loud, so aggressive, Delilah actually jumps. Her pretty face turns pale, and without another word, she flees.

I watch her go, horrified by my actions. I've never lost my temper like this. And for something so petty and baseless. She was trying to help. I tried to take her head off.

Unbidden, the image of my father standing over a much smaller version of myself with his fist raised flashes into my head. He had loved using his size and strength to intimidate those weaker and smaller than he was.

My stomach lurches, the room tilting sickly. "Fuck."

Crunching over debris, I roll out of the room and into the hall. "Delilah?"

But even as I call out, I catch sight of her car through the upper windows as she drives away.

Delilah

I won't cry. I will not cry. Nope. Not going to happen.

My lids prickle, and I snarl a ripe curse. My car bumps over the driveway as I speed along, my hands gripping the wheel hard enough to make my fingers throb. Macon's shout still rings in my ears.

That asshole. Bullying, mean . . . jerk.

We've always bickered, but he's never screamed at me like that. The force of his rage had been palpable. It shook me to the core.

Nothing is worth this crap. I had a life. A good one. I didn't put it on hold to be verbally abused.

My vision blurs, and I take a breath, trying to steady myself. I'm on the road, heading toward the highway. Away from here. Away from him.

"Shit." I left everything behind.

With him.

"Doesn't matter." I'm not going back. I'll have it shipped. Hell, he can throw it all out. I don't care. I was insane for offering myself up like this anyway. I'll take Mama on a nice long vacation. If she's not here to learn about Sam, then she'll never know.

My phone rings, buzzing away on the seat beside me. A quick glance, and my stomach bottoms out. It's him. The asshole.

I ignore it for three ring cycles. Part of me wants to throw the phone out the window. But I'm not a coward. I might have needed to . . . regroup. But I'm not scared of Macon Asshat Saint.

I answer with the built-in car speaker. "What?"

His voice comes at me from all directions, very deep yet very soft. "I'm sorry."

I drive for a couple of shocked beats because an apology without preamble is the last thing I'd been expecting.

"Delilah?"

I clear my throat. "What?" I ask with slightly less acerbity.

His sigh is a whisper of sound in the small confines of the car. "I'm sorry."

"You already said that."

"It bears repeating."

"True," I concede, driving along. The Pacific glints with orange sparkles as the sun races toward the horizon. Only then do I realize it's on my left side, which means I'm heading north to God knows where. I pull into the parking lot of a seaside taco stand, too distracted to drive safely, just as Macon starts talking again.

"I don't know what came over me. I wasn't myself. I've never . . . never shouted at someone like that."

"Figures you'd choose to start with me."

He makes a sound of self-derision. "It was inexcusable. I don't know what to say to make up for it."

It's on the tip of my tongue to tell him nothing can atone for his behavior. But then I think about how he'd been in pain, embarrassed, frustrated, unable to free himself. I'd seen it play out, clear as day in his eyes, the tightness of his expression and the way he'd thrashed around like a wild animal caught in a trap. And I'd blustered in, ignoring his requests for privacy, convinced I could fix it. That he should behave and listen to me.

I absolutely loathe being managed or babied. Why should Macon feel any differently?

Cringing, I glance out the window and notice a second restaurant boarded up and overlooking the northwest side of the lot. It's basically a dilapidated beach shack, but it has great outdoor space with premium sea views. There was a time when I'd dreamed of owning a place like this. A place I could run and be inspired by. I'd willingly put my dreams on hold for Macon. For Sam. For Mama.

"Delilah?" Macon's hesitant query draws me back to the present and him.

"Yeah?" I whisper before clearing my throat again.

He takes an audible breath. "It won't happen again. I swear."

I snort at that, looking down at my scarred-up chef's hands. "You won't lose your temper? Macon, you might as well say you're going to stop breathing and still live."

He laughs at that, but it sounds tired and weak. "Okay, I deserve that. You're right; I can't promise I won't argue with you."

I roll my eyes, but he can't see it. Even so, I have the weird feeling he knows perfectly well what I'm doing. Maybe it's because I can all but picture his face, not smiling, but the corners of his eyes crinkled in wry humor, his expressive mouth forced into a hard line. He'd have that expression whenever we'd call a stalemate—because we'd never been able to concede to a truce.

"I won't lose my temper in that way again," he says. "I promise."

Doesn't every man start by saying that? I shouldn't even be talking to him. But somehow I am, because I know I, too, would have screamed at him if the tables had been turned. Somewhere inside me, I felt safe enough to take his call. My fingers drum on the steering wheel. For once, he's utterly silent, letting me take my time replying. Macon can be as patient as the day is long if he is after something he wants.

I glance at the old restaurant. Sometimes dreams shift and change. Such is life. I can drive off, leave this place, chase a new dream, leave *him*.

"Come back," he says as if hearing my inward yearnings. "I'll let you wing another tomato at me."

My lips twitch. "It isn't as fun if you aren't trying to get away."

Come back. Why do I want to? What is it about him that has me feeling more present than I have in years? He makes me perversely excited. Makes me want to forget about daydreams and live in the right now. Damn it, I want to return. I must be sick. Twisted. A masochist.

With a sigh, I turn away from the view and put my car into drive. "You do it again, and I'm gone. Our deal is considered fulfilled."

"All right."

"Fine." I glance at the phone as though I'll somehow find him sitting there instead. "But I'm off for tonight. I don't want to see you. Or hear from you."

Wry humor colors his voice. "Fair enough." He pauses. "You'll see and hear from me tomorrow, then, Tot."

He hangs up before I can reply. Bastard. Always getting in the last word.

God, I truly am twisted. I should dread going back and facing him. Instead, I find myself driving a little faster.

I never could resist a challenge.

CHAPTER NINE

Macon

I hang up on Delilah before I do something ridiculous like try to chat with her as she drives back home. She's made it clear I need to go away and leave her be. I'm more than willing to do so; it's not as though I want to face her right now. I wouldn't be able to look her in the eye.

With a grunt, I maneuver my ass off the wheelchair and attempt to lower myself to the floor. It all goes wrong, and I land hard on my hip. Pain sparks and shoots like fireworks. Something seeps into the back of my pants. Great. I'm on my dinner.

North walks in as I'm reaching around me to pick up shards of a plate.

"Well, this is a sight."

I don't bother glancing up. "You need something?"

"No. But it looks like you do." He crouches next to me and starts putting some of the mess on the dented tray. I bite back the request for him to go. He's almost as stubborn as Delilah, and the fight has gone out of me.

"What the hell was all that?" he asks.

Wincing, I lift my thumb to my mouth and find a sliver of glass stuck in my skin. "Guess you heard."

"I wouldn't be surprised if they heard it in Orange County." North pushes my chair back and slings an arm under my shoulders. No asking with him. Just action. And though it chafes to get help from anyone, I'm no longer in the position to bitch about it.

He gets me in the chair. "Shower time."

"Fucking hell." Yeah, I'm not being mature about this. But I'm not having a good time adjusting to the fact that I cannot get my ass in the shower without assistance. My balance is off. With busted ribs and wrist on one side and a busted leg on the other, I can't get into a steady position without massive pain right now.

North has been helping. I should hire a professional nurse, but my level of trust is near zero, and though I don't like the situation, North has a matter-of-fact, deadpan way of dealing with me that makes it bearable.

Pride is a strange beast. We tend to think of it as doing things for ourselves, not leaning on others. Was it my pride or my ego that made me run Delilah off when she tried to help? An itchy, tight twist in my gut makes me think that maybe true pride is more about being able to accept a situation for what it is with grace.

Whatever the case, my respect for those who have had to readjust their way of life and work it out with dignity and grace has increased tenfold.

I'm getting dressed again when Delilah slams her way through the house and shuts herself in for the night. The woman does not walk on light feet. Despite my low mood a smile threatens. She moves through a space like a storm, crashing about and leaving a mess in her wake. Always has.

When we were teens, the bold way she occupied the world around her fascinated me. For all appearances, she was a shy girl, not liking the spotlight turned on her. The clothes she chose, the way she wore her hair, all of it was designed to blend into a crowd. Logically, she should have crept through life as well. But no. Some part of her might have wanted to hide, but Delilah's true nature was to shine bright.

For someone who drew the eye without effort yet secretly hated the attention, I realized even then that she was my true opposite. And that we were both somewhat twisted.

I killed the vital light in her pretty face tonight. Shouted like a tyrant.

"I'm such an asshole."

North, who had returned with his impeccable timing, raises a brow. "You think? Seriously, Saint, what was that? You practically took her head off."

Grunting, I settle onto the couch set up in my bedroom's sitting area. "I don't know. I'm off lately." I pinch the tense spot between my brows. "Even before Delilah showed."

"You need to tell her about the accident."

Accident. I suppose it was. A sick, oily sensation slides down my throat. I swallow it away. "I will."

North gives me a long look before tilting his head to the side. A small crack rings out as he works through a neck kink. I'm in a shit mood; he's tense as fuck.

"What's with you?"

He stops fidgeting. "Martin is here."

"What, now?" I ask more out of irritation than anything. Of course he shows at this hour.

"I told him you might not have time for him, but he insisted on waiting."

"Where'd you leave him?" I ask, not exactly liking the idea of Martin having free rein in my house. I doubt he'd do anything so crass as to snoop. But he's too observant by far.

"He's in the den." Judging by North's tone, it's clear he knows exactly why I asked.

The den is fairly cut off from the rest of the house. Which also means if Delilah has an itch to leave her room and visit the kitchen, she won't encounter us. I've never hidden that I've searched for Sam. But the topic of Delilah's sister has a bad effect on all of us. I have no desire to rub salt in tonight's open wounds.

I find Martin comfortably lounging in my favorite leather chair by the dead fireplace, glass of Pappy Van Winkle in his hand. Martin is a prime example of a life lived hard and fast. Lines already fan out from the corners of his eyes and bracket his thin mouth. His brown eyes are always hard, even when he's amused.

It wasn't until I moved to LA that I noticed the small details of people's looks. But it's part of the culture here. You quickly learn to assess a person's wealth, health, and position of status with a glance.

I offer North a drink, but he shakes his head, then leans a shoulder against the closed door.

I pour myself a glass and sit opposite Martin. My fingers curl around the cool, sharp edges of the cut-crystal glass. "You find her?" No use mucking around with polite chitchat with Martin. Besides, I already know the answer. If he had, she'd be here.

"The girl is a ghost." He frowns, and there's a flash of irritation in his eyes; then it's gone. "I'd be impressed if it wasn't my job to find her."

North looks off, barely holding in a grunt. Talk of Sam puts him in a shit mood as well. Jesus, is there anyone who isn't adversely affected by my ex-partner in misery?

I should be disappointed Sam is still missing. I don't want to think about why I'm not. "Don't take it too hard. She's had a lifetime to perfect her act."

He makes a disgruntled sound and finishes up his drink in one quick gulp. "So have I."

"Leave it be for now."

The request punches into the room with the force of a bomb, and both men gape at me. Hell. I'm shocked as well. It wasn't what I'd planned to say. But now that I have, I lift my chin and stare back. "We have more important things to focus on now."

I swear North mutters, "Like Delilah?" But he gives me a blank look when my head whips around, and I glare. But I can't form the denial. Shaking off my disquiet, I set my glass, still half-full, aside. "I'd rather hear about the other matter."

I need to know my household is safe.

Martin sits forward, resting his wrists on his thighs. "Michelle Fredericks. A real estate agent from Pasadena. I'm thinking that's how she found your address."

The collar of my shirt hugs too tight around my neck. I swear the damn thing shrunk in the wash. "And you're sure she's the one who was with Brown?"

Lisa Brown, my stalker. I can't say the woman's name without feeling slightly ill. I don't care if she's troubled. I just want her far away from me. She was arrested for reckless endangerment and stalking but is out on bail. They slapped her with a restraining order, but it's only a piece of paper, not a guarantee. And Brown wasn't alone the night my car went off the road.

I can tell myself as much as I like that my shitty behavior tonight was all about pride. In some ways it's easier than admitting the fear that lingers, the nightmares. Long ago, I told myself I'd never be afraid of anything again. Too bad emotions don't listen to orders.

Martin hands me his phone. There's a picture queued. It's a headshot, cheaply done and cheesy, the kind you see on real estate signs. A fairly attractive woman in her mid- to late thirties with dark-brown hair smiles back at me.

"Is it her?" North asks.

I stare at the picture, my fingers shaking before I can control them. "I don't know." I remember the scent of strong, cheap flowery perfume. One of the women had been brunette. "It was a blur." Blood and rain tend to do that.

"She's friends with Brown," Martin puts in. "They both belong to a Facebook fan group. Saint's Willing Sinners."

North makes a gurgling noise at the back of his throat, and I know he's holding in a laugh. I flip him off with a glare, but there's no heat behind the action. I'd laugh, too, if it wasn't for the memory of being hunted, being treated like a thing while trapped in that crumpled wreckage.

Martin pins me with a look. "And she was here the other night."

Ice runs through my chest. I shove the fear back. "What?" It isn't a question. More like the beginning of a threat.

North shoves away from the door. "The cameras didn't pick up a thing."

"Easy," Martin says, bland as dry toast. "She didn't come close enough to the house. Just sat in her car two gates down the road. My guys were watching her."

It's that knowledge that lets me sleep at night. And it's that knowledge that also makes my skin feel too tight. All my hard-earned freedom has once again been whittled down to tightly controlled monitoring. The restrictiveness of it yanks at my neck like a choke collar, and for an airless second, I'm back under my father's watch.

No. This time I'm the one in control.

"We need to report this," North says. "Have them arrest her."

Martin shakes his head. "She hasn't done enough to warrant any charges. None that we can prove at the moment, anyway."

"But if she was there . . ."

"He's right." Sighing, I reach for my drink. "We don't have any proof."

"At the very least, we can report her as a person of interest," North pushes.

"Already did that." Martin pockets his phone. "They're going to question her. In the meantime, we keep vigilant. I haven't seen Brown around, but that doesn't mean she lost interest."

"Fucking great," I mutter under my breath.

North lets Martin out, and I head back to my room. It's early. If this had been a month ago, I'd be at an exclusive bar, surrounded by people I barely know, letting their chatter lull me into a mindless calm. I'd feed off the energy of everyone and everything, all the while remaining apart from it. Not a perfect life, but adequate. Enough to stop me from thinking about things best left in the past.

Now, all I want to do is take a painkiller and crawl into bed. I slow down as I near Delilah's door. The house is so quiet I can easily hear the television playing. She's watching *About a Boy*.

A memory hits me, as bright and painful as a spotlight.

We were on the big brown sectional couch in her family room, watching this very movie. Delilah was fourteen, chubby cheeked and wearing a thick braid that ran like a dark snake over her hunched shoulders. She was curled up on one end of the couch, while Sam and I were tucked into the other.

As usual, Sam leaned on me until I lost feeling in my shoulder and tried to nudge her off. She found her way back, digging her bony elbow into spots she knew annoyed the hell out of me.

Hugh Grant tossed out a quip that made me laugh. Delilah laughed too. It hit me that we kept laughing at the same times. She must have realized the same because she turned my way, and our gazes clashed. We always tried our utmost not to look at each other, so it was a visceral punch whenever we failed.

The inevitable reaction of heat, tightness, frustration, and a twisting sense of wrongness ran through my system. And inevitably, I covered it up by opening my big mouth. "Got a crush on old Hugh?"

Hugh Grant played Will in the movie. Cool rich guy who cared for nothing but getting laid and having fun.

She pursed her lips, giving me that withering look of hers, the one that I'd been found lacking. "Well, he's witty. Intelligence is definitely a plus."

"And rich. Don't forget that."

"Being wealthy is part of what makes him a useless asshole."

Sam, who'd been picking at her nail polish, piped up. "He's old, but he's still hot. I'd date him."

Delilah's snort spoke volumes.

"Delilah is more of a Marcus lover," I said, daring her to look back my way. Marcus was the oddball of the story. Awkward, alone, abused by his classmates, and terrified of losing his mother, the one person who he felt truly loved him.

Surprisingly, she smiled, a sad, sort of secretive gesture, and rested her chin on her knees, all but wrapping herself into a tight ball on the couch. "You're right. If there's anyone to love in this movie, it's him."

She cast me as the hapless Will type and her as a Marcus. Part of me was dying to tell her that out of everyone in the movie, I identified the most with Marcus too.

I don't remember what I actually said. Probably something obnoxious. The memory fades, leaving me alone in the hall, listening to the muted sound of Delilah's laughter drifting through the silence.

I want to knock on her door, ask her to let me in so badly my hands shake. But I move away instead. We both made promises. Like them or not, I intend to keep mine.

CHAPTER TEN

Delilah

"So this is where you find all those delicious fruits." Macon ambles along the stalls of the outdoor farmers' market I've taken him to, his face half-hidden beneath the brim of a faded-green baseball hat.

"Among other places." This is one of my favorite markets, as it's tucked in a valley and shaded by towering eucalyptus trees. "The sellers here always offer the best produce."

Earlier, we went to the doctor's office to have his temporary cast removed and replaced with a soft cast and walking boot. Macon made an offhand complaint about being cooped up for too long, so I told him to come shopping with me. For all his whining, he wasn't keen on going out in public. Which had me asking if he was a chicken or simply another lazy, pampered star.

At those fighting words, his nostrils flared. "Fine. But we're taking North with us."

"Right." I cringed, feeling like a heel for teasing him. "Security. I just assumed since we're going somewhere unplanned . . ."

"Things can get out of hand when you least expect it," he said tightly.

"I'm sorry I called you chicken."

"But not that you called me lazy?"

"Asks the man who needs his smoothie brought up to him."

A brief gleam of acknowledgment lit his eyes before fading. "I know it sucks, Delilah. But this is your life now."

My life. Inexorably tied up with his.

All in all, our tentative truce is going as expected. Which is to say, we still find ways to squabble like chickens going after the last piece of grain.

Now, however, he's like a puppy finally let out of his pen.

"It smells so fresh here. Where do you want to go first?" He has a cane—mahogany with an amber top—that he loves because it looks like the one from *Jurassic Park*. I told him that if he wants to channel his inner John Hammond, he really should be wearing a white suit as well. Unfortunately, he didn't go for it.

"It's your first time here." I put on sunglasses so I can see without squinting. "Have at it."

Smiling wide and joyfully, he takes another survey of the place, then heads for a stall selling fruit and inspects a mango. North keeps an unobtrusive distance away. They warned me that when we went out on the fly like this, North wouldn't be our friend. He'd be working, constantly scanning for trouble.

"Can I have a sample?" Macon asks the guy manning the stall, a young hipster with a full beard and a tattoo that says "Grow It Green" along his inner forearm.

"Have one on the house, Arasmus."

Upon hearing the name of his character, Macon does a double take as if he's gauging how intense this potential fan might be. Then his easy good-ole-boy smile is in place. "Kind of you."

That smile used to grate on me like nails ambling down a chalkboard. But there is no denying its efficacy. When Macon smiles like that, people react.

"Thanks . . . ?" Macon trails off in question.

"Jed," the seller replies as he takes a mango and begins to prep it, slicing the fruit along each side of the pit and then scoring a crosshatch along each half.

"Jed, I'll share it with my girl here." Macon grasps my elbow and gently tugs me to his side.

His girl? I cut him a glance, but he's not looking my way—I can only assume it's intentional.

Jed gives me a quick smile of acknowledgment, but his attention is purely on Macon. "Man, that scene where you chopped off Thieron's head with one swing of your sword, then gave that war cry and tore his army apart . . . fucking beautiful. You gonna finally marry Princess Nalla?"

"Could be," Macon says as if he too is speculating. Then he winks. "Or maybe not. You'll have to watch."

Jed beams like it's his birthday. "Knew you wouldn't give up the goods."

"Where would be the fun in that?" Macon says in good cheer.

Jed asks for a picture with Macon, and I dutifully use his phone to take a couple of shots of them holding up mangos. Then we're on our way, each of us armed with luscious ripe sections of mango.

"Well, you charmed the hell out of that guy. I'm fairly certain he'll be singing your praises for the next year, at least."

Macon huffs out a laugh. "Charm? More like bullshit. I'm the king of bullshit." He says this without a hint of pride or self-pity, so detached he might as well be talking about someone other than himself.

"You always were," I murmur, but without any rancor.

Macon's coffee-dark eyes are thoughtful. "You're the only one who ever figured that out."

"I'm teasing, Macon."

He shakes his head, faintly smiling. "No, you aren't. I am the bullshit artist, and you're the one without verbal impulse control."

I stop short. "Verbal impulse control?"

"Don't pretend it isn't true. You blurt out what you're feeling all the time. It was one of the easiest ways I could get to you."

"Oh, really?"

"Yep. All I had to do was push one of your buttons, and I knew you'd give me so much more when you blew."

"You don't have to sound so pleased about it."

He slings an arm around my shoulders and gives me a good-natured squeeze. "Aw, come on, Tot. You're smart as a tack. You knew what I was doing."

Admittedly, I did. I just hadn't known *he* knew how easily he played me. I should have, though. Macon is likely one of the smartest people I've met. Strange thing is, I don't think he'd say that of himself so easily.

"Well, shit," I mutter.

Macon laughs, his head tilting back with the force of it. A couple walking past glance at him, then do a double take. Macon's stubble has graduated to a beard, and the hat he wears is low on his brow. But there are those who recognize him anyway.

"Why weren't we always like this?" he asks, studying my face with genuine curiosity. "Why weren't we trying to make each other laugh?"

"Because we were too busy trying to kill each other."

"Time wasted on your part. Clearly, I'm indestructible." He seems pleased with the idea.

The sun is shining, and the air holds a hint of the sea. He still has his arm around my shoulders, his torso pressed against mine. It feels good, this half embrace. Too good. It creates the unwanted illusion that I could rest against him, and he'd hold me up for as long as I needed it. I can't understand this feeling. By all accounts, a half hug from Macon should put me on full alarm. In truth, I don't think we've ever willingly touched.

I try to think back to a time when we had any prolonged physical contact as kids and draw a blank. Rattled, I step away from the warmth of his arm. He lets me go easily as if this isn't a momentous occasion, and instantly I feel foolish.

Of course it isn't a big deal. People tease and hug each other all the time without any weird ulterior motives. Inwardly, I shake my head at myself and move on.

We stop under the shade of a eucalyptus tree. Macon takes a bite of mango, licking his lip when juice threatens to roll down to his chin. I'm momentarily distracted by the sight.

"Have you watched *Dark Castle* yet?" he asks, oblivious to my rapt attention on his mouth.

"Ah . . . not as of yet."

"Not as of yet?" Wry amusement laces his voice. "Is it the sex scenes I'm in or just my nudity in general you're avoiding, Grandma?"

My eyes narrow in a warning that does nothing but make the corners of his eyes crinkle with sly humor.

"Neither." *It's both, actually.* "I just haven't had time to trudge through two seasons' worth of beheadings, disembowelings, and brothel visits."

I'm clearly not fooling him a bit. "How about I have the studio send over a highlight reel instead?"

"It's almost as though you want me to see your bare ass."

"More like I want to see your reaction to my bare ass," he says with a quick wink.

I huff out a breath. "Juvenile."

"With you? Guilty."

We share a quick grin, but his fades.

"It's why I went into acting, you know."

I'm about to unwrap my mango half but stop at his words. "You want to explain that non sequitur?"

"The bullshitting. I spent my entire life pretending to be someone else; I thought, why not try it professionally?"

"Pretending?" I repeat stupidly.

Color floods the crests of his cheeks, and he clears his throat. "I was never fully myself with anyone."

My voice comes out as a whisper of sound. "Why couldn't you be yourself?"

"I didn't know how," he says back, just as low. "No one in my house ever did."

Macon shifts his weight onto his bad leg, winces, then leans back on his good leg. He clutches the smooth egg-shaped amber knob at the top of his cane hard enough to turn his knuckles white. "That's why I loved going to your house. For better or worse, you all were entirely yourselves. It was beautiful and strange to me, as if I was watching a beloved play, but the actors were speaking in a foreign language."

For a moment, I can't move. The crowds of people drift by, and I simply stare at Macon and wonder if I've ever really seen him. I'd recognize his face anywhere. I used to see it in my nightmares. Though older, his features haven't changed: the same sculpted cheeks, square jaw, and bold, high-bridged nose. The same well-shaped lips that manage to appear both uncompromising and wonderfully soft. He still has a freckle at the corner of his right eye. On a woman it would be called a beauty mark. And yet this Macon is something entirely different—willingly showing me pieces of himself that aren't perfect.

I want to ask him why his family weren't themselves, why he felt the need to play a part. But it's clear that regret for speaking too freely is creeping up on him, his gaze darting around as though he'd rather look at anything but me.

Whether he wanted to or not, Macon gave up a private piece of himself. One that I doubt anyone has ever seen. I feel . . . humbled.

"Oh, my family were ourselves all right," I say with a light shrug as if the air between us hasn't become too heavy with old ghosts. "To the point of oversharing. Don't tell me Sam never mentioned 'Family Grievance Night.'"

A protracted, shocked laugh escapes him. "No. What?" He grins, easier now. "Do tell, Ms. Baker."

Ordinarily, I'd take the horrors of Family Grievance Night with me to the grave. But he shared with me. I can do the same for him.

"Whenever we started bickering too much for Mama to take, she'd sit us all down as a family, and we had to 'air our grievances.'"

Macon is clearly a hair's breadth from cracking up. His eyes are glossy with restraint. "You mean like Festivus?"

I cringe, remembering too well. "But without the pole."

A snort rings out, and he runs his hand over his mouth.

"I'm pretty sure Mama got the idea from *Seinfeld*. Whatever the case, it never went well."

"You don't say."

"Inevitably we'd end up squabbling so badly that—"

"You engaged in the Feats of Strength?" He waggles his brows, biting his lower lip in an ill-concealed attempt to hold back a full grin.

"Might as well have," I admit ruefully. "Mama would threaten to turn the hose on us and lament about where she went wrong." If I close my eyes, I can picture it now: Mama with her hands on her hips, a frazzled look about her. "I once made the mistake of answering that ending Family Grievance Night would be a good start in fixing the error."

He laughs freely. "Oh, man, I'm so sorry I didn't know this then. I would have found a way to attend."

"I would have been scarred for life if you had." I shake my head. "I can't believe Sam never told you."

"Why would Sam tell me about it?"

I stop short, my gaze searching his face to see if he's serious. He appears genuinely confused.

"It was a nightmare for both of us. You and Sam were in each other's pockets all through childhood. I assumed she told you everything."

The tendon along his neck stands out as he looks away, his brows drawn tight. "Sam did most of the talking, and I'd pretend to listen. But it was never about anything personal. She'd complain about her hair or if someone was being a shit to her, and I'd nod along. Truth is, I found her boring as all hell."

My mouth falls open. "But you . . . she . . . God, Macon. You were with her on and off for years. Why would you do that to yourself if you thought she was boring? Why would you do that to *her*?"

His lips curl in a parody of a smile. "You don't get it, Delilah. The feeling was entirely mutual."

"How do you know?" I challenge.

"Easy. She told me."

"Bullshit." Sam had thought Macon was the bomb. She loved him for a time.

He scratches his chin. "Let's see; if I recall, she said, 'I don't particularly like you, Macon Saint, but aside from me, you're the best-looking person in this school, so we really should be together.'"

I wince. That sounds exactly like something Sam would say. "And you agreed?"

His nose wrinkles as if he smells something off. "No, I couldn't have cared less what people thought of me. But if I was with her, other girls wouldn't bother to approach me."

Everything in me goes still, and I feel the bottom drop out of my stomach as understanding finally hits. "You're gay."

"What? No." His brows wing upward. "Why the hell would you think that?"

I lift my hands in confusion. "You're describing Sam as a beard, Macon. You went out with her to keep girls at bay."

The crests of his cheeks flush again. "Oh, for the love of . . . I did not keep Sam around because I secretly liked guys. Sam was safe, Delilah. She didn't ask questions, and she didn't really want to get to know me. I was a loner stuck in the role of town charmer. Sam suited my purposes because she played the part of devoted girlfriend and kept people from getting too close. That's all."

I really don't want to examine the purely selfish reasons that I find myself relieved to know he's not gay. But his confession depresses me. "Life isn't a play," I find myself saying. "You don't act out roles in real life."

"Just because you're an open book doesn't mean everyone is." His brows lower as he leans closer to me. "Most of us pretend to be something we're not. It's only to a select few that we really show our true selves."

"I'm not an open book."

"More like newsprint." He gives me a level look. "I can read you like a headline, Delilah."

I huff out a breath. "Okay, I'm fairly open, but I do get it. Everyone has a public self and a private self. I'm only saying that it's kind of sad, you and Sam sticking together for those reasons."

"Why do you think I found you so annoying?" Macon quips. "Because you damn well knew we were fakers."

I smile, showing teeth. "I thought you two were plastic. Not faking a relationship."

"Brat," he says, amused.

Thing is, I'm amused too. It's easier now, hashing things out with Macon. Which is a surprise. People grow up; I know that. But usually you're there for the growth, the steady change of character. Seeing is believing. I hadn't been around Macon for a decade. I hadn't seen the change from boy to man. And though he might look and act more mature, my instincts react as if no time has passed. My first impulse is to think the worst of him. Only slowly but surely, he's making me reassess that.

Rolling my eyes, I unwrap my mango and take a bite. It's richly sweet and perfectly ripe. Like Macon, I find myself scrambling to wipe away the juice that runs free.

He watches beneath lowered lids. "Missed a spot." The blunt tip of his thumb brushes the lower edge of my lip, just at the corner—a place

I never thought to be particularly sensitive. Yet that small touch sends thick chords of shuddering pleasure through my body.

That damn spot fairly hums now, a little tickle, and it's all I can do not to lick it. Macon stares at my lips like he knows I still feel his touch. When did he get so close? The scent of his skin and the heat of his body carry on the breeze, moving over me like warm cotton.

I want to lean into that warmth, soak him up. Something catches my eye. North stands a few trees away. I'd forgotten he was here. He isn't watching us—but scanning the perimeter—and is far enough not to overhear. But the sight is enough to snap me out of the haze I'd been pulled into.

I swallow down my bite of fruit. "Don't flirt, Macon. It won't make me more biddable."

The intensity of his gaze plucks at my skin, but his expression remains neutral. I want to squirm. I'm vastly aware of how well he can read me and wonder what my expression gives away.

But then he simply smiles, all easy and relaxed. "Damn, you caught me out."

I eye him warily because he relented a bit too easily. "Mm-hmm . . ."

He nods in agreement. "It was stupid, thinking you'd fall for that." His voice lowers as he takes a small step forward. "You're completely immune. Always were."

My voice doesn't appear to be working properly. "Right."

Macon rests a hand on the tree trunk, his big body angling toward me. I press my back to the tree, all too aware that his inner arm almost touches my cheek. God, he has pretty eyes. I have issues.

A smile plays about his mouth as his gaze lowers to my mouth. His voice pours over me like hot syrup. "Doesn't matter what I say, does it? I could tell you that watching you suck on that juicy bit of mango was one of the erotic highlights of my life. That I want to lick the pink, pouty curve of your lower lip to see if it's sticky sweet."

Gently, he touches the swell of my lip, and I feel it deep within my sex.

"Such a pouty fucking mouth," he whispers. "Always frowning at me with that plump lower lip."

I. Cannot. Breathe. I am flush with fever-bright heat.

And it is all Macon's fault.

Macon, who watches as my breasts rise and fall with increasing agitation. Macon, who makes a pained grumble deep within his throat.

The tips of my breasts graze his chest with each breath I draw. His own breath hitches, and I make my move, leaning just close enough so that my mouth is by his ear. He doesn't move an inch, but I see the tremor run through his shoulders.

I find myself smiling, though I'm too hot, too weak kneed to be truly amused. "Macon?"

He makes a sound that is the approximation of "Yes."

I allow myself one nuzzle, the briefest brush of my nose against the curve of his ear—loving the way he tries to suppress a shiver—and then I make my voice hard and firm. "Bugger off."

Macon rears back as though goosed, his brows raised high in surprise. His gaze clashes with mine, and then he's laughing—a wry, self-deprecating sound that's just a bit too forced. "For a second, I thought I had you."

"Not a chance," I say, making my own show of laughing the moment off.

But when we resume shopping, walking close enough that our arms occasionally brush, I wonder who is the bigger bullshitter here.

CHAPTER ELEVEN

Delilah

The next day, when North pulls around with the car, Macon tells him we're dining out for lunch. "We"—not him. I don't want to be a "we." I especially don't want to have lunch with his agent. If the one-sided phone conversation I'd overheard is anything to go by, the woman is already dead set against me. Not my idea of a good time.

"No, I have menus to plan and a list of frivolous crap to take care of."

Macon gives me a deadpan look. "None of the tasks I ask you to do are frivolous."

"Oh, really? Sending some chick a batch of cardamom cupcakes with lavender frosting made by a specific baker that I have to drive all the way out to Laguna Beach to pick up, because of course they don't deliver, isn't frivolous? Hell, I can make those myself. I can even put *happy birthday* on them in little gold letters like you wanted." Frankly, I'm surprised he hadn't specified what font should be used.

"But they wouldn't be from her favorite baker," he tells me, then makes a sound of exasperation. "She's my makeup artist. The woman I have to spend hours in the chair talking to. She needs to know she's appreciated."

I roll my eyes. "You don't have to bribe people with goodies, Con Man."

"Everyone here does."

"So being yourself isn't enough?"

At that, he shoots me a slanted smile that doesn't reach his eyes. "Why, Ms. Delilah, are you saying that my personality is capable of winning people over?"

"You could charm the skin off a snake if you wanted to, and you know it."

His chuckle is smug, and I turn away to look out the window so he doesn't see my reluctant smile.

North takes us to Chateau Marmont, an old Hollywood hotel that looks like a castle holding court over Sunset Boulevard.

We're whisked to a table on the terrace, nestled between rustling palms and heavy red hibiscus flowers. I want to scoff at the location because it's definitely a place to see and be seen, but it's also lovely in that way of LA restaurants, a secluded little fairyland of grace and beauty.

I order their take on a moscow mule and sit back with a content sigh. Now that I'm far away from the doctor's office and soaking up the warm sun, I'm happy.

The drinks are arriving when a harassed-looking woman in a dove-gray Dior day dress hurries over.

"I'm sorry I'm late, darling," she says to Macon, forestalling his attempt to rise by giving him a quick kiss on the cheek. "Traffic on the 101 is a beast."

It's always a beast. But I suspect she knows this and is more concerned about making a grand entrance. The woman is tall and thin, her long dark-brown hair flowing in perfect waves around her face. I know the effort it takes to have your hair turn out that perfectly; either she puts aside a few hours to get ready in the morning, or she has a standing reservation at a salon.

Regardless, I'm impressed and a little envious. I'd resisted washing my hair for as long as possible, but my own blowout gave up the ghost with this morning's shower, and I am not nearly as adept with the flat iron as my stylist. Which means my hair now floats too thick and fluffy around my head.

Karen takes a seat and plunks her elbows on the table with a dramatic sigh. She's older than Macon and me, maybe five years, and there's a hardness about her, as though the lines bracketing her mouth were made by frowns instead of smiles. "Well," she says, eyeing Macon. "You're looking much better."

"Out of the wheelchair, at any rate," he answers before taking a sip of his iced tea.

"Thank God for that," Karen says expansively. "The studio wants you looking strong and healthy, or they'll start worrying you'll be unfit to play the role."

I frown at the idea that Macon has to hide the fact that he's been seriously injured. The man has months to heal, for pity's sake.

I don't realize I'm swinging my crossed leg in agitation until the tips of Macon's fingers touch my knee. The contact is firm and fleeting, but it's enough to grab all my attention. Abruptly, I halt and uncross my legs.

"Karen," he says. "This is my new assistant and chef, Delilah."

It's as if I've magically just appeared at the table and she's seeing me for the first time. Her blue eyes do a quick inventory. "I see what you mean," she says to Macon, dismissing me with a turn of her shoulder.

My eyes narrow.

"Wherever did you find her?" Karen asks, oblivious.

"976-BABE," I say with a smile.

The entire table seems to freeze, and they all gape at me. But then North swallows down a snort. I stare at them in turn. "Oh, come on. *Pretty Woman*? 'Welcome to Hollywood! What's your dream?'"

117

"Yes, dear, I know the movie." Karen gives me a pitying look. "I simply didn't connect the line with you."

Heat prickles over my cheeks. I know what she sees and what she doesn't. Compared to the stars she works with, I am fairly plain. I don't stand out in a crowd. I don't wear couture or smile on command.

I know this, and yet that doesn't give her the right to treat me like dirt under her shoe. It's taken me years to truly understand that I don't have to take other people's crap lying down.

Wisely, Macon leans forward, partially blocking my sight line with his big shoulder. Or maybe he just wants to create an obstacle between my fist and his agent's face.

"You had a script you wanted to show me?"

Karen brightens. "Oh my God, do I. This one is top secret, so I really don't want to say too much here."

"North and Delilah will know whether you tell them or not," Macon says. "Because I will."

Her nose wrinkles. "It involves a particular comic franchise and a new superhero . . ." She trails off suggestively.

"Holy shit," North murmurs, looking impressed.

If it's the franchise I'm thinking of, I am too.

"Marvel," Karen adds with a little wiggle in her seat. "Can you believe it?"

Macon sits back and rubs the stubble on his chin. "No shit." Though his voice is subdued, I can see the excitement he's hiding. It's there if you know where to look, in the slight tremor of his hand that rests in his lap, in the way he holds himself too still. Macon wants this.

How could he not? If his character becomes popular, he'll be able to write his own ticket. And while Macon clearly doesn't have to worry about money, the fact that he could command a high salary would equate to power. In La La Land, as my mother continues to call it, power means everything.

Karen nods slowly. "They're impressed with your work on *Dark Castle* and have asked for you specifically."

Macon shifts in his seat. "Okay." He glances at me, and our gazes clash and hold. The restaurant seems to fade, and there is only us, Macon looking at me as if to say, "Can you believe this crazy shit?" Thing is, I can. There isn't any limit to what this man can accomplish; I've always known that much.

"Okay," he says again in affirmation, his eyes still locked with mine, and then he turns, and the spell is broken.

A small frown works its way along the sides of Karen's mouth as she looks at us, but it quickly smooths over, and she puts all her focus on Macon.

After ordering lunch, he and Karen map out possible plans to get him the role while North offers training routines he can do with Macon to work around his injuries.

And I eat.

It's not that the conversation isn't interesting. I simply have nothing to add. Occasionally Macon asks me to put a date or note down in his calendar. I do but then notice that he appears to have perfect recall of other dates and contract points, and I wonder if he's simply giving me busywork, especially when Karen tells him that she'll send over all the information anyway.

I'm typing in one such date when Macon's fork comes drifting over to my plate and spears a piece of my black-truffle arancini. "Hey. Get your own."

He is unrepentant and steals another bite. "But it's so good."

"Then you should have ordered it. Take another bite, and I'm biting your hand."

He goes in for a piece, and a fork duel ensues.

"Stop eating my food."

"But yours is better."

"I know. That's why I ordered it."

119

"Come on, Tot. Just one more bite."

"No. Eat your damn salad. It's good for you."

"I hate salad. Fuck the salad."

"You first, salad boy."

We're snickering now, our forks clanging as they thrust and parry. A loud exasperated sigh cuts into our fun.

"You're acting like children," Karen says, wrinkling her nose.

Macon straightens, his brows drawing together. He looks at his fork as if he's never seen one, his thumb running along the tines. The transformation of his expression is like a slow unfurling, from confusion to irritation to bland remoteness. He sets the fork down and is all business once more. "Delilah brings out the worst in me."

I want to snort but don't. There's something about his manner that makes me feel as though he's set me aside as easily as he did the fork. When am I going to learn? I'm pissed that I forgot how easily Macon can draw me in, only to drop me off a cliff when I least expect it.

And I'm pissed at myself for feeling chastened by Karen, of all people.

She gives me—not Macon—another reproachful look, then turns to him. "You should listen to your assistant. She clearly understands about fattening foods."

Her tone is not kind. And I'm done being polite. Or quiet.

I turn to North, who is sprawled back in his chair, blue eyes alight with undisguised anticipation. An ally I desperately need. "Tell me something . . ."

"Anything, babe."

I kind of love him just then. Because I know, *I know*, he's calling me babe to irritate Macon. It's in his eyes and the way his mouth twists to hold back laughter.

"Do agents in this town take Cliché Bitch 101 classes around here?"

A muscle in his lower jaw twitches while Karen huffs out a sound of annoyance.

"Pretty sure they offer a special discount at UCLA."

We both grin.

"All right," Macon cuts in. "That's enough."

I shoot him a look. *Tell that to Ms. Sunset Boulevard.*

And he returns one of his own. *Behave.*

Make. Me.

His answering grin is crafty. "Later."

"Later for what?" Karen demands in a snit.

"To perform my other services." I dab the corner of my mouth. Because fuck her.

Macon chokes on a sip of his water. North, however, just laughs, a big booming sound.

"I like her," he says to a glowering Macon.

"Well, I don't," Karen snaps before leaning into my space. "Watch yourself. I could eat you for breakfast." Her gaze flicks over me. "Well . . . maybe for dinner."

Rage surges up my body. "You can eat a bag of dic—"

Macon grabs hold of my wrist, gently tugging me back down to my seat. "Apologize." For a hot second, I think he's talking to me, but for once, his laser gaze is on Karen. "You've been antagonizing Delilah since we got here. Which isn't a good move since she's going to be around for the foreseeable future."

There is a tense silence in which Karen clearly contemplates swallowing her tongue to avoid speaking. But she does, eventually, spitting out the words between clenched teeth. "I'm sorry if I implied you were anything other than a light meal."

Oh, the things I want to say to that. But it will only make things worse. Still, the evil pixie on my shoulder goads me to give the woman a tepid smile. "Apology accepted. I'm sorry for implying you were a bitch." I should have said it flat out.

A bare nod, and Karen is back to chatting with Macon, going on about numbers and scripts she wants him to read.

We're sitting outside in the sunlight, and yet it feels like dark walls are closing in on me. I move to take a sip of my ice water, but a warm weight on my wrist halts me. Macon is still holding on to me, my clenched fist resting on the top of his thigh. A jolt goes through me, and I tug my arm.

He lets me go immediately, not even looking my way. But I feel the ghost of his touch long afterward, like a phantom, maniacally reminding me that this is my life now, tied to a man who has been my enemy. We aren't that now. The problem is, I don't know what we are or how I'm supposed to survive living with him.

It stretches out before me like a long gloomy road. A road I put myself on. Damn it. But I can't think like that. Because there is a small silver lining. According to the agreement, if Sam returns at any point before the year is over, which she *will*, then I get paid for the months I've worked—rent-free. I am going to take that money, combine it with the money I've saved, and start my life again. Start a restaurant. Something all mine.

And yet I can't shake the heavy feeling of defeat that rests on my shoulders as North drives us back to the house. Maybe Karen got to me more than I'm willing to admit.

Macon sits in the front with North, silent and staring out of the window. North catches my eye in the rearview mirror, and concern tightens the friendly laugh lines around his eyes. Though North doesn't say a word, somehow Macon senses the direction of North's gaze. His eyes narrow, and he shoots a glance my way. Whatever conclusion he comes to has his expression going dark. But he sits back in his seat and resumes his brooding out the window. Which is fine by me; I have no desire to talk.

Only I'm not given much of a reprieve. As soon as North drops us at the front of the house and drives off to the garage, Macon pulls me under the shade of a lemon tree. Those yellow fruits, heavy with juice, dangle over his head like golden raindrops as he starts in on me without pause. "Let's get one thing clear—"

"If this is about not being nice to Karen, I swear to God, Macon, I will nut you where you stand and leave you for dead."

A protracted laugh escapes him. "I don't care about Karen; she was being a shit." He ducks his head so that we're eye to eye, and there's a glint in his. "And keep my nuts out of this. They're entirely innocent bystanders here."

"They're attached to you, so I call them fair game."

His eyes crinkle briefly. "You never played fair, Tot."

"Stand back, will you? Your hypocrisy is smothering."

If anything, he moves closer. The scent of lemons mixes with the buttery warmth of his skin. I catch a hint of the mint iced tea he drank at lunch as the deep syrupy roll of his voice touches my ear. "I don't care what you do on your days off—"

"Wait, I actually have days off? Color me shocked—"

I nearly yelp when he tweaks my earlobe with his finger. "Tuesdays and Thursdays, starting next week, brat." His thumb smooths over my lobe before drifting away. "Now, will you be quiet and let me speak?"

I'm assuming it's a rhetorical question and bite my lip as I angle my head back so I can glare at him properly. His expression is part aggrieved, part reluctantly amused. But it quickly turns black.

"Your personal life is your own," he bites out. "But North is off limits."

Of all the . . . I'm not remotely interested in North, and I know North isn't interested in me either. Apparently Macon is clueless. And I have no intention of enlightening the jerk. I suck in a breath, hold it, and let it out slowly. "Oh, really?"

"Yes, really. I don't need the aggravation of my staff members avoiding each other when the sex goes stale. And believe me, it will."

I want to laugh. I want to slap his face. As it is, my breathing comes on quick and fast. "Which means North is really only off limits while I work for you. Good to know."

A streak of red spreads across the tops of Macon's cheeks, and I swear the man growls. It rumbles in that wide chest of his as his mouth tightens. "He's not for you, Delilah. Unless, of course, you're into having Sam's leftovers."

As if I've been slapped, my breath hitches. Oh, that was low. Not only to me but to North as well. My face feels tight and hot. And for an instant, something that looks like guilt flickers in Macon's brown eyes, but it's quickly smothered by stubborn self-righteousness and a pugnacious lift of his chin.

"Well then," I manage, "I guess that leaves you out of the running too."

The second I say the words, I want them back. Horror whips through me, cold and bright. Why did I say that? Why? *Why?*

And, God, the smug grin that creeps across his firm lips. His lids lower a fraction, that smile growing—the picture of a self-satisfied male. "Nice to know you were considering me, Tot."

With that, he turns on his good heel and gracefully limps back into the house.

CHAPTER TWELVE

Macon

"I'm in trouble."

North glances my way. We're in the media room of my house, looking over sword-fighting footage from last season's *Dark Castle*. In a week or so, my wrist and ribs will be healed enough that I'll be able to take up modified training again, but until then, I'm staying fresh by watching and discussing moves with North.

"You'll be fine," he tells me. "I don't know a person in the stunt business who hasn't broken a bone or ten. Sure, it'll hurt like hell at first, but you'll bounce back. Besides, you're the star; we'll work around what you can't do when the time comes."

I should let him believe I'm talking about getting into shape, but clearly I'm in a mentally weakened condition because I elaborate. "Delilah is the trouble."

North's grin is small but smug. "Ah. The pretty Ms. Baker is throwing you for a loop, eh?"

"Pretty?" I narrow my eyes at him.

"What?" That smug grin is growing. "You don't think she is?"

"I've got eyes, don't I?"

Delilah is pretty. Quietly pretty. She will never be the first person everyone looks at when entering a room. Especially not in LA, where beautiful women bloom like flowers in a well-tended garden. But among a bouquet of perfect roses, Delilah is much like her namesake flower—unexpectedly vivid and complex—making you realize that roses are boring in comparison.

I don't tell North that. Instead I glare at him. "Touch her, and we'll be wearing matching casts, even if I have to pay someone to put you in one."

He laughs. "You're getting in a twist for nothing. But don't worry; I'll stay far away."

I grunt but then shake my head. "No, don't keep your distance. The crazies are still out there. I won't have her hurt because someone wants to get to me."

For one cold second, I'm back in my car, the road falling out from under me, knowing I am going down. Despite the terror, the main emotion that grips me is regret. I regret too many things in this empty life of mine. Delilah getting hurt because of me will not be another. "Watch over her whenever she leaves the house."

North's lips compress. "Understood."

I know he does. North is golden like that.

"Are you sure it's a good idea to keep her here?" he asks.

"Probably not. She drives me nuts. Just this morning, she kept me arguing for thirty minutes on the difference between clarified butter and ghee, which I finally said means fuck all to me since my stupid diet doesn't even allow me to sniff butter, much less taste it."

North chuckles.

I rub a hand over my mouth, hiding my smile. "And then she has the nerve to tell me that's too bad since she's been cooking all my meals with clarified butter anyway."

Fuck if I hadn't loved every second of our argument. Yep, we're definitely flirting. Angry flirting. Is there a word for that? There should be.

"What the hell is ghee?" North asks, earning a sidelong look from me.

"Man, explore the multicultural soup that is the American experience." When he just stares me down, I elaborate. "As far as I can tell, it's like clarified butter but prepared differently and used in Indian cooking. You'll just have to google the rest because I am *not* going through Delilah's lengthy explanation. Once was enough for a lifetime."

Which is mostly true; witnessing the pink wash of color on Delilah's cheeks and the irate flash of her eyes made it worth it. That and every time we argue, her tits tend to jiggle. Call me a pig for noticing, but I do, and I enjoy it every damn time it happens.

North's smile fades. "I don't know why you're keeping up with this pact. It's goddamn medieval."

My insides tighten uncomfortably. "I'm not breaking our agreement. It would hurt Delilah's pride." And I've stomped on that in the past enough to never want to do it again. "Besides, the arrangement will likely draw Sam out of hiding. Even she isn't heartless enough to disrupt her sister's life to this extent."

North doesn't look like he believes that shit for a second. I don't blame him; it's a weak argument, but the deeper truth is one I can barely say to myself: I can't let her go.

Something is waking up in me or settling back into place. I don't know which, but everything in me wants to hold on to the sensation and soak it up.

"It's complicated," I mutter. "Delilah and I never got along. Her mama used to say we fought like rats over a scrap. But I respect Delilah. Always have."

"You know," North starts in, "it's kind of funny—"

"And there goes my hope that you'd drop this."

"All I was going to say is that if you'd introduced Sam and Delilah to me at the same time, I'd have thought Delilah was your ex, not Sam."

I shift in my chair, trying to get comfortable. "Sam is much more my type."

The women I hook up with are happy to take attention away from me and keep the spotlight on themselves. Hell, my "type" started with Sam. But the truth is, I haven't been attracted to her in a long time. And even then, it'd been a mild interest at best.

It is an astonishing thing to realize that I have never been so hot for a woman that I lose my head, forget myself in her. Sex has never meant much to me. An itch scratched, but not something essential. Men aren't supposed to admit that their sex life is lackluster and has always been that way. It feels like a failure.

North studies me now, his eyes seeing far too much. "You never eyed Sam like she was . . ." He trails off with a shrug.

"Like she was what?"

"Butter."

I snort, but it has no conviction.

"Delilah, on the other hand—"

There's a knock on the door. Speak the devil's name, and she will find you.

"Yeah," I call out, eager for a reprieve.

Delilah sticks her head in, her hair glowing in the light of the projector. "Hey. Y'all busy? Because I have cookies."

"Cookies," I repeat. Lord, this woman tempts me.

Her smile is wide and impish, making her cheeks plump like a chipmunk's. "Don't worry; they're healthy."

North and I exchange a look.

"Well," she says, carrying in a plate, "as healthy as cookies can be."

"Which means they suck," I mutter, disgruntled as hell over my restrictive diet.

Her eyes flash. Extraordinary eyes, the color so light brown it's startling. I've never been able to meet her gaze without feeling it deep in my gut. I wonder if she feels that weird hot zing that zips through the air whenever we're together.

If she does, she's not showing it. Instead she smiles brightly at North. "I guess that means these are for you."

"Hey!" I protest, reaching for the plate.

Since I'm slowed down by my broken body, she easily evades me. "No, no, I insist. I wouldn't want to serve you sucky food, Mr. Bossy Butt."

Bossy butt?

North is grinning as he eats a cookie. "It's good. What is this?"

Delilah beams. "Flourless dark chocolate with peanut butter chips. It's high in protein."

"I could eat an entire platter of them," he says.

Delilah practically purrs. "You can have all the cookies you want."

Fucking hell. One instance of jealous stupidity, and I'm paying for it.

"All right, brat," I cut in, reaching again. "Give me a cookie."

"Brat?" She sets a hand on her wide hips. "Is that supposed to convince me to give you one?"

"Are you or are you not my cook?"

Her eyes narrow, but I keep mine on the plate. She might dump those cookies on my head, and I'll have to be quick. "That's twice you've played your little lord-of-the-manor card."

I grin, having fun. "What was the promise? Oh, right. The third time I do so, you make a jerk-off gesture."

Delilah sets a hip against the back of North's chair as she faces me. I don't like the proximity of her butt to his head. At all. But she's smirking at me with those pouty lips. "Let me save you the trouble."

With her free hand, she makes a loose fist and pumps it. The gesture is expected, but not the bolt of heat that punches through my gut and goes straight to my cock.

Fuck. I can practically feel her hand on my swollen flesh, the tug she'd give me. Biting back an internal groan, I give her a lazy smile. "Looks like you've had some practice with that, Tot."

Practice some more. I'm here all week, willing victim.

She doesn't blink. "I'm multitalented, Con Man."

"I just bet you are." My dick is rapidly rising, getting heavy in my pants. Hell. *Calm yourself, Saint.* The request is easier said than done. She's locked eyes with me, unwilling to back down. And she has no idea what she's stirring up. It isn't anger I'm feeling.

I'm in so much trouble. *It would help if you stopped flirting with her, dickhead.*

Clearing my throat, I glance at North, who looks on avidly.

"Butter," he says.

I envision nut punching him.

Delilah frowns his way. "Pardon?"

He becomes the picture of innocence as he grabs another cookie. "I was wondering if you used butter in these."

Her gaze darts between North and me. I will kill him if he lets on what he really meant. I keep my expression neutral and sweat it out.

She stares at me for a beat; then her gaze turns cheeky. "I used clarified butter."

With a groan, I run a hand over my face. "All right. I surrender. You're the greatest chef on earth, and nothing you cook or bake ever sucks. Now can I please have a cookie?"

"Hmmm . . ." She pretends to ponder the question. "Nope. I don't think so."

"What!"

"You're right. These aren't healthy enough for you. Whew, you really dodged a bullet there, Con Man." Quick as a blink, she reaches out and ruffles my hair. The unexpected physical contact distracts me enough for her to scamper off, cackling like a witch.

"Delilah Ann Baker," I shout after her. "You're going to pay for that!"

Mad cackles are the only reply.

Silence rings out, and I remember North.

His expression is smug but sympathetic. "You're right. You're in trouble."

Delilah

It pisses me off to no end that a twinge of guilt nips at my belly when North asks if I want to drive with him to Beverly Hills. Macon had no business trying to order me away from North. And I need to go; Karen has demanded that I pick up a few scripts for Macon from her office. She doesn't trust it to couriers or sending via email. I might as well have been asked to pick up the Ark of the Covenant.

Since North has a bit of an Indiana Jones flare about him, I figure he's a good escort.

"Okay." I grab my purse from the hooks by the side door. "But I'm driving."

North halts. "I'm the driver. It's in my employee contract."

"Since you're not carting around our employer, your point is moot."

North crosses his arms over his chest, an unmovable mountain. "I am a trained stunt driver."

"That's nice. I'm sure you do a great job on stunts."

Pulling out my keys, I head for my beloved MINI Clubman that's been sitting idle and ignored in the driveway. North follows in a huff, and I shoot him a look over my shoulder. "Are you going to whine about this?"

He puts a hand to his chest as if affronted. "I never whine."

"Good. Get in the car."

I hop into the driver's seat and run a hand over the steering wheel. "Hey, baby. Mama's back."

North gives me an amused look as he shuts the passenger door. "You going to talk to the car the whole time? If so, I might actually start whining."

With a laugh, I turn the car on, and we head out. It isn't until we're driving down the highway that I talk again. "Until now, you seemed to be a fairly laid-back guy. Does it really bother you so much that a woman is driving?"

He pinches the bridge of his nose and turns his attention to the blue streak of the ocean just outside his window. "Saint will have a fit," he mutters.

"Macon? Why, because we're running errands together? Tough shit." Okay, I'm still grumpy and still feeling guilty, damn it.

North casts an amused smile my way. "Why would he care if we're running errands?"

I wisely refrain from illuminating North. "You tell me."

The big man glances out the window as if he's contemplating jumping out of the speeding car. With his credentials, he'd probably do a graceful roll, then dust himself off before walking to Beverly Hills.

"The accident," North bites out. "It's made him . . . cautious."

It's clear North feels he's sold out Macon's privacy by admitting this. And I don't blame Macon for having certain fears about driving. If I'd careened down an embankment and gotten wrapped around a tree, I probably wouldn't get in a car for months.

North's voice is subdued. "He told me to drive you anywhere you needed to go, whatever the case."

The car hums along the road as I grip the wheel and think.

"That's why you asked if I wanted to come with you to Beverly Hills. You knew Karen wanted me to pick up the scripts."

"I'm meeting a colleague in the same building," he protests before his shoulders slump. "But yes, that was the motivating factor."

"And here I thought you enjoyed my company." A thick silence is my answer, and I can all but hear him wincing. With wide eyes, I glance at North. "Oh my God, you got the lecture, too, didn't you?"

His smile is wry. "The 'if you so much as look sideways at Delilah, I'll break your legs' lecture? Yes."

A shocked laugh bursts out. "Mine wasn't quite so violent. More of an irate warning." My lips purse. "That arrogant . . . pain in my butt. I can't believe him."

"No fraternization between employees is a fairly standard clause." He doesn't look as though he believes that's the reason Macon ran interference. I don't either.

Macon has been sticking his nose into my love life ever since we were kids. Every boy I showed any interest in was immediately told of all my supposed faults. They were run off with the effectiveness of a deployed stink bomb. I never believed jealousy was the motive. Macon did it out of spite. And now he's doing it again.

"First off, I didn't sign any employee contract, and there is no handbook. We both know that. Secondly, Macon said that because he's an asshat. No, an ass bonnet with flowers on top."

North laughs but then gives me a wary glance. "You weren't . . . I mean, I think you're great and pretty, but—"

The tips of his ears turn red as he squirms in his seat. And the devil in me can't help but respond. "But what, North?" I give him a sappy look. "Don't you like me?"

He clears his throat. "Of course I do, but . . ."

"It's Macon, isn't it? Trying to get in the way of our love."

North pales, blinking rapidly as his mouth falls open. For a second, I imagine he's contemplating jumping from the moving car, but then his expression clears with a rush of color and the narrowing of his eyes. "You're fucking with me, aren't you?"

The laugh I've been holding in bursts free. "I'm sorry. You were just so nervous about offending me."

"Sorry. That was bigheaded of me, eh? I just . . ." He smiles tightly. "You know what? I'm going to shut up now."

"Just to be clear, I'm not over here crying in my soup. I'm not interested in you that way." I give him a sidelong look, still smiling. "Not that you aren't pretty."

He snorts and shakes his head. "Now I understand why Saint doesn't know if he's coming or going with you."

Laughing, I turn onto the next highway. So many LA highways. "It's awkward as all hell talking about this. Really, I'm annoyed on principle. And Macon just annoys me in general."

"Probably because you two are so much alike."

"Alike? Ah, no."

"Both of you are uncomfortably blunt, proud, stubborn—"

"Hey!"

North grins, tilting his head in my direction. "I don't find these qualities faults. I've known Saint for two years, and already, he is my closest friend. You're both exceedingly loyal too."

"Loyal? Macon? Are we talking about the same person?"

"If you can't see his loyalty, you aren't looking," North says quietly.

Something uncomfortable twists in my belly. Guilt, frustration, I'm not sure, but I shift in my seat.

"I know Samantha took the watch." Anger twists his lips and fills his blue eyes. "I know you're working here to pay him back, which makes you a fucking saint in my book."

I glance away, embarrassed and upset with Sam all over again.

"But I figure that's a pretty bitter pill to swallow, regardless. So you should know that even though Saint can be a dick now and then, it's clear, to me at least, that his actions toward you aren't motivated by some old feud."

I'm the one now fighting not to squirm in my seat. "I don't know what to say."

"You don't have to say anything." North shakes his head, chuckling under his breath. "This *is* awkward as hell. But I wanted you to know you're valued here. Shit situation or no."

"You're a good egg, North."

"Just trying to keep the peace, ma'am." He thumbs up the brim of an imaginary hat.

I laugh, feeling lighter. "So what's your story?"

"I have to have a story?"

"Everyone has a story. Some are boring, some aren't, but everyone has a story."

"My family is in the stunt business—dad, brother, sister, me. That's how I met Saint; I'm his stunt double on *Dark Castle*."

"Really?" I wouldn't mistake him for Macon for a second, but aside from the hair color, they do have roughly the same build and height.

"It's colored black during filming," he says, seeing the direction of my gaze. "The fake beard itches like hell, though."

While I haven't watched the show, I have seen pictures of Macon as Arasmus. He's often in Roman-style leather body armor and heavy fur capes, his hair roughly chopped and sticking out at all angles, a full beard covering his jaw. I've never been one for beards, but Macon works the barbarian look.

North stretches his legs out. "Since Saint and I both do the sword-fight shots, I was also responsible for training him. Then that crap with the crazed fan and the accident happened—"

"What?" I cut in shrilly. "What fan?"

"Hell, you didn't know?"

"How could I know?" My grip is a vise on the wheel.

North swears under his breath. "Saint said he was going to talk to you about—"

"What happened?" A sick lurch tilts my insides, and I have to swallow hard. "Please, North."

His jaw twitches, but then he relents. "He has lots of fans. Some of them get a little more attached, lose touch with reality. We managed to keep this part out of the news, but two women tried to follow Saint home one night and kept too close for comfort. Whether accidentally or on purpose, they hit his bumper. It was raining; roads were slick. Saint lost control of the car. The women stopped too. But only to take some pictures of him in the wreckage."

My back teeth meet with a click. "Jesus."

Shock tingles through my veins. If you'd have asked me last month if I'd react like a protective mama bear over Macon Saint, I would have laughed. I'm not laughing now. I'm sick.

I think of Macon hurt in the dark while some shitheads took pictures of him, and I have to fight the urge to turn the car around and comfort him. The sensation is almost dizzying and completely unfamiliar when it comes to Macon.

"Why didn't he tell me?" I swallow hard. "He should have told me."

"Yes, he should have. But try not to be too hard on him. It's like pulling nails to get him to talk about it." North rubs a finger along his temple as he frowns. "He thinks that if he'd kept his cool, he wouldn't have lost control of the car."

"That's ridiculous. He was being *stalked*. I would have been terrified."

"Macon loves to be in control. And he doesn't ever admit to fear."

"This is true," I mutter, then expel a breath. "Jesus. I can't believe someone did that to him."

"Stalking . . . it's a shitty aspect of fame."

"And there's more of these people?" My voice is wispy, fear for Macon pulling at my throat. "Crazies who stalk him?"

He considers his answer. "It's hard to tell who is going to act out. But Saint and the studio agreed to have him guarded while he's recovering. Once shooting starts up again, I'll go back to stunt work and training, and Saint will have another bodyguard detail assigned to him if he wants it."

If he wants it? He had better.

My thoughts halt. When had I become so invested? No, this is normal. Of course I care; Macon is a human being. Anyone with a lick of compassion would care. But that doesn't explain how personal it feels or the way ice has settled in the pit of my stomach. I'm afraid for *him.* Specifically.

Rattled, I then reach down to turn on the radio. North and I maintain a thick but not uncomfortable silence as we drive along, listening to the Strokes.

———

Two hours later, my somber mood has turned to annoyance. Karen has left me in the waiting area of her office suite. It's a very nice area, with shining concrete floors, exposed ductwork, and colorful modern art on the blinding-white walls.

There is one wall dedicated to her clients, featuring pictures of Karen laughing it up with Hollywood A listers and up-and-comers. Macon's picture features Karen leaning on his arm, her fingers trying—and failing—to wrap around his big biceps. Macon stares back at the camera, a faint, polite smile on his face.

There is something almost chameleonlike in his looks. Sometimes, he is the dark and brooding Byronic hero; in other lights, he's the all-American athlete; and then you look again, and he's a marauder—intimidating and brutish. And yet no matter what, he is still Macon; the symmetry of his features, the undeniable beauty of him, is always there.

I glare at that face now, my butt sore from sitting in a leather chair so narrow I swear it's designed to weed out undesirables based on ass width alone. There are two other people stuck here with me, a pretty young woman who's probably no older than nineteen and reminds me of Lorde and a guy around my age who is Matt Bomer handsome. Both are tense but trying not to appear that way. Both have been waiting less time than I have.

Karen's assistant catches my eye and quickly looks away. She's beautiful too—must be a requirement—and wearing stilettos that are too small. I should know; I spent a good fifteen minutes trying not to stare at the toe crotch bulging from the tops of her shoes.

The fact that I'm even thinking about toe crotch settles it. Enough is enough. I can either try to get past Ms. Heels—and I'm guessing that's easier said than done despite the fact that I'm wearing Keds—or I can annoy the hell out of Karen. Annoying Karen sounds much more fun.

I am a woman of few talents. I cook, I bake, and I know songs. I can carry a tune, but I'm not going to win any awards. But I have the ability to remember song lyrics. Dozens of them.

Setting my purse down, I smile around the room, making sure to catch everyone's eye. Not surprisingly, they all return my look with varying levels of caution. Weird might work on Sunset but not at a high-level talent agency. Well, at least not for them.

"At first I was afraid." Slowly I rise. "I was petrified."

Lorde's look-alike's eyes go wide as I really start singing "I Will Survive." Mr. Blue Eyes grins. And Karen's assistant frantically picks up her phone.

Throwing my hands wide, I give myself to the song, selling it for all it's worth. I add in jazz hands because every performance is that much better with a little shimmy.

Blue Eyes begins to clap and egg me on, while the young woman—who quickly hurried to the other end of the room—laughs into her hands.

By the time I'm standing on the chair, doing some weird version of the bump and belting out how I will survive, Karen is in the room, red faced and huffing. From the doorway comes enthusiastic clapping, and

I find North and another man watching. North gives me a thumbs-up, which earns him a glare from Karen.

Given that I'm standing on the world's narrowest chair, my curtsy isn't as grand as it could be.

Karen steps forward, flailing as if she's torn between pulling at her hair or me. "What are you doing?" It comes out in a loud hiss of sound.

Sweating and panting, I jump down from my perch. "Warming up the pipes," I tell her. "However, I'm much better with an accompanist."

"You are *not* amusing, Baker."

"That's Ms. Baker to you. And neither is waiting for endless hours just so you can try to put me in my place." I take a drink from my bottled water. "Now, give me the damn scripts before I start in on show tunes, and believe me, I know them all."

I have a stack of scripts in my hands in ten seconds flat.

Chapter Thirteen

Macon

SweetTot: I'm looking through your social media pages.

Delilah left with North about an hour ago. I welcomed the reprieve, knowing she was still pissed at me yet having no idea how to fix it. I take it as a good sign that she's actually texting. Then again, she might just be bored.

Miss me already?

Yeah, I'm counting the seconds until I see you again. [Insert eye roll here]

Laughing lightly, I respond.

Hide behind eye rolls all you like. I know the truth, Tot.

Uh-huh. Seriously, though, Macon, your accounts are a disaster.

What's wrong with them?

Personally, I thought they were okay given that I hate maintaining them and feel like a fool every time I post.

They're so wooden and stilted. And OLD. You never update!

What did you expect? I AM wooden and stilted. And I hate updating.

You forgot old. You're old too.

A snort echoes in the silence of my living room. I sit back in my chair and get more comfortable.

I'm a few months older than you so . . .

In spirit, Macon. You're old in spirit.

It's not the years, it's the mileage.

She responds with an eye-roll emoji. Don't quote Indy. You are no Professor Jones.

I bite back a grin like she might see me, even though she's far away.

You can't make that assessment until you've seen me handle a whip.

I can picture her making a face.

Anyway . . . You need to fix this. Show them just a little bit of the real you.

Sitting up, I hesitate for a second before answering.

What is the real me?

Little dots appear on my screen, then pause, then appear again like she's deliberating on how she wants to respond. I sweat it out, needing to know. When the text finally appears, though, I'm almost afraid to read it.

Better than what you show. You're funny when you want to be.
You know, in a sarcastic way.

Oh, well, thank you. [Insert my sarcasm here]

I'd never admit it, and I'm suddenly grateful no one can see me, but her words leave me uncomfortably warm. I've never been good with compliments. I don't know how to handle them from Delilah. At all. I cover the moment by quickly texting before she can.

Consider social media another addition to your duties.

You want me to pretend to be you? Are you feeling all right?

Yes. And yes. Why do you ask?

Because I could make your life hell. I could post ANYTHING.

Snorting again, I shake my head.

But you won't.

I know Delilah too well. Everything she does, she makes sure to do perfectly. It would hurt her soul to put out bad or embarrassing content. Not because she'd worry about how it reflected on me but because she'd know it was her work, and it couldn't be subpar.

Damn it, you're right. Ugh. Okay. I'll help you. But I'm not doing it on my own. I'll give you tips, but it has to come from you for the content to be authentic.

I could push the issue, insist she take it over entirely. And then I'd feel like a dick. I already feel like that enough around her anyway.

Deal. But I'm NOT posting torso shots or crap like that.

Another eye-roll emoji follows.

You always thought too highly of yourself, Macon. And you will if I say you will. Abs = love.

So . . . you love my abs? I knew it. My butt is pretty awesome too, isn't it?

Sorry, Delilah has left the building.

Look, you don't have to beg. I'll send you a picture.

Don't you dare!

I lift up my shirt, take a quick picture of my abs, and send it.

Asshole!

Now, Delilah, don't get kinky with your requests. I draw the line at ass shots.

ARGH!

Laughing, I leave it at that. She doesn't respond again, which is kind of a disappointment, and I'm left not knowing what to do. Ordinarily, I'd be out—visiting acquaintances, jogging along the mountain paths, whatever I could to occupy my mind.

With North and Delilah out, the house is still and quiet. The distant crash of the sea against the shore is a constant hum. An hour rolls by, too still, too quiet. I get up and walk slowly from room to room, chasing the sun as it slants through the massive windows. I know every inch of this place. It is all mine.

Growing up, nothing was mine. Not even my bedroom. It could be invaded without warning. There was no safe space. I used to dream of my own place, design it in my mind's eye—where it would be, how it would look. I grew up in a mansion, so I knew all about beautiful spaces. That didn't interest me as much as thinking about light and space. A place to breathe freely, see everything around me with clear eyes.

The pool shimmers in the afternoon sun. I'm not yet allowed to go swimming, but damn if it isn't tempting. To the best of my knowledge, Delilah hasn't gone near the pool. Did she even swim? The last time I saw her in a bathing suit was when she was thirteen. She caught me looking a few times—much to my horror—and hadn't been pleased. I can't say I blamed her. I was pissed as well—both at being caught and over my lack of self-control. It was a relief when she stopped going to the lake with Sam and me to swim.

Only, it left me alone with Sam. The realization that without Delilah in the equation, that hanging out with Sam was an exercise in patience and boredom was an ugly shock. Shortly after, I made certain we always went out with a big group of friends.

With that regrettable memory prodding my back, I turn away from the view and head for the kitchen. Delilah has left me a lunch. There's a note with instructions, as if it wouldn't occur to me to take the cellophane wrap off the plate before I ate my food. Smirking, I set the note aside and am pulling the carefully wrapped plate out of the fridge when my phone dings.

It's from North.

Someone's gone viral. lol

I grow cold inside. Have more photos surfaced? I paid a lot of money to gather up the majority of the photos of me in the wreckage. But I might as well have tried to hold water in a sieve. North sends me a video link.

Hell, video?

Gritting my teeth, I click the link. And find my mouth falling open.

I'm so shocked I'm not sure I can trust what I'm seeing. But there Delilah is, standing on a chair in what looks to be Karen's outer office and belting out Gloria Gaynor with such feeling it almost makes up for her terrible singing voice. Almost.

Delilah shimmies and shakes, setting all her abundant curves in glorious motion. She is completely uninhibited. And she is magnificent.

A laugh bursts out of me. I laugh so hard my bruised ribs protest. But I can't stop. It keeps tumbling out. I laugh until tears leak from my eyes. And just when I finally get myself under control, I break down and start all over again.

I can't help it. The video is just so Delilah and yet not. It's the Delilah I always suspected hid under the surface, yet so much more. It's clear she's performing to piss Karen off, and it's obviously working judging by Karen's screeches.

I'm suddenly extremely sorry I wasn't there to witness all of this in person.

The second viewing only gets better.

I'm wheezing with laughter when the phone rings. Karen's name flashes on the screen, and I know I'm in for an earful. I can't control my voice when I answer.

"Oh, good," Karen snaps. "You're laughing. Clearly you've seen it."

A snicker escapes before I clear my throat. "Twice, actually."

"Are you going to do something about it?"

"Such as?"

There's a sound of utter disgust. "Fire her, obviously."

"For that?" I unwrap my lunch and find a cold Moroccan-style chicken-and-bulgur salad. "It was the best laugh I've had in years. I'm kind of thinking she needs a raise."

Well, I'd give her one if she was working for a salary. Ah, that pinches. Right in the guilt department. I shake it off as Karen launches into a tirade.

"She is completely unprofessional with that little stunt."

"And I'm sure it wasn't at all instigated," I add dryly.

"What are you suggesting, Macon?"

"I know Delilah. She doesn't act out so much as she reacts. What did you do?"

A huff comes over the phone. "Not a thing. I was going about my workday—a day that includes making your career shine, I might add—when I heard her god-awful caterwauling."

Caterwauling is a good word for Delilah's singing. My lips twitch, the urge to lose it once more rising up. I swallow it down and take a bite of my lunch instead. Jesus, the woman can cook. I take a bigger bite, practically shoving the salad in my mouth, suddenly starving.

"You cannot be serious about keeping her around," Karen says. "Even without her poor behavior, she's an utter embarrassment to you."

I freeze, fork laden with food halfway to my mouth. "Karen," I say calmly. "I appreciate that you're upset, but that's the last time you speak about Delilah that way."

She's silent for a beat. "You're taking her side?"

"There aren't any sides—"

"After all these years of working together, all I've done for you?"

"Cut it out, Karen. You were a shit to her at lunch. And—"

"So was she!"

"This is beneath you," I say in a low voice. "Making comments about her weight or appearance isn't what I hired you to do. I know you are better than that."

I want off this phone. I want to eat my lunch. Actually, I really want to see Delilah and tease her about the video. Yes, I'm a little bit childish when it comes to Delilah.

Karen sniffs, collecting her dignity. "All right. I concede; that wasn't well done of me."

I don't say a thing.

"I don't know why she irritates me," Karen mutters.

But I do. Delilah sees right past people's bullshit. Even if she doesn't call a person on it, they somehow know she sees them. It chafes if the person doesn't like who they are on the inside.

"She's an acquired taste," I say, reaching for my salad again.

"What's going on with you two?" Karen asks, sharper now.

"Aside from being employee and employer?" I quip. "Nothing."

"Defend the woman all you want, Macon, but she clearly isn't a professional assistant."

No, she really isn't. "She's a hell of a chef."

"Macon," Karen begins, then hesitates before rushing on. "Does she have something on you? Is that it?"

I start laughing again. Hard.

"This isn't funny," Karen says. "Something is not right between you two."

Where to begin with that?

She takes on the tone of a worried mother. "If I need to handle this . . ."

"There's nothing to handle," I cut in. "I'm hanging up now. My salad is getting cold."

"Salad is already cold!"

"So you see my problem. Bye, Karen."

"What problem? Macon—"

It is far too satisfying hanging up on her. I've done it before. She's hung up on me before as well; it's the relationship we have. But this is the first time I've been irritated on behalf of someone else.

I text North again.

Don't tell D that I know about the video.

North answers a few seconds later.

If I told her, I'd have to confess that I sent it. I don't have a death wish.

Smart. She would definitely kill you.

Luckily, you piss her off more. Having seen her in action, I'd sleep with one eye open if I were you.

Snorting, I hit play on the video again, and a smile erupts as Delilah's terrible voice fills the kitchen. I find myself eyeing the front door, waiting for her.

———

Delilah

"So . . . ," Macon drawls as he walks onto the upstairs balcony where I'm sitting, painting my toenails. "You had quite the day."

I don't look up from my work. One bad swipe of Cherry Sundae will show for miles. "What, did Karen call to complain?"

He plops his big frame onto the Adirondack chair beside mine. "She's always complaining." His attention drifts to my toes. A small smile plays about his lips, and he taps his long fingers on the arms of the chair. Macon leans back, but his gaze remains on my feet as if he finds the process of my self-pedicure fascinating. "Somehow, I don't think she'll try anything with you again."

Pressing my lips to my bent knee to hide my smile, I finish off the last toe. "She'd better not. I studied up on Rodgers and Hammerstein during my shower, and I'm not afraid to belt out a stirring rendition of *Oklahoma!* if needed."

Macon snorts. "If she messes with you again, I'll provide backup."

I pause and dab at a small spot on my toe. "That's right; you starred in our junior-year musical." Unlike me, Macon has a wonderful voice— deep and resonant. I still kind of hate that he wore suspenders and sang "The Surrey with the Fringe on Top" and still managed to make all the girls swoon.

Silence falls, and Macon stares out at the Pacific, where the sinking sun has turned tangerine in a violet sky. That smile of his grows secretive and quivering around the edges as if he's holding on to his composure with great effort.

"Macon Saint, you're itching to say something. Spill it."

He full out grins. "Well, Ms. Delilah Baker, it appears you've gone viral."

"What?" My voice rises as panic sets in. "What!"

Macon pulls out his phone and flicks on the screen. And the horrifying sound of me singing at the top of my lungs comes out.

"I'll give you this," he says, laughing. "You really sell it."

With a screech, I launch myself out of the chair and at the phone. Macon holds it up out of my reach while his other arm wraps around my waist and pins me against him. Only then do I realize that I've basically thrown my body over his in my attempt to get to the phone.

"Give me the phone," I cry, still struggling.

"Not a chance." I don't know how he manages it, but I find myself sprawled on his lap, arms tucked against his chest. I'd find his strength impressive if I wasn't in full panic mode. He holds me prisoner with one arm. "We'll watch it together."

Since I can't move, and he still has the phone, I can only groan and slump against the wall of his chest. "Fine. Torture me; I give up."

Chuckling, Macon hits replay. And there I am, singing loudly and obnoxiously and dancing like a fool.

I let out a sound that is somewhere between a moan and a wail. Whatever it is, it is pitiful.

Macon, however, is extremely entertained. "Is that the Funky Chicken?"

"Yes." Unable to take it, I burrow my face into the crook of his neck. His breath hitches, but he doesn't move, and I'm unwilling to move either. Macon makes for a surprisingly nice shelter; his skin is smooth and warm and smells of musky citrus. I almost can't hear the stupid video. Almost.

Laughter rumbles in his chest and vibrates along his skin. "Oh, man, look at you go, my 'Tiny Dancer.'"

"Shut." I punch his chest. "Up."

"Two hundred thousand likes and counting."

"Noooo." I press closer to his neck. "Make it stop."

"Oh, come on," he says, suddenly softer. "This video is a thing of beauty. People love it. You're a badass, Tot."

With a sigh, I lift my head. Despite my utter humiliation, a smile threatens. "I didn't know what else to do. She left me waiting for two hours."

Macon's happy expression dims a little before he gives me a conspiratorial look. "Let's put her profile on Tinder and say she's into diaper play."

I snicker. "And disco."

"Diaper disco."

We both chuckle softly. He doesn't stop me when I take the phone from his hand. The video is over, and I force myself to look at it again. Nope, just as embarrassing the second time around. But it hits me that the angle of the shot is coming from the doorway to Karen's office. "Oh my God. She's the one who filmed it and put it on YouTube. That bitch."

Macon peers down at the screen. "I'm pretty sure it was Elaine, her assistant." His eyes gleam with glee. "You want me to have her fired? Disposed of?" He's clearly joking and clearly enjoying the hell out of himself.

"No," I mutter before hiding my face once more. "Just weigh my feet down with rocks, and fling me into the ocean."

The warm weight of his hand slides to my hip and rests there. "That would be a massive waste of talent." His voice is lower now, competing with the sound of the waves. The chair creaks as he adjusts a little, and I sink farther into the cradle of his lap, my head on his shoulder.

"I'll say one thing," he says after a moment. "Life with you isn't dull."

My smile comes out as a hum. The sun is no more than a tiny pinpoint of orange light atop an indigo sea now, leaving the sky violent shades of hot pink, lavender, and teal. Evening breezes play over us, carrying the scent of the ocean. It's getting cold, but Macon's body is warm and solid against mine.

"This place is utterly beautiful," I whisper. "I haven't said so before, but I love your house. Actively love it."

He stills for a second before his fingers drift along the curve of my hip. "I do too—every board, window, and shingle. It's too big for one person—hell, it's too big for two—but it's private, comfortable, and of course there's the view." Resting his head against the chair, he expels a long breath as if letting go of the day. The lines of his body seem to sink into relaxation. "I know I've had it easy when it comes to money. But every morning I wake up here and am grateful."

My eyes drift closed. A warm lassitude fills me. I could sit here all night, listening to the steady beat of his heart and the even cadence of his breathing. Reality crashes over me. I'm sitting in Macon's lap, cuddling him.

Holy hell.

As if pinched, I jump out of his embrace and scramble to my feet. He eyes me cautiously, clearly expecting an argument. Or maybe it's disappointment in his gaze. I'm too unhinged by the idea that I've been snuggling with him to figure it out. I've been on his damn lap, and it hadn't felt weird or wrong; it had felt normal, right, *good*.

Seriously, what the great hell, Dee?

Macon peers up at me, one thick brow quirked as if to say, "You're the one who made yourself comfortable all over my lap." Yeah, I did. Why did I do that? I take a step back, and my butt rests against the balcony railing. I have to think about something other than how very good it felt to be in his arms. I have to put an end to all this soft, dangerous emotion. He's my boss. I'm here because of Sam. And then I remember . . .

"Why didn't you tell me about the stalkers?"

His good humor shatters like dropped glass, and he stares back at me, stone faced. "North?"

"That's not an answer."

His fingers flex, and I've a good idea he's imagining wrapping them around North's neck. "I meant, did North tell you?"

"Who cares who told me?" I stretch my arms wide in frustration. "You should have."

"Why?" His chin lifts belligerently. "It was over and done by the time you arrived."

"Is it? You mean to tell me they were caught and are now behind bars? That you have North as a bodyguard and are worried about me going out on my own because everything is just peachy?"

A curse snarls out of him, and he runs a hand over his face, the bristles of his burgeoning beard rasping against his palm. With an aggravated sigh, he sits back with the grace and arrogance of a king. "They're not in jail. Yes, I am taking precautions, and that includes having you protected."

A chill races down my spine. "Jesus, Macon! When you said you had security concerns, I thought you meant in a 'let's be extra cautious and vigilant' way. Not that someone had actually stalked you!"

"Well, now you know."

"Don't you dare be blasé about this. You should have told me. Not North, you. It should have been you!"

"I know!"

I'm not sure who is more surprised at his admission. We blink at each other before his eyes narrow in that pugnacious way of his.

"Why didn't you tell me?" I grind out.

"Because I hate talking about it." The tendons in his neck stick out as he turns his head and scowls into the growing night. "It makes what they did real."

Shit.

"I hate what they did to you," I say quietly.

His snort is both snide and doubtful. I forgive him for it because I'd be lashing out too.

"I do, Macon. It was wrong, horrible."

The tense set of his shoulders eases a smidgeon.

"If it was me," I go on, "I would be so angry. I'd want to . . . well, if I'm honest, I'd want to punch them in the face."

Slowly, his gaze turns back to mine. Wry amusement lingers in his dark eyes. "You always were bloodthirsty." He leans his head back against the chair. "Shit, Delilah. What can I say? It messed me up. I hate it. But I should have told you."

"Did it ever occur to you that Sam might be in real trouble?" Fear bolts through me. Because she truly might. My breath comes short and fast.

But Macon snorts. "No," he says as if it's the most ridiculous idea on earth.

"No?" I lean toward him, my body humming with anger. "What if someone hurt her trying to get to you? That's a possibility, you know. Don't shake your damn head at me! She might have gotten in their way or—"

"Delilah," he cuts in blandly. "You're not living in a crime novel. Sam didn't get carried off or hurt by my stalkers."

"How do you know? Things happen, you patronizing ass—"

"She's the one who told them where I'd be." He stares back at me, unflinching, pissed off. "If anything, she ran when she found out what her loose tongue cost me."

Rocking back on my heels, I struggle to understand his words. "She . . . wouldn't. She's not that low . . ."

"She is absolutely that low. The woman who ran me off the road confessed that she paid Sam a thousand dollars to get ahold of my schedule."

Horror prickles over my skin, sears me from inside out. Macon lets me absorb it. I can't look him in the eye. Whipping around, I clutch the rail and stare at the now inky sea. "Fucking bitch."

The chair creaks behind me, the sound of Macon rising. He comes to stand beside me at the rail. "Not the exact words I used, but yeah."

Now I understand. There was no way Macon would let Sam get away after that. The fact that he even considered my offer and didn't pursue vengeance stuns me. I'd be out for blood.

It takes me a few tries to find my voice. "Do you . . . do you regret the deal we made?"

The crash of the sea grows louder in our shared silence. When he answers, his voice is low and wary. "No."

I turn to him. He's staring off into the night, the lines of his body hard. When I made my offer, I thought he was the one getting the better deal. That my begrudging services were something of greater worth to him. Now, I have to wonder . . . "Why did you agree to it?"

I watch his jaw work, tensing and releasing as though he's sorting through multiple answers. His coal-dark eyes finally find mine. There's nothing in his expression when he gives me his answer. "I really don't know." He huffs out a humorless laugh. "I'm not sure of anything anymore."

He leaves me standing there, shocked and unsettled as all hell. I stare out at the waves glinting in the waning light. Somewhere out there is my sister.

"Damn you, Samantha," I whisper with a sharpness that scrapes my throat. If she were here, I'd make her face her mistakes. If she were here, I would no longer have to be. I could escape, go back to my orderly life, and forget about Macon Saint—or the terrifying truth that I am in real danger of falling for him.

CHAPTER FOURTEEN

Macon

Karen and my publicist, Timothy, keep texting to see when I'll be "back to normal." I am not ready to go back to my normal schedule. I won't admit it to anyone, but the idea of being formally "out there" with the eyes of the world watching my every move has me breaking out in a cold sweat. Given my profession, this is a problem.

I didn't lie to Delilah; talking to the mango seller about Arasmus and *Dark Castle* was enjoyable. It was gratifying to know my work gives others pleasure. But it wasn't my work that caused those two women to stalk me. I was a thing to them. Sometimes, in the still of the night, when I'm not guarding my thoughts, they'll creep up on me, those grasping fingers, the flashing light of their cameras. I might have bled out and died before they finally called 911. And I can't help but think that going out in the public eye will draw more of their kind.

It pisses me off that I care.

A little more time, I tell myself. That's all I need. A little more time to regroup, heal. And then I'll be good. Just like new.

Until then, I'm sticking to the house. And there's one place I find myself gravitating toward.

The kitchen.

It has become a living, thriving beast in the center of my once quiet and orderly house. There's no ignoring the new heart of my home. It won't let me. I constantly hear the sounds coming out of it: clanks, sizzles, muted thumps and bangs. A cacophony of sounds. It should annoy me, but it intrigues me instead. What tasty delights will come from those sounds? What new dish will bring me to my knees and make me beg for more?

Scents waft from the kitchen, dancing around the halls to find me and tickle my nose. Warm and comforting and mouthwatering. "Come closer," those scents seem to say. "Come see what we have for you."

Come.

How can I ignore that?

So I don't. I follow the siren's call and find the siren herself at the very center of activity.

Delilah moves with utter confidence in her kitchen—because it is unequivocally hers now. This is a prima ballerina performing a solo. Not a fast-paced, frantic dance, but slow and easy, controlled power in motion.

Knowing that she hasn't yet noticed me, I simply watch her work, admiring the curves of her body as she reaches for a spoon to taste a sauce. The pink tip of her tongue flashes as she licks her lush top lip. Something hot and tight clenches low in my gut at the sight. Then she's moving again, adding a spice to her sauce; a flick of her wrist controls the temperature on the stove.

My body remembers the feel of hers, the way she cuddled up in my lap for those few mindless minutes. I was surprised enough that she did it. I simply held her, afraid to make any move that might startle her away. She was warm and soft, her tan skin smelling of butter and cinnamon sugar. I wanted to sit there all night and breathe her in.

I wanted to let my hands roam over those plump curves and learn each one. It was an act of careful coordination to keep her from noticing just how much she affected me. It was worth the painful dick and the aching gut of lust because in that moment, she felt perfect.

She turns back to the center island and the cutting board there and sees me. The loose-limbed ease of her body dies. She's all twitchy now, eyeing me like a feral barn cat as if I might try to lash out and catch her.

Tempting.

As though she suspects the direction of my thoughts, she straightens and adopts a casual pose like she never sat on my lap, never let me pet her as the sun set. "Don't tell me you're hungry again."

No mention of the cuddle or the uncomfortable conversation about Sam. For that, I'm grateful. Maybe it's for the best that we don't talk about Sam. Ever.

I move farther into the warmth of the kitchen. "Since you got here, I'm always hungry."

She can make of that what she wants.

She's been bent over a stove, so the flush on her cheeks might be from the heat. Or maybe not. She nods toward a pressed tin container on the counter. "I made some oat bars. Nothing exciting, but they're on your approved list."

"I think we both know how I feel about that damn list."

The corners of her lips curl in amusement. "Yes, we do."

I stand at the end of the counter, close enough to be within touching distance but not crowd her. "What are you making now?"

She's got two pots going, one of them covered.

"A bordelaise sauce." At my interested look, she grabs a spoon out of the canister filled with clean ones that she keeps near the stove and dips it in the pot before handing it to me.

The sauce is a glossy mahogany, and when I slip it into my mouth, I close my eyes and groan. Rich, deep, dense—I don't have the words to do it justice.

I open my eyes to find her staring with an unreadable expression on her face.

"God damn, Tot." I lick the spoon, desperate to get another taste. I whimper this time.

Delilah watches me, and her nostrils flare like she's sucking in a quick breath, but her voice remains smooth as old silk. "Don't worry; I won't be using much of it. Just a spoonful on top of a flat iron steak. Shouldn't be too many calories."

I cut her a reproachful glare. "Don't you dare skimp. I'd bathe in this if I could."

With a husky laugh, she takes my spoon and puts it in the sink. "As delightful as that image sounds, let's keep the sauce on our plates."

"That's not half as fun." I pull out a stool and sit to alleviate the ache in my leg.

Delilah eyes me. "You hurting a lot today?"

Since she's already taken me to task for denying my pain, I answer her truthfully. "Yes."

With a hum, she starts on a turmeric latte. I don't know how much they actually reduce pain, but it's soothing and something made just for me. I accept her gift and curl my fingers around the cup, stealing its warmth.

Delilah has opened up a journal and is reading heavily marked pages. The leather-bound journal looks much like the ones I use, though hers is battered and splattered with various food and oil stains. She jots down a note in the margin of what looks to be a recipe, then catches me watching her.

"My recipe journal." She closes it. "Early on, we're taught to write things down. Memories can fade. But I also use it to develop recipes or make note of an idea."

Her slim hand, as battered as her book, rests protectively over the cover. She eyes me warily as though I might poke fun at her. It touches a nerve deep within that her trust in me is so thin, that my past actions caused this lack of trust. So I give her the only thing I can: my own vulnerability.

"I journal too." I take a sip of latte. "Not recipes, of course. But notes about my role. Or what happened on set that day, so I'll remember it when I'm old."

Her butterscotch eyes grow wide. "Truly?"

"It is so surprising?"

She blinks and gives a little shake of her head. "Yes. No. I don't know. I guess I can't picture you taking the time to write things down."

"Everything important to me, I write down." Shrugging, I palm the cup again. "Or I do now. Back when I lived at home, I wouldn't dare. Nothing in my room was safe from being confiscated."

Her lips part in surprise. Yeah, I don't suspect she had any idea how truly confined I was as a kid. An old discomfort rolls through me, as ugly and itchy as a hair shirt. I shed that past long ago, but some things never truly go away; we just try to forget them as best as we can.

"I got into writing after high school." After the letter. Another twang of regret plucks me. I don't mention that damn letter. I have some pride. "Helps me gather my thoughts."

Delilah nods slowly, her eyes still wide and on me. "It does," she says after an awkward second. I get the feeling she's more surprised we have something in common. I'm not. Even when being around Delilah made me want to tear out of my skin just to get away from her judging eyes, I knew we were forged from the same metal.

"Why did you become a chef?"

She visibly jolts at the question, clearly not expecting it. Her palm, still on the journal, makes a slow, smooth circuit of the leather. "Aside from loving to cook?"

She's evading, and we both know it. I hold her gaze, letting her see that I won't hurt her here. "Aside from that, yes. You could have cooked for yourself and done something else."

Delilah licks her upper lip. It's a quick nervous gesture I saw her do dozens of times when we were kids. But she never was one to shirk from answering—at least not with me—and she doesn't disappoint this time either. "I went to college because it was what I was supposed to do, you know?"

I nod. Because I did the same. Follow the track society set for me.

"Don't get me wrong; I enjoyed it. But the closer I got to graduation, the more scared and less satisfied I became. What the hell was I going to do when I got out? I felt . . . stifled. I had this urge to create . . . something."

"Like something's pushing against your insides, wanting to get out."

"Yes, exactly!" Delilah's words flow with more ease. "I asked myself, what was it that I most enjoyed? And I realized it was cooking. Food was my joy."

"So you followed your joy."

Her slim finger traces the edge of the journal, the one that looks almost exactly like mine. "A mentor of mine once told me that food is a commonality that binds us all. We all need to eat to survive. But in eating, creating dishes that gave us pleasure, we developed a story of our humanity as well as the story of who we are as individuals. Food is tied to so many of our memories."

"I once read a quote that good food heals our soul."

"The right dish certainly can." She leans toward me, her gaze intent and bright. "Give me a memory of food that makes you happy."

She wants to heal me with food? Strange thing is, I'm fairly certain she's already doing that.

I answer without thought. "Grilled cheese sandwiches your mom used to make us after school."

She blinks, pink lips parting, but recovers quickly with a warm smile. "Yes." In a flash, she moves to the fridge and pulls out a few packs of cheese.

"You've been hiding cheese in there?" I say with mock outrage.

She smirks. "I'm not going to forgo cheese. You never look in this thing, do you?"

"It makes it worse if I do."

Delilah puts the cheese on the counter, then goes about gathering bread and butter. She has a thick loaf of farm bread that she cuts in slices.

"You're going to make me a grilled cheese? Actually cheat?"

From under the fan of her lashes, her eyes gleam. "I won't tell if you don't."

I fall just a little further under her spell, my walls crumbling in places I never thought they'd weaken.

"And I'm not making it," she adds, taking out a frying pan and turning on the stove. "We are."

I stand and stop by her side. "I can make a grilled cheese, but not like your mama's. They always come out too dark on the bread and too cold in the center."

"That's because you haven't learned the proper way."

Together, we construct the sandwiches, using a blend of muenster, because it was what her mother favored, and provolone, because Delilah thinks it adds a deeper flavor—and liberally buttering the bread because, Delilah informs me, it's all about the butter.

"Now," she says, laying two sandwiches on the hot pan. "Here is where you learn that cooking involves all the senses. Taste, yes. But also sound. Listen. The butter is sizzling. No sound means it's not cooking the right way. The pan is either too low or too hot."

We listen to the sizzle.

"Sight," she says. "We need to see that beautiful butter hopping and bubbling around the edges of the pan."

Dutifully, I watch. How can I not? She is in total command.

"Smell." She wafts her hand over the pan, letting the warm scent of browning butter and bread wash over us. "This is more important when you're adding herbs and spices. Does the dish smell as it should? It's something you learn on the way. Flip the sandwiches."

I take the spatula from her and do as asked. The bread is perfectly browned.

"Feeling. You have to feel how the food is behaving. The texture of it. Now, with grilled cheese, you don't want to cook it too fast, or the cheese won't melt. Hear how the sound has dimmed?"

I nod.

"We need to add more butter; turn the heat down just a bit."

She walks me through the entire process, teaching me to control the heat, baby the sandwiches to get them how I want. All the time our shoulders are brushing, our moves in coordination for a common goal. A sense of calm spreads over me. I'm not thinking about work or the outside world. I'm not angry or empty. I'm filled up. I'm here, with her.

We get the sandwiches on plates, and she hands me a knife.

"The best part. Cutting it open." Her brow wings up in warning. "Only cut on the diagonal. Down the middle is a sin against grilled cheese."

"Please," I say, with feeling. "As if I'd sink so low." I make the first cut and am rewarded with a fine crunch of sound, followed by the ooze of gooey cheese. Perfection.

"Taste. Take a bite," Delilah urges with childlike excitement.

It's just a sandwich. A kid's treat. It feels like more.

I take a bite.

"Close your eyes," she says. "Tell me what you think when you taste it."

You.

Me.

Delilah wearing braces, her thick hair pulled back in a tight ponytail that highlights the roundness of her face. Her gold eyes glaring at me from opposite her mother's kitchen table.

Home.

Safety.

A tremor goes through my gut. I open my eyes, wanting to step away from the counter. From her. But she's watching me with rapt eyes. Waiting for an answer.

"I remember those days," I say thickly. "Your mama yelling at us to wash our hands or we wouldn't get a snack. I remember how we all ate those grilled cheese sandwiches quickly so each bite would be just as crisp and oozing, and she'd warn us that we'd burn our mouths with our gluttonous eating habits."

Her gaze holds mine, her voice soft now. "And we didn't care because it was too good to eat slowly."

"Yeah." The air is thick with memories—and us. I have the insane urge to step into her space, touch her cheek. Just touch her.

Delilah blinks, and the spell is broken.

"This is almost exactly like your mama's," I say to fill the silence. "But better."

She makes a dubious face. "No one makes them better than Mama."

"You do."

Flushing again, Delilah pours us iced tea, and we eat in relative silence.

"So you're a chef because you want to evoke memories?" I ask after a time.

"Not exactly." She wipes her hands with a napkin. "So we agree that food evokes memories, but a chef is doing something a little different. She's telling you a story through food. If she does her job correctly, she's taking you on a journey, making you taste things in a new way, making you stop, think, and appreciate the food. A chef not only feeds you; she gives you pleasure. She illuminates."

Heat sweeps under my collar, and I struggle to get it under control, but damn she makes it sound almost illicit.

Unaware of my struggle, Delilah continues, "Good food is theater in a way, but the audience participates."

"We're both entertainers," I say with a start of surprise.

"I guess we are," she agrees after a second.

"So why catering? Why close it down?" I can't help myself. I want to know her as she is today, not as she was before.

Her words come out with measured slowness. "When I was in New York, working the line, all those monstrous hours, I used to dream of catering, where I could slow things down, have a bit of a life outside of cooking."

Her smile is wry. "But then I got to LA and started up the business. I became stuck with the strange whims of my clientele, worrying about parties and how they would go. My creativity faltered." Shaking her head, she shrugs. "I found I didn't want that, either, which makes me wonder. Do I have what it takes? How can I if the thought of constantly working turns me off?"

A frown works across her face, and she ducks her head as though she doesn't want to meet my gaze. She probably thinks she's said too much.

"When we're filming," I say. "We have such long hours I lose track of days. Hell, sometimes I'm so tired I don't even know who I am anymore. It's exhausting. Sometimes, I want to say, 'Fuck it, I'm done.' But then I think of not working anymore and feel empty. I never expected acting to fill a void in me, but it does. So I keep going."

The moment the words are out, I feel the truth of them. I love what I do. And I'll be damned if I hide away because of one bad incident. No more hiding out. No more fear.

My breath comes easier than it has in weeks. "That you want more out of life than constant work doesn't mean you aren't a chef. It means you are human."

The expression on Delilah's face is one I haven't seen before. It almost looks like gratitude. I don't know what to do with that. She shouldn't feel grateful. I'm the one holding her back. The knowledge wraps itself around my throat and squeezes. She shouldn't be here in Sam's place. I should let her go. I should say it. But I can't seem to make my mouth form the words.

Delilah takes a long breath and lets it out slowly. "In a weird way, being here has helped put things into perspective."

"What do you mean?" I ask through stiff lips.

She tilts her head back and sighs. "A chef has to discover who she is and how she wants to express that to the world. What is the story she wants to tell?" Her big soft eyes meet mine. "I closed the shop because I realized I didn't exactly know the answers to all that."

"And being here helps?" I want it to be true, but I can't believe it. I'm a hindrance, not an asset.

"I don't know if *help* is the right word," she drawls with slight humor. "More like I'm learning about myself through adversity."

I wince. "Ouch."

Her laugh is light and oddly carefree. "Don't look so pained. It was my choice."

Sadly, that doesn't help a bit.

"And when this is done?" The thickness in my throat swells, making my words rough. "Will you still go on that tour?"

She worries her bottom lip with the edge of her teeth. "You know, for the first time in years, I'm not looking forward. I'm just concentrating on right now." She appears to find this surprising, almost funny, if her huff of laughter means anything. "I don't want to think about the future."

In that we differ. For the first time in years, all I see is the future. It's dark and empty, and what scares the ever-loving hell out of me, what makes me get up and leave the kitchen a short while later, is that it will be because she's gone.

Chapter Fifteen

Delilah

Macon and I do not mention that evening on the porch. Whether this is by silent, tacit agreement or it simply doesn't register as any big deal to Macon, I don't know. I can't ask because, as stated, I refuse to speak of the incident. It's a struggle not to think about it, either, but I manage. Mostly. There are occasional flashes of memory—how very good it felt to rest on him, how very delicious he smelled, or the heady feeling I got just hearing the deep rumble in his chest when he laughed. Those unfortunate snips of memory I push away as quickly as I can. But they disturb me. Mostly I'm disturbed by how easy it was to cuddle up to him.

But in the dark of night, when I'm huddled under my covers alone and too sleepy to fight it, a trickle of regret will steal over me. It was more than comfortable there with Macon. For the first time in my life, I felt *seen*. And for an all-too-brief moment, it was perfect.

And then there's Sam. I know without a doubt I won't see her until she's good and ready to be found, that guilt and shame have pushed her into hiding. This is far worse than the time she disappeared for a month after blowing a semester's worth of tuition on a weekend in Vegas with her girlfriends. Daddy was alive then and mad as hell. She only came slinking back when she ran out of money, and only then—I'm convinced—because she knew Daddy wouldn't actually kill her.

She's got no such assurances when it comes to Macon.

Good God, she sold his trust and his literal safety. I *know* that's why she left. The watch was probably an impulse theft, a quick way to get cash. Ugh. Everything feels turned on its head. I want to protect my mother's tender heart as much as ever. But I also want vengeance for Macon. I don't want to leave him alone in this. If, at age seventeen, someone had told me that I'd feel protective of Macon Saint, I'd have laughed my ass off and called them a liar. Now? Damn it, I don't know. The hurt and still very vocal girl in me says get the hell out of here and protect yourself. The adult in me says that maybe Macon isn't so bad. Maybe he could be . . . what? A friend.

I shake my head at that, scared and freaking confused. And I work. Work always helps.

We settle into a routine of sorts. Macon goes about his business—whatever that may be—and I plan my menus and, after getting Macon's okay, set about planting a vegetable garden along the side of the property. The place already has a good amount of lemon, avocado, and olive trees dotted around. Something I take advantage of as much as I can.

The assistant aspect of my job isn't the greatest; I'm either shopping, picking up Macon's meds and whatever else catches his fancy, or bringing meals. But mostly I field his calls. So many calls. And Macon doesn't really want to accept any of them. I've become the queen of giving lame excuses.

His issues aside, there is one personal issue I have to manage, and fairly quickly. I hunt Macon down and find him in the kitchen, pouring a cup of coffee.

"I have a problem," I say without preamble.

"Oh? Is it sex related?" With a brow waggle, Macon leans against the countertop. He's tall enough that his butt rests on the top of it. The perfect height that, if he wanted to, he could set a woman on that cool marble, spread her legs, and . . .

What is wrong *with you? Stop thinking about sex, you hussy.* A shudder moves over my shoulders, and I push those thoughts away. Push, push, push. So many unwanted thoughts. It's getting crowded in my mind now, harder to hide away from things I don't want to address.

"Hardly. My mother keeps texting me. She wants to know about my new job and is asking questions."

"So answer her." He pours me some coffee and slides it my way. "Or are you having trouble with what you should say?"

I shake my head. "No, I'll tell her . . . something. I'm not sure what at the moment, but it'll come. Thing is, I owe her a birthday lunch."

Macon pauses and looks at me from under his straight brows. "You were preparing her brunch when I first texted."

"I never finished." I set my cup down. "I want to go home and host a makeup brunch."

"This is your home now," Macon says in a quiet tone. "Host the brunch here."

My home? It doesn't feel like that in the slightest. "Here? You'd be okay with that?"

His dark eyes are guileless. "Why wouldn't I? I love your mother."

"I know." After he befriended Sam, Macon was at our house at all hours. Mama took him in like a stray puppy. There was always a seat open to him at our table. Even when he was being a shit to me.

"You two need to put aside your stubborn pride and mend this rift, Delilah," my mother said when I complained. *"If that boy needs safe harbor from his homelife now and then, I'm not going to deny him because you have a bee in your bonnet."*

To this day, I have no idea why she thought of Macon's visits as a safe harbor, given that his favorite pastime at my house was to dog me at every opportunity.

I shake those memories aside. If I think of them for too long, I'm going to want to throw my mug at him. I have to live with my nemesis now. The past needs to stay in the past.

Macon is frowning at me as if he's working things out in his head. Maybe he's remembering things as well. Sometimes I wonder how he views our past. Does he imagine himself the wounded party? I suppose he was at times.

Whatever the case, he crosses his arms over his chest and gives me a level look. "Quit trying to pick a fight, and call your mother, Tot."

Patronizing . . . I bite my bottom lip and shake my head. "All right, then, prepare to be invaded."

Macon raises his cup in salute. "Bring it on."

———

Exactly one day later, Mama and her best friend, JoJo, descend upon Macon's house with wide eyes and gaping mouths.

"Well," my mother says. "I can see why you'd give up trekking around Asia if you get to work here. It's simply beautiful."

So far, I've told Mama the bare minimum—that I took a job as a personal executive chef—and left out the part of assistant because I knew she wouldn't buy it. I insisted that the pay and opportunity were too good to pass up, all the while fighting down the bitter taste in my mouth that came from lying.

When she pushed for more, I promised to fill her in when she came for lunch.

We have the house to ourselves. Macon and North are down in LA, doing God knows what. I think they made up an excuse in order to flee.

Mama's blue-gray eyes, so like Sam's, are alight with interest. "Who on earth are you working for, Dee?"

"Let me guess." JoJo grabs my wrist in excitement. "Someone famous. It has to be. Famous people value their privacy," she says to Mama.

Maybe it's because they've been friends for so long, but despite the fact that Mama is pale and blonde, and JoJo is dark and brunette, they look remarkably alike. Both wear their curly hair cut in bobs that pouf out like triangles around their delicate faces, both are of a height, and both love to wear loose-fitting capris and flowing tunics in various animal prints. Standing together now, they look as if a cheetah collided with a zebra.

Unexpected tears prickle behind my lids, and I have the urge to rush over and beg for hugs. Because the two of them together make me feel like a kid again, safe and protected. I always looked upon them with awe, wanting to be as uniquely confident as they were when I grew up. I still want that confidence.

JoJo is on the move, investigating the great room for clues. "So," she says, peering around. "Who is it? A movie star? Big producer? Musician? Tell me he's handsome."

"Maybe her boss is a woman, Jo." Mama smiles at me. "Put your sexist auntie JoJo out of her misery, and tell us, sweetheart."

Auntie JoJo flips Mama the bird under the guise of scratching her eyebrow. As much as I'd love to see them go at it—because their squabbling can be epic—I take a breath and confess. "It's Macon."

Mama tilts her head as if she's misheard. "Macon?"

Dully, I nod.

Her mouth slowly drops open. "As in Macon Saint?"

"Macon Saint?" JoJo parrots. "Sam's childhood beau?"

Ugh. I hadn't really thought of Macon in those terms lately. It somehow makes it all worse—Sam's theft, the fact that I'm taking up her debt, all of it.

I clasp my hands tightly. "Yes."

They exchange a long look.

Mama's voice is subdued. "I see."

I fear she does and scramble to reassure. "It's a great opportunity. Macon is famous. Chefs get a lot of exposure working for famous people." I fear that sounds as horrible to their ears as it does mine.

But JoJo gives me a kind look. "This is true. And if I do say so myself, *Dark Castle* is my favorite show. Have you seen it, Andie?" she asks my mother.

"No. Or rather, I viewed the first few episodes." Her pale cheeks pinken. "But then there was *that* scene."

"Ah, that scene," JoJo says, failing spectacularly to hide her grin. "I must say, it was a shock to see . . . that."

Yes, "that" being Macon's ass. It seems the whole world has seen his ass except for me. I'm beginning to feel sorely left out.

Mama's color deepens. "I couldn't look. It was like seeing my own son . . . you know. For Pete's sake, how was I supposed to watch after that? It isn't as though I could do a search. 'Will Macon Saint have sex on *Dark Castle* tonight?'"

I snicker and quickly swallow it down. "I haven't watched either."

Big mistake.

Mama's expression turns sharp. Another glance at JoJo has my honorary auntie suddenly finding a deep interest in the view.

Mama moves close to me and sets a cool hand upon my wrist. "You know I'm not one to question your choices, Delilah, but you're truly working for Macon Saint? Living with him?"

"I'm not living with him. I live on the property." It sounds lame even to my ears.

She shoots me a quelling look. "Macon has his good and bad points, just like anyone else. But the two of you got on like gas and fire. He's the last person I'd expect you to work for. Now, tell me what is going on with you." Her eyes pin me to the spot. "Is it money? Has it something to do with Sam? It must, what with the way you've been desperately searching for her."

My mother isn't stupid. I knew she'd figure some things out. So I have my excuses planned.

When lying, it's best to stick as closely to the truth as possible. You'd think Sam taught me that, but it was my daddy. Trick is, I have to tell my mother a twisted version of the truth for her to believe it.

With a sigh, I meet her gaze. "Sam stole money from me."

Mama's expression crumples. "Oh, Sam, my misguided baby. My stupid, misguided child." With a shaky hand, she cups my cheeks. "Tell me everything."

I feel like a heel. A horrible, lying heel. "She took my savings, and I'd already closed up shop, as you know."

Grimly, my mother nods.

"Macon had heard about my catering through friends and happened to call at an opportune moment. He offered me a job as his assistant and chef. The pay is enough that I can save up to go to Asia next year."

"This won't do," Mama says. "I have some money—"

"No, Mama. Absolutely not."

Her lips purse. "It's my money. I get a say—"

"Not with this." I lay a hand on her shoulder. "I've already given my word. I won't turn back on that."

With clear reluctance, she nods. And I smile. "Besides, look at this place. I'm not hurting here. It's beautiful, and the work is easy."

She glances around and then shakes her head. "It is. But it won't stop me from tanning your sister's hide when I find her."

"I'll help you do it. But you know Sam won't turn up until she's good and ready." I take her elbow and guide her back to where JoJo is staring out of the living room window and undoubtedly eavesdropping the whole time. "Now, who's hungry for lunch?"

JoJo takes my free arm. "I'm starved, doll."

I lead Mama and JoJo out to a table set beneath a vine-covered trellis on the north side of the lawn. There is much oohing and aahing over the ocean view before they inspect the table. I managed to find a natural linen tablecloth, some tumbled glass votives, and a large chrome-and-wood hurricane lamp. Mixed with his everyday creamware plates and Mexican-style glasses, the setting is as nice as I can make it.

"This is lovely, pumpkin," Mama says, touching one of the sprigs of rosemary I tucked into the linen napkins. "You didn't have to go through all this trouble."

"It's your birthday lunch, Mama. And it was no trouble."

"I can't believe this view." JoJo sighs as she stares at the ocean. She turns our way, and her salt-and-pepper curls lift in the breeze. "That boy has excellent taste."

"He always has." Mama takes the seat I pull out for her. "Thank you, dear. Though I will say, I had no idea TV acting paid so well. Oh, don't give me that look, Dee. I know it's tacky to mention money, but we're family."

I roll my eyes and pour her a glass of sweet tea.

JoJo takes the seat to her right. "He's a star in one of the most popular shows on cable, Andie. I expect it pays well."

"Not this well." Mama waves a hand in the general direction of the lawn.

Knowing that Macon might return home at any moment makes me itchy. I cringe to think of him overhearing my mother and her best friend being gossips.

"Lemonade or sweet tea, Ms. JoJo?" I cut in before they can say more.

"Lemonade for me, angel." She leans past me to look at my mother. "This is likely from his family money. Turns out Cecilia's family was richer than a shiny-toothed television evangelist."

"I knew they had money, but not to that extent."

JoJo gives a careless shrug. "Old money doesn't like to be showy."

Mama nods sagely, and I press my lips together in irritation.

"Does it really matter if Macon comes from money?" I snap without thinking.

Mama grimaces and sets her cool hand on top of mine. "Of course not, baby." She smiles brightly. "Well, obviously you two have made nice this time around."

A noncommittal hum is all I can manage.

"I always thought Macon was secretly sweet on you."

I can't help but snort. "Sweet on me? Not a chance. His loathing was real."

"Now, I know he could be . . ."

"An asshole?"

Mama pretends to be shocked. "Language, Delilah."

It's JoJo's turn to snort. Though my mother has excellent manners and is the soul of kindness, she also curses like a trucker when she thinks her children aren't around to hear. I don't consider that a flaw, but it is amusing when she tries to put on airs.

"He was horrible to me," I say firmly.

Mama waves a hand. "That doesn't mean anything. You know, they say boys are meanest to the girls they like the best."

"I hate that saying. Meanness is meanness. To tell a girl that there's some sort of benevolent action behind it all is to say that it's okay for her to be victimized."

Mama stares up at me for a moment, then shakes her head. "You're right, pumpkin. I don't know why I said that."

JoJo snorts again. "Because you and I were raised with 'boys will be boys' tossed in our faces." She sits back in her chair and turns her face to the sunlight. "I say it should be 'dicks will be dicks, and a misbehaving dick deserves a knee to the balls.'"

Mama and I look at each other and then start to laugh.

"Well," Mama says finally with a faint gasp. "There you go, Dee. If that boy gets out of line, knee him in the balls."

"Hopefully I won't give her cause to do that," says a deep, amused voice behind us.

I'm ashamed to say we all jump like escaped convicts.

Macon stands, leaning slightly toward his good leg, the sunlight glinting in his black hair. A slight smile plays on his lips. His gaze meets mine, and a flush of . . . something goes over me.

"You're back." I try not to make that sound like an accusation. And fail.

A taunt flares in his eyes. "I am."

He lingers a second longer before turning his attention to my mother.

"Mrs. Baker, Ms. Davis, you're both looking well."

"As are you, dear boy," JoJo drawls. "So handsome. You have the jawline of a young Robert Redford, even if it is hidden by all that scruff. Now come over here, and give your elders a proper kiss on the cheek."

I barely refrain from coughing "cougar" under my breath.

Macon grins and strides forward, making it look effortless even with a cane and a severe limp. Dutifully, he leans down and kisses both JoJo and Mama on their presented cheeks. As he pulls away from Mama, he gives me a sly wink before straightening, and I know he's going to put on a show—sweet, gallant Macon Saint.

"I hear felicitations are in order, Mrs. Baker. Happy birthday."

Mama all but titters. "Why, thank you, Macon. And please call me Andie."

His smile is all charm. "I don't think I'd be able to. It would feel disrespectful. You've always been Mrs. Baker to me, ma'am."

Lord, help me.

But Mama soaks it all up. "Sweet boy."

Traitor.

"Look at you," she goes on. "All grown up."

"That I am."

"I'd read on Twitter that you'd been hurt." Mama glances my way as if somehow I'm responsible. I bristle, but she's back to patting Macon's hand. And I try to wrap my head around my mother trolling through Twitter.

"I'll be fine in no time, Mrs. Baker."

"Yes," I add. "He just needs to rest." *Go rest, Macon.*

His brow raises as if he hears my silent demand. And I get a look that says, *Not on your life, Tot.*

"We're about to have lunch," Mama says, killing my hope. "You should join us."

Oh, hell no. "I'm sure Macon has other plans—"

"Why, I would love to, Mrs. Baker. How kind of you to ask."

He goes to grab an empty chair from across the way, and I glare at Mama, who gives me a pinch under the table. I rub my thigh and get up. "I'll just be a moment. Help yourselves to the fruit plate."

Grumbling, I head for the kitchen with Macon's rumbly voice haunting me as I go. I'd made Macon a plate of food and left it in the fridge. I add it to our lunch, tempted to sprinkle some cayenne on it. Wily interloper. He'll charm Mama, and all I'll hear about for months is how sweet and wonderful Macon is.

When I return, he's holding center court at the table. He sees me approach, and his eyes light up with mischief. But he doesn't say anything as I set down my massive tray on the sideboard and begin to serve lunch.

"Why, Delilah," Mama says. "This looks wonderful."

I've made squash blossoms stuffed with pimento cheese mousse—because my mother loves pimento cheese—and for the main course, lobster salad on fresh sweet potato rolls and a simple roasted-corn succotash and jicama-fennel slaw as sides.

"Delilah is a great chef," Macon says. "Since leaving Shermont, I hadn't given much thought to food. Then Delilah comes back into my life, and I find myself craving all the time."

An awkward beat falls over the table. He said it with a straight face, but damn him, his words have me hot and bothered and thinking of sinful cravings that are most definitely bad for me.

JoJo clears her throat delicately. "Good food will do that to you."

Macon quirks a brow my way as if to silently say, "Indeed."

I cut him a glare and attack my sandwich with vigor.

Silence descends as we eat, but then Macon wipes his lips with his napkin and turns my mother's way. "Perhaps you can settle an argument, Mrs. Baker."

"Don't tell me you kids are going at it again."

For some reason the words hit me entirely the wrong way, and all I can picture is Macon and me truly going at it. Against a wall, all hot and sweaty. And hard. So very, very hard . . . I reach for my lemonade and spill some in my haste.

The tops of his cheeks become slightly ruddy. "Er . . . no, not exactly. Delilah tells me she's named after an aunt who drowned in a pie."

I make a face at him, and he returns it while my mother is distracted by taking a sip of tea.

"Ah, yes, Great-Aunt Delilah, smothered by strawberry rhubarb."

"I didn't know *rhubarb* was involved," Macon exclaims as if the addition of it makes all the difference.

"Cuts the sweetness of the strawberry with a little tart," JoJo explains.

Completely straight faced, Macon nods. "I like a little tart with my sweets."

I struggle not to roll my eyes.

"Personally," Mama goes on, "I can't stand to eat strawberry rhubarb pie anymore. Reminds me of death," she confides in a lowered voice.

With a groan, I rest my head in my hands.

"I much prefer a nice buttermilk pie or coconut cream," she tells Macon.

"Chocolate chiffon is my favorite," JoJo puts in.

Macon keeps his eyes firmly off me as his mouth twitches. "I'm partial to warm peach."

"Oh, for the love of pie," I exclaim. "Would you please tell us why I was so named, Mama?"

She gives me a chiding look. "Your patience leaves much to be desired, Delilah."

Macon clearly struggles not to laugh. "I'm always saying that, but she thinks I'm picking on her."

"If your leg wasn't broken, I'd kick it," I say sweetly before giving my mother a pleading look. "Go on, Mama."

"It was your father who picked the name. He did so love his aunt." She takes a bite of her lobster roll, then dabs her lips with a napkin. "I wanted to call you Fern."

"Fern?" I rear back. "Do you know the amount of verbal abuse I would have gotten at school over Fern?"

Macon clears his throat, then presses a fist to his mouth like he's trying to force it to behave before speaking. "It would have been a lot."

"Mostly by you," I add with some asperity.

His grin is quick and unrepentant. "Probably."

"I told her not to do it." JoJo helps herself to another squash blossom. "I said, 'Andie, your girl will hate you for this. You want her to at least make it to her teen years before she tries to kill you.'"

"What's wrong with Fern?" my mother asks, spreading her hands in exasperation. "It's from my favorite book, *Charlotte's Web*."

I can't . . .

Macon's broad shoulders are shaking, his face red behind the fist he still has covering his mouth.

I lean toward my mother. "Then why didn't you name me *Charlotte*?"

179

Mama blinks at me as if I'm off my nut. "I couldn't do that! Charlotte dies at the end. It would have been bad luck."

Agitated heat blooms over my chest. "Aunt Delilah died! By pie!"

Macon loses it with a great burst of rolling laughter. He laughs so hard he leans back in his chair, holding a hand to his chest. He laughs so hard his eyes turn into little triangles of glee.

All the women at the table are momentarily stunned by the spectacle because Macon Saint full-on belly laughing is an undeniable thing of beauty. He's so jovial that it makes me start to smile. Before I know it, I'm laughing too. Mama and JoJo fall under his spell as well, and soon we're all laughing like a bunch of loons under the yellow sun.

Chapter Sixteen

Delilah

SammyBaker to DeeLight: Why is there a viral video of you singing on a chair?

DeeLight: Sam! WHERE THE HELL ARE YOU?

Had to get away for a while. Don't worry. What's with the singing?

That's all you have to say? What about this mess with Macon?

Don't worry about him either. I'll deal with that when I get back.

R U Kidding Me? When? When are you coming back?

A few months. Just need to take care of some things.

Months! Damn it, Sam!

Good chat, D. Turning my phone off now.

Sam!

Sam!

———

"Fucking bitch!" I toss my phone across the bed and lean back into the pillows, my nerves jumping and sizzling like hot oil. After all this time, she finally texted. And jerked my chain, giving me next to nothing. I'm so pissed and shocked I don't know what to do.

I can go to Macon, tell him . . . what? Sam's definitely hiding out, but hey, she's coming back in a few months, which means, technically, I win the bet. Only I don't know if she's bringing back the watch or exactly *when* she's returning. No, he'll just get worked up into a froth like I am. And for nothing. Because that's what she gave me.

Why did she text? She'd seen my video? So despite her claims, she is using her phone. And she is coming back. I believe that much. Girl can't stay away forever. She's too damn nosy and too damn used to being the center of attention.

I'll let her get comfortable again, wait until her guard is lowered, then send out another feeler. That's all I can do. Pushing it will just make her dig in her heels.

Grumbling, I roll out of bed and head for the shower. She's managed to ruin my morning and leave a sick, ugly feeling in my stomach. The craziest thing about my situation? I hear Macon moving around in his room and find myself in the same predicament I awake with every day—excited to see him.

———

In the four weeks since the accident, Macon has been in self-imposed seclusion. He's slowly getting better; the black eye fades away; the slash over his brow heals to a faint scar that merely gives him more of a rakish appearance.

While his leg is still in the walking boot, his wrist and ribs are now unwrapped. He works out with North every day, doing a modified routine.

Being more mobile clearly makes him antsy. And he soon tells me to accept an invitation to a charity luncheon on Saturday. Which is fine—I'm glad he's getting out of the house and back into life—only I have to go too. It's a daytime event, which means fairly casual, but I'm still stuck in a little black A-line dress and sensible heels, trailing behind Macon as he walks the red carpet, camera flashes going off like starbursts, people calling out his name.

North blends with the crowd, his job as bodyguard not as needed with all the security manning the event. I'm met by Timothy Wu, Macon's publicist. The energetic man's enthusiasm tires me out within minutes, but I have to say he totally rocks a pinstripe suit and yellow polka-dot tie.

Timothy takes me under his wing, and together we answer press questions, take numbers, and run interference whenever someone he deems unacceptable tries to get too close to Macon. I quickly learn about press-publicist vendettas and backbiting.

"That bitch," Timothy hisses in my ear after waving off a woman with promises to keep in touch. "She completely misquoted Macon in an interview. Made it sound like he was ungrateful for his success with *Dark Castle*."

One thing I know for certain about Macon is that he never takes his work for granted.

"Then why did you agree to set up another meeting?" I ask Timothy.

He shrugs lightly. "Her magazine is too popular to ignore her."

That pretty much sums the whole thing up. Here, Macon is a commodity, a product carefully crafted and handled. It isn't that he's fake; his genuine nature is still there—that's what makes him so appealing—but it's as if a glass wall has been dropped between him and everyone else. And what we get to see is a picture, not the true man.

Everyone here is the same. All of them walking around in their own glass cases—everyone in on the lie. I hate it. Hate that I have to trail behind, acting as though the most important thing in the world to me is Macon's image and what people think of him.

I am a chef, not an assistant. I want to learn how to make noodles in Hong Kong, Tokyo, and Shanghai. I should be taking wok lessons with my friend Sammy in Beijing. We met in cooking school and exchanged emails when he took a job at a luxury hotel in China. Visiting him was my first stop.

The invitation is open ended, but the wait chafes. Sam's texts chafe. She'll come back soon. Great. Wonderful.

I miss my kitchen, miss the rhythm and flow of it when my staff and I were preparing a big dinner. I miss the scents of good food sizzling in hot pans. I miss the alchemy of food. Cooking for Macon is challenging in that I have to come up with health-conscious meals that taste so good he doesn't know what he's missing. So far, I'm only half-successful because the man wants his desserts, and he wants them badly.

Sitting with other assistants at a table in the back of the room, I try to suck it up. I shouldn't complain; I signed up for this, begged Macon for a chance to make amends. And Macon hasn't been the asshat I expected him to be. That's part of the problem. I like him. I'm attracted to him—that's an understatement. My body is not my own anymore. He's taken control of it, made it fluttery, overheated, wanting, needy. I'm a strange mix of giddy and anxious all the time.

Worse, my mind isn't my own either. I think of Macon when I go to sleep, and I think of him again when I wake up. And for once, thoughts of Macon aren't haunted or angry but of things that make me smile—his ridiculous jokes, the way his eyes crinkle when he smiles, even the way his jaw works when he eats an apple.

"Lord," I mutter, taking a sip of white wine. I disgust myself. I'm sitting here all . . . moony. While he's up at the front, chatting with a tableful of equally beautiful people.

By the time the event is over, I'm contemplating trying hypnosis to get the man out of my head. We're to meet up outside, where a line of cars is pulling forward to pick up celebrities. Over the sea of people milling around and conversing, Macon spots me. The stern expression that is his natural resting face lightens, a subtle curving of his lips, a lift of his slanting brows. But it's the emotion in his eyes that gets me. When Macon looks at me, it's as if I'm the only thought in his mind. It's always been that way, only now, instead of seeing resentment and irritation in his eyes, I see genuine pleasure.

In that moment, everything melts away: the horrible tension in my neck, the tetchy feeling in my belly. Warmth and a flutter of anticipation fill me instead. Macon still uses a cane—this one is ebony with a silver skull handle, which makes me smile—but he wields it well, his gait more of a swagger.

He looks every inch a star, ruggedly gorgeous, in a gray bespoke suit that emphasizes his height and capable shoulders. He doesn't wear a tie but has his white shirt open at the collar, exposing the hollow of his throat. He steps to my side, his hand touching my elbow. "There you are." As if I'm a child he lost track of.

I bite the inside of my cheek because the snappish feeling returns, and it isn't his fault that I'm moody.

"Here I am," I reply as people jostle us.

His hand slips to the small of my back, guiding me around two Oscar winners. "You should have sat with me."

I try not to stare at one of my childhood crushes, who apparently is my height—you learn something new every day. I tear my eyes away before I'm caught gaping like a rube. "Macon, it was a twenty-thousand-dollars-a-plate function. Staff doesn't sit with the stars."

His firm lips go flat. "Next time, I'll buy you dinner, and we'll sit anywhere we damn well please."

Don't make me like you any more than I already do. But I can't say that without revealing too much, so I give him a weak smile. "That's sweet of you, but I don't mind. You're working."

He makes a noise of dissent under his breath. "I kept forgetting you weren't there, and I'd lean over, wanting to whisper something in your ear, only to find Chris looking back at me as if I'd lost my mind."

My lips twitch. Chris being Chris Chadsworth, one of Hollywood's hottest stars. "Maybe he thinks you're sweet on him."

"Oh, I'm sure my hand on his knee clinched that." He winks when I laugh, but something in my tone must give me away because his expression quickly turns concerned. "What's wrong?"

"Nothing is wrong." Nothing I can fix, and nothing I wanted him to notice, at any rate. I'm not going to complain to him, and it irritates me that I let any cracks show. I try to make my voice lighter. "I'm a little tired; that's all."

It doesn't fool Macon for a second. His eyes move over my face as if he can somehow read my mind if he looks hard enough. "No, something is bothering you. Tell me what it is. Please."

It's the gentle "please" that gets me. At this point, evading his questions will only make him latch on and try to weed them out, thinking the worst.

"I feel out of place here," I confess in a low voice.

The tense line of his shoulders relaxes, and he ducks his head so his lips are closer to my ear. "I do too. Everybody here does."

I cut him a disbelieving glance. "Don't patronize me, Macon. It isn't necessary. You fit here like hand to glove. And I sincerely doubt your colleagues feel out of place."

"You'd be surprised," he says dryly, but he lets out an expansive breath. "Let me clarify, because you're both right and wrong. There are times when I am working, and I feel like I've finally found my place, my people. And that feeling? It's fucking awesome, Tot. A relief. But right on the heels of that is this dread that it can all go away in an instant. Unless you're absolute Hollywood royalty, most of us here never truly feel at ease."

"That's how it is to be a chef as well."

Dark eyes sharpen as he peers down at me, and a cloud forms over his fine features. "You're miserable doing this, aren't you?"

I can't deny it, so I look away. Between the folds of my skirt, his hand finds mine. He links our fingers together, giving me a slight tug so that I have to look up at him. I see the remorse in his eyes. "You are."

"Macon . . ." I push away all my self-pity, ashamed that I let it show. "I'm fine."

"No." His grip becomes a little tighter. "You're not. Let's end this deal. Reopen your catering business, and do functions again. You can use the kitchen at the house until you get back on your feet."

"No," I say firmly. "We had a deal. I'm not running scared. I can take it."

His brows lower. "I don't want you to 'take it.' I was a dick to agree to any of this when I knew I was only doing it to give you a hard time."

Warmth runs over me like a balm. "It was my idea, and we both know it. I'm not leaving you in a lurch, Macon. It wouldn't sit right."

With a huff of clear frustration, he runs his free hand over his hair. "I don't want this anymore," he rasps, so low I almost miss it over the din of the crowd. "Not if it comes at the expense of your happiness."

I don't know what to say. Our arrangement sits like a cloud over us, but so does Sam's theft. In the dark corners of my mind, I wonder if my reluctance has anything to do with Sam. Or if it's all Macon.

"My happiness was never part of the equation," I whisper, more to myself than to him.

Macon opens his mouth to retort but catches sight of something behind me, and his body jolts as if hit. Blood drains from his face, turning his skin the color of sun-dried mud. I step toward him, my fingers touching his wide wrist, and find his pulse racing.

"Macon . . . ?" But I then see what he sees, and my mouth dries.

The man striding toward us is an older, grayer version of Macon. Same beautifully carved bone structure, same slanting brows and coal-dark eyes. Only his mouth is different, thin and flat with a bitterness that appears to be a permanent affliction. There is a bloated look about his neck and face from hard drinking, a reddened cast to his puffy skin.

George Saint wastes no time with pleasantries as he stops in front of his son. "Knew I'd find you here, prancing like a peacock in front of the press. Always were desperate for attention."

Macon has regained some of his color, and his voice comes out hard and sharp. "I'd say something about the pot calling the kettle black, but you don't have enough self-awareness to get it."

George Saint narrows his eyes, and while the gesture is reminiscent of Macon's, it holds such cold ugliness that in that instant, they look nothing alike. "I thought I beat the disrespect out of you. Clearly I should have hit harder."

My blood runs ice cold at his words, and I expel a breath that hurts when it leaves my lungs.

Though he doesn't look my way, Macon hears me and shifts his weight, his wide shoulders half blocking my view as if he's trying to put a wall of defense between me and his father. "The only thing your hits taught me was to hate." Macon's words are nails punching deep. "But understand this well. I hit back now. And I hit much harder."

George's florid skin pales before the red returns with a vengeance. "You owe me my due, boy."

"I left you in one piece," Macon snaps back, though his voice is low and strong. "Given what I wanted to do, you ought to thank me."

"I will end you," George hisses, spittle wetting his lip. "Tell everyone who you really are. Worthless, spineless little shit—"

"No!" The word erupts from my mouth like a shot. Somehow I've spoken without planning to, rounding past Macon and stepping into George Saint's space without realizing it. But I'm not backing down. Rage colors my world a blinding white, hazing the edges of everything. It surges through my blood like quicklime. "You will do no such thing. You will leave this place and crawl back under the rock from which you came."

I'm in a fine fix now, my body shaking with rage. "This man is the best of you, the only good you will ever know. And you will have to go through me to ever touch him again."

The din of the crowd returns full force when I, at last, run out of steam. But I am no less enraged—merely resting. And then Macon moves, just as his father seems to step forward. It all happens at once, a sort of strange, ugly dance in which Macon wraps an arm around my waist, tucking me to his side as he also straightens, his stance so menacing that George Saint falters.

"Enough." One word from Macon's mouth. A threat and a promise. Whatever George does will be met with the impenetrable wall of Macon's resolve.

His father's cold eyes land on me. "I recognize you now. The dumpy Baker girl with the big mouth. Used to fight like a cat with my boy. Knew he wanted to hate fuck you then. Told him not to bother since he had the beautiful slutty sister begging for it." He sneers at his son. "Should have known you wouldn't listen. Slumming now, boy? Must be a new chunky kink."

Macon's grip on me tightens even as my breath catches painfully in my throat. He clearly feels my reaction, and his hand spreads wide and warm over my side.

"Shut your ugly mouth while you still can," he says to his father. Against my cheek, his heart beats swift and light into his ribs. Tremors go through his middle, but he hides it well. "If you think for one second you're safe because we're in public, you're wrong."

So far, no one seems to have noticed our argument. People are laughing and chatting in groups. But that could easily end with one good hit.

"I think," George Saint says, leaning in, "that you'd snivel and plead just like you did as a snot-nosed boy."

Macon doesn't move, doesn't show an inch of emotion, but I feel the recoil in his body, the hurt that he undoubtedly hates acknowledging. Because family, whether we like them or not, has the power to tear our hearts out. They know just where to twist the knife in.

My hand goes to his chest and presses lightly against his racing heart. "Come away now," I say, looking up, the whole of my attention given just to him. "There is no reason for you to be here anymore."

His eyes have a sheen, but he blinks, a sweep of thick black lashes, and his gaze is clear. "No reason at all," he agrees in a soft voice. "Come on, honey."

He turns us to go when George Saint lashes out a final time, his ugly barbs finding their mark on my skin. "Put on your airs, girlie. But I know you're nothing. A by-blow, unwanted and left behind. Only picked up by the Bakers because they felt sorry for you."

Macon halts, his long body humming like a struck tuning fork. I, on the other hand, am numb. It serves me well when I place a hand on Macon's back and urge him forward, silently pleading with him to ignore the hateful man who gave him life. And he does. His arm is firm around my waist, holding me up, as he guides me away.

CHAPTER SEVENTEEN

Delilah

There is an incessant ringing in my ears as I walk along with Macon, a pained smile plastered on my face. I suppose he's wearing some semblance of a pleasant expression as well, but I can't make my body work enough to check. The entirety of the nasty encounter with Macon's father probably took all of two minutes. And yet it was enough to feel as though I'm coated in a sticky grime from inside out. A greasy lump of emotion slides down my throat, and I swallow convulsively.

Blindly, I let Macon lead me, the crowd ebbing and swelling around us. And then we are at the car, North stepping up to open the back door for me. But Macon touches his arm, leaning in so that no one else can hear. "I need the keys."

Whatever North sees in Macon's eyes is enough to sharpen his gaze. He gives Macon a quick nod. "In the ignition." Shutting the back door, he then opens the front passenger door for me. His eyes hold concern, and I give him a tight smile as I get in.

Inside the big Mercedes SUV is blessedly cool, the air running in a steady hum, Sia playing softly on the radio. Shaking slightly, I lean back against the plush leather as Macon rounds the car. With an impatient grunt, he tosses his cane in the back and then slides into the driver's seat with deft ease, even though he has a broken leg, and the walking boot isn't small.

"Should you be driving?" I can't help asking. My voice is like gravel, my throat hurting as if I've been screaming. He shoots me a quelling look, something wild in his eyes as if he's holding on by a thread, and I lift a hand in placation. "Right. Carry on."

Another grunt, and we're off, smoothly pulling out onto the road. Neither of us says a word as he maneuvers through traffic without hesitation. Horrible accident or no, it becomes clear that Macon is an excellent driver. Memories of sitting through driver's ed class with him when we were sixteen flit through my head. He'd been the teacher's pet then, something that annoyed me as usual. The more so when he beat my class record time for parallel parking by one measly little second.

I glance his way now and find him staring grimly at the road. Sweat peppers his temple, and his jaw begins to twitch, but he keeps on driving with determination as if he just needs to get to his destination and everything will be okay.

Oddly, he's not heading back to Malibu but south toward Hollywood. I don't question it but relax as much as I can and watch the passing scenery with disinterest. He turns the car into Griffith Park and heads for the loop trail. At the first empty overlook, he pulls over and turns off the car. In the silence, the engine quietly ticks.

Macon draws in a breath, then leaves the car, shutting the door behind him. I scramble out of my seat and follow. The air is sweet with the scent of eucalyptus and wildflowers and hot in the afternoon sunlight. Macon paces for a moment, then leans his forearms on the roof of the SUV. His shoulders hunch as he struggles for a breath.

With a violent curse, he slams his open hand on the roof. "Fuck. Fuck. Fuck." Each curse punctuated by a hit to the car.

Silently, I watch him, afraid to get too close, afraid to move too far away. His eyes squeeze tight for a long moment, and then they open wide, his gaze landing on me. "Are you all right?" His voice cuts into my tender skin.

"I'm fine." I don't sound it, but I don't think he'll argue. "Are you?"

He ducks his head again, his jaw working, then turns to glance out at the city below. His thumb drums upon the metal roof in a hollow rhythm. "I'm sorry."

"For what? Your father's despicable behavior? Or that we had to deal with him? I can assure you, neither is even remotely your fault."

His smile is dark and pained. "Feels like it, though. Fuck, I hate him."

"He is a hateful man," I reply softly.

Macon makes a noise of agreement, but it ends up sounding strangled. He ducks his head again, his fists clenching, and I don't know what to say to make it better. I'm still reeling both over what George Saint said to Macon and the nasty way he treated us.

Macon's flat voice breaks the silence. "Remember that time in seventh grade when I was distracted and collided with you in the science hallway, and you accused me of doing it on purpose?"

Given that I seem to have a photographic memory when it comes to Macon, I do. The memory doesn't sting anymore but fills me with wry amusement. "Distracted, my aunt Fern. You denied it. Said you didn't see me. But I'd yelled out a warning right beforehand, so how could you not have known I was there?"

Deep grooves line his tight mouth. "The reason I didn't hear was because I had water in my ears from the night before when my father held my head down in the bath as punishment for coming into the house with dirty cleats."

Horror flows over me in a ripple, leaving my head light and my stomach heaving. "Macon . . ."

"Don't." He holds up a hand, his eyes both hard and pleading. "Just . . . don't."

I halt, giving him the barest nod of understanding. There are times for comfort and times when an ounce of sympathy can break you.

Sadness shadows his eyes. "All those years, from the very first, you always seemed to know exactly what made me tick, and I swore you could see my every weakness. I assumed that somehow you knew I'd been beaten. It was so humiliating that I'd lashed out. I hated you because I thought you saw my shame. I thought you saw it every time you looked at me."

"No," I whisper thickly. "I had no idea that he . . ." I can't finish without wanting to rail at the sky or turn around and hunt down George Saint.

Macon's snort is weak and without humor. "I know that now. And I feel so stupid for my assumptions. And for befriending Samantha instead of you. Empty, shallow Sam, who would laugh at your discomfort and encourage my pettiness. I saw her as an ally. She and I were alike that way, lashing out at others until it became our idea of fun."

Rooted to the spot, I search for something to say, but I'm struck mute.

Macon shakes his head softly and squints up at the sky. "So you see, I'm more like him than you think."

That gets me going. "No. Not even a little. You said it yourself. He taught you to hate. The fact that you're even worrying about being like him makes you nothing like him at all."

Far from comforting him, my words seem to hit hard. His shoulders bunch under the fine wool of his jacket as his lips flatten. "He always used to say I was nothing like him. A complete disappointment." Bittersweet eyes glance my way. "That it was to my good fortune I was his spitting image, or he'd think I was the plumber's child."

"He didn't deserve you," I snarl, giving the words Macon said to me about Sam back to him. "And he never will."

A humorless smile barely touches his mouth. "He thinks he deserves the money, though. He's been trying on and off to sue me for it since my mother died."

"Truly?" Though I'm not shocked. Not in the slightest.

His expression turns grim. "Problem is, he signed an ironclad pre-nup." At the sound of my surprised breath—because I was not expecting that—he meets my eyes. "My grandfather rightly believed my dad was a grifter. He insisted on protecting my mother's assets. Dear old Dad got nothing but what he made on his own."

"I'm astonished he agreed to it."

"I think the idea was that he'd say yes to gain my mother's trust, then charm her into tearing it up." Macon swallowed with effort. "A failed plan since he couldn't keep his temper for very long."

Growing up, I barely saw Macon's mother, but I remember her well—petite, bone thin, with chestnut hair that always fell in a sleek sheet to the tops of her shoulders. Her eyes, the color of a winter lake, were wide and round and haunted. There was a fragility about Cecilia Saint that made a person want to both protect her and feel just a bit sorry for her.

"Did he . . . did he hit her too?"

"No." Something like gratitude softens his voice. "He knew better. You know the sad thing? She was divorcing him when she died. I found the papers. He hadn't yet signed."

We're both silent for a moment. My throat is thick and sore, the need to give him a big hug fairly strong. But I stay still. "I'm sorry, Macon. I'm sorry the wrong parent left you and the shitty one keeps finding ways to hurt you."

A car drives by, kicking up dust and swaying my skirts. Macon doesn't flinch but studies me with solemn eyes. "You're adopted."

The ghost of George Saint's hateful words punches into my heart. "Yes."

I am not ashamed of the fact. How could I be? Not a single person has control over their birth. And yet there were times when it chafed knowing that Samantha was of Mama's and Daddy's blood, and I was not, as if that one little point made me the lesser daughter.

It didn't help that Sam was beautiful and popular while I was the problem child, always getting into rows with Macon or whoever else gave me trouble. But I was also ashamed for feeling that way because my parents loved me with all they had. They never treated me as anything other than their beloved if not somewhat awkward daughter. So I tried to bury those feelings so far they couldn't touch me anymore. Their lineage became mine. They were all I had. They were everything. But the worry, the need to please and protect, always pushed right back up to the surface.

"Your father was wrong about one point. I wasn't a pity case. They adopted me because they wanted a child and couldn't conceive. But it's a long process. Mama was pregnant with Sam—a complete surprise—when the paperwork for me came through. She always said she was doubly blessed." I hung on to those words for years. They shaped me.

There is a pensive air about Macon, and he clenches his hands together where they rest atop the roof of the SUV. "I didn't know. How did I miss it?"

I understand what he's saying; I am short, curvy, dark haired, and brown eyed. My skin is light beige in the winter and golden brown in the summer. Mama and Sam are blonde and blue eyed, tall, thin, and milk white in the winter and slightly less milky in the summer. Daddy had the ability to tan deep bronze, but his hair was blond as well, his coloring on the cooler spectrum, whereas I am all warm tones. Which all meant that if you saw us all together as a family, I stood out as different.

"I honestly don't know—everyone else in town knew—but even back then it occurred to me that you hadn't noticed."

Somehow we've ended up standing close together, our arms nearly brushing. He tilts his head to meet my gaze, his brows drawing together. "How did you figure?"

"Because you would have said something about it."

Macon grimaces. "I'd like to think I wouldn't."

I can't help choking on a bittersweet laugh. "Macon, you always went for the jugular. Hell, you got the whole school to call me Tater Tot." Shaking my head, I stare out over the hazy valley. "I still have nightmares about all those fucking *tots* falling at my feet. You still call me Tot, for Pete's sake."

For a long moment, we stand there, me breathing a bit too hard, my chest rising and falling—and Macon staring at me as though he's never seen me before.

But then he blinks, a slow sweep of those thick lashes. "Did you ever find out who your birth parents were?"

"No." I lean my butt against the car. "Mama and Daddy offered to help me connect with my birth parents. But I didn't want to."

Shaking my head, I sigh and study my sensible black pumps, now chalky with road dust. "I was afraid to open that particular box. What if my birth parents ended up together and could have kept me? What if they had a kid right after me and didn't give him away? What if they were horrible people? Or what if the story is just so sad it breaks my heart? My list of fears were—*are*—endless."

With a shrug, I face Macon. "It seemed better to leave it be. Besides, I have parents. The fact that they did not conceive me doesn't make them less my parents."

"They're great parents," he says fondly. "I used to wish they were mine."

"Not anymore?" I tease.

A strange look enters his eyes. "That would make us siblings, so no."

"Don't worry; I find the thought of you being my brother just as distasteful." Not in the way he probably thinks, but I'm not saying that.

"I should hope so." He gives me a quick wink.

I'm silent for a second. "Maybe someday, I'll do one of those DNA kits and see what I'm made of."

"I can tell you that," he says easily. "Sugar and spice and everything nice."

"That mean you're made of puppy-dog tails?"

Macon shakes his head. "Never did understand that one."

The past suddenly seems both a distant memory and far too close to my skin. Lost in his own thoughts, Macon stares out at the city sprawl all hazy in the sun. Lines of strain mar the skin around his eyes. "I was a dick in high school."

Another small laugh escapes me. "Yeah, you were."

"And you were a brat."

I swiftly look his way. "What?"

Macon's chin lifts a touch. "As I recall, *you* said it didn't matter how good looking I was, I'd always be ugly on the inside. A worthless soul who would never find redemption."

A thick, heavy feeling pushes through my chest as I meet his gaze and the hurt lingering there. I genuinely wounded the implacable "I don't give a fuck about anything or anyone" Macon Saint. He never showed an ounce of tender emotion when we were kids, never let me see anything other than that perfect facade. But he is now, and I can't ignore it.

"Damn," I whisper, clenching my hands. "That was a shitty and overly dramatic thing to say."

"Yeah." His hand brushes against mine. "You always had a way with words."

Slowly, like he's afraid I'll bolt, he touches the tips of my fingers with his, and by some silent agreement, I lace our fingers together. The edge of his thumb strokes a soft path over my knuckles. I hold still, afraid that any movement will end the spell and he'll stop. I don't understand him. Here we are, remembering the worst of our fighting, and yet he touches me as if he loves the texture of my skin and can't stop himself.

"God, Delilah." He sounds angry at himself, and that grimace returns, twisting his features. "The things we said to each other. We were horrible."

I have to laugh, and it feels good, despite the lingering tightness in my chest. "We were fairly terrible."

He hums in agreement.

I blow out a breath. "I'm ashamed of myself."

"Don't be. We can't change the past, and you didn't know." His fingers twitch, and he leans my way. "When I call you Tot now, it's out of affection. But I'll stop using it if it hurts you."

I find myself hesitating. "It pissed me off at first, but now . . . I'm used to it."

"Used to it," he repeats, disbelieving. "Like an annoying hangnail?"

He's clearly laughing inside.

"You're the hangnail, Macon," I say blandly, teasing now.

He flashes a quick grin, but it fades as his gaze turns inward. "I guess I am, at that. I'm sorry I caused you pain all those years ago, Delilah. I was an unhappy person back then, and you took the brunt of a lot of it, unfortunately."

A lump rises in my throat. His expression is steady, the breadth of his shoulders stiff as if waiting for my censure. I swallow thickly. "I shouldn't have said those nasty things to you either. They weren't true."

He lets my hand go. The loss of his touch takes the lightness from me. And an air of melancholy settles over my shoulders. I wrap my arms around my middle.

Blinking up at the sky, I take a deep breath and let it out. "Well, today has been a day."

"A shit day," he agrees with a husky laugh. "With dry chicken and uninspired roasted vegetables."

"I wasn't going to say it, but yes."

He shoves his hands into his pockets and studies the horizon. The sun is riding low in the sky, obscured behind the haze of smog. "How about we do something entirely unlike us and call a truce?"

A truce. Which means we'd be something closer to friends. Macon Saint as my friend is something I never thought I'd say, but it feels right. *Friends* I can handle. I think.

"All right." I clear the thickness from my throat. "I'd like that."

He gives me a measured look that sends a frisson of heat over my chest but then winks, all easy charmer. "Good. I wouldn't like to think my chef might poison me one day."

With a gasp, I put a hand on my chest. "I'd never stoop to poison. If I wanted you dead, I'd go for the jugular."

"I'll hold you to that, Tot."

Chapter Eighteen

Macon

Timothy arrives at the house chipper as fuck, which does nothing to help my headache or my own shit mood.

"I come bearing gifts," he announces, setting a big box on the breakfast nook table.

I follow him farther into the kitchen. "Somehow I doubt that."

He grins wide. "You're right." After taking the lid off the box, he pulls out a fake ax and plunks it on the table before an empty seat. "You've got stuff to sign."

The show and I have made an effort to give away autographed memorabilia for charities. Throughout the year, I host ball games and fun runs for kids or travel around with my costars to meet and greet certain groups, but until I'm up for travel, it's down to signing things and having Timothy and his crew distribute them.

"Do you think my social media pages are shit?" I find myself asking as I sign whatever he hands me.

He pauses. "Hmmm . . . let me see . . . I do recall saying as much, oh, I don't know, about fifty times over the past year."

He delivers his sarcasm so sweetly.

My mouth twists. "I remember." And I do. Faintly. Problem is, as PR is my least favorite part of the job, I tend to block a lot of things. Timothy knows it and makes it as pain-free as possible. Which is why he's worth his weight in gold.

He helps himself to a glass of Delilah's sweet tea and makes an appreciative noise.

"Careful." I fight a smile. "That's the real deal and probably about a thousand calories."

I'm fairly certain Delilah keeps it on hand just to torture me. I snuck a glass yesterday and drank it down like a sailor who found a lost cask of rum. A lump swelled in my throat at that sweet taste of childhood. Specifically, my childhood at the Baker house.

Timothy hesitates, glass halfway to his mouth, then shrugs and takes another sip. "Fuck it. I'll do extra cardio today."

I sign a small poster of me dressed as Arasmus. "Some days, I really do miss living in the South, where I could drink my sweet tea in peace."

"Take me with you," Timothy says. "Because this stuff is divine. Where'd you get it?"

"Delilah makes it."

"I like that girl."

I sign a faux leather gauntlet, writing along the edge of it. "I'll be sure to tell her."

"No need. She knows. And where is your superchef slash assistant today?" He glances around the kitchen as if she'll suddenly pop up from behind the counter.

"In her room." She hasn't come out yet, even though it's eleven. Nor did I get my morning smoothie. I'd give her shit, but I don't really want to. Dealing with my father left us both bruised but brought us together in a way that was both unexpected yet inevitable. Nothing between us is how it should be. The problem is I don't know how to make us right. Or even if there is an us.

Whatever the case, it's not like her to hide out. I clench my pen and focus on the repetitive work of autographing.

Timothy sets his empty glass down. "So tell me, why the sudden interest in your social media?"

My shoulders stiffen. "No reason. Just thought I'd ask."

"Right. I totally buy that. Completely." He takes a seat on the banquette and drums his nails on the tabletop, watching me. "Delilah gave you shit, didn't she?"

"Why do you think it was Delilah's idea?"

"Because she's smart and clearly not afraid of you."

At that, I smile faintly, but it fades just as quickly. "She thinks it's sad. A bad reflection on the real me."

"It is." Timothy pulls a small compact from his bag and checks out his reflection. With a frown, he starts to touch up his foundation with efficient pats. "But we'll work on it."

"Delilah said she'd help me." I stop, cringing inwardly when one of Timothy's perfectly groomed brows lifts.

He snaps his compact closed and tucks it away. "Since you're open to touchy subjects today, I've been meaning to talk to you about how we're handling these next few months."

I sit back in my chair, flexing my stiff wrist. It's mostly healed, but signing isn't doing it any favors. "What do you mean, 'handle'?"

"You were run off the road by a fanatic, Saint."

"I am aware."

"There's speculation about whether you're affected by this."

My pulse thrums in my temple as I gesture to my body. "Obviously I'm affected. What did people expect?"

His gaze is placid in the face of my growing agitation. "I meant mentally."

Of course he did. I glance away.

Timothy sighs. "How could you not be? It would have freaked me the fuck out. But you don't want them to see that." His voice takes on a note of unwelcome sympathy. "You need to get out there more often. Let them see you strong and unbroken."

A harsh laugh breaks free. "I am not fucking broken, Tim."

"Bad choice of words." He reaches out as if to pat me, then obviously thinks better of that bad move. "Look, we got great feedback after the luncheon. People want to see you living your life. The industry wants to see you. So let them see you."

"Fine, I'll go out more," I mutter.

He bites the corner of his lip, and I know I'm not going to be happy. "Thing is, Saint, it would look better if you were seen being happy."

"Happy?" I run a hand over my hair. "Okay, I'll bite. How exactly am I supposed to be happy?"

"I think you should go on a date."

"A date." *Oh, fuck no.*

He scoots forward. "Now, don't give me that look. Let me explain first."

"Then hurry up and explain."

"Going out on a date brings speculation away from the accident and focuses it on your love life."

"Seeing as I don't want anyone focusing on my love life, that's hardly an inducement."

Timothy sucks the inside of his cheek as if he's trying to hold back a retort. "Anya Sorenson. Do you know her?"

The question catches me off guard. "Yeah, sure. She's doing great work on *Gauntlet.*"

"Yes. But she's new. She needs some good press."

"And you think being seen on a date with me will give her that." I snort. "Come on. Really?"

"Yes, really." He smacks my forearm. "Stop being obtuse. You're hot right now. Could be hotter. But you're still one of entertainment's most desirable single actors."

I roll my eyes.

"So if you go out with Anya, it will both help her with a PR boost and get people talking about you in a new, upbeat way. Come on; she's great and a huge fan of yours. Her publicist says they'd really appreciate the help."

I hate that he makes sense. And that he's set me up to feel guilty if I turn Anya down. There's only one problem. "Man . . ." I rub my tired eyes. "I don't think I'm up for dating."

"I get it. But it isn't dating. It's a date. Basically an acting job, if you think about it. You've done it plenty of times."

I have. Numerous fake dates set up by my publicist. All to create an image I'm not sure I like anymore. It would be a lie to say I didn't enjoy some of the dates. Truth is, I enjoyed the fringe benefits of them a bit too much. Oftentimes, they started as an arrangement, but both of us had been more than willing to end the night with casual sex. A nice release from all the pressure with someone who knew exactly how the system worked.

I have to force myself not to look toward the kitchen doorway that leads to the hall and, beyond that, Delilah's room. Going on a date with Anya shouldn't feel like a betrayal. I'm not cheating. Delilah and I have only just called a truce. Hell, she's my employee. The fact that I can't stop thinking about her doesn't matter. Nothing can come of this . . . whatever it is, anyway. So why not go out, get on with my life? Get her out of my head.

"All right. I'll do it."

"Great," Timothy all but squeals. Thankfully, he keeps it to a minimum before picking up his phone. "How about tonight?"

I choke out a laugh, the pressure of an unwanted emotion sitting heavy on my chest. "Don't waste time, do you?"

"What's the point in that?" He shrugs, busy texting Anya's rep, if I had to guess. "It's not like you can get time back. When it's gone, it's gone."

Delilah

"Delilah." The voice drifts through layers of warm sleep, peeling them back and tugging at my elbow. "Delilah . . ."

Frowning, I burrow down farther into my bed and ignore it. I know that voice, and I don't want to listen to it. Sleep is my friend. My happy place. A blunt-tipped finger grazes my neck. The touch skitters over my skin and down my spine. With a strangled cry I flail around, my arms caught in the covers.

A masculine chuckle has my eyes popping open. Macon sits on the edge of my bed, grinning down at me with evil satisfaction.

"You ass chapeau," I hiss. "You know how ticklish I am."

Thus far, he's never used this particular ammo on me, though I dreaded it in my younger years.

"Ass chapeau is a new one." He glances at my neck as if contemplating another go at it.

I narrow my eyes and haul the covers up. God, he smells good. I want to curl over and inhale him. *No, down girl. Bad, bad, bad Delilah.* "Why are you in my room?"

He's sitting too close. Close enough that I feel his body heat. Now I know from experience that he'll feel warm and strong. A perfect perch to rest on. I pull my blanket up higher in defense.

"You wouldn't answer your texts." Macon holds up my phone as evidence. "You have this on silence."

"Yes, I do that when I don't want to hear my phone," I deadpan. "Hooray for technology."

He cuts me a sidelong glance and flicks the phone off silent mode. A barrage of questions comes at me in an authoritative clip. "Why are you still in bed? Did you know it's eleven thirty? What's wrong?" He crosses his big arms over his chest and waits for an answer with impatience.

Something about Macon tugs at my core. I am aware of him on a level that I'm not with anyone else. Is it because of our past? Or is it just base attraction? Likely both. I know he wants to be friends. Friends who flirt. I know this, but I can't yet trust it.

Macon clears his throat, his brows lifting. I haven't answered him, and he's obviously not going to go away until he knows why I'm in bed.

"I have my period," I say. "I feel like bloated death, and I don't want to get up." True. But also not true.

The left corner of his lips twitches. "You're just gonna come right out and say that, huh?"

"Should I be ashamed of a normal bodily function?"

The tops of his cheeks turn ruddy, and he grunts.

Not really an answer, so I curl up on my side and try to get comfortable again. Earlier, I'd been a twitchy ball of throbbing distress, but a couple of pain meds have me nice and relaxed. "I'm going back to sleep now. Make your own breakfast."

"I already did." He leans closer, bringing the scent of the sage soap he uses and something purely Macon. The scent of him is so familiar, burned into the many layers of my memory, that in my weakened condition, it makes me feel like I'm home. I don't like that idea one bit. I stare up at him with a brow raised to question his invasion of my personal space.

He huffs out a breath as if I'm cute in the way angry kittens are, then returns my look. "You going to get up at all?"

So much for repressive glares. "Nope. Make your own lunch too."

"Delilah."

The warning in his tone has me snorting. "You really don't want to mess with me right now, Con Man. I have superhuman powers bestowed upon me by the period goddesses."

Sadly, there is no such period goddess, only an evil she-devil who makes my life a living hell once a month. I'm weak as twenty-second tea and abnormally tired. My boobs hurt, too, and there is no way

I'm wandering around Macon's house without a bra. Hence, my self-imposed day in bed.

Also, not entirely the whole truth. I need a break from Macon. He's too much for me right now. I shouldn't be craving the sight of him. I should be able to think of things other than Macon's laugh, Macon's teasing ways, his dark honey rumble of a voice. Argh! I'm doing it again.

"Shoo," I mutter. "Go away before someone drops a house down on you too."

Macon rolls his eyes at my *Wizard of Oz* quote and then hauls himself up, using his cane for leverage. "Fine. But I'm giving North the employee-of-the-month award."

"Unless the award is a chocolate cupcake that is delivered to my mouth in the next five minutes, I don't care."

He snorts, but a ghost of a smile is in his eyes. "Sorry, I award red velvet."

"Pfft. Be gone with you, then." I wave him off, knowing he isn't so easily dismissed but finding small gratification in teasing him.

As predicted, Macon doesn't move but rests a hand on his hip and peers at me from under the dark fan of his lashes. All the humor bleeds out of his expression, and I find myself frowning. If I didn't know better, I'd think he's hesitating. The moment pulls tighter between us, and he lets out a breath, squeezing the back of his neck with one hand. It is unfair how good that makes his bunching biceps look.

"Take the whole day, then," he finally says. "I'm going out tonight."

The way he says it has my hackles rising. I shouldn't care; he can go wherever he wants. But there's something almost guilt laden about the way he looks at me. Why would he be guilty?

"Okay," I say, drawing the word out. "Have fun."

His lips press together as if he's fighting some internal battle, but then his chin rises. "If I'm not back for breakfast, I'll text."

Ah. That's why. My stomach does a weird, sick lurch. He's going on a date. It should be expected; while I might call him an asshat, there's no denying he's gorgeous. Hell, he's famous. That right there would get him laid even if he needed to wear a bag over his head and had chronic halitosis.

Shit, I'm too quiet. I shrug my shoulder as if it doesn't weigh a ton. "Kind of you to let me know."

His expression turns stony, and I find myself replaying my words. Was I too flippant? Not enough? Whatever the case, I clearly didn't convince him that I am unmoved. And that is not okay. It's a struggle to play off tired grumpiness when a lump of inconvenient and unwanted jealousy sits heavy on my chest. But I try. "Is that all? Because the ibuprofen is kicking in, and I'm getting sleepy again."

Macon's nostrils flare with an indrawn breath, but he gives me a bland look. "Nope. That's it. See you tomorrow, sleeping beauty."

Tomorrow? As if it is now a sure thing that he isn't going to come home. As soon as he leaves, shutting the door quietly behind him, I pull the covers over my head and curse my damn raging hormones. I miss him as soon as he's out of sight. Damn that too.

CHAPTER NINETEEN

Delilah

I didn't lie when I told Macon I needed rest. Well, rest and wallowing. As soon as he's gone, I tuck into a quart of coffee fudge ice cream that I hid beneath a bag of frozen peas, knowing that Macon hates peas and would never think to look behind them. Yes, I've become that chef, managing her client's diet even when not around. Bah.

Bitterness coats my tongue, and I can't blame the ice cream. Tossing the empty carton into the kitchen trash and cleaning off my spoon, I find myself at a loss of what to do next. I've slept too long, and the house is too empty. Outside is a wall of darkness, and the lights in the kitchen reflect my face back to me in the window. I look tired and puffy. And there is a zit on my chin.

"Lovely," I mutter, instantly wanting to mess with the thing. Determined to rally, I march to my room, slather on a pore-tightening mask, and take a long hot shower. Bundled up in my robe, I put out an SOS call to my friends.

In high school, I used to think I'd get out of my small town, find my people, and fall into a glamorous life similar to *Sex and the City*. Didn't happen that way. I made friends, but over the years those relationships have changed. People move away, get married, get mired in their careers. Some are even having kids now. Which all means there's little time for hanging out in bars, and I talk to friends less and less.

Now, I'm starved for some conversation, anything to get my mind off things. Predictably, some friends are busy—it's Friday night, after all—but Jia answers, asking me to come visit her and Jose at their restaurant. They are two of my favorite people, and the thought of hanging out with them gives me a boost of energy needed to get dressed.

Before I head out, I sit on the edge of my bed and pick up my phone. No messages. Why would there be?

Macon won't text; he's on a date.

Good.

Great.

Wonderful.

Loneliness washes over me with such stunning force I actually suck in a sharp breath as though it might drown me. The backs of my eyelids prickle with uncomfortable heat. I take another quick breath and find myself texting, even though I know it's useless.

DeeLight to SammyBaker: I don't know where you are or what you're doing. I shouldn't even care anymore, but I do. What I didn't get to tell you earlier is that I'm living in Macon's house. I'm constantly reminded of what you did—I know you told those stalkers where he'd be. I'm so ashamed of you for that. Maybe I could understand if you would TALK TO ME. But you're hiding. Damn it, Sam, this needs to end. Macon deserves better than what you gave him. Yes, Macon. He's not so bad. Not anymore.

I hit send, then rapidly type out another. It feels safe, somehow, texting to someone who won't get the message. Like a silent confession.

DeeLight to SammyBaker: I like him, Sam. I like him a lot.

Quickly, as though Macon himself might sneak up on me and see what I've written, I close the text screen and head for my car. It's only when I'm at Jia's that I realize the texts to Sam didn't bounce back to me this time.

———

Macon

I used to be decisive. It was one of my best qualities. I reflect on this bitterly as I pop a piece of sashimi in my mouth and chew like it's tough steak instead of silky, fresh tuna. God damn, even the taste of the food makes me think of her. Delilah—the woman destroying my decisiveness.

I should be thinking about the woman sitting in front of me. Anya Sorenson. She's utterly stunning: big liquid brown eyes, high cheekbones, full lips, and flawless skin of mahogany brown. Anya has the natural shine of a star. People catch a glimpse of her, and they end up staring. She's surprisingly easygoing.

I like her. And I'm being a shit date. I swallow down my food and bring up a smile. "How are things over at *Gauntlet*?"

Anya pauses, chopsticks midreach for a piece of avocado roll. "It's wonderful. Perfect."

Her smile is bright. But the edges are strained.

"You're exhausted, aren't you?"

Her smile falls. "God, do I look exhausted?"

The worry in her expression is one I commiserate with. We're not allowed to appear tired and worn.

"Not at all." And she doesn't. She's as luminous as ever. "I'm simply speaking from experience."

With a soft sigh, she lets her shoulders slump. "It's insane, isn't it? I feel wired, like I'm constantly humming."

It's one reason some actors get into drugs—to stay that way, or we're afraid to actually crash and burn.

"I've learned to catnap like a boss." I snag another piece of sashimi. "It helps."

"I can't seem to turn my brain off." She waves an elegant hand through the air in a helpless gesture. "It's just running at full speed all the time."

"Lines repeating in your head? Even the ones that aren't yours?"

Anya's expression is wry and knowing. "Hell, I even remember the instructions my director gives the crew."

We exchange grins. Somewhere to my left, I feel the presence of a camera. I hear it click to take a picture. A quick look catches the guilty party—a guy setting his phone down too fast, his gaze shuffling away from my own. I don't mind, though. That's why I'm here—to be seen with Anya.

At least, in part. When Timothy proposed a date with Anya, that's how he sold it. But the reason I agreed is a little more muddy. I needed to get out of the house, away from Delilah.

She's avoiding me anyway, making it perfectly clear that she wants no part of getting in deeper with me. Okay, we haven't outright discussed the issue. Because every fucking time I try, she scuttles off like a crab being chased by a gull.

I know Delilah as well as I know myself; she's running scared. I don't blame her. I'm not exactly peachy right now either. It's a shit thing to realize you're falling for your old enemy. Makes me question everything. Makes me hesitant. I hate hesitation, damn it.

My gut churns, and I focus on my date—who is supposed to remind me that there are plenty of women in the world. One is as good as any other.

Total bullshit. If people were interchangeable, we'd never grow attached to someone. It's painfully clear now that Delilah cannot be replaced by Anya.

Anya, who is smiling at me, her eyes warm and inviting. "You know, there is only one thing that gets my mind off work now."

She's close enough that I catch a hint of her perfume. It is a punch to the gut to realize it's the same as Delilah's. I recognize the scent: apples and brown sugar, smoky caramel. Only it's different on Anya. Not worse. But different, oddly less enticing. It doesn't get my cock to rise the way smelling it on Delilah does.

Jesus, I'm in a bad way. I resist the urge to tug at my collar. "Oh?" What were we talking about again?

"Sex."

Right. "Sex."

Anya's glossy lips curl in a sly smile. "Hot, sweaty sex. You know the kind that makes you forget your own name?"

I gulp down some ice water, something inside my gut curdling. Do I know that sex? No. No, I fucking don't. I know how to please a woman. I've spent years learning how to best get them off and begging for me. And why? So they don't notice that I'm not as blown away as they are, that I'm only partially engaged.

Resentment is a bitter taste in my mouth. I have been more present while flirting with Delilah than any time I've had my head between a woman's legs. How fucking sad is that?

Why the hell did it have to be Delilah? Why her? Anyone else, and it would be easy. I'd relish falling. Fuck, I'd dive in with a running jump.

Why couldn't it be Anya, eyeing me with interest and waiting for a reply?

"Sex does a body good," I say. A stock line followed by my trademark smile.

I'm sick of both.

Anya licks her bottom lip, then glances around before her gaze meets mine once more. "You want to get out of here?"

Part of me wants to whimper because she's making it so easy. And part of me wants to smash my fist into the table. Because I don't even

214

feel a stirring of interest, and I know I would have two months ago. I would have taken her back to her place and rocked her world.

And then gone home as lonely as always, you sad sack.

My back teeth meet with a click, and I have to force my body to relax. I don't want to hurt Anya's feelings. I just don't want to fuck her.

"Anya, I think you're lovely . . ."

Her smile fades. "But you're not into it."

Rubbing the back of my neck, I give her the truth. "I'm into someone who isn't into me. I tried to get over that tonight. I'm sorry. It was shitty of me."

"Hey." She reaches out and covers my hand with hers. "We've all been there."

"*There* sucks," I mutter.

She laughs. "Very true. But I'll tell you this; avoiding it isn't going to make it go away or get you out of Suckville."

I give her hand a light squeeze. "I really do wish I wasn't stuck in Suckville. You're a great date."

Her smile is wide. "In another life, we're probably really hot together, you know."

"Probably," I agree. But I'm lying. Instinctually, I know it wouldn't matter what life I lived; I'd find my way back to Delilah.

Suddenly, I can't breathe. I need to get out of here.

It takes too long to end the date and get back home. But when I do, the house is still and dark, only the front lights on. On silent feet, I make my way upstairs, not wanting to wake Delilah, but come to a halt when I find her door open and her room empty.

She's gone?

I hadn't expected that. A humorless laugh escapes. So damn sure I'd find her here waiting. Such is hubris.

I don't bother turning on the lights as I head downstairs for a glass of water. Delilah has been experimenting with flavored waters in the hopes that I'll somehow find them more palatable and less boring than all the regular water I have to drink.

Her ploy worked. I find myself anticipating each batch. The current one is cucumber, mint, and strawberries. I pour a glass and sit my ass down on a chair in the great room.

In the dark, I text North.

Do you know where she is?

I don't bother explaining who "she" is to North. He'll know. He answers quick enough.

No. Check the feeds.

The house has cameras set up by the front door, along the driveway, and all around the front gates. Even though only North and I can access the feed, I refuse to put cameras anywhere else. Instantly, I'm reminded that Delilah is out there and so is one of the women who stalked me.

If Delilah were accosted or hurt by a stalker obsessed with me, I don't know what I'd do. The air in my lungs grows thin. My thumbs shake as I type.

She was supposed to stay home. She was supposed to be guarded.

Mathias is watching Fredericks. She won't get anywhere near Delilah.

Cold comfort when the house is empty, and I don't know where Delilah has gone. I don't care if it's spying; I pull up the feed. And there she is, looking edible in a clinging wrap dress and wearing those red fuck-me heels again. She went out shortly after I did; it's one o'clock in the morning now. Oh, how the mighty have fallen. I told her I was going out all night, making it pretty damn clear I was hooking up with someone, and did she stick around, get jealous? No. She went out on her own. As she should. Only, now I'm home alone, and I feel like a fool. For many reasons.

I don't have a name for the emotions roiling around in my gut, but I don't like them. Setting down my phone, I close my eyes and breathe. I have to believe she's safe. Doesn't stop the other thoughts from crashing in.

Never in my life do I regret my youth more than at this moment. I bullied Delilah out of fear and ignorance. There's no excuse for it, and I have no idea how to make up for what I've done. But I have to because this need for her is only growing stronger, deeper. I care for her. A lot.

Everything could go up in flames if things go south between us, and I'll lose her completely. But sitting here in the dark, waiting for her to come home just so I know she's safe, just so I can hear her voice and see her face, makes it perfectly clear that I can't keep pretending that I don't care.

Question is, does she want me? I've caught her staring when she thought I wasn't looking. She doesn't seem to realize I feel her gaze on me like a hot hand stroking my skin. Every. Damn. Time.

I think of the way she snuggled into my lap with complete trust and contentment. It was a moment of perfect rightness. Had it felt that way to her? Maybe. Maybe not. Once she realized what she'd done, she lit out of there as if her ass was on fire.

"What am I doing?" My voice is a rasp in the dark. I press a hand over my aching eyes, soaking up the warmth.

I don't chase women. I am a loner. It works for me. If I let people in, they might see something they don't like. Delilah already sees things wrong with me. She always has. And here I am contemplating laying down my pride for her. When pride is the only thing that has kept me going, I have to wonder if it's worth it.

Delilah

The Uber drops me off at the doorstep. The windows are darkened; only the front drive and hall lights that I left on are glowing. The sight of it almost enough to sober me up and take away my happy buzz.

But no, I'm not going to think of *him*. Nope. Nope-ity-nope-nope.

I let myself in and am greeted with the silence of an empty house. The unwelcome thought of where Macon is sits heavy in my stomach. Leaning on the wall for support, I kick off my heels, one of them flying farther than intended. It pings on a wall, and I snort before stumbling toward the kitchen. I need to drink some water to head off a hangover.

To combat the awful quiet, I start singing "Comfortably Numb" again, snickering between lyrics because I know how goofy I sound.

"Are you singing Pink Floyd?"

Macon's deep voice coming from the dark has me yelping loudly. I spin so fast I have to grab one of the columns that frame the great room so I don't fall on my ass.

Macon sits in a low-slung armchair by the window, the light of the moon shining down, turning him into a picture of grays and whites. His dark eyes glitter as he stares at me.

"Jesus wept." I press a hand to my pounding chest. "You scared the spit out of me." Literally. I think I spit. I wipe my mouth just in case. I don't acknowledge the little happy flips my insides are making at the sight of him. My body is a stupid traitor to my will.

Macon doesn't move. "Where have you been?"

It's not quite a demand, but there is a certain sharpness to his tone that gives me pause. I walk past him and go into the kitchen to help myself to a glass of cold flavored water. I take a long drink before I return to him.

"I went out for dinner."

One of his thick brows lifts. "Must have been someplace nice." His gaze glides over my body. "Like your dress, Tot."

218

Why that makes me feel naked, I can't say. My knees are weak, and I throw myself into the corner of the couch, all elegant grace. "I went to Jia's."

This time both his brows lift. "I think I've underestimated you."

A soft snort escapes me. I could let him think I have some magic clout that gets me into exclusive restaurants whenever I want, but I'm too buzzed to lie. "I'm friends with the owners."

"Jia and Jose?" He sounds impressed. "I've never met them. Ate at their restaurant, but they weren't there that night. Food was almost as good as yours."

My snort is much louder now. "Flattery will not get you a smoothie at sunrise tomorrow."

His smile is thin. "It is tomorrow, and I'm sleeping in."

All at once, I remember that he isn't supposed to be here. My head lolls on the couch cushion as I peer at his still frame in the shadows. "Why are you here?"

"I live here," he says in that same low, slightly off voice.

"I thought you were going to be *out*."

Macon looks away, giving me his tight profile. "I did go out, remember? Now I'm home."

Elusive ass. He knows what I'm asking. I roll my eyes and trace the condensation on my glass before taking another long drink. Hydration is key. "Bad date?" I venture. *God, let it be. No, that isn't nice.*

The corner of his mouth makes a bitter curl. "I wouldn't call it a date exactly." Macon's gaze collides with mine. "Timothy set it up. Anya is a star in another series the network is promoting. They thought it would look good for us to be seen together."

Anya Sorenson, beautiful, bright, looks like a supermodel. Every interview I've seen her in, she appears genuinely intelligent and kind. Right. Great.

Macon's gaze slides away again, going back to some distant point only he can see. "Anya was into it . . . willing." He waves a lazy hand as if to fill in the blanks.

I fill them in just fine. A burning sensation rises up my chest. I think it's heartburn. "I don't know why I need to hear that."

He huffs out a humorless laugh. "I don't fucking know either, Delilah." With a sigh, he leans his head back and rubs a hand over his face. "I don't know anything anymore."

Ordinarily, Macon is in perfect control. That he seems to be sliding off kilter worries me. "Are you drunk?"

"No. Why? Do I look drunk?" He smiles as though the thought amuses him.

"You're sitting in the dark," I say shortly. "Making vague and morose statements. It's a little creepy."

Macon cuts me a glare. "Didn't feel like going to sleep."

"Okay, sure."

His glare grows glacial. "And you weren't home."

"Were you waiting up for me?" I don't know how I feel about that. Mushy? Nope. I'm too sick at the thought of Macon and "willing" Anya to be mushy.

He frowns and looks away. "No."

Liar.

"So what? You gave Anya a ride on the Macon train and then were so exhausted you had to sit here in the dark, thinking deep thoughts?"

"The Macon train?" he chokes out, then shakes his head. "Fuck, Delilah, your mouth . . ." He pinches the bridge of his nose. "There were no Macon rides."

I let that settle, but my insides continue to flip and flutter. "Why not?"

Oh my God, shut up, drunken Delilah.

He looks as surprised at the question as I am. But then his expression grows cagey. "I didn't want to."

"You didn't want to have sex with a hot and willing woman?"

Seriously, you need to shut up.

His gaze narrows on me. "You really want to go down this road?"

Swallowing thickly, I lower my eyes. "No. It's none of my business." I lift my hand in a helpless gesture. "I'm mouthy when I'm buzzed."

"You're mouthy when you aren't too."

I pretend to put on lipstick with my middle finger.

Macon almost smiles, but he's still pissy about something. His fingers drum an idle rhythm on the chair arm, his gaze turning inward. We're both silent for a minute.

When he speaks, his words come out measured and slow. "You ever come to a crossroads in your life? When you think you have everything figured out, and then you realize you know nothing? And you have no clue which way to go from there?"

He glances at me as if he truly wants to know. And my heart begins to beat a little harder.

"Yes," I whisper. Truth is, I'm there now.

"What did you do about it?" he whispers back.

The glass is wet with condensation; my hands are too cold. I grip the glass tighter, feel the skin stretch over my knuckles. "Mama used to say the brain can lie to you, but the heart always knows the truth." I shrug. "Problem is, most of us would rather believe the lie than face the truth."

His burning stare licks over my skin, exposes things I don't want exposed. "What would you rather believe, Delilah? The comfortable lie or an inconvenient truth?"

I don't like the way he looks at me, angry and resentful, tense and alert, as if he needs my answer but doesn't *want* to need it. There is too much riding on my answer, and I don't even know what the correct response should be.

"I think that if my heart was ready to hear the truth, no lie my brain could come up with would matter."

Macon draws in a breath and lets it out, his chest moving with the action, but there is nothing relaxed about him. If anything, he's tighter now, heavy and tense in the chair.

"I think you're right," he says dully and then turns to look out the window once more. "Take some aspirin before you go to sleep."

Dismissed. I feel it as effectively as if he walked out of the room. But I'm the one who gets up and walks away.

Chapter Twenty

Macon

I wake up hungry. Let me amend that; I wake up more hungry than usual. I want something sweet and creamy. I want to slide my tongue through honey-slick sweetness and eat until my mouth grows tired and my body becomes laden with satisfaction.

Problem is, it isn't sweets I'm hungry for. Last night, everything became crystal clear. I want Delilah. No one else will do. Sam, the watch, my broken trust— those things are part of the past. If I want a future, I have to let them go.

Delilah might want me, but she clearly isn't willing to risk any complications. Which leaves me in a predicament. Ignore this increasingly painful need, or tell her in no uncertain terms how I feel and try to find a way to work it out. My gut tells me to fight for Delilah. My head tells me to proceed with extreme caution. Since I'm not certain of anything anymore, I get up and start my day.

After a grueling workout with North, who doesn't go easy on me despite my bad leg, I head for the kitchen and the promise of a smoothie Delilah texted that she has waiting for me. She stands there, frosty glass in hand, the sunlight that shines through the windows setting her golden-brown hair and tan skin aglow.

A lot of skin. So much gloriously curvy skin is on display. She's wearing dark-green boy-short bikini bottoms and a fitted white T-shirt that flirts with the edges of those tiny Lycra shorts, taunting me with potential glimpses of more smooth, dusky skin.

I swear to all that's holy my knees go weak. I bobble a step and try to play it off as due to exhaustion instead of sheer fucking lust. "Damn, I'm beat."

Her expression is wry as she hands me the glass. "North going easy on you again?" she teases.

My hand shakes as I take a long drink. Whatever she's concocted tastes creamy and spicy, like cinnamon oatmeal cookies laced with coffee. It hits my system with a welcome kick and runs icy cold down my parched throat. I set the glass on the island counter with a sigh and then run a hand over my face.

"Easy?" I repeat with a snort. "Yes, that's exactly what I thought while whimpering like a small child on the floor."

"At least you admit to crying."

I flash a quick, tight smile. "I was clinging to his leg, pleading for my life."

Evilly, she laughs with glee. "What happened to manly stoicism? Sucking it up and all that."

I give her a look of mock outrage. "And where would that get me? Alone? In pain? Without you to wipe my fevered brow?" *Please come up to bed with me and wipe my brow. I'm so damn fevered.*

"Where do you come up with this stuff?" She's clearly trying not to give in to another round of laughter.

"I'm a lit major," I say easily, even though we're standing so close my shoulder is rubbing against hers, and it's distracting as hell. "I have an endless supply of melodrama stored in my brain."

Despite my attempt to put her at ease, Delilah edges away and cleans out my glass. "You should probably take some ibuprofen and a shower."

I don't want her to go yet. Seeing her makes my day brighter. Desperate to keep the conversation going, I set my hand on my heart as if struck. "That's all you have to say to me?"

"What? Did I forget your birthday?" she quips, biting back a smile.

"I'm in serious pain here. Where is my sympathy, woman?"

A laugh bubbles over her lips, and I feel like I've won a damn medal. "Fine, then," she says, looking up at me with a patronizing expression. "Poor Macon; want me to kiss your boo-boos and make it better?"

You have no idea how you tempt me, woman. "Would you?" I'm not above fighting dirty. I reach for the hem of my shirt and start pulling it up, exposing my abs. "Because I have this spot here—"

"Ack, stop." She's laughing again, but a fine blush spreads across her cheeks. Bingo. "Pest. I'm not kissing anything."

I let the shirt fall back into place. "Tease."

"Flirt."

I grin without remorse, then get distracted by the gleam in her butterscotch eyes. She's looking at me like I'm a snack. I don't think she even knows she's doing it, but it's enough to make my hunger return full force. I'm this close to drooling. Just to be sure, I run my thumb and forefinger along the corners of my mouth and am gratified to find her watching the movement. She licks her full bottom lip. The gesture is so explicitly hungry that my abs clench, and my cock stirs.

Down, boy. Take it easy.

"Been thinking, Tot . . ."

Her eyes narrow. "Probably best if you don't."

Probably. But where would that get us? "I want a dessert."

She turns and starts wiping down the clean counters like it's her new mission in life. "I'll go to the farmers' market and get some ripe fruit."

"Not. Fruit." Fact is, I can't eat a mango anymore without wanting to suck on Delilah's tongue. "Something rich and sweet and creamy." And now I'm thinking about sinking to my knees before her. Behind the kitchen island, I reach down and adjust myself. Having zero experience with flirting, I don't think I'm doing a proper job of it. I'm only getting myself riled up here.

Especially since Delilah's expression remains deadpan. "I don't think any of that is on the approved list."

"I think you bring up that damn list to annoy me, Tot."

"This is true." She doesn't bother to hide her glee.

Like a bee to nectar, I drift closer. "Come on, Delilah. Cheat with me. Just a little?"

Shaking her head in clear exasperation, she tosses the cloth into the sink and faces me. "All right, just this once. Name your poison."

She isn't in my arms. My mouth isn't on hers. But it's still a victory, and I rub my hands together in anticipation. "Let's see . . . oh, God, the choices. Your Totally Toffee-Chip Cookies? Your Mad Monster Chocolate Cake?" I stop to think of all the deserts Delilah has made over the years. "Ah. I know . . . Bountiful Banana Cream Pie. That's what I want."

It's as if I've kicked her. Her happy expression ices over into something hard and angry. "You shithead. You total dick weasel."

"Dick weasel? Why? What'd I do?"

She scoffs in disgust. "Of course you don't remember. Typical."

She darts past, giving me a wide berth. I'm left standing alone and bewildered. Why would she be pissed about her banana cream pie? She made the best ones I've ever tasted. The fact that I haven't had a taste since we were thirteen and I still remember how good they are should tell her . . . the memory rises up like a ghost.

The annual summer pie contest. Delilah at thirteen, wearing a pretty blue-and-white summer dress without a bra. A young brainless me realizing that Delilah had breasts. Words were said. Pie was thrown.

"Oh, shit." The heavy thump of my walking boot beats a rapid staccato as I rush to follow her. "Delilah. Wait. Shit . . ."

I catch up to her by the pool. "Okay, I remember . . ." *Don't laugh. Don't laugh.* But, God, that pie had flown. The splatter was spectacular—a virtual Rorschach test of banana and whipped cream. "But come on, you have to admit in retrospect it was kind of funny."

She rounds on me in a fine fury. "I don't have to admit a thing."

I soften my tone, but a smile escapes. "It wasn't that bad."

Delilah's hands clench. She eyes the pool as though she's contemplating throwing me into it, then takes a threatening step in my direction before halting. "You called me *banana tits*." A flush washes over her face. "Do you know how embarrassing that is to a thirteen-year-old?"

Right. I was thinking about where the pie landed. She got so mad at me that she threw the pie at my face. Only quick reflexes born from years of avoiding getting hit saved me from a face full of Bountiful Banana Cream Pie. Mean old Mrs. Lynch, the pastor's wife, wasn't as quick. The pie hit her square in the face.

I clear the laughter out of my throat and straighten my shoulders. "Yes?"

"Yes? Was that a question or an answer?"

I rub the stubble on my chin, trying to figure out how to diffuse this bomb. "In hindsight, yes, I can see that. But I was a kid—"

"It was sexual harassment!" She throws her hands wide. "You called attention to my breasts in front of everyone. I would never do that!"

"Now, hold on. In ninth grade, did you or did you not tell the girls in your gym class that you'd seen me changing out of my swimsuit, and I had a 'thimble dick'?"

Her mouth snaps shut.

I laugh, shaking my head. "And we both know that was complete bullshit."

"Okay," she amends. "But I'm not going around leaving thimbles all over the house now, am I?"

"I'd probably laugh if you did."

Her eye twitches. "You're missing the point. You know your dick isn't the size of a thimble."

"I do, but you seem pretty confident about that fact too. Have you been taking peeks, Delilah?" I tease, wanting to keep the conversation on my faults.

"I might not have seen it, but I know enough to . . ." She falters and blows out a breath. "What I mean is, *my* lie was a made-up exaggeration. Yours, unfortunately, wasn't. I had a complex about the shape of my boobs, and your asshat comment made it worse."

"You think I was disparaging your tits?"

"Kind of hard to think otherwise." Her tone is so pained everything in me stills.

For the first time, it fully hits me what I'm facing when it comes to Delilah. Yes, we've said evil shit to each other over the years. Yes, we were both accountable for our shared bad behavior. But I unknowingly did damage that has left wounds that still haven't healed. While she was disparaging of my character, I picked apart her looks. Like an asshole. It's clearly shaped the way she thinks I saw her—see her still.

Some might say she should have gotten over it already. But I know damn well how negative words can dig into your soul with sharp claws. I've spent a decade avoiding my father, hating him, and all he had to do was throw a few well-placed words my way, and I was that hurt, bewildered boy once more. Is it any different for Delilah? Somehow I doubt it.

Shaking my head, I lower my voice so she'll be forced to hear it. "No way. Not for a fucking second."

She blushes. "Oh, for the love of—"

"Tot, please believe me when I say that the sight of your tits in that thin top was the erotic highlight of my young life." She has to know what she does to me. How can she not know?

Delilah sucks in a breath as though I've shocked her, but her gaze slides away. "Stop saying 'tits.' It's crude."

"Fine. Breasts. Happy?"

"Hardly."

I duck my head so I can catch her gaze with mine. "I was into them. Really into them. Okay?"

She bites her bottom lip, clearly struggling to believe me. "And yet you had to tease me about them."

"It was shitty, yes. But a necessary diversionary tactic to my thirteen-year-old lizard brain." I take a small step closer. "I didn't want anyone to notice that I had a raging hard-on. And forgive me for panicking, but it was my first public sight-induced erection."

Her snort is sheer disbelief. "Your first?"

"Yes, ma'am."

"Bullshit."

"Why would I lie?" I huff out a laugh, remembering the fine pain of that childhood embarrassment. "Can you imagine my horror, going hard as a pike upon seeing the shape of my greatest nemesis's tits?" I put my hand to my heart. "God, you have no idea. I was like Pavlov's dog after that. One sight of your breasts, and there I went, fucking hard as a rod no matter where I was. Made me grumpy as hell."

I'm still like Pavlov's dog when it comes to her. She just has to be around, and I'm drooling. Like a damn dog.

"You . . ." She sucks in a breath. "I can't believe you're telling me this." She starts to smile. "Mrs. Lynch never forgave me, you know. She used to call me that horrid banana-pie girl and then scuttle off in the other direction as though I was preparing for another pie launch."

I burst out laughing, doubling over. "Oh, shit . . ." I try to stop. Honestly, I do. But my mind keeps replaying that moment in slow motion. Evil old Lynch's pinched mouth going wide in horror, the wet slap of pie as it hit her face. I lose it again, and I hold up a hand as if to say, "Give me a moment here."

"You're just asking for a dunk in the pool at this point," Delilah deadpans.

I wipe my watering eyes and straighten. "Okay, I'm good."

She raises a brow, and my lips quiver. Delilah gives me a grudging smile, her hands going to her hips. The action thrusts out her breasts. And all my good intentions fly out the door.

"You're staring at my boobs." Her tone is wry but somehow not insulted.

"I am aware." I should be sorry, but I'm not. "I'm staring at your peachy butt, too, if we're being totally honest here."

"Macon."

I glance up at her. "Your body is fucking luscious, Delilah. Bitable in the best way possible. A juicy peach, a sweet apple covered in caramel. Do you know how much I'd kill for a caramel apple right now, Tot? And me stuck on this hell diet. It's a torment, I say."

"I don't think this is very professional," she says weakly.

"I should hope not." God, I love teasing her. Her whole body lights up when I do it. Foreplay. Does she realize that's what we're doing? "I was just thinking—"

"What did I say about you thinking?" she warns.

"They don't look like bananas now, Tot."

"Oh my God, you're terrible." But she's grinning now. Fighting damn hard not to show it, but definitely grinning.

"More like peaches. Ripe, juicy peaches."

She sways in my direction before catching herself doing it and shifting her weight. "You called my butt peachy." A dry complaint. "My boobs can't be peaches too."

"Maybe I have a thing for peaches."

Somehow, we're only a foot apart, the space between us humming with *something*. It licks over my tender skin, tickles the back of my neck. *Take it slow, Saint. She's skittish. Back off.* My body resents this greatly and strains toward her warmth.

Her voice is a thread, drawn tight. "You're still staring."

"Paying proper respect," I amend quietly. "You don't ignore a body like yours. It would be rude."

"Pretty sure you have that backward." She's breathless now, her glorious breasts rising and falling with agitation.

I lean down, take in the warmth of her scent. "Come on, Tot. I've grown up, seen the error of my ways. Give me your bountiful banana pie."

Again she sways into my space, laughing softly. "Pervert. You're not getting any pie from me."

I hum, heat and need making my head swim. "But I have this craving."

She's whispering now. "Disappointment can be character building."

"I'll need my strength for that. How about peach pie?" *Kiss me, Delilah. Or let me kiss you. I'm not picky.*

The pulse at the base of her tanned neck visibly beats. The scent of her skin is like honey.

"I thought you wanted banana cream," she says, a dazed look in her eyes.

The tips of my fingers touch the collar of her shirt. "I don't think pie is what I want anymore."

Her breath leaves in a whoosh. I'm more aroused than I've ever been. I want to press up against her and ease the tight ache in my dick. But the moment is gone; she's backing away. "I'll make you pie later. I'm on break now."

A nice reminder meant to set us firmly back into our places of boss and servant.

I might have walked away, let it go. But she whisks her shirt off, revealing a tiny sixties-style bikini top and that body with curves for miles. She is glorious, her peachy ass swaying as she drops the shirt like a dare, then saunters to a lounger. Yeah, I might have let it go if she hadn't looked back, a quick glance as though to make certain I was still there.

I'm still here, honey. And I'm not going anywhere.

Delilah

What was that? I swear I almost kissed Macon Saint.

My heart is beating like an angry metronome. I'm tender and flushed between my legs. All from a little banter with Macon. I want to lie to myself and say it wasn't anything different than the light meaningless flirting we've been doing since I walked into his office all those weeks ago. Except it isn't meaningless anymore. Something fundamental has changed.

Macon's direct gaze has always been powerful, capable of evoking a visceral reaction: annoyance, rage, suspicion, resentment—anticipation, amusement, attraction, craving. Today, he looked at me with intent. With lust.

If it were anyone else but him, I'd already have dragged the man upstairs. But it *is* Macon. And this . . . lust, this need for him is weird for me. I don't know what to think. Sex has always been about pleasure for me. I have no doubt sex with Macon would be incredible. But having sex with Macon would mean opening myself to every vulnerability I have. Never mind the fact that we have to live together afterward—with the knowledge that we've been thrust together by Sam's theft.

Our relationship is based on a mutually uncomfortable deal and an unexpected attraction. Sexual release is fleeting, while the awkwardness of regret can linger like a bad odor. Walking away from him was the right thing to do.

Only it isn't so easy to shake. It's as though my insides have outgrown my skin, leaving me bloated and tight. I'm twitchy and irritable and wanting to burn off this unstable energy within me.

Damn that man. Damn his six-foot-two canvas of tightly packed muscle and unfairly gorgeous obsidian eyes. Damn him for not staying in the mold of ex-enemy and current employer but insisting on blurring the lines and upending my nicely ordered world.

God, I nearly moaned when he wiped his face with the bottom of his T-shirt, revealing the hard slab of his lower abs. Lord, but he's beautiful, nicely defined but big and strong. A fighter's body. My mouth went dry at the sight of the V and those glorious abs, swooping down and disappearing behind the low line of his sweats.

The weather isn't helping my mood any. The sun blares hot overhead. Growing up in the South, the term *hot* meant something entirely different than it does in LA. There, *hot* meant feeling like you were walking into a sauna whenever you stepped outside. Here, *hot* is brighter, intense sun and heat that makes your skin tight. It's rare to feel that sort of heat in Malibu. Usually, the ocean breeze cools a body down. But today, nothing stirs up on the bluffs.

I close my eyes and try to take my mind off everything. A shadow blocks out the sun, and I squint one eye open to find Macon looming over me, his dark gaze traveling over me in lazy perusal.

The bikini I'm wearing is modest by today's standards, and yet I feel utterly naked, all too aware of my nipples still stiff from our last conversation. Macon's attention slides down to my belly and thighs.

God, I hate that I want to squirm. When I put on my bikini, I liked the way it lifted and cupped my boobs and how the bottoms covered my butt and cut across my hips at just the right point to flatter my body. But now, all I can think about is that my belly has a pooch, and my thighs have little dimples.

But I don't move. I stare up at Macon with raised brows. "May I help you?"

"What a question," he murmurs, still staring at my body. He's finally shaved, exposing the smooth, clean lines of his face. It makes him look younger and reminds me of the boy I knew before.

He shakes his head slightly, and a smile tilts his lips. "God damn, Tot, you look like Honey Ryder in that suit."

"From *Dr. No*?" My snort is loud and inelegant. "Hardly."

Macon's lazy gaze slides up to meet mine. "Totally. A softer, lusher Honey." As if he can't help himself, he glances down again, and his teeth catch on his lower lip. "Damn . . ."

I can't help it; my nipples tighten even more, a pulse of heat and anticipation going through me. Call it feminine instinct—call it a moment of insanity—but I arch my back, just enough to lift my breasts a bit higher. Macon's eyes widen, his lips parting. And I flush hot, all the while pretending that I'm simply moving around to get more comfortable.

But I don't think I fool him. He makes a sound low in his throat, his breath kicking up. I'm pinned to the lounger by his stare. And despite the little insecurities that plague me, the avid interest in his stare makes me want to do foolish things, spread my thighs just enough to draw his attention there, to stretch again so that the full length of my body is on greater display. My muscles quiver with that need.

So I frown up at him instead. "Go away. You're blocking my sun."

Unfortunately, he leans in closer. A bead of sweat trickles down the side of his neck. Normally, I'm not real big on sweat. I don't like the smell, and I don't like the feel of someone else's on my skin. But Macon smells of sweat and soap, and it's doing something to my hormones because I want to haul him down, dip my nose into the hollow of his throat, and draw in a deep breath. All I can think of is how it would be to slip and slide against that firm skin, my own body fever hot and dripping.

Jesus.

His deep voice surrounds me, all lush heat and promise. "Now, I can see you've been thinking things through in that suspicious brain of yours, maybe coming to a few realizations you didn't expect, and it's throwing you for a loop. So I'm going to ignore the rudeness because I was where you were earlier, and it's no picnic." Grim humor curls his lips before they soften. He dips closer and speaks just above a whisper. "Let me know when you've figured shit out. I'll be waiting."

With that enigmatic statement, he straightens and walks off, leaving me frowning up at the clear blue sky. I can't settle down. His words have kicked up my heart rate, and the anxious tightening in my belly has returned tenfold. I might have been able to remain on the lounger, stewing in my thoughts, only I spot Macon heading toward the rough stone stairs that lead to the beach.

"Of all the stupid . . ." I grab my T-shirt and put it on before scrambling off the lounger. He's a little less than halfway down when I finally catch up to him. The stairs are fairly wide and set at a forty-five degree angle along the cliff face. But they are also roughly carved and have hidden slick spots where the sea spray has hit them. "What the hell are you doing?"

Macon glances over his shoulder as he hobbles down another step. "The Pachanga. What does it look like I'm doing?"

I hustle down the stairs until I'm behind him. "It looks like you're being a complete idiot."

"You say the sweetest things, Tot. Really." He keeps creeping down the stairs, his cane at the edge of the stone. The sight nearly gives me vertigo.

"Macon, you could fall, and you're busted up enough as it is, don't you think?"

"Hell, the boot comes off tomorrow. I'm just taking a little walk to get some air."

"Take it tomorrow, then."

"I'm not going to fall." His foot wobbles, and he halts to shoot me an accusatory look, as if I somehow caused it. "Unless you've come to tell me you figured out what I already know or have the sudden urge to take a walk with me on the beach, quit hovering."

"Quit speaking in riddles. It's annoying."

"Quit being obtuse," he counters. "It doesn't suit you."

"Why don't *you* quit being stubborn." At the small landing, I scramble around him, skirting the edge of the stone, and hop down on the stair in front of him.

Macon utters a ripe curse. "You call me stubborn. You could have fallen just then."

"I needed to get in front of you." I don't know how to explain it without sounding like a mother hen, but the thought of him toppling down these stairs and becoming more battered—or, God forbid, breaking his damn neck—makes my blood run ice cold. Not that I think he'd appreciate the concern.

Storm clouds gather over his face. "And why is that?"

"So I can break your fall if you tumble."

Wrong thing to say, apparently. His skin goes ruddy, his mouth working as if he's lost his voice. But then it booms out. "Of all the stupid, *stubborn*, foolhardy—"

"Stop ranting. It's bad for your blood pressure." I'm in front of him now. All is well. At least if we can get safely to the sand.

His nostrils flare. "You honestly think you could catch me? Delilah, I'd squish you like a grape if I fell."

"I'm hearty. I can hold you up."

"You're a grape," he repeats. "A succulent little grape."

"There you go again, comparing me to food."

Dark brows snap together as an evil light enters his eyes. "Yep. And one day I'm going to eat you right up. Now move your butt. I want off these stairs."

He dogs my steps the rest of the way down as if somehow it's his responsibility to make sure I don't fall. Typical male. I'm shaking my head when we finally reach the sand.

"There," I say, hands on my hips. "You're down safely. Now call when you need assistance back up, and I'll come get you."

"Call when I . . . ? Oh, for the love of fuck." He runs a hand over his face as if trying to quell his temper.

That's my cue to go. "Well, I'll be seeing you."

I take one step, and he's on me. "Oh, no you don't," he says with a dark laugh. "You followed me down here; you're damn well keeping me company now."

"You're too moody for company."

"Your fault, Tot."

I dodge, trying to get around him.

He lurches forward, his hand outstretched as if to grasp my elbow.

A few things go wrong. His cane, which he's reliant on, sinks into the sand—because canes and sand do not mix—and his step bobbles as he tries to correct his stance. I sidestep in the wrong direction, and my foot meets with a slimy lump of seaweed, which causes me to yelp and hop the other way, colliding with Macon's teetering form.

We go down like timber.

The sand is soft but not enough, and I let out a hard breath when I land. Macon's heavy bulk falls on top of me, our hips colliding. He reacts quickly, though, catching most of his weight on his elbows. I'm surrounded by him, his arms bracketing me, his hips nicely cradled between my spread legs. I'm so aware of how warm and solid he feels and the way my body suddenly wakes up that I can't breathe for a long moment.

"Shit, Delilah," he says on a husky chuckle. "Are you okay?"

His eyes search mine, genuine concern in their dark depths. I smile despite the growing warmth between my legs and the increased pace of my heart. "Oh, God, you were right," I say with an exaggerated wail. "I'm a grape. You squished me like a grape!"

He laughs, a slow, deep rumble of sound, and I try my best not to notice how that makes certain things push and prod in areas that are growing more sensitive. But I do. My thighs clench as my nipples tighten beneath my flimsy shirt and bikini top.

I don't know what he sees in my eyes, but his laughter dies down, his lips parting on an indrawn breath. His gaze grows slumberous, sliding to my lips and holding there.

The air heats and swells between us. The blunt tip of Macon's thumb touches the corner of my mouth, where a hair clings. He lifts it away before caressing the edge of my lip. Every nerve in my body fires with pleasure.

I see the knowledge of that in his eyes, the answering want. His head dips closer, our breath mingling, becoming one.

"Delilah . . ." He gives me every chance to say no. But I don't. I can't.

His lips brush mine, and then I'm the one surging forward, meeting his mouth. Or maybe we move together. All I know is that we're kissing as if it's sweetly painful, like we've waited so long it's almost too much to bear. And it's so good. So very good, the feel of his mouth flowing over mine, learning the shape of me as I learn the shape of him.

He makes a noise deep in his throat, a protracted groan, a needy request for more. Liquid heat pours over me, my mouth opening to his. He tilts his head, his tongue sliding in for that first taste, and I slowly break apart beneath him, my mind going hazy, my body on fire. God, I need more. I need everything.

There's no more hesitation. No more careful touches of tongue to tongue, lips softly questing. Just base hunger. Macon kisses me as if he's parched, his jaw wide, tongue thrusting deep, so deep. I arch against him, held down by his chest, his fingers grasping my hair. That small bite of pain drives me frantic, kicks my lust up.

We become hot breaths, nips, licks, small wordless sounds. He's surging against me, hard cock moving over my sex, grinding into the tender swell of my clit. And I wrap my leg around his hips, wanting more. The action shifts our positions, and the thick crown of his cock notches against my opening. It feels so damn good I moan into his mouth, my hips pushing up on him.

He shudders, suckling the plump crest of my bottom lip, and rocks into me—only the barrier of his sweats and my bikini keeping him from entering. But it's enough. Enough that I feel that fat head pushing and nudging there but leaving me unfilled, empty.

My muscles clench sweetly, wanting relief, needing more. I slide the flat of my tongue against his, whimpering, undulating against him. He groans long and pained, his whole body moving with his stunted thrusts. We're going at it like sweaty teens, dry fucking each other in the sand. And I don't care. I want his clothes off. I want mine gone.

A wet slap of water crashes into us—ice cold and briny. It's in my eyes, salt in my mouth. A startled cry leaves me. Macon shouts in surprise. We both scramble to our knees, a tangle of wet limbs, shock making us clumsy.

For a second, I don't know what the hell happened, only that I'm soaked, my hair hanging wet and sandy in my eyes. Then it dawns on me that we're on the beach, the sand beneath me now sodden. I glance back at the ocean. A rogue wave hit us, leaving behind foamy brine and bits of seaweed. Being on the bottom, I received the brunt of it.

Macon and I stare at each other as if in a daze, and then he bursts out laughing. God, he's gorgeous when he laughs, eyes like dark stars, mouth wide and happy. I think about how we must have looked, sprawled on the sand, lost in each other, a wave crashing over us. *From Here to Eternity*, it was not. Just cold, salty, and gritty.

I start to laugh, too, letting it take me over. Better to laugh than think about how hot I'd been, how damn needy. The sound soon dies down, and we're left slightly panting and staring at each other. Macon's smile is lopsided. Gently, he reaches out and tucks a wet strand of my hair back from my face. "Wave got you good, Tot."

The tips of his fingers trace my cheek, and I find myself leaning forward. Good Lord, I think I'll want him forever.

His hand cups my jaw, holding me. "Let's go upstairs."

Upstairs. To his bed. Or mine. And then . . .

The thought of tomorrow has me moving back, fumbling to my feet.

Macon's gaze follows my body, a smile still in his eyes. "Eager. I like it. You know, if I'd have known how agreeable you'd be after a kiss, I'd have kissed you in high school."

He sounds so much like the Macon of old, the one who used to taunt me, that my skin grows cold. "To shut me up, huh."

Macon rises more slowly than I did but much more gracefully. "You gotta admit, kissing is better than fighting."

It's so easy for him to brush off the past. I can only assume it's because our shared past didn't leave scars on him like it did on me. I don't know how to feel about that. "That was a mistake."

He blinks, his body rocking back on his heels. "A mistake."

Panic claws up my throat. I was practically humping Macon on the sand. What the hell was I thinking? "An aberration—a small flight from reality."

"I get the picture," he cuts in irritably. "And that is bullshit." He pushes a hand over his wet hair. "It was fucking perfect. Right up until you decided to run from this."

Again, he makes it sound so easy. He, who has the least to lose. Then again, everything has come easily to Macon. He expects the world to fall right in his lap. I'm just another fool for him.

My chest grows tight, and words fly from my mouth. "I don't even know what this"—I wave my hand between us—"is."

His lips pinch. "About fifteen years in the making by my count."

"Fifteen years? Are you saying you *liked* me back then? Because I won't believe that."

A scowl darkens his features, and he sets his hands low on his lean hips. "I wasn't mooning over you, if that's what you're asking. But there was always something, Delilah. I don't know what to name it. Not love. Not hate. But something. Like an itch that wouldn't abate. You were always there, under my skin."

Under my skin. That was the truth of it. "So what, now you want to scratch that itch with sex?"

He laughs without humor. "You think this is just about sex? You think if we fuck that this"—he copies me and waves his hand—"is going to go away? Think again, sweetheart."

The smarmy tone has me seeing red.

"Oh, you make me so . . . so mad!"

"And why is that?" He takes a step closer. "Why do I make you mad, Delilah?"

"Because you always do! You always have."

Oddly, this seems to calm him, but he doesn't let up, his tone staying hard and insistent. "Do you hate me now?"

"No." There's a weight on my chest, and he's making it heavier, agitating my blood.

"Then why do I make you mad?" The bastard's gaze is relentless, too calm and practical.

"I don't know!" But it's a lie.

And he knows it too. "Maybe it's because you want me as much as I want you."

I stare back at him, my lips puffy and sore from his kisses, my sex still slick and tender.

His shoulders set in a line of pure stubbornness. "Because I do. In case that wasn't perfectly clear." He gestures toward his pants and the impressive bulge that has only gone down slightly. "I want you. I've been wanting you since you walked into my office with those fuck-off heels and red lips. And I'm not too proud to admit it."

Unlike me, his tone implies.

"Wanting and having are two different things. I work for you. No, scratch that, I'm working off a debt to you—"

"I've said that I don't want this debt between us anymore." He throws up his arms in frustration. "I regretted agreeing to it as soon as the words were out of my mouth. But seeing you again . . . for the first time in years, I felt something other than being utterly fucking numb, and I pushed my doubts away. Because it meant having you around again, even if it was under shitty circumstances."

"Are you saying you only agreed because you wanted me under your thumb?"

He snorts. "Don't give me that self-righteous look when that's exactly how you sold the proposition. Did I take advantage? Yeah, I did. But it was never about control or payback. It was the only way I knew I could be close to you. We parted with so much hate and hurt between us. I wanted a chance to get to know who you are now. For me to show you who I am." Macon leans close, his breath heated, his gaze a dark challenge. "I'm not lying about my motives or the way I feel. Question is, why are you?"

I can't breathe. I'm panicking. I can't help it. Years of insecurities don't just up and go after a few weeks of tentative friendship and rising lust. I am falling too hard and fast. If I have sex with Macon, I will be all in, open and vulnerable in every way. When it comes to this man, I have only ever experienced disappointment and hurt. Truly letting him in terrifies me so much I feel light headed, struck mute.

He shakes his head once like he's trying to dislodge the truth. "You keep resisting my offer to dissolve our agreement. Why? Why did you make it in the first place? Was it really all about Sam? Or was it something more?"

Macon watches me like a hawk, ready to pounce.

Panic surges. It rings in my ears and turns my lips numb.

I cut a hand through the air. "This discussion is over." It has to be.

He narrows his eyes, his chin jutting up. "I don't agree."

"Too bad." I turn on my heel and head for the stairs.

His voice follows, irate and hard. "I never thought you were a coward."

The words hurt because he isn't wrong. "Now you know better."

CHAPTER TWENTY-ONE

Macon

I pushed too hard, said too much. Maybe I shouldn't have touched her, but in all that happened today, it is the one thing that didn't feel wrong. Whether I wanted to admit it or not, I have wanted to know how it would feel to be kissed by Delilah Baker for as long as I can remember.

To be kissed *by* her. There's a distinction in that. It meant she looked past all the animosity, all the misunderstandings and fuckups, and wanted me anyway. It meant that she forgave me. I can only laugh at myself for being a fool. She might have wanted me in the moment—that heady, mindless moment of unadulterated lust—but the second her sense returned, she looked at me in horror.

Not great.

North comes to help me up the stairs. The fact that Delilah obviously sent him both chafes and amuses me. Neither of us says a word, and North leaves me once we get inside the house. I'm grateful for his silence; it can't have escaped his notice that both Delilah and I are covered in wet sand.

Alone, I head for my office and take a seat. Delilah needs space, and I want to give it to her. I could have gone to my room and showered off, something I desperately need to do, but we might have run into each other again. Awkward as fuck.

Maybe she's right. If we give in to this desire and things go wrong, we'll be stuck together in a fresh sort of hell. Stupid hubris. I should never have taken her offer. It's trapped us both. But if I hadn't, she wouldn't be here. Delilah would have remained a past regret, a break that hadn't healed right. As it is, she is more like a Ghost of Christmas Past now, reminding me of all the ways I've fucked up. I should end this. But I can't. I fucking *can't*.

With a sigh, I rest my head against the chairback and wince as pain slices along my spine. Yep. Definitely pulled something.

The sound of Delilah's bedroom door slamming shut grabs my attention. Right then. Stay away from the angry woman. Fuck it. I don't need her. I had a life before Delilah. A good life.

Flipping through my phone, I read a bunch of texts for work.

Carl, my director, is looking forward to getting back to work: translation—*are you up for this, Macon?*

Timothy wants to know if I want another date with Anya. No thanks, Tim.

A couple of my costars want to know if I've heard any rumors about the new script. Unless a character's death is imminent, which affects our contracts, we're kept in the dark as to what will happen each season. The producers don't want to take any chances that a spoiler will get out. They don't need to worry about me; I don't have anyone to tell.

And that's when it hits me. I don't have anyone.

North is my friend. But we are both kind of closed off. It isn't the sort of deep connection that makes me feel like I have an anchor.

I've never had someone whom I could turn to in the dark of night, when the world feels a little too empty and cold, and find comfort.

Sitting here sticky and wet with sand and ocean muck, I realize that the one person who might fill that empty space has just given me the brush-off, convinced we can't work.

A grim smile pulls at my mouth.

Delilah might be right. We might be a disaster. We might live to regret it. But she's completely off her nut if she thinks I'm going to let this go without a fight. Because if there is one thing I know to be true, it's that everything worth having in my life is worth fighting for.

And I will fight for Delilah.

———

Delilah

I'm pissed. Pissed at Macon and pissed at myself. This isn't a fairy tale; this is real life. I can't switch gears that easily. I can't just slip from a lifetime of thinking of Macon in terms of ribald hate to . . . what? Lust? Is this simple lust or something more? And if it's more, then what is it? A fling? Forever?

His accusations, the questions he laid forth burn through my skin and settle like a hot stone over my heart. I considered the offer I made to Macon a sacrifice for family, a necessary arrangement to protect my mother. But Macon's confession made me wonder. He said he'd been numb until I came back into his life. I'd been numb too. So . . . *dead* inside. I cannot deny that from the moment I realized it was Macon texting me, something woke up and paid attention.

And I cannot deny that I like his attention. That must make me some sort of sicko to virtually enslave myself just to get more of it. I truly don't know if I refused to end our arrangement so I wouldn't be able to leave him, but the fact that I can't reject the theory outright is distressing.

"Argh." I groan into the tiled wall of my shower, the hot water pounding on my back doing little to ease my stiff body. "I'm an idiot."

A great prideful idiot trapped in a net of my own making.

If we didn't live together, I'd feel safer to explore this new thing between us. I'd have the ability to go to my own corner and lick my wounds if things went south. I don't have that here. We haven't even had sex, and it's awkward as hell.

I hide out in my room for the rest of the day. Damn if I'm not edgy, wanting to seek out Macon's company. I feel the pull of him as if there's a hook attached to my breastbone that leads directly to him. I know without being told that he's in his room just as I am in mine. The side of my body that faces his room is cold, and I find myself rubbing my arm in agitation. By the time the sun sets, I'm downright twitchy.

It's almost a relief when he texts.

ConMan: I need you.

My stupid mind takes this the wrong way, and my insides flip. But I shake myself out of it.

FearTheTater: Clarification?

You'll have to come to my room for that ;-)

I bite back a smile. This Macon, the side of the man I never knew before, does not hold grudges. He disarms me at every turn. This Macon is fun. I can't help but have fun with him.

Don't winky face me. Answer the question.

Such a hard ass. Fine. I need you to help me.

With?

His voice, sounding oddly hollow, comes from the direction of his room. "Get your peachy butt in here, Tot!"

I text him a reply.

Seriously???

"Completely serious," he hollers. "I'm not going to shut up until you get in here."

"Juvenile," I shout back. Why he can't come into my room is beyond me. And why it has to be in his room, I don't know. But it feels like a trap.

"Nonsense," I mutter to myself, tossing my e-reader aside and hauling my "peachy" butt off my bed.

Macon's room is like mine on steroids. It's bigger but still manages to be cozy. He has a fireplace, a glorious affair of cut white stone reaching up the coffered ceiling and a reclaimed-wood mantel. The gas hearth is a line of flickering flames over crushed ceramic coals.

I pointedly ignore the large Mission-style paneled bed, plump with rumpled linen covers as if he's just rolled out of it. Macon leans against the wall by the bathroom. His skin is ashen, pinched lines framing his mouth and pulling at the corners of his eyes. He gives me a protracted smile. "Hey."

"Hey."

Despite our text exchange a moment before, now that we're facing, our awkwardness is at stellar heights. I try not to think about his mouth, how he tastes, those soft greedy noises he makes. God, I try, but it's just there, floating over my skin and making me hot. His eyes hold the same knowledge, a flicker of lust going through them. But a shadow of pain overrides that, and I snap out of my haze.

"What's wrong?"

A grimace tightens his mouth. "Here's the thing. And this in no way makes you right about my going down to the beach . . ."

"Sure," I drawl.

His nostrils flare on a shallow breath. "I *might* have pulled something when we fell."

"Might have?" I notice how gingerly he's holding himself. "Where?"

"My sides, back, shit . . . I don't know. My torso. The whole area is not good." He swallows thickly and closes his eyes for a second.

"Why didn't you say something earlier?" I snap, wanting to touch him if only to provide comfort but fearing it will hurt him worse, fearing I won't stop at one touch.

Macon's brows knit as he glares. "My mind was on other things."

I refrain from blushing. Which is a feat, considering my mind can't seem to get away from those "other things."

Macon makes a noise of stifled pain. "It wasn't an issue until I reached over to turn on the taps, and everything seized up."

Two years ago, I decided to try one of those boot camp, "We'll make you feel the pain until you cry" workouts. I went home and moved the wrong way while pulling out my house keys, my back clenched, and I ended up on my floor for an hour until my mother arrived to help me. The agony was real.

"Okay," I say softly. "Have you taken anything for the pain?"

"I'm already on meds for my leg," he grits out, his expression slightly sullen as if he doesn't want to admit it. "I've taken all I can."

"You should be lying down. On the floor. Really, it'll help."

His lip quirks with tight discomfort. "I need to soak in the tub first."

Only then do I realize he's still sandy, tiny bits of ocean detritus sticking to his temple and on his neck.

"Jesus, why didn't you clean off before?"

"Because I couldn't fucking move?" A small sound leaves him. "North usually helps with this, but he's out."

"Is it wrong that I find that kind of hot?"

Macon cuts me a look as though he can't decide whether to laugh or roll his eyes. "Whatever gets you going, Tot." His humor wanes. "I've been standing here for too long, trying to shake it off and get my ass in the tub, but it isn't working. Would you please, for the love of all that is holy, turn the taps on for me?"

Right, he needs my help. And I've been fantasizing about hot male shower action. "Sure."

Macon's bathroom is . . . wow. As big as my bedroom back home, it has a copper gentleman's soaking tub large enough for two tucked into a windowed alcove to take in the view. The fireplace in the bedroom is double sided, open to the bathroom. The flicker of firelight gives the room a golden glow.

"What?" Macon asks when I stand there gaping.

"All that's missing is a bottle of champagne and some lounge music to make this a perfect seduction cliché."

He cuts me a sidelong look. "I can barely move, but I'll make note of that for later."

Grumbling, I walk over and turn on the taps that are in the middle so that a person can comfortably lean their head on either side of the tub. "How hot do you want it?" I ask over my shoulder as Macon hobbles in, wincing with each step.

"Just this side of cooking me." He stops by my side. His dark eyes suddenly appear a little boyish. "Can you, ah, put bubbles in?"

I grin wide. "You want a bubble bath?"

"Hey. The bubbles help keep in the heat, and they smell nice."

The man is a good ten inches taller than me, with shoulders twice as wide. The world knows him as a barbarian warlord king-killer on their favorite show. But he is adorable just now.

"You don't have to convince me," I say lightly. "I love a good bubble bath."

"Do you now?" he murmurs under his breath but then gives me an innocent look when I glance back.

He wasn't kidding about his love of bubbles. Multiple bath gels and a nice wide loofah wait on a rack by the tub. I eye it, and he shifts his weight as if being caught out. Not hiding my smile, I pour some gel into the water rushing from the faucet. The scents of bergamot and warm vanilla fill the humid air. It's a subtle fragrance but delicious, like sticking your nose into the warm crook of a well-groomed man's neck.

I shake my head at my wandering mind. Time for me to go. Only Macon's lips are still pinched, and he's wearing a sandy, damp shirt that clings to his chest and shoulders. That shirt isn't going to come off easily.

Damn. Damn. Damn.

"Can you lift your arms?" I ask, my voice a little thick.

"Do I have to?" His expression is one of dread.

"Come on; man up, and let's do this."

He smirks, but that quickly fades as he tries to lift his arm. "Fuck."

Ordinarily, I might have been flustered pulling off Macon Saint's shirt. But it's such a slow, awful process, with Macon gritting his teeth, breaking out in a cold sweat of pain, and me wincing in sympathy, that we both sigh in relief when it's finally off.

His broad chest heaves as he leans a hip against the wall. "Fuck the bath; just put me out of my misery, Tot."

"Drown you in the tub?" I suggest, turning off the water.

"That will take too long." He moves to rub his face but halts and swears under his breath.

Poor guy. I glance at the full tub. The copper sides are high, swooping up on both ends. A small teak stool is next to the tub, but that's about it. Hell. Taking a deep breath, I brace myself for torture. "You're going to need help getting in, aren't you?"

For a second his expression is totally blank. We stare at each other, facing the inevitable.

His smile is slow and melting. "How much did it cost you to ask that?"

"It's fine." *Lie!* "I'll close my eyes."

A low chuckle rumbles. "I don't mind if you look."

"I bet." I wouldn't mind, either, but I'm not going to do it.

Oh, but it's a challenge to keep my eyes closed. His warm, hard side presses against mine as he makes small shifts of his hips to lower his sweatpants. Doesn't help that when I fumble around to grip his waist, I get a handful of what must be the best bubble man-butt I've ever touched. And he calls *my* ass peachy.

Face flaming, I wrench my hand away, but he laughs all the same.

"Copping feels, Ms. Baker?"

"Get in the tub, Con Man."

He grunts. We bobble once, and I'm terrified we'll topple again, but he gets in with a clumsy splash and a muffled oath. Winded, I rest my hands on my thighs, then straighten.

Macon's amused voice drifts over me. "You can relax now. I'm decent."

Decent. Ha. Nothing about the picture he makes is decent. Arms resting on the sides of the tub, bubbles frothing over his tan chest, he looks like sin. His pecs are large and prominent and lightly furred with dark hair. A bubble dangles from one of his tiny nipples, and I have the urge to touch it.

A smug smile remains in his eyes as, with a long groan, Macon relaxes against the tub. His injured leg is propped on the far side of the tub, exposing a good length of massive thigh. From beneath lowered lids, he looks at me. "Thank you for helping."

So meek. So deceptive. So damn tempting.

A constellation of fragmented shells and sand floats in his ink-dark hair.

"Damn," I mutter. "You need to wash your hair."

A snort escapes him. "Not fucking likely. I'm not moving a muscle. You'll have to scoop my cold and pruny body out of this tub at some point."

"Well, that sounds fun."

His grin is quick and wide. Then he sinks a bit deeper. "It'll keep."

It won't, and we both know it.

"I'll wash it." The words are dragged out.

Macon quirks his brow, a frown growing. "No."

Rejection hits between my ribs. "What? Why not?"

"You looked like you wanted to throw up just offering. I'd rather not suffer through your martyrdom." He gives me a dismissive glance, then closes his eyes, leaving me to gape at him.

My hands meet my hips. "I am *not* being a martyr!"

"You're doing a good job of leading up to it." He lies there, not a care in the world, soaking in his damn bubble bath. But I'm not fooled. His eyes might be closed, but his attention is on me, baiting like the master he is.

"Do you want me to wash your hair or not?"

Dark eyes snap open and level on me. "Yes, I want you to wash my hair," he rasps. "Yes, I want you to touch me. I want a lot of things from you."

Well, hell. I find myself sinking to the teak stool by the tub, my hand curling around the edge.

Macon's gaze bores into mine. "Question is, what do you want from me?"

I can't lie now. Unfortunately, the truth isn't very helpful. "I don't know."

He nods as if he knew it was coming. "So let's talk this over."

It's the last thing I expect him to say. Men I've known never want to talk things out. But Macon simply sits there, king of his tub, patiently looking at me for confirmation. It's so disarming all I can say is "Okay."

He studies me as if trying to think out the best plan of attack. The air is humid around us, thick with the heady scent of his bath, the bubbles making a soft hiss as they fizzle. And Macon lying naked beneath it all.

"Are you pretending to be attracted to me because of our arrangement?" he asks bluntly.

"What?" I sit straight. "That's insulting."

He shrugs a big shoulder. "Do you think if you fail to put out, I'll hold it against you?"

Of all the . . . my hand twitches as I imagine pushing his fat head under the water. "Are you trying to get me to dunk you?" I grit out.

He grins. "Just getting the bullshit out of the way."

"Okay, okay, I get the point." I drag my finger through a clump of bubbles resting on the rim. "This is new."

I'm not talking about the tub, and we both know it.

"Not that new."

"New enough. Up to the time you accidentally texted me, I thought of you as Macon Ass-Chaps Saint."

He huffs a laugh. "And you were Delilah Judgy-Eyes Baker."

"Judgy-Eyes?"

He smiles, totally pleased. "Asks the woman currently giving me judgy-eyes."

I flick the side of his head. Macon chuckles slow and easy. "Just proves my point."

Something inside me goes quiet and warm. "I don't think you're an asshat anymore."

All humor fades from his night-dark eyes. His gaze, hazy and heated, lowers to my mouth. "I can't stop thinking about you."

My resistance melts like warm butter in a hot pot. "I think about you too."

The muscles along his big arms clench as he grips the tub. "I want to be near you all the time. And when I am near you, it isn't enough; I want more."

We're leaning into each other, not touching but sharing the same air.

Macon's lips part softly. He licks them, then meets my eyes. "I can't pretend anymore."

I want to rest my head on his shoulder, crawl into the tub with him, clothes and all, and hold him close. It scares the crap out of me. "No," I agree. "We can't go back to how it was before."

Macon stirs, the water sloshing, but he doesn't touch me. His lashes are spiky fans, his skin glowing bronze in the lowered bathroom lights. "I know you think everything comes easily to me, Delilah. On the surface, it's true. But when it comes to here"—he presses a fist to the center of his chest—"I'm fucking lost. I don't know about normal relationships; my parents certainly didn't have one."

He wipes a hand over his wet face and then stares out of the window, where the night sky is black as velvet. Lines of concentration pull at his mouth. When he finally looks at me, his expression is drawn tight, frustration darkening his eyes. "When I'm on location, it eats up hours, days, months. It isolates me, and I forget to be social. Fuck, half the time, it messes with my mind, and I start acting like whatever character I'm playing."

I nod because I don't know what to say, and Macon rubs his face again, water tinkling with the movement. "It can be lonely as fuck. But I'm used to being lonely."

The thought makes me ache.

Macon's eyes hold mine as if he's willing me to understand. "I was okay with all of that. And then you came back . . . Delilah, you are the only person alive who truly knows me for me. That used to piss me off. But now? It feels like a lifeline."

A lifeline. I've never been that for anyone. And I tried to snap that connection with him. Remorse is a cold fist in my throat. "I'm sorry for how I reacted on the beach. I shouldn't have lashed out like that. It's just . . . it's a leap of faith for me, all right? As the person with all the power here, you have the least to lose."

"Delilah," he says with a dry laugh, "if you think you don't have power over me, you're completely deluded. Haven't you been paying attention? One word from you has the power to bring me to my knees."

As if it is any different for me? He can cut me like a blade without even half trying.

A frown works between his thick brows. "I get that it's hard to switch gears. We were at each other's throats for years, and now we're not."

"I'm trying," I whisper, the urge to trace the waterdrops along the sharp line of his jaw almost overwhelming.

"I know."

And I realize that he truly does know. He's trying too.

"We're ending the deal," he says. "It has to end for this to work."

Nodding, I lean a little on the tub. "And Sam?"

The corners of his lips pull tight for a second; then he lets go of another breath, this one resigned. "I stopped looking for her a while ago."

"Since when?" I'm more than a little surprised.

"Since the first week you were here. The watch is gone. Only Sam can bring that back. And I cannot punish her without hurting you or your mama, which is something I'm no longer willing to do."

Goddamn Sam. I don't want her deeds hovering over us. The sooner she returns, the freer we'll be. Macon might have given up searching, but I won't. I've been too lax with that. But for now . . .

"I'm sorry," I say. "For all of it. I hate what Sam did."

There is kindness in his eyes as his hand edges toward mine. Our pinkies touch. "I know, honey."

The small point of contact feels like a caress along my entire side. "I'd move out and put some distance between us, but my house has been rented."

"So stay." His pinkie strokes the edge of my finger. "I don't want distance. But if it really bothers you to live here, move into the guesthouse.

There's room." He says this freely, but his expression is akin to a man sucking on a lemon.

I laugh, the sound husky and raw in the bathroom. "You're actually pushing me to live up there alone with North?"

The sour expression grows. But he shrugs those massive shoulders, water rippling as he moves. "I'll do whatever it takes to earn your trust."

And right there, he has it.

"I'll stay here." It comes out in a whisper. But he hears it just fine and releases a breath as though he's been holding it.

"Okay. Good." With an impish glint, Macon sinks a little farther into the bath. "Now about us . . ."

"Can we take it slowly?" I blurt out. My body doesn't want slow. It wants now. But the shy girl I once was has more control over me than I realized. And she's cautious.

"We can do anything you want." He pauses, rubbing the corners of his mouth. "Define *slowly*."

It's cute the way he thinks I can't see him plotting my sexual downfall.

"As in we don't immediately have sex."

Macon frowns. "I don't like that definition."

I laugh at his disgruntled look. His answering smile is small and repentant but just a little wicked as if he enjoys teasing me. Crazy thing is, I enjoy it too. I try to be stern, though I'm probably failing at that. "Macon, I just got to the point where I only want to kill you some of the time instead of all of the time."

Macon chuckles. "There *is* that improvement."

We share a look, a lifetime of irritations and misunderstandings, grudging respect and mutual admiration flowing between us. We're changing, neither of us knowing exactly how to do it, but we're trying.

"We can go at whatever pace you set." His thumb glides over the back of my hand in a slow, seductive circle. "However, I have a proposition."

"Why do I get the feeling you're leading me into trouble?"

His answering smile is lopsided and growing. "It's only trouble if you don't like it."

"Stop giving me those sexy eyes."

"Sexy eyes?" He chokes on an incredulous laugh.

"You're looking at me like you . . . you . . ."

His eyes gleam with wicked intent. "Want to stick my head between your thighs and slowly lick you until we both come?"

A strangled sound leaves me as a pulse of pure lust hits my sex. I want to touch myself, press against that ache to relieve it. "Macon . . ."

"Because that's what I'm thinking half of the time," he goes on levelly. "When I'm not thinking about kissing your soft mouth or easing up your top to finally—fucking finally—see those gorgeous tits."

"Macon!"

"Delilah," he shoots back with cheek.

God, I want him to do all those things and more. I want to strip him down, lick his warm skin. Lick him up like ice cream melting off a spoon. Why did I say anything about going slow?

Whatever he sees in my eyes has the smile slipping off his face, replaced by something distinctly hot. "I won't touch you tonight. Instead, you touch me."

"Touch you?" My pulse kicks up and starts to strum.

"Yes." He rests his arms on the sides of the tub. It draws my attention to the breadth of his shoulders and the carved definition of his biceps. "Put your hands on me; get comfortable with being close to me, taking what you want. Nothing is off limits."

Oh, God. I want that. He is acres of smooth, slick skin and rippling muscles. I'd touch him all night and then lose my ever-loving mind. "How is that not sex?"

"Because it's only you touching me." His gaze glides over me like liquid silk. "Do you want to?"

The breathy "Yes" is out of my mouth before I can think.

His nostrils flare, the look in his eyes pure temptation. "Then touch me, Delilah."

My fingers curl around the tub, holding on. Just holding on. "It won't go anywhere. That would be a tease."

"I want you to tease me."

Part of me still can't believe we're here, talking about this. That he's naked and willing. "You do?"

His throat works on a swallow. "Yes, I fucking do."

"Even if you won't get anything out of it?"

A shuddery breath leaves him, and his nipples go tight. "If you're touching me, I'll be getting something out of it." That dark voice works over my skin like warm honey.

"God . . ."

"I won't move a muscle," he promises. "Unless you ask me to. Now, woman up, and stop stalling."

I can't help but laugh. "Woman up?"

"I figured you'd object to 'man up.'"

"You figured right."

"You're still stalling."

Shaking my head, I soften. Then get up.

CHAPTER
TWENTY-TWO

Delilah

"Where are you going?" The slight alarm in Macon's voice is gratifying.

"To get your shampoo." I grab the bottle out of the massive walk-in shower, then head back to him, setting the stool behind him. Macon's shoulders tense. "You need your hair washed, remember?"

"All rational thought has left my head at the moment."

I laugh, but he doesn't move as I fiddle with the handheld sprayer by the faucet. Warm water jets out. "Lean forward a little, if you can," I tell him, feeling the odd need to speak in hushed tones.

Macon lets out a little sound of pained protest but rises enough that the water can flow down his back instead of out of the tub. It's a good reminder that as much as I want to touch him, and as much as he obviously wants me to, he's also in pain. As gently as I can, I rinse through his hair, holding a hand by his forehead to keep the water out of his eyes. I feel his careful breaths, almost as if he's afraid to move, and the heat of him. God, there's so much heat coming off him.

When his hair is wet, I turn off the taps. "Rest back again."

He does and then groans when I start massaging the shampoo into his hair. The sound goes straight to my core. I work slowly. Slower than I should, but it feels good to have my hands on him. My fingers glide over the hard curve of his skull, down to the thick cords of his neck.

"God," he whispers. "Please don't stop."

His muscles are so strong here that it hurts my fingers to dig in, but his noises of pleasure and the way he leans into my touch keep me going.

Foam rises around my hands; water trickles down the tan column of his neck to wander over the hills and valleys of his wide-set shoulders. My lips swell with the need to follow those waterdrops, press against his wet skin. I bite the inside of my cheek.

Macon sighs, his lids lowering, and I move closer, my breasts hitting the back of the tub. I push along the rise of his shoulders. They're like silk over granite, slippery wet and warm. He grunts, and I do it again. He leans into my hands, whimpering softly. I take the moment to rise and turn on the taps again. We don't speak as I rinse the shampoo from his hair.

It's a strange thing, taking care of him this way. I'm turned on—more than I thought I could be. It's a low hum in my body, the lush swelling of my breasts, of my sex. It's in the painful tenderness in my nipples and the sensitive edges of my lips. I want to savor him like I do fine dark chocolate, letting each bite melt on my tongue, lingering over the delicious taste of it.

But that isn't what I find strange or surprising. It's that I like taking care of him. Behind all the bright and searing lust is warmth and contentment. He is in pain, and I am helping to take some of the burden off. That lovely homey feeling tempers everything and makes it possible for me to keep my focus.

The legs of the stool scrape overloud as I move around to his side and face him again. Lids half-lowered, he waits, his breath coming in soft, barely there pants. Everything in me draws tight. My hand drifts to the hard swells of his pecs. Macon visibly twitches at the contact, but neither of us says a word.

Slowly, lightly, I stroke his chest, teasing him. Lord, but he's built on a heroic scale, solid and thick. My fingertip brushes his beaded nipple, and he grunts low and tight. I swirl around the tip, making him shiver despite the steam coming off his wet skin.

He licks his parted lips but stays utterly still, taking my torture. The trickle of water, the harsh rasp of our agitated breathing surrounds us. I slide my hand lower, idly feeling all that smooth, slick skin. And then I see it—the wide, engorged tip of his cock rising out of the dissipating bubbles to lie hard and needy on his flat stomach.

We both still. I am looking at Macon Saint's cock. I go a little light headed. Macon's dark eyes shine with both a question and a dare. He's coiled so tightly his body hums with it, but he doesn't move. He won't unless I ask him to.

I slip my hand beneath the warm water. He's hot and thick and fits against my palm just right. A low, tortured groan leaves him, and his head falls back against the tub edge. Gently, I work him. And he takes it, his expression almost pained. He's panting heavily now, flushed along the cheeks as his hips begin to rock helplessly in time with my strokes.

The sight is so patently sexual, so insanely hot, that my sex swells and slicks. I press my legs together to alleviate the pressure. My hand moves up and down his long length, a steady rhythm. "Is this what you needed?" I rub my thumb over his tip on the downstroke. "Me tugging on your big cock?"

"Oh, shit," he whispers, his throat working. "Oh, shit. Delilah . . . I . . ." His wide chest hitches on a caught breath.

The tips of his fingers turn white as he grips the edge of the tub. He's tensing, all those finely wrought muscles clenching. I jerk at his cock, squeezing a bit harder, going a bit faster.

"You needed it, didn't you?"

"Yes," he says, panting. "Fuck yes."

Macon's eyes close, his brow pinched. He licks his lips as he moans—whimpers, really. That I've reduced this strong, stoic man to this quivering mass has my head spinning. I want to crawl in the damn tub with him. Sink down onto this beautiful dick and take him. But this time is for him.

"Are you going to come for me, Macon?"

At the sound of my voice, his eyes snap open. The heat in them sears me. "You want to see me come, Delilah?"

"Yes."

His lashes flutter. "Then make it hurt, honey."

The next downstroke has the water frothing. I give him no mercy, pumping him, pulling on his cock as he grunts and thrusts. He's panting, his straight brows knitted in a look of near pain, but he keeps his gaze on me, silently begging for more.

"You're beautiful," I whisper, squeezing his shaft. His nostrils flare as his hips lift, and a long, agonized groan tears from him. He comes in a fine arc over his chest and sinks back into the water with a shuddering sigh.

I gentle my hold but stay with him until he is limp and replete. We fall silent until suddenly Macon moves, grasping the back of my neck to haul me close. His kiss is quick but messy, like he's all wrung out but needs to convey how much he liked what I did.

The dark fringe of his lashes are clumped and wet from his bath as he stares into my eyes. "Thank you."

He kisses me again to punctuate the sentiment.

I smile against his mouth. "You're thanking me for a hand job?"

He huffs out a laugh, his lips tickling mine. "I'm thanking you for trusting me enough to give one."

CHAPTER TWENTY-THREE

Delilah

Make it hurt . . .

With a gasp, I wake up in my bed, flushed and fevered and wanting him. I'm slick and swollen between my legs, the soft linen sheets almost coarse against my sensitized skin. I've been dreaming of him. My hand still feels the imprint of his hard dick, the weight of it, the girth.

"Sweet Jesus," I mutter, wiping an unsteady hand over my damp brow.

I actually jerked Macon Saint off in the bath. And it was glorious, gorgeous, hot as hell. His orgasm was the sexiest thing I've ever witnessed. Logically, I'm glad I asked to take it a bit slow. Physically? I want to fuck him and forget the world.

Cheeks burning, I take a long cool shower and then pour myself a glass of juice from the little bar set up in my room. It's early, not quite sunup. Part of me wants to go to Macon now, tell him . . . what? Do me? Can I touch your cock again? Pretty please.

I laugh at my neediness. A little decorum, Delilah. Just a little.

But I'm happy. And slightly shy at the prospect of facing him. I mean, I jerked off Macon. Macon Saint. The world truly has turned over on its head. Butterflies go to war in my belly, and my fingers are twitchy with anticipation.

Humming "Where Is My Mind?" by the Pixies, I sit back and watch the sun rise over the Pacific. I'm almost totally relaxed when my phone rings.

Picturing Macon on the other end, having come up with some new devilry to tempt me, I answer without looking. "What now?"

I'm teasing, and I know he'll get that. But there's a protracted silence, then a soft, feminine laugh. "And here I thought you'd be happy to hear from me."

My entire world screeches to a halt. "Sam?"

I almost can't believe it. I glance at the bedroom door, my heart trying its best to pound its way out of my chest. Part of me wants to run and find Macon, tell him that Sam is on the phone. But she'd only hang up, and he'd probably *blow* up.

"The one and only." Her voice is light with false bravado.

My back teeth clench. "Where are you? Where have you been? What the hell, Sam?"

"Whoa." She laughs, but it's tight with annoyance. "I didn't call to get grilled."

"You had to expect it," I retort. "I mean, come on!"

Sam sighs expansively. "Yeah, I know. I know, okay. I'm a shit, and this is bad."

"Bad? Macon could have been killed. This is beyond bad, Sam."

"Hey! I didn't know that lady was a stalker. She said she was press and only wanted to get a good picture."

"And that's okay? To sell him out to the press?"

There are times I can't believe we were raised in the same house. How is it that I'm more like my parents and not of their blood, and Sam is so very off?

"Oh, please, Dee. Macon is famous. Having his picture taken is part of the job. They offered me good money for something he'd have to deal with anyway." She pauses and has the grace to sound sheepish. "Or that's supposed to be how it went."

"Well, it didn't. And as soon as you realized how badly you messed up, you ran instead of dealing with the consequences."

"I never claimed to be perfect," she says sullenly. "I know I'm a jerk here. All right?"

"And the watch?" My heart is thudding, hard and pained.

"I needed money. I panicked."

Sure. Right. Great.

I take a deep breath, but it doesn't work. I want to strangle her. Slowly. "You have to come back."

"I know." So very sullen.

"And return the watch. Please tell me you still have his mama's watch."

"I have it. I couldn't . . . I didn't sell it, all right." Her pissy tone irks. "I'll come back soon and fix everything."

Somehow I doubt it. "Soon? Where are you?"

She's silent for a second. "Stop asking, Dee. I'm not going to tell you. And that's not why I called."

"No?" I want to laugh, but I'm not at all amused. "Then why the hell did you call?"

"You said you were living with Macon."

Don't think of him naked in the tub.

"Because I am. I'm working off your debt."

Do not think of the damn tub!

She sucks in an audible breath. "What the hell, Dee?"

"What do you mean, 'What the hell?' I told you I was cleaning up your mess. What did you think I meant?" A cold laugh escapes me. "That I had paid him back for a three-hundred-thousand-dollar watch? Jesus, even if I had that kind of cash, do you honestly think it's okay for me to pay for your theft?" My voice has risen several octaves, and I find myself panting.

Sam's voice is just as sharp. "I didn't think you paid him, no. I thought . . . well, hell, Dee. I thought you'd do your thing and reason with him. Make him back down."

Good God, that's just what I tried. She knew I would. I feel a fool.

"He didn't want to be reasoned with," I hiss. "He was going to the police. And I had to protect Mama from that worry. You know how weak her heart is!"

Sam curses under her breath, then speaks more calmly. "I didn't think. But you're right. Mama wouldn't take it well." She sounds almost sorry. Almost.

"No shit, Sam."

I can practically see her narrowing her eyes in a glare.

"But you didn't need to work for him. He was bluffing."

"I was there, Sam. He was ready to make that call."

"He was *bluffing*. Macon loves Mama, as much as that man can love anybody. He wouldn't do anything to risk her health." She snorts. "You forget, I know him. More than anyone."

Blanching, I fall back against the chair. My gaze goes blindly to the ocean beyond as that feeling of foolishness increases. In the prideful little corners of my mind, I always thought I knew Macon better than anyone, that I understood him on some weird, not entirely safe level. But Sam is right; she hung out with him all the time. Despite what Macon said about them not truly liking each other, they were partners in crime for their entire childhoods.

I don't have that with Macon. I don't even have that with Sam.

The shy, lonely, awkward girl I was returns full force. My lower lip trembles. I bite down hard. I will not cry. I haven't all these years. I'm not about to start now. Especially for something so useless as being jealous of Sam and Macon.

Macon's voice whispers in my head, *"Delilah, you are the only person alive who truly knows me for me."*

He said it with such conviction.

She's talking again, more persuasive now that she's scored a direct hit. "You cannot trust him, Dee. Do you hear? He's a professional actor and a manipulative son of a bitch."

"I can't pretend anymore."

He was sincere. I'd know it if he wasn't.

Despite my unsettled thoughts, I scoff. "That's rich coming from you."

"Which means I know what I'm talking about. Do you know how many times I witnessed him bullshit someone? He'd tell them exactly what they wanted to hear, and they'd fall right into his palm."

He was Sam's boyfriend for so long. What am I doing even thinking of taking up with Macon? It violates sister code. Ex-boyfriends are definitely off limits. Especially Macon. I was the third wheel in their relationship; most of the time, I was their enemy, the outlier in their united front of all things anti-Delilah.

The writhing feeling within takes a nauseating turn, and I gulp down juice.

A sigh gusts from her end of the phone. "I'm sorry that you ended up in this position. I truly didn't realize you'd do this for me."

"I did it for Mama," I say automatically, my voice wooden. I feel as hollow and brittle as an old log. My lips feel numb.

"Whatever the case," she says, tossing the distinction away. "I'm sorry. But you texted that you like Macon. Don't. He's never cared for you. Did you forget about prom?"

I hadn't forgotten. I just didn't want to think about that anymore. But the girl in me? She's curling in on herself, Sam's reminders burning through the skin like so much acid. I don't want to believe Sam. I want to believe in Macon.

"If he's acting kind," Sam says, "it's to keep you happy and in your place."

Funny thing is, she might as well be talking about herself. That knowledge depresses me. "He's not that good of an actor, Sam. You forget, I know him too. Maybe not as well as you do . . ." Everything in me screams out that it's not true; I do know him better. But is that truth or vanity talking? "I know when he's bullshitting and when he's not."

"What exactly is going on between you two?" Suspicion laces her voice.

I don't tell her about last night, the kissing, the growing attraction. I don't tell her about getting closer to Macon or the way he's opening up to me. It would feel like a betrayal. At some point, my loyalties have shifted.

"A working arrangement." The lie tastes bitter on my tongue. We're more than that. More. "Given the circumstances, Macon has been really good about everything."

God, if only that point would sink into my head too. Stupid insecurities. Stupid Sam for stirring them up.

She hits me again, right where I'm most tender. "You didn't hear half of the ugly things he's said about you. He couldn't stand you, Dee. You think that just goes away? Hell, you wouldn't even watch *Dark Castle* because the memory of him was so repugnant to you, and that was only a few months ago."

Her words fall over me like hot tar, sticking and burning. She has to know she's hurting me. That she's willing to do it to get her point across hurts too. "That's really unfair, Sam. People grow up. I grew up. Macon did too."

"This is what I'm talking about! You're letting your guard down. Macon will use it to his advantage."

"Why? To what purpose?" I shake my head and huff out my exasperation.

"To use you as bait and lure me back home."

269

"Then take the bait," I snap. "Come back, and end this."

And then we'll know. A trickle of fear goes down my spine. What will happen if she returns?

"I will. Soon."

"That isn't good enough. I have to tell him you called."

"No! Don't you dare!"

"Why not? He should know."

I can practically hear her thoughts racing.

"He'll get in an uproar again, and it'll be relentless. You tell him, and I'm not going to come back."

"Oh, that is low." I can't punch Sam, so I punch the padded arm of the chair. "Really low."

"Am I wrong? He'll be back in a black mood, gunning for me."

She's not wrong.

"If you're unwilling to leave that house . . . ," Sam begins, making it sound like a question.

"I'm not leaving. I made a promise." I don't tell her the other truth: I don't want to leave. Not yet. I've grown attached to this place, to Macon. Is that a weakness? Stupid of me? I don't know. Sam's muddying the waters even more.

"That's what I thought," she says. "So don't rock the boat. I'll come back as soon as I can. And I'll bring Macon his damn watch. But don't you dare fall for his act, whatever it might be."

Sorry, sis. I'm already falling.

"You're being melodramatic."

"Am I?"

"Yes. And I'll give you a month. After that, I'm telling him."

A month is more than generous. Even though I feel like a traitor to Macon by keeping this secret.

"Fine," she says. "But I'll know if you tell him."

That's why I'm agreeing to this. Because he'll absolutely start up texting her again. He'll want her to return immediately. And like before, his threats and texts won't bring Sam back. She has to do that for herself.

I feel small and irritable and suddenly don't want to hear the sound of her voice. I can't believe I've been anxious to get a call from her. "Just get your ass back here with the watch."

"I will," she promises with a drawl. "And you remember your past. Remember who Macon is."

She hangs up, and I'm left holding the phone in my numb hands. Remember who Macon is? Or who he was?

———

Sam's phone call festers. I try to shake it off, but her ugly words keep playing over in my head. I can't rid myself of them. They remain even when I go to my happy place, the kitchen. They ring around my head like an unfortunate earworm as I chop onions, my eyes smarting and watering.

"Shake it off," I mutter, patting at the corner of my weeping eye with my sleeve. "They're just words. Doesn't mean she's right."

"Are you crying?" Macon stands at the entrance to the kitchen, a frown on his face. For a moment, I simply look at him, remembering the bronze of his skin, beaded with water, the way he came in my hand with a groan that seemed ripped from the deepest part of his wide chest.

My face blazes with heat. He must notice; a slow, lopsided smile unfurls. Those inky eyes hold tenderness and mischief.

"Onions." I set the knife down and go to wash my hands and splash my face with cool water. "This one is particularly fierce."

He takes his time walking over to me, that small pleased smile playing on his lips. And here I am, jumpy as a cat with fleas. Stopping before me, he reaches out and gently touches my cheek, catching a water droplet I missed when I dried my face. I try not to flinch. But I do.

271

The frown returns. "You all right?"

I know he's asking about more than the damn onions. "I'm good."

The frown remains. "Something is on your mind."

It isn't a question. That jumpy, twitchy, ugly feeling grows nearly intolerable.

"What is it?" he asks in a low, concerned voice.

It's Sam. She called and burst my happy, horny bubble. She cut me off at the knees and reduced me to that insecure teenager.

Sam called.

I'm not supposed to tell you.

I hate her.

I hate that I wonder.

I hate that I'm doubting you.

My mouth opens, but nothing comes out.

"I see those thoughts racing behind those pretty eyes, Tot. Tell me what you're thinking."

"Macon . . ." I lick my lips.

His soft gaze shutters. "Are you regretting last night?"

"No," I whisper. "Not exactly."

"Not exactly," he repeats flatly.

"I'm just having a moment." I stare down at the counter. My sister eviscerated my self-confidence. "I'll be okay in a bit. Just . . . give me some space."

That clearly doesn't sit well with him. His chest lifts on a breath, and he makes a fist as though he's trying not to reach for me. But then he shakes his head once and cups my cheek. "Let me in, Delilah. Please. I want in so badly."

Tell him your piece. Get it out, or it will continue to fester.

But the truth hurts and makes me ashamed that I'm not able to let my past go. Words work like broken glass against my throat. "I want to be with you. I do. But there are things . . . my mind . . . sometimes it gets stuck on repeat."

"Repeat?" A furrow appears between his brows. "What does that mean?"

I can't tell him about what Sam said without telling him about Sam's call.

My fingers curl into the folds of his soft cotton shirt. "I woke up today . . ." *Excited. Until Sam. Now I'm . . .* "It's not logical, okay? And that's the most frustrating thing about this. But like it or not, we spent a decade lashing out at each other, and I still have those scars. For years, whenever I looked in a mirror and saw flaws, whenever I heard that voice in my head that said I wasn't good enough . . . Macon, it was your voice I heard."

A sound leaves him, small and pained. He looks utterly wrecked. "Shit." His jaw bunches tight as he ducks his head. "Delilah . . . shit." He slams his fist against the counter.

"Don't do that. You'll hurt your wrist again." I reach for him, but he brushes me off.

"You think I care?" He doesn't yell; his voice is a ghost of itself, which somehow makes it more horrible. "When you've just torn me wide open? It fucking guts me that I've done this to you." He lifts his hands in supplication. "I don't know what to do. I don't know how to fix this."

With another curse, he turns away and glares at the floor as if it might hold some answers.

"Maybe you can't. Maybe it's too late for us." Clearing the air hasn't made anything better. It's worse. So much worse.

Macon's head snaps up. "No." He moves as though he wants to hold me but halts a few inches away. He doesn't touch me but lowers his head until we share the same air. "No, don't say that."

"I'm sorry, Macon. I shouldn't have said that. I'll get over it." I will. *I will.* "It just hits me sometimes."

"I don't want it to hit you." His voice is sharp and rough. "I want you to feel safe with me. Always."

"I want that too. Without hesitation or reservation." A lump clogs my throat, and my voice comes out in a rasp. "But sometimes what we want isn't what we get."

The corner of his eye twitches. "Delilah, I've known that my whole life. The only difference here is that it hurts more than I can handle."

———

Macon

I walked away. I couldn't see that look in her eyes. Regret. Shame. A mistake.

Every inch of me hurts. There is a crushing weight in my chest, claws grasping at my throat.

I'm Macon Saint, untouchable, the one everyone wants to be near. I am nothing. Stupid, disrespectful, lazy boy. That's what my father always called me. Though I've tried over the years, I can never fully rid myself of that old hurt. Just a glimpse of his face, the memory of his voice is enough to yank me back into that shell of a boy who felt small and helpless. How can I fault Delilah for having the same knee-jerk reaction to the things I said to her?

Some things you can never forget. Like the moment I saw that girl on a red bike coasting along the road, weaving back and forth in a serpentine pattern. Nut-brown skin and glossy brown hair streaked with copper and gold spoke of days spent in the sun. She appeared happy and well fed. Carefree. She didn't sit on her seat but balanced on the pedals, humming some tune off-key as she glided. A butterfly girl in the sun.

Her dark eyes caught sight of me, and a knot of dread formed beneath my breastbone. I didn't want her to see me. My face was hot and throbbed in time to the beat of my heart. It was probably red and swollen at my cheek where my father had hit me. But she didn't heed my warning glare and rode over.

She had chubby cheeks, a snub nose, and eyes the color of the butterscotch candies our maid Janet sometimes slipped me when no one was looking. And she was bigger than me. By at least a few inches. I knew she'd just moved into the neighborhood.

I knew the house. It was one of a dozen bungalow-style houses built sometime during the 1920s. Nothing like the monstrosity of a mansion I lived in, looming at the end of the road. I'd seen two girls running around on the lawn while their father watered the pink rhododendrons and laughed at their antics.

She was loved.

She looked at me on that first meeting with those strangely golden eyes surrounded by dark lashes. Looked at me like she saw it all: the pain, the isolation, the sadness. I couldn't breathe from all that looking. This pretty, happy girl on her bike had everything I wanted: a sister, parents who loved her. She belonged in the world, and I didn't.

Rage choked me, thick as grits sliding off a hot spoon. Stupid boy. Lazy, disrespectful little shit.

She peered at me and seemed to come to some conclusion. "Maybe you'd like a friend?"

A friend. I didn't have friends. Didn't want them. Didn't want her. That choking rage took root and found a voice. I spit it out like bitter blades. "You stupid or something?"

Butterscotch eyes widened in hurt.

Stupid boy.

Stupid.

Stupid . . .

Regret presses in on me. If I could go back to that moment in time, I would. I would have told that sweet little girl yes. Yes, I needed a friend. I needed one so badly. Someone to show me what simple kindness was so I'd know it when I saw it. So I wouldn't push it away with both hands.

But I can't go back. I chose the wrong girl to cling to back then. I let my father win, became the stupid boy he so often accused me of being. That boy still lives, grown to a man everyone calls Saint. The devil with an angel's name.

Everyone except her.

She thinks we're a mistake. For her, I am one. I understand that now. I don't want it to be true. But I understand it. And there is only one thing I can think of to fix this. I have to let her know everything.

Chapter Twenty-Four

Delilah

I flee. To the safest place on earth—my mama's kitchen.

"Now then," Mama asks when I'm settled at the battered round oak table I've eaten meals on since childhood. "Why are you here looking like someone kicked your dog?"

"I don't have a dog, Mama."

Her red lips purse. "It's an expression."

"It's a terrible expression. Who would do that? Why would I want to picture it?"

"Stop evading, Delilah Ann. Out with it."

I take a deep breath. "I heard from Sam."

She doesn't move, but I see the relief in her eyes. "I knew she'd turn up sooner or later. Though I'd hoped for sooner."

Says the woman who cried on the phone at two in the morning.

"She only called. She won't tell me where she is."

"No, I don't suppose she would." Mama gets up and starts fussing with the yellow daisies she's put in a blue-and-white Chinese vase. "Do you know, when she was five, she broke Grandma Maeve's Waterford punch bowl and hid in the attic all day rather than come out and face the music? Scared the bejesus out of us until we found her. Lord, but she was defiant, even then. Not a lick of remorse."

"I don't remember that."

"Likely you were too young." She tucks a daisy farther into the vase. "I believe we distracted you by putting on *The Lion King*."

"That movie always made me want to cry," I whisper, wanting to cry. But the tears won't come. At this point, they'd be a relief.

Mama turns, and her silver brows knit. "Baby, what did Sam say to upset you?"

Because she knows us too well.

"She reminded me of how Macon used to be. All the ugly things."

"And you let it get under your skin."

Shame washes over me. "Yes."

"I see." She sets the vase on the table, then moves off.

"And then I told Macon that I couldn't get past it."

"I gather you two squabbled over that."

Squabbled wasn't the word. I gutted him.

My head feels too heavy to hold up, so I let it rest on the table. "I like Macon Saint." My confession is muffled against the oak.

"Like him?" my mother asks from somewhere nearby.

"You know . . ." I wave a hand over my head. "Like him."

I can hear the laughter in her voice. "As in you're mentally drawing little hearts around his name?"

I sit up to glare properly.

She smirks. "What was that expression you and Sam used to use on me when you were kids? Oh, yes . . . well, duh."

I swear, I might not have come from her womb, but sometimes it scares me how similar our snark is. "How long have you been waiting to use it on one of us?"

Mama smiles as she washes a few dishes in the sink. "Too long." The light of the sun shines through the window and hits her soft blonde bob. There is more silver than gold now, but it only highlights her delicate beauty. Her eyes twinkle with mischief. "Of course you like him. And he likes you. That much is obvious."

"Is it?" I trace a groove in the table.

"Well, it was at lunch." She pulls a carafe of her homemade sweet tea from the refrigerator and pours us both a glass. "The way that boy looked at you . . ." She trails off, shaking her head with a bemused smile.

"How did he look at me?" I insist despite myself.

Mama eyes me thoughtfully. "As if he suddenly realized you were the reason God created sexual pleasure."

"Mama!" I could have gone my whole life without hearing my mother say the words *sexual pleasure*.

She sniffs. "Oh, don't be such a prude."

"Prude, huh?" I sit back and drum my fingers on the table. "That mean you want to hear details about my sex life?"

A little spasm runs over my mother's face, and she fluffs her hair, definitely avoiding my gaze. "I suppose if you really need to get things off your chest, I could . . ."

I burst out laughing. "Relax, Mama. That would thoroughly scar us both."

She lets out a breath and holds a hand to her chest. "Thank the Lord. I still haven't gotten over the birds-and-the-bees talk we gave you."

"You mean when you and Daddy played Cole Porter's "Let's Do It, Let's Fall in Love," and I got all confused about educated fleas doing it?"

She flushes pink. "Probably not the best way to explain; I'll grant you that."

We both laugh, but mine dies down first. "Daddy always loved the classics."

"I miss that man," Mama says wistfully.

It makes my heart hurt. "I do too."

"There were times when he'd make me hit him over the head with a pillow, but I loved him something stupid." She shakes herself out of her reverie. Sharp blue-gray eyes pin me. "What is going on between you and Macon?"

"It's complicated. Macon and I . . . kissed. And he . . . I . . ." A flush hits me. I can't talk about this with Mama. But no one else knows our history. No one except Sam, and she's gone. Not that I'd be able to tell her about *this*.

My mother is silent for a moment, drinking her tea and frowning slightly. "You're working for him," she says finally, her expression stern. "And living in his house."

"We decided to end that arrangement."

"Living together?"

My cheeks heat. "Working for him."

"Well, that's good." She opens her mouth, then closes it, then opens it again. "He was Samantha's beau."

I hate the term *beau*. It sounds so old fashioned, but there's also something so much *more* to it than *boyfriend*—a solidity, a sense of time and history. It makes me cringe. Because I hadn't even been thinking of Sam when I kissed Macon. I rarely do think of her in conjunction with him anymore. I am now, however. It twists and curls in my belly like an agitated snake.

I don't want to tell my mother about how Macon viewed Sam. It isn't my place to say. Still, I can't keep from cringing.

Mama notices and makes a small tsking noise. "Although I have my doubts over how serious they ever were."

I grip my glass a little harder, my hands slipping on the condensation. "And yet you brought up their relationship."

She does a double take as if she's just realizing something, and her lips purse. "Lord, I didn't even . . . no, honey, I didn't mean you should be ashamed or guilty about being drawn to Macon. I was merely thinking in terms of complications." She reaches across the table. Her smooth, cool hand wraps around mine. "You and Macon make more sense than he and Sam ever did."

Shock has my heart tripping. "Why would you say that?"

"Sam and Macon never sparked the way you do. They were . . . flat, off in a way. They brought out the worst in each other. Oh, not how you and Macon would engage in petty bickering, but something darker. They made each other less than they could be."

"I can't believe it. You never said a word."

She half shrugs and sips her sweet tea. "Maybe I should have stepped in and said something to Sam. But she seemed to need Macon at the time. And he did too."

I draw a circle through the condensation on my glass. My head hurts. Everything hurts, really. A constant low throb of discomfort.

I don't know how much of my thoughts show on my face, but Mama watches me with a fond yet distant gaze, as if remembering another time. "But you and that boy . . ." She smiles faintly. "Showers of sparks. You light each other up."

I eye her sidelong. "You used to say we were like gas and oil. And that was *not* a good thing."

She bats that away with a flick of her wrist. "Gas and oil are combustible. Not ideal when you have two children fighting. But it's an entirely different matter when you're talking about love."

Groaning, I rest my head in my hands. "No one said anything about love."

"Then what are we talking about?" She sounds exasperated.

"I don't know," I say weakly.

With an audible sigh, Mama touches my arm again, forcing me to look at her. Empathy lines her eyes. "Darling, you and Macon . . ." She pauses, wrinkles deepening over her forehead. "There is no one on this earth I know of who has the ability to get to you like that boy does."

"Don't I know it."

Her tone is soft and understanding. "It means you care. You've always cared what he thought of you. And while I'd love to see the two of you finally click, tread lightly, baby. I don't want you hurt. And I fear this one will hurt quite a bit if it doesn't go the way you hope."

I know all this. I knew it when I fled Macon's house.

"Why does my past with him haunt me? I don't want it to." Fisting my hands, I heave a sigh. "Why can't I fully forgive him?"

"I don't know, Dee. It's easy for those on the outside looking in to say, 'Get over a hurt; move on.' But some wounds fester no matter how badly we want them to heal."

"I want to be with Macon free and easy. I was so close to letting all that old baggage go, Mama. Then Sam calls and reminds me of the horrible things we've said and done to each other." I groan again and press the heels of my hands to my eyes. "The old fear and animosity returned to sit on my skin like sludge."

"What does Macon have to say about it?"

"He was crushed." God, the look in his eyes. I need to go home, see if he's all right. When did Macon become my home?

Her "hmm" has me inwardly cringing. "Did you tell him exactly how you feel? Or just point out his misdeeds?"

Swallowing, I blink up at the ceiling as though it might have the answers. "I always fumble when it comes to Macon."

My mother keeps talking—gently because she truly does know me. "The fact that you're willing to even try with Macon Saint speaks volumes. Don't beat yourself up for taking your time getting all the way there."

"You're supposed to have a magical solution to make it all clear and easy," I mutter.

"Ha." She slaps a hand on the table, her wedding ring—which she has never taken off—clinking on the wood. "You wanted me to give you permission and tell you it was a good idea to pursue him."

"Well, duh."

Her eyes narrow, but she can't hide her smile. "When things come easily, we don't fully appreciate them." She stands and smooths her skirt. "I may not have a clear solution, but I can offer you a grilled cheese sandwich."

"God, yes," I groan. But then I think about how of all the dishes in Macon's life he could have mentioned when I asked him for a good food memory, he picked grilled cheese. Were we really his best memories?

A leaden ball falls in my belly, and I suddenly don't want grilled cheese. But it's too late. My mother gives me a pleased nod and heads to the fridge.

Despite myself, the scents of frying bread and butter whet my appetite. I eat my sandwich slowly, my eyes closing with each bite because there is nothing else like her grilled cheese to bring me back to being a young girl, her whole life ahead of her. I hated being a teenager. I was filled with impatience to get on with the adventure of living my own life on my terms. How little I knew then. A fierce longing for those awkward yet wonderfully ignorant days nearly overwhelms me now. I'd go back there if I could.

And yet a persistent voice whispers in my head, exposing the lie for what it is. Because I want something else much more.

———

Part of me wants to stay in my mother's kitchen forever, that simple place with its florid fruit wallpaper and yellow cabinets. But when night falls, I return to the perfection of Macon's house and find the place oddly quiet.

Come morning, I'm sitting at the kitchen table, running over menu ideas in an effort to do something productive. I didn't sleep well last night. Macon has kept his distance, texting to say he needs some time to think as well. And though it's my own damn fault for opening my mouth, I feel the loss of his open affection keenly. Why did I have to say anything?

Yes, I have emotional scars. Everyone does. The point is you don't run from them; you work through them. I could be that scared, reactionary, closed-off girl of my childhood, or I could grow up and take at face value what Macon clearly wants to give me.

I'm about to get my ass up and go search for him when he appears. Dressed in a rumpled, faded gray T-shirt and a loose pair of athletic shorts that hang low on his hips, it's as though he just rolled out of bed. He runs a hand over his spiky hair and peers at me with eyes that are bruised and puffy.

Regret pushes through my middle, a thick ugly knot that has me pressing a hand to my stomach. I'm the one who put those lines of strain at the corners of his mouth. It's because of me that his shoulders, usually straight and proud, now hang low.

"Hey." His voice crackles in the silence.

I clear the lump in my throat. "Hey."

Macon makes a noise in the back of his throat as he slowly approaches. He's holding a slim package in his hand, about the size of a paperback novel. The brown packing paper is wrinkled and battered as though it's endured a particularly rough time with the postal delivery.

Watching me with wary eyes, he takes a seat. Thick thighs parted, elbows on his knees, Macon studies the box he holds loosely in his big hands. His thumb presses into a corner of it as he begins to speak in a voice like sandpaper. "I know you didn't want this before—"

"Wait." I put a hand to his wrist. "Hold on. What do you mean, before? What is that?"

He frowns. "You've never seen it?"

284

After a moment, he offers me the box. And I accept it with all the hesitation of a person accepting a bomb.

My name and childhood address are on the front, and Macon's old address is on the top left corner. A big red Return to Sender stamp covers the label. On the top right corner, those same words are repeated, written in familiar handwriting, only I can't tell if it belongs to Mama or to Sam; their script is too similar.

I lick my suddenly dry lips. "I've never seen this."

His frown grows. "You didn't return it?"

"That's . . ." My voice breaks, and I try again. "That's my mother's handwriting. Or Sam's. I can't be certain which one."

His lips pinch, and I know he's thinking this is yet another instance where Sam might have messed with us. "Well . . ." He gestures to the package with a lift of his chin. "It's for you."

I run my fingers over the label, feeling the old slashes where Macon's handwriting all but carved out my name in ink. The date on the stamp has me pausing. "You sent this to me the week after . . ."

"After the prom," he finishes, raw and tight. "Yes."

I eye the package anew as if it might truly be a bomb. But Macon is leaning toward me, the lines of his body tense as if he's bracing himself. He wants this badly.

With shaking hands, I slowly pull apart the paper.

Macon's harsh voice cuts through the silence. "I thought you were the one who returned it."

Pausing, I lift my eyes to his. "Would it have mattered if you knew it hadn't been me?"

"I would like to think I would have delivered it in person, had I known someone hid it from you. But I was an immature prick at seventeen. I can't say for certain what I would have done."

My hand smooths over the box.

"Open it," he says. "Please."

The old packing paper crackles under my hands. Inside is an envelope, my name printed on it in big block letters, and a slim robin's-egg-blue box. My breath catches because I know the color of that box. The words *Tiffany & Co.* are embossed in black on the front. Curiosity has me itching to open it, see what's inside. But the letter calls to me in a stronger voice—in *his* voice.

Carefully, I set the box on the table and open the letter.

Macon's handwriting isn't pretty—some letters are crammed together with frustrated impatience while others pull wide as if unraveling. The ink is dark, words etched into the paper with determined force. For a long moment, I simply hold the ruled paper, so obviously sheared from one of his old school notebooks.

I'm afraid to read it. But Macon's dark eyes are upon me, waiting. His hands curl into fists. I give him a quick, weak smile as if to say, *I'm going in. It's okay; I won't run.*

And then I turn my attention to the page. Instantly his voice is in my head, that slow butter-and-honey drawl that used to work like burrs upon my skin but now sinks into my heart and makes it beat both harder and stronger.

———

Delilah,

My mother once told me that if you have something truly important to say, write it in a letter. Not an email or text or typed out. But to put pen to paper. A person's handwriting, the places they press harder on the page, the blots and errors in the ink, show their soul. Put your thoughts in a letter, and the receiver has a record of it forever, not just a memory but something they can pull out and touch when they need a reminder.

Since my mother rarely gives me any advice, I've decided to heed hers now. Plus, I'm much better when I can think of things I want to say instead of spitting out whatever bullshit nonsense flies from my mouth.

I am sorry for what happened at prom. Things went too far. I should have

That sounds weak even as I write it. I don't know the right words to say. I don't know why things always get out of hand between us. But I do know that I can't stand living in my skin when I think of you as you were that night. That should never have happened.

I was in the wrong. I'm often in the wrong—especially when it comes to you.

I don't expect your forgiveness. I don't really need it. I won't be in your life anymore and that's probably a good thing. You deserve better than what you got from me. From a lot of people.

So, no, I don't expect your forgiveness, but I hope that you won't hurt anymore.

Maybe you don't remember, but you once said that the stars overhead gave you hope because, even though it took years for their light to reach us, their starlight still gave us joy when we looked upon them. And I sneered at you because I didn't have any hope or light in my life. But I could never shake the thought that if Delilah Baker remained hopeful that she'd eventually burn bright, despite all the shit that got thrown her way, who was I, with all my advantages, to stop trying? I hated you for that too, Delilah. I hated that you were the only one who could ever scratch the scabs that cover me. You made me bleed when I didn't want to.

And now I've made you bleed too much. Why does it feel like it's my wound too?

Doesn't matter. I bought you this because it reminded me of stars. I figure you can wear these stars around your neck and always remain hopeful. I understand if they remind you of me instead and you don't want my gift. In that case, sell the damn thing and use the money for whatever pleases you.

—Macon Saint

P.S. This is my last piece of dignity and you are welcome to it. Your face is familiar to me as my own. Now that I know I won't ever see yours again, it feels as though a part of me has died. Do you really think it is because you are my enemy?

My breath is caught somewhere between my heart and my throat. I can't seem to set it free. Blinking rapidly, I clutch the letter in my hands and finally face him. There is too much in his eyes: wariness, yearning, sorrow, regret, but no hope. His walls are up, though it's clear he's fighting through them.

Hearing Macon's voice from the past has opened both of us wide. He's so still he might as well be frozen. When he speaks, the words crackle like fragile glass. "Are you going to open the box?"

I haven't yet touched the box. I'm afraid to. The letter implies he gave me a necklace, but I fear seeing it might break my bruised heart. His letter nearly did me in. I want to tell him things, hold him close, and cry for both of us. He, the proud and messed-up boy whom I hated so much, and me, the proud and defensive girl who always seemed to seek him out whenever she wanted a fight.

I'd long forgotten what I said about the stars. They were words tossed out in the moment. But they clearly imprinted upon Macon and meant something to him. Strange how the knowledge now makes the stars more meaningful to me as well.

I smooth a hand over the slightly textured surface of the blue box. "Macon . . ."

"Open it, Tot." His voice is old velvet. I cannot refuse the request.

"Oh. Oh, my." With trembling hands, I lift the necklace free. The chain is a delicate thread of gold that holds a well-spaced row of tiny diamonds glinting in the sunlight. He got me Diamonds by the Yard. "Macon . . ." My breath hitches. "It's beautiful."

His brows knit together as he looks at the necklace. "I thought rose gold would complement your skin well."

A small helpless laugh escapes me. "I'd love this even if it didn't."

He nods as if satisfied. "Okay, then. Good."

Unable to stop myself, I lift the necklace to the light, admiring the sparkle of the diamonds and the mellow luster of the gold. "It's absolutely beautiful. But why did you keep it? You could have returned it, couldn't you?"

"Yes," he says slowly, still frowning. "But it wasn't mine to return. It was yours."

My mouth falls open. "But . . . you thought I'd sent it back. It's been a decade, Macon."

"I am aware." His expression is dry. "Doesn't change the fact that it is still yours. Whether you accept it or not."

"I can't," I whisper, my fingers curling around the thin chain in protest, even though my mind says I have to let it go.

His lips form a determined line. "Then back in the safe it goes."

"Macon . . ."

"Delilah." He leans closer, his big shoulders bunching. "You're not hearing me. The necklace belongs to you or no one." Coffee-black eyes peer at me from under the sweep of thick lashes. "You're under no obligation to wear it, but don't expect me to return the thing either. It's a decade too late for that."

"Stubborn."

His grin is quick but fond. "Says the most stubborn woman I know." The easy expression fades, and he takes a breath. "I meant every word I wrote. And I know it isn't enough . . ."

"Words never feel like enough," I say. He winces, and I continue in a soft rush. "When you're the one saying them. But that doesn't mean they aren't. You opened a window to your heart. You gave me your trust. You didn't have to do any of that, but you did. And it means something."

He seems to consider this but then draws himself upright, a new, deeper tension moving over his features. "There's a bit more."

"More?"

Macon reaches into his pocket and pulls out a small bundle of folded papers. "I could tell you all this. But it's the past that's haunting us now, so I think it's better if you hear it from the me that you used to know. It isn't exactly pretty, and some of it I am ashamed of, but these, too, are yours."

He sets the bundle on the table before me. "Read them. If you want to end this afterward, it will hurt badly. But I won't stop you. We've played enough games over the years. I don't want what's between us to be another one."

Gray edges my vision, and I expel a hard breath. I want to tell him that it will never be over for me, but he doesn't wait for my answer, doesn't even meet my eyes; he simply nods toward the papers. "Go on. I have nothing left to hide."

With another breath, I unfold the pages. The letters are all clearly written on whatever paper must have been on hand: stationery, spiral notebooks, a rumpled scrap. The ink is different on each one: some in black, some in blue. One is scrawled in smudged pencil lead. The top letter is the oldest, dated a few months after my family moved to Los Angeles, the black ink scrawled so hard there are small punctures where the pen pushed through the paper.

———

D—

My mother is dead. The doctors say it was an aneurism. Personally, I think she simply did not want to be here any longer. I empathize.

I can't cry. I keep trying but nothing happens. There is just this fucking heaviness, a thick black ball in my throat. But no tears. You never cried. No matter how badly we argued, I never saw you shed a tear. Neither have I. Which makes me wonder why it is that we can't cry. Are we some kind of broken? Or do you cry when no one is looking? These are things I find myself wondering at odd times. You know, in those moments between trying to cry so that I can grieve. I do grieve, but not in the way I expected.

Point of fact—and I'll only confess this to you, who will never receive this letter—I am happy too.

She left everything to me. The house, the money, everything.

It isn't the money that makes me happy. It's the freedom.

Freedom, Delilah. That's what she's given me.

I know you think I always had money. I had nothing. It was all hers. Her family money. A small allowance is all I got. He—my father—wouldn't allow me to work. No Saint would be seen laboring for money. Which is a load of bullshit since he came from nothing, he just didn't want anyone to know it.

That necklace I sent—the one you want no part of— was the sum of all my savings. Years of squirreling away my funds. My ticket out of here. I wanted you to have it: a penance for all my misdeeds. Melodramatic on my part, don't you think?

Doesn't matter now. You don't want it. And I have more money than I need. Obscene amounts.

The money allows me to breathe free.

For the first time, I can breathe.

And it's all because my mom is dead.

My happiness is a twisted thing.

Are we all so fucked up, Delilah? Or is it just me?

Whatever the case, I'm getting out of here. Packing up and going to Berkeley—not my father's alma mater, Alabama, as he demanded. Because, fuck him.

Anyway, the funeral is tomorrow. If you were here, would you hold my hand? I'm guessing no. But I wonder, if I held yours would you let go or would politeness keep your hand in mine. I wish I could find out.

—Macon

———

"I would have held your hand," I whisper, my hands shaking. "If I had been there, I would have done it."

But Macon is gone. At some point, he left the kitchen. I hurt for him, for the pain and confusion that is so clear on the page. I want to cry for him. But he's right; I never can truly manage it. I had no idea he couldn't either.

It's his voice in my head now, telling me to keep reading. I pick up the next letter.

———

Delilah,

I graduated today. Magna cum laude in classic literature—a degree my father would have hated. Not that he was here to tell me. There was no one here to see me graduate. I did my walk, congratulated my friends, and went home.

Do you know what I found waiting for me?

A letter from D. Baker.

I thought it was from you. I swear, it was as if your ghost walked up behind me and licked my neck. Took me forever to open the damn thing. I thought, maybe she regrets returning the necklace. Maybe she knows I'm in California and wants to meet up.

Stupid, huh?

It wasn't from you, Delilah Baker. It was from Darrell and Andie Baker. Yes, your parents sent me a card offering best wishes upon my graduation. I have no idea how they knew or how they even found me; I haven't talked to a Baker since the night of the prom.

They sent me a card with a hundred dollar bill inside. Me. The guy who tormented their eldest and dumped their youngest. I couldn't believe it. I sat there, holding the card with that crisp Benjamin staring up at me, and laughed.

I inherited three hundred and thirty-one million dollars from my mother, (Yes, you read that correctly. I couldn't believe it either when I was informed) and your parents, thinking I was a poor college kid all alone, sent a little something to start me off in life.

If I was able to cry, I think I would have done it then.

So here I am writing to you, wanting nothing more in this world than to be at your parents' dinner table, eating your mom's famous roast chicken and throwing peas into your hair when they aren't looking—just to see you flip me the finger in new and creative ways. I want that so badly, my chest fucking hurts.

Maybe it's your graduation day too. If so, I hope life gives you everything you want, that you find someone who loves you, that you live each day to the fullest. That maybe, in the darkest corners of your mind, you think of me just a little bit.

—M. A. S.

———

A smile wobbles on my lips. I want to seek out my mother, give her a big hug for caring about a boy she hadn't seen in years. She was right; he needed us. And I hadn't seen it. Pressing a fist to my lips, I force myself to go on.

———

Hey Tot,

You probably hate that name, don't you? Thinking it's an insult, a commentary about your appearance. Maybe it started out that way, me trying to put you down, put you in your place—somewhere far from me, where you couldn't make me feel like I was bleeding from the inside out. But I don't think of it that way anymore. It makes me think of you as a hot little bite I want to sink my teeth into.

Truth? I'd wanted to do that even when I said the words. I always wanted to sink into you. Didn't matter if you drove me crazy, I wanted it so much it made my teeth hurt. Would it shock you to know that? Piss you off? Probably both.

I miss you, Tot. Can you believe it? Yours is the voice in my head, haunting my dreams, pushing me forward.

I'm in a casting office now. Sweating my balls off, waiting for them to call my name. I'm reaching for the stars, Delilah.

I hear you smirking, that sugar and arsenic-laced voice of yours saying, "Of course you'd have to try to become famous, Macon Saint. You always did like attention on you."

How well you knew me. And how little you knew me.

I <u>did</u> want attention. But <u>only yours.</u> I have no idea why since, whenever I eventually got it, I'd act like a foolish shit.

Truth is, I'd rather be someone other than me. I want the fantasy instead of reality. So I'll act. I'll say words that are not mine and breathe easier while living in someone else's skin.

How can I not want it? "We are such stuff as dreams are made on" and all that crap.

I'm shaking now, Tot. Nearly sick with anticipation and worry that they'll see right through me, straight into my rotten core. But I have you to bolster me. I'll go in there and pretend it's you I'm talking to. It will be easy then, thumbing my nose at your skepticism, proving to myself and you that I'm not a worthless soul as you once so aptly put.

Your hate gives me strength.

I'm probably a selfish fuck for feeling that. No, I know I am. But it's true.

Fuck, I miss you. Why? Why do I miss you so much?

You'll never answer because there's no way in hell I'm sending this.

But I do.

I

Miss

You

Delilah

Ann

Baker

My little

Hot

Tater

Tot—

———

I choke out a laugh. Irritating and boorish man. Oddly sweet man. His hastily scrawled words send tingling warmth over my breasts and up my thighs. Shaking my head, I spy the bold slashes of his next letter, the handwriting bigger than usual, taking up more space on the page.

———

Behold! I am Arasmus, bastard son of Jon'ash, brother of King Ulser of the Braxtons.

I have been exiled to the Sorrow Lands, forced to fight for my food, my shelter, my existence. Until . . .

Well, production hasn't let me in on the rest. I'm sure it will be epic and angst-filled, and if my character manages to live through this season it will be a fucking miracle. If you've read any of the Dark Castle books, you'll notice heads have a way of separating from key characters' necks. We're not following the books to the letter, so I'm not certain of Arsamus's fate.

Makes my neck hurt just thinking about it, though.

But for now? I party.

Or I will tonight.

At the moment, I'm in my car, writing in this damn notebook I still have in the glove compartment.

Writing to tell you that I hate you once more.

I hate you, Delilah Ann Baker, cold and cruel Tater Tot.

I hate that I just got the call from my agent, telling me that, yes, I . . . Macon Saint, a virtual nobody in Hollywood, landed the coveted role of Arasmus in Dark Castle . . . the most anticipated series to come to cable in decades, and who do I immediately want to tell?

You.

Fucking <u>you</u>.

Why? Why is it always—

YOU?

The impact of his words hits me like a blow, and I sit back in my chair and stare out of the window. It's almost too bright in here, the sunlight bouncing off the walls, making my eyes burn. For a moment, I was in that car with him, huddled down in the seat, feeling his frustration, his rage. The way he thought of me was so similar to my reactions to him—it's eerie.

I'm afraid to read the last, knowing that he hates me in it, and I am the ghost he wants to be rid of. Oh, how I regret my words to him earlier. Ghosts, I realize, are just that: long dead. They can't hurt us unless we let them. But I owe it to both of us to finish.

———

Hey Tot,
I won an Emmy.
It's heavy and cold. And the best thing I've ever received. And the worst. Because it feels like a lie. Why didn't they see I was full of shit? Why did they think I deserved it above the others? Those fine and true actors who know what they're doing. Who are real.
I never feel real.
Do you? What do you dream of now? Is it of being a famous chef?
A friend handed me your catering card. Said your food was incredible. As if I needed telling. It always was.
I carry the card in my wallet, but I don't look at it much. I'll be tempted to call if I do.
What would I even say? We're strangers now. Nothing to each other but an ugly past.
At least I am to you. To me, you are something different.

You have no idea that tonight, when I stood at that podium and said,

"I thank the stars for leading me here. Nothing is possible without them."

I was speaking of you.

Anyway, I just thought you should know.

Or the "you" that is in my head.

Always yours,

—Macon

———

"Oh, God," I whisper in the empty silence. My eyes burn hot when I press my cold fingers to them. "God."

The diamond necklace on the table winks at me, and I pick it up. It's so fine and light I barely feel it against my skin, and yet it's the most substantial and real gift I've ever received. Macon gave me everything he had when he bought me this, even though he had little hope of my forgiveness or friendship.

There are eleven tiny diamonds on the chain. Eleven. The age I was when I met Macon. The number on Macon's high school football jersey. Come May, it will be eleven years since we fought at prom.

He's still giving me everything he has.

It takes me two tries to get the necklace on. It settles like gossamer upon my skin. Then I'm rising.

CHAPTER TWENTY-FIVE

Macon

There's something cathartic about doing the thing I most feared. Even if I don't know how Delilah will react to my letters, she has them now. She'll read them and know all those secret thoughts I never expected to tell anyone. I'm glad she has them. They belong to her.

Doesn't stop me from feeling agitated as hell. I can't seem to settle. I pace my office, then my room. I don't want to be in my room. I can see the bath from here, and I cannot look at that damn bath without thinking of her slim, capable hand on my cock . . .

"Shit."

I push open the balcony doors and step out. The sun is hot and bright. I turn my face into a breeze and breathe deep. The air smells of salt and sea and sweetgrass. I let it calm me as much as I can, but nothing truly helps. I'll only settle when I can face her again.

I'm sitting in the chair I once cuddled Delilah in, my knee bouncing, my gaze on the horizon, when I hear a noise and look up.

She stands a few feet away, her big eyes glassy. Is she upset? Happy? I'm too worked up to get a proper read on her.

I stay completely still as she walks my way, those rounded hips swaying. God, I love the way she walks. I love the way the sun gilds her skin golden brown. I love the way her butterscotch eyes always seem to see right through me. I love . . .

"Hey," she says, stopping before me.

I scramble to my feet, then regret it because I'm looming. She doesn't back away, though, but tilts her head back and stares at me as though she's seeing me anew. Her slim hands cup the rough scruff of my cheeks, and she kisses me, gentle explorations of her mouth. I draw in a sharp breath before letting it out slowly as I stroke the delicate line of her jaw, the warm curve of her neck.

Delilah touches me as though I might soon fade away. She kisses the bridge of my nose, the skin at the edges of my eyes. I rest my forehead against her, my breathing growing deeper, faster. I brush my lips against her with every other kiss she places upon my skin because I need that contact, however brief.

"Delilah," I whisper, my thumbs caressing paths over her temples. "All the things I've said—"

"Are in the past." Her lips press to my cheek. "I wish I was there. I wish I had known."

"You were there. You were always with me." She has to understand this. I sit down and pull her onto my lap. "That's what kills me, Tot. When I thought of you, it drove me on. I didn't feel alone. You say I'm the voice in your head, telling you what you aren't. I want to be the voice telling you all the things that you *are*. Talented and funny and fearless as hell."

It's then that I notice she's wearing the necklace. I trace the chain, stopping at a glinting diamond. "That you are beautiful to me in the way of stars."

"Macon . . ." Her fingers comb through my hair. "I shouldn't admit this, but even when you were at your worst, when I'd be dreaming of tarring and feathering you and leaving your carcass out for the birds to pick over"—I laugh at that—"I admired your arrogance."

"Did you?"

As if to steady me, she rests her palm on my chest, surely feeling the hard beat of my heart. "I used to channel that arrogance. If I ever became intimidated or felt less than, I used to think, 'What would Macon Saint do?'"

My smile grows wide, and she returns it.

"So you see. It wasn't all bad. You were there with me, too, giving me strength, forcing me to be better than I thought I could." Her touch is warm and steady along my jaw. "I made a deal to stay here, expecting the worst, but I found the best man I've ever known."

Her words punch into me. It's sweet pain. A small voice in me wants to say I'm not good; I'm not remotely the best. But if she has to believe in how I see her, I have to do the same.

Her gaze searches my face in wonder. "I'd told myself I made that deal with you for my family, but when I walked into your office, I felt alive in a way I hadn't for ten years. I know now that I made that deal for me too. I'm here for you, Macon. That's the honest truth."

Expelling a long breath, I grip the nape of her neck, holding on. "We going to do this, Delilah?"

"Yes, we're going to do this."

Weirdly, it feels as though I've been waiting my whole life to hear that.

———

By silent agreement, Delilah and I spend the day together, simply soaking each other in. We hang out like we did as kids, only this time, it's Delilah who is curled up against my side when we watch movies. It's

Delilah whose hair I stroke. I'm content to stay that way all night. That is until the sound of Delilah's stomach growling loud and insistent rings out. She turns bright red.

I burst out laughing but quickly quell it when she glares. "I'm sorry. But you are so fucking adorable."

Delilah makes a face and slaps the side of my arm. "Ass."

I laugh again and quickly kiss her cheek. "I'm hungry too. Let's get some dinner."

The sun has sunk entirely, and the sky is purple in the twilight. I hadn't noticed. Rising, I offer to cook. Delilah raises a brow.

"What? I can cook," I protest. "It's nothing close to what you do, but I can manage simple meals."

"I believe you." Delilah rises from the couch, distracting me with her body. "I was just thinking maybe we could go out."

Go out. For normal people this wouldn't be a problem. For me, it's something different. Call me selfish, but I don't want to share Delilah right now. Out there, I will have to because people inevitably notice.

She clearly sees my hesitation. "Nothing fancy, totally casual. We can even eat in the car if you want," she adds with a brow wiggle like she's enticing me to sin.

"Now I'm intrigued."

"You'll love it," she says as we go to change. "Besides, I want to show you something."

It strikes me just how dangerous it is to live with Delilah because getting ready for dinner feels like we're something more than just starting out. It's comfortable in a way I've never experienced. Real in a way I only allow myself to dream about in the darkest corner of my mind.

All this time, I worried about hurting Delilah, but now I wonder if I'm the one who will be left stripped bare and empty. I shrug the worry aside. We said we'd try. That's all anyone can do.

Delilah takes me to a small taco stand down the coast, tucked between the highway and the sea. The rocky inlet has enough room for the cars, a parking lot, and another cottage-size restaurant that's closed for business.

The taco stand, however, has a long line. No one looks at us as we wait, huddled in our hoodies against the wind that's blowing over the sand. The rich scent of grilled meats and frying vegetables has my stomach grumbling.

"See?" I say, looking down at my stomach. "He's just as noisy."

"Ass," she mutters.

"That's Mr. Asshat," I remind her with a nudge of my elbow.

Delilah smirks and then rests her shoulder against mine. I'm inordinately pleased.

At the stand, I let her order, insisting that since she knows the menu, she can pick what's best. Taking our beers, I secure a seat at one of the picnic tables set under multicolored string lights.

Delilah returns with two boxes and sits at my side. The selection is simple: a pork, a fish, and a beef for each of us. It's how they're made that makes me groan.

"Damn," I say around my bite. "That's good."

"So good." She licks a drop of aioli at the corner of her lip as juices run along her fingers and drip into the box.

We eat in relative silence, enjoying the food and our beers. Around us, families, couples, and groups of singles chatter and laugh. Contentment steals over me. I don't have a lot of experience with happiness. But I soak it in.

"You see that place over there," Delilah says, breaking our easy silence.

"The blue shack of a restaurant?" I squint at the faded sign. "An old crab house?"

"Yeah." She wipes her fingers with a napkin. "Apparently, they weren't any good, and you can't expect to stay open serving crap. Especially next to this place."

Delilah stares at the old place, her expression thoughtful like maybe she's seeing it in a way I can't. Tension visibly creeps along her shoulders when she turns back to me. "I've been thinking about opening a restaurant there."

Carefully I set down my beer. This place is ten minutes from my house. She'll be near me. I want that. Fiercely. I want her happiness more. "Would it be a good idea to open next to such a popular place?"

"I wouldn't be serving tacos, so it isn't direct competition. It would benefit both, I think, because people who love good food would be drawn here." Her hands start to move as she talks, getting more excited. "I'd strip that awful blue paint off, bring it back to an old beach-cottage look. I'm not certain about the menu, but it's starting to take shape in my head. Comfort food, but not heavy. Quality ingredients, a mix between simple and complex—" She stops, and her lips quirk. "I'm boring you."

"Hardly. I like hearing you talk." I take her hand and thread our fingers. Because I can. Finally. "It'll work, Tot."

She shrugs but can't hide her smile. "Well, there's a lot of stops between an idea and reality. I don't have the money or a backer—"

"I'll do it. I'll back you. Hell, I'll buy the place if you want."

"No. Macon, no." She softens her rejection by leaning against me. "It's a generous, lovely offer, but I don't want that between us. Business has to stay business."

"And we're not business." We started off that way. Until now, I didn't truly comprehend how much I wanted that arrangement behind us. It does funny things to my insides to hear her say she's here because she wants me, not what I could do for her, not because of that damn deal.

"No," she says happily. "We're not."

"Okay." I take another look at the restaurant. "But I can still help. I know a guy—"

Delilah bursts out laughing. "Oh my God. Please don't say he's in the mob."

I tweak her earlobe. "No, smart-ass. He's a restaurateur who happens to be looking to new expansion."

That gets her attention. "Who?"

"Ronan Kelly."

"You know Kelly?" She makes a sound of amusement. "What am I saying? Of course you do. Hot successful men run in packs."

My chin rests against the top of her head. "Hold on a second. What's this about *hot*?"

"Ronan Kelly is hot. Insanely hot. It would be hard not to notice that."

I grunt. "I'm not sure I like that *you* notice."

"I have eyes, don't I?" She runs a finger along the top of my thigh. The muscle tightens in response. Her hum is pleased. "Macon Saint, jealous. Who would have thought?"

"It's not the first time with you," I admit in a low voice.

But she hears. And grins. Because Delilah is evil.

"North?" She huffs out a laugh. "We have zero chemistry. If you were thinking clearly, you would have seen—"

"Not North," I cut in. "Although, yes, I was a touch irritated."

Delilah snorts but then stops and looks up at me. "Who, then?"

It's my turn to grin. "Matty Hayes."

"Matty Hayes? From high school? Seriously?"

"The way you used to stare at him like he was a god?" I roll my eyes, fighting a laugh. "Annoyed the hell out of me."

Her lips quirk. "How ironic, given that when I think back on that day, I realize that I, too, was probably jealous."

It's probably bad of me to be so pleased. "Do tell, Ms. Baker."

The wind whips a strand of her hair over her mouth, and she brushes it aside before she speaks. "You and Sam were always a couple. I had no one. I felt like a third wheel, and it sucked."

Pressing my lips to her hair, I'm silent for a moment. Sam. Always Sam, lurking like a ghost between us. At this point, I don't care if I never see her again. "You were the glue that held us all together, and you never knew it."

Delilah huffs. "Yeah, well, at the time, I'd have preferred a boyfriend. I'd only had one kiss up to that point. And that was only because of that stupid party game The Shed."

I freeze, my insides seizing up. Then my heart starts to pound with some weird mix of shock and satisfaction. "That was your first kiss?"

"You remember me in school; I wasn't exactly popular." Her eyes narrow. "Why do you ask?"

Hell.

"Macon . . ."

"Okay." I hold up a hand. "In the spirit of our newfound sharing and honesty, I have to confess that it was me."

"What was you?" she asks darkly.

"In the shed. With you." I clear my throat. Hell. "I kissed you."

"What?" Her hiss carries over the area, and a couple glances our way.

Taking her hand, I help her up, grab our trash, and dump it before walking with her toward the old restaurant. "I drew a number, went in the shed, and waited. A girl came in. About five seconds later, I knew it was you."

"How?" she whispers, still shocked.

"Delilah, we may have been enemies, but I knew your scent like I knew home."

"Please. I smelled like any other girl back then."

"You stumbled or stubbed your toe on the way in and muttered 'shit sticks' under your breath." I chuckle at the memory. "I was shocked as hell. And turned on—as much as a thirteen-year-old kid could be."

Her pretty mouth falls open. "Oh my God. It was truly you?"

"Yes."

"You knew it was me, and you kissed me anyway." She stares up at me like she's seeing me anew. "Why?"

"I wanted to know how it would feel." I take a step closer. "I knew it was you, and I was strangely relieved that I wouldn't have to kiss anyone else."

Her gaze turns hazy as if she's remembering. "You were sweet."

"So were you." My hand drifts up to cup her jaw. "I liked it."

A frown wrinkles her brow. "Why did you pretend you kissed Sam?"

Shrugging, I turn and study the restaurant. "I liked it too much. And there you were, glaring daggers at me throughout the party. Seemed safer, easier to ask Xander to switch numbers and pretend it didn't happen."

Delilah is silent. A frown works between her brows. "You started dating Sam that night."

She doesn't say it, but we both know the truth. Everything changed that night, for the worst. The wedge between Delilah and me grew wider.

"I made a lot of mistakes in my life," I say quietly. "I don't want to make more." Glancing at the restaurant, I take Delilah's hand in mine. "Do you want me to call Ronan?"

She doesn't answer immediately but stares at me. "All right," she says finally. "Yes, please."

"Consider it done."

"Thank you, Macon." She startles me with a short amused laugh. "I should be giddy at the thought of meeting Ronan Kelly. But all I can think of is that kiss and how I'm so glad it was you and not that dickhead Xander."

I tug her into a hug. "Yeah, well, I'd rather you think of kissing me instead of thinking about meeting Ronan, so I'm not complaining." What I don't tell her is I'm increasingly convinced I want her to be the last woman I kiss, the only one. The fact that she might not feel the same scares the hell out of me. My history of retreating from situations I can't control has me holding on to her a little tighter.

Don't fuck this up. Somehow, I'm afraid I will.

CHAPTER TWENTY-SIX

Macon

"I've come bearing refreshments." Delilah stops in front of the double-wide lounger I'm sitting on reading scripts.

We spent the morning apart. I wanted to give Delilah time to get used to being with me. It wasn't easy. I wanted—needed—to know if she was all right. Maybe I just wanted to see if she'd come find me. Yes, I'm a needy fucker.

I move the pile of scripts to the far side of the lounge to make room for her. "Hand it over, and sit," I say, making her roll her eyes at my order. "What do you have for me this time?"

Delilah often grumps about me comparing her to luscious foods, but I can't help it. I can't think of a time when Delilah hasn't been taking care of the people in her world by offering them food and drinks. For Delilah food is love. Truth is, that more than anything pushed me to take her up on the offer to be my chef; I wanted to be cared for by Delilah even if I received it in the most circuitous of ways.

"Pimm's cup." Delilah gets comfortable, bending her tan legs as she leans back. "My favorite lazy-day afternoon drink."

I take a long drink and let the taste of Delilah's lazy day slide down. It's crisp, sweet, a burst of freshness. Kind of like Delilah.

"How's the leg?" She sits forward and peers at my calf.

Earlier, I went with North to the doctor's to get my cast off. The first sight of my emaciated leg wasn't heartening. I wiggle my toes, and the weakened muscles along my leg shift beneath my pasty skin. "Looks like hell, but it feels good. No pain or twinges."

"And your back?" Her lips twitch as she carefully keeps her eyes on my leg. Is she remembering the spectacular attention she gave my dick as I soaked away my aches? I hope so.

"Good as new. You must have magic fingers."

A furious blush graces her cheeks, but Delilah doesn't say anything as she picks up a script and starts reading it. Chuckling, I relax and drink my Pimm's, enjoying every damn icy-cold sip. The sun is low in the sky, getting ready to set, and the sea goes quiet as if waiting for that final kiss of light.

"Are you thinking about doing this movie?" she asks, the ice cubes in her glass clinking as she drinks and reads.

"I am." I lean over and glance at the script. She's reading the superhero one. It's supposed to be top secret, reveal on pain of death. But I trust Delilah. "Why? I thought you liked comic book heroes."

When we were kids, we used to camp out on her family room couch and watch the *X-Men* animated series. Delilah wanted to be Rogue, despite the fact that the character could never touch another person without risk of killing them.

She meets my gaze for the first time today. "I love them. Seeing you in this would be . . . I don't even have the words. Surreal. Awesome."

"I like those words," I tease. "But? What?"

She bites her bottom lip, clearly considering her words. "I guess it depends on what you want out of this career. You're basically playing a superhero now, only with swords and leathers. If you play one again . . ."

"I run the risk of being typecast," I finish, understanding dawning.

"Then again, these movies are insanely popular." She smooths a hand over the script. "You can easily become a superstar."

"Who will quickly fade when he gets too old and beat up to play those roles anymore."

She chuckles but shakes her head. "Not necessarily."

With a sigh, I lean my head back and stare at the sea. "I need to diversify, take on different roles. But all these"—I gesture to the pile of scripts—"are basically for action films."

"Nothing wrong with being an action star." She copies my pose, stretching her curvy legs out. Her little toes are painted bubblegum pink now. Why I find that cute as hell is a mystery. "Look at Harrison Ford. He's one of the biggest stars of all time. The majority of his movies are action films."

"Yes," I agree, deadpan. "All I have to do is somehow land roles in movies as epic as *Star Wars* and *Indiana Jones*, and I'm all set."

She gives me a nudge. "If anyone can own this town, you can."

"I don't know if I want to."

My confession has her turning on her side to face me. "Are you happy?"

Something deep inside my gut tightens uncomfortably. "What a question," I quip with a huff of laughter.

Her gaze is steady and serious. "It's a hard one, isn't it? Sometimes, I'll ask myself, and I have no idea what the answer is. Which probably means I'm not."

I set my glass and hers on the pavers and then turn to lie on my side so that we're face to face. "Maybe we're not meant to be completely happy at all times," I say. "I'm happy on the set, when things are flowing. Good conversation with good friends makes me happy." I move closer, resting fully on the lounger. She's close enough that all I'd have to do to kiss her is lean over. "I'm happy when I'm with you."

Her gaze goes slumberous as she studies my face like she's taking in the details and committing them to memory. "Would it surprise you to learn that I'm happy when I'm with you too?"

"Yes," I say truthfully, my heart thudding in my throat. "But I'm damn glad you are, Tot."

Her smile is small but pleased. Neither of us says anything more. I'm content to lie here and simply be—because she's here, and that's all I need right now. Slowly, creeping like she's afraid I'll bolt, Delilah edges closer. I wait it out, pulse thrumming. Her warm leg collides with mine. I let out a breath, and my leg slides between hers.

The sun sinks, hot orange on the cool-blue ocean. We could be watching the sunset. We're watching each other instead. Curled up close, our limbs intertwining. The evening light turns Delilah's skin caramel, and her eyes gleam like old gold. She's so beautiful she makes my heart hurt.

I press a kiss to her cheek and am rewarded with the sound of her breath hitching. I want to explore her mouth for hours, days. I'm beginning to think I'll want it for endless years. For now, I'll do as she wishes and go slow, starting with chaste, relatively innocent touches. My reward is her hand smoothing along my neck to rest there, warm and lazy. I feel that soft touch down to the bone, a throb of warm happiness that lingers.

She snuggles closer, her calf sliding along mine. It feels so good I'm momentarily distracted. My arm wraps around her waist, securing her against me. Her body is all curves and warmth. I'm trying my best not to get distracted by her breasts or the way they tease along my chest with her breathing. But damn, I want to touch them.

"Macon?"

"Hmm?" I stroke her arm, touch her fingers. If I'd known on that fateful prom night that wrapping myself up in Delilah would be this good, I'd have hunted her down, thrown myself at her feet, and begged.

"Have you been avoiding me today?"

My hand pauses at her waist. "I wanted to give you time to get used to this." Us. We were an *us*. Fucking unbelievable.

She worries the inside of her lip with her teeth as her thumb brushes my jaw. "I thought as much." Her gaze lowers to my mouth. She has my total attention now. "Thing is, I missed you."

I can't help myself. I lean in and kiss her like I've wanted to all day, deep and sweet. She makes a small pleased sound that licks along my skin, and then her mouth opens to mine, the gentle touch of her hand turning into a desperate grip.

I'm not going anywhere. I tilt my head, drawing her halfway under me, knowing she has no idea how much I relish the freedom to touch her, taste her. "This okay?" I whisper before suckling her plump lower lip. "Kissing you like this?"

It feels okay. More than that. And she's responsive. But I want the words. I need to know she's as into it as I am. Delilah hums into my mouth, tickling my lips. Her body arcs into mine, pressing those glorious tits against my chest.

"Yes," she says.

Yes. My new favorite word.

A grin slips free. Then I lose myself in Delilah. I've never kissed like this, kissing because it feels so damn good my body throbs with lust. I swallow down her soft sounds, learn the contours of her mouth. The simple slide of her tongue along mine has my dick so hard it hurts.

Delilah kisses like she does everything else—all in. She kisses me like I'm an indulgence, a secret treat. And it turns me on so badly my movements become clumsy, fumbling and uncoordinated. I want to touch her everywhere, and my hands can't decide where to start.

I've never felt like this.

By the time we part for air, we're both panting slightly, and my hand is halfway up her shirt. A little closer, and I'm in heaven. But she pulls back, a pretty blush spreading over her cheeks.

"Damn," she murmurs, glancing at me with a wry smile.

"Damn?" Leaden with lust, I can only lie there, trying to control myself so I don't reach for her again.

Blushing, she shakes her head as if to pull herself out of a fog. I want to pull her back into it.

"I never thought I'd be making out with you on a lounger," she says. "I never thought . . . realized it would be so . . ." She takes an unsteady breath. "So good."

Her confession sends another bolt of heat through me. I cup the back of her neck and kiss her again. Harder, maybe a little fucking desperate. Because she's killing me here.

Delilah's leg climbs up my side, her body curling around mine. Her hands fist my shirt, the short strands of my hair. Aggressive, greedy. A grunt leaves me, and I roll to press her into the lounger, when she makes a sound of protest, and she breaks off.

Her lips are swollen and parted as she gasps. "I . . ." I suckle her lower lip. She murmurs a sound of approval, licking into my mouth before trying to talk again. "I think we should . . ."

"Stop?" I'm hard as wood; my abs actually ache with need. *Take it slow. She wants slow.* I'll give her anything she wants. "Okay. Give me a minute—"

She touches my cheek and gently turns my head to meet her gaze. There's so much heat in her toffee eyes that my mind goes blank. "Forget what I said about taking it slow. I want you now."

It takes me a second to catch up. But my dick immediately pushes at the base of my shorts, trying its best to get out. This is probably the moment I should try to reassure her, tell her I'm fine with waiting. That there's no rush. That's not what comes out of my mouth.

"Oh, bless you."

She laughs, the sound muffled against my lips as we tumble back, and I kiss her like I need air. "I was never any good at waiting," she says.

I kiss along the smooth, fragrant skin of her neck, my hands filling with her sweet ass. "Never fucking change."

She nips my earlobe. The tips of her fingers tickle my waist as she gathers up the edge of my shirt. "Take this off. Take it all off."

So demanding. I swear, I nearly come from that alone: Delilah Baker ordering me to get naked. Jesus.

"Yes, ma'am." I pause. "Wait. Here?"

There's a reason I'm protesting the location; I just can't focus enough to remember what the hell it might be.

"Yes. Here." She lifts her head. Hair mussed, golden eyes dazed, she smirks, and it is damn sexy. "Unless you have some objection—"

"Here's good. Kiss me." I groan when she does. "That sassy mouth." I delve into it, taste her flavor. "God, Delilah. Give me another taste of that tart mouth."

She hums, and her hand slides down to cup my dick. Ah, sweet relief.

"No, wait. Shit. Condom." A breath shudders out of me. "We need a condom."

A whimper of protest sounds in her throat as she leans her head on my chest. I take the moment to clutch her close, grind my hard-on against her heat. She whimpers again, and I clear my throat. "Upstairs. Now."

We both scramble off the lounger.

The trip to my room is a clumsy dance, broken up by frequent stops because I keep pushing her up against any available surface to kiss her mouth, eat at it like it's my last damn meal. I'm starving for Delilah.

She's just as hungry, tearing my shirt off in the hall. It drops somewhere in our wake. Her strong, deft fingers trace along my abs as we struggle to find the bed.

316

"God, Macon. You are so fucking . . ." Her pink tongue flicks my nipple. I'm not ashamed to admit I whimper. She smiles. "Gorgeous."

I've been called that in some form or other my entire life. It's never meant anything. Until now. Because she doesn't look at my body when she says it. She looks straight into my eyes. She looks at me like I'm hers. I'm damn close to begging her for mercy. And she isn't even naked. I need to fix that.

With a grunt, I haul her close, wrap my arm under her plump ass, and pick her up. She makes some protest about my leg, but she doesn't know how strong of a motivation I have. I carry her the last few steps into my room, my lips never leaving the haven of hers.

When I finally put her down, everything changes. We fall quiet, staring at each other. I'd say she is shy, but that's not it. Lips parted and swollen with my kisses, Delilah meets my gaze. She's soaking this moment in the same way I am. I want to remember this, the way the light caresses her burnished skin and sets the flyaway strands of her hair aglow, the way her eyes are wide and wondering. I draw in the scent of her skin and lean closer, needing her warmth.

Smiling a little, she grabs the bottom of her shirt and tugs it off.

"I wanted to do that." I barely recognize my voice it's so rough. Because she's standing there, those glorious tits encased in a pale-pink lace bra.

Her smile grows. "You can do it next time."

"There's going to be a next time?"

"I guess that depends on how good you are this time."

Cheeky. Stepping closer, I trace the strap of her bra, gratified to see little goose bumps lift on her skin. She sways toward me, her palm resting on my chest. I hold her gaze as I reach behind her and release the hook. Her bra slides onto the floor.

No, this is what I'll remember for the rest of my life. The first sight of Delilah's breasts. I've dreamed about them for far too long. My first wet dreams were about them, how they might look, feel, taste. I knew nothing.

She is full and ripe, the skin paler here, delicately capped with dusky-honey tips. It gets me so hot I'm shaking. My hand cups their soft, plump weight, and she shivers too. I want to say something like "Finally" or "What took us so long?" but all that comes out is the most important thing. "You're beautiful."

Her lids flutter, her breath hitching when I rub the tips of my thumbs over her silky nipples. Those sweet buds tighten, and it's all I can do not to swoop down and suck them hard. As it is, I tweak them, and she keens. The sound goes straight to my dick. "Get in my bed, Delilah. And get comfortable, because you aren't leaving it anytime soon."

CHAPTER TWENTY-SEVEN

Delilah

It's almost surreal, stripping down in front of Macon, like I'm watching it happen from outside myself. That we're finally in this place. Somewhere, in the back of my head, I'm as nervous as an inexperienced teen. But then our gazes collide, and I forget to be shy or wonder how we got here. Because there is only him and the way he makes me feel.

Like I'm a newly minted version of myself, re-created into something glorious, something essential. He does that to me with just one glance. I want to shine for him. Only him.

He doesn't look away as he shoves his shorts off and stands before me, naked and hard. I've seen pieces of him in the bath; now I have the whole picture. I've never seen a more beautiful sight. And then he's on me, wrapping me up in his arms. His body is hot and solid and so much bigger than mine that I'm enveloped.

The bedding sinks beneath me as he presses me down, dragging openmouthed kisses along my neck. "Anything you don't like, honey.

Anything you need, tell me." Big hands, rough with calluses from sword fighting, skim down my sides. "Anything."

With a noise of want, he cups my breast, then leans over it. His mouth is hot and wet, and I groan, arching into him as he sucks my nipple in deep. He releases me with a long satisfied lick and then does it all over again.

"Macon . . ." It's a plea. For more, for it everywhere.

He seems to know this because he looks up at me from beneath the fan of his lashes as his wicked tongue flicks over my other nipple. "It's my turn to play."

Play he does, suckling my nipples until they're swollen and stiff and gleaming, then rubbing the flat of his fingers over the sensitive tips—a slow, heavy circle. The action is so lewd, so basely sexual, that I writhe and moan against him, my leg hooking over his trim hips in an attempt to bring him over me.

But he resists, his focus all on me. He makes his way over my body, learning every curve and hollow—gentle little kisses of shuddering pleasure, slow wet kisses of greed. When he gets to the rise of my hip bone, he pauses. His big hands settle over my thighs, gripping them lightly. His gaze, dark and hot, meets mine.

"Spread these thighs, Tot, and show me what I've been dreaming about for far too long."

Slowly, I open to him. I feel the exposure in the soft stretch of my inner thigh muscles, the cool rush of air against my wet sex. My breasts jiggle with every shuddering breath I take. Macon's attention is rapt. He licks his lower lip, and I clench deep within me.

With a groan, he lowers his head and kisses my pussy like a man deprived of air. Pleasure jolts through me, hot and sharp. I writhe against that slowly questing mouth of his. He fucking feasts, and I can't help but put my hand on the back of his head to hold him there, urge him to take more.

God, the feel of his tongue sliding and searching; my clit becomes so swollen and sensitive I'm half trying to get away. But he won't let me. The sight of his broad shoulders between my legs, the fan of his lashes shadowing an expression of sheer greed, has me teetering on an orgasm. He stops to place a soft, firm kiss right on my clit like it's something he has to do, this bit of utter affection at the height of his lust, and I fall.

Arching against the bed, I come and come. Macon kisses me again, his hand soothing my quivering belly in gentle circles, then rises to hover over me. "Of all the flavors you've given me," he says roughly. "That was my favorite."

God. I lick my dry lips, my breath catching. "You can have a taste anytime you like."

His expression is one of male satisfaction and pure heat as he slides his palm down my belly and over my poor, teased sex. I'm so slick and ready two of his thick fingers slide right in. We both groan, his forehead resting on mine. "You need me in here, don't you, Tot?"

"Yes." I'm panting now, my body flush and shivering.

He keeps fingering me, downright dirty about it. "How do you want it?"

I cup the back of his head, gripping the damp strands of his short hair. I tug him down until we share the same air. "Macon, do you know how many nights *I've* dreamed about that thick cock of yours pushing into me?"

He shudders, a hard breath punching from his lips. "Shit. Tell me."

"So many frustrated nights." I lick his upper lip. "I want it deep and hard."

All sense of play evaporates. He gets a condom, but his hands are shaking so hard, and he drops it. He huffs out a laugh. "Hell, I'm too worked up." His hot gaze collides with mine. "Put it on me?"

I try, but I'm shaking too. Softly laughing, we put it on together. His abs clench as I brush a hand over his balls, his dick flexing with impatience. There's no more smiling. His expression is almost fierce as he cradles my cheeks and kisses me. I feel it in my knees, down my back, in my heart.

Then he's sliding over me, making room between my thighs. Every bit of him is big and strong. Hard biceps bunch and strain as he holds himself over me, his erection pressed hot against my belly.

He cants his hips just enough to slide through my wetness, but he doesn't enter me. Not yet. Dark eyes peer down at me. I forget to breathe because what I see there isn't just lust. Gently, as though I'm a dream, he ducks his head and places a feather-soft kiss on my swollen lips.

"Delilah."

That's all. Only my name.

It's everything.

My arms wrap around the thick column of his neck. I'm surrounded by his heat, the fresh scent of his skin, the unsteady rush of his breathing. I take a small sip from his lips, then tell him what he needs to hear. "Yes, Macon. Yes."

A breath shudders from him. He holds my gaze, those expressive eyes shining black in the light. The first push spreads me wide. My chest hitches. He fills me in a steady invasion. So thick. So perfect.

And all the time he watches me.

He's too big for ease. He has to work for it, a little in, a little out, each time sinking deeper.

And still he watches me.

Pleasure pulls tight. And then he's all in. He holds there, throbbing and shaking.

"Oh, fuck," he rasps. His kiss is hot and demanding, almost desperate, as if he can't get enough. "What you do to me . . . you have no idea, do you? How you make me feel."

"Yes, I do. You think it's any different for me? Feel my heart." I put his hand between my breasts. "It's racing. For you."

There are no more words. Macon moves, the power of his body undulating over me. We move together as though we've been doing this forever, like we already know each other perfectly. Maybe we do.

He isn't a selfish lover. He gives me everything, touches and caresses with such dedication and attention that I feel cherished. And he fucks with such greedy relish—sucking at my skin, thrusting into me with deep grunts of pleasure—that I feel adored.

But in the end, he rolls onto his back, taking me with him. Stretching his arms overhead, he grasps the headboard. "Ride me, Delilah. Take what you need."

All that power laid out before me. The high crests of his cheeks are flushed. Sweat trickles down his temples. Every inch of him is hard and tight with lust. I sink down onto his cock, and we both groan. I take my pleasure, luxuriating in his body. I don't let up until he's groaning and crying out my name.

We come together, falling into each other, wrecked.

Nothing will ever be the same again.

CHAPTER TWENTY-EIGHT

Delilah

I'm hosting a dinner for Ronan Kelly, one of the most powerful restaurateurs in the business. I know this to be true, but part of me has a hard time believing it. For all his fame and business savvy, Ronan is a hard man to pin down. Much like Macon he's rumored to be both a social recluse yet is adored by many. He is in his midthirties, is the son of Irish immigrants, and has the Midas touch when it comes to restaurants.

And he's coming to dinner. All because Macon asked him to. I could kiss Macon for that. For a lot of things. I knew sex with him would be good, intense. What I didn't realize was how close I'd feel to him. Sex is something I understand. It's pleasure and release. Intimacy is different. I thought I understood it. I've had boyfriends. But I knew nothing. Because this thing between Macon and me is changing the very makeup of who I am.

He's not getting under my skin; he's becoming part of it. I don't think I can walk away from him now without tearing a good chunk of myself apart. It's both frightening and comforting. If tonight goes as planned, my life will change yet again. I'll be one step closer to my dream. And it's all due to a text that wasn't even meant for me.

I'm ashamed to say I haven't wanted to think of Sam. At all. Sam now equates to guilt. Guilt for not telling Macon about her call. Guilt about sleeping with Sam's childhood boyfriend. Guilt for even feeling guilty about that. What a mess.

A small, childish part of me is glad she's gone. Out of sight, out of mind, and all that. But pushing something away won't fix anything. My sister is flawed. But she's family, and she owes it to all of us to return.

Sitting heavily on the bed, I reach for my phone and send a text before I can think better of it.

> **DeeLight to SammyBaker:** Everything has changed. I just wish you were here. I have so much to tell you.

I give her a good twenty minutes. She doesn't answer. I have to resign myself to the fact that she's not ready to come back. Swallowing down a lump of disappointment, I get dressed and focus on tonight.

I'm so damn nervous I can hardly keep my hands from shaking as I smooth out my hair and apply my makeup. The Delilah in the mirror has round cheeks that are too flushed and amber-brown eyes that are too big and shiny—scared. I leave off the blush, since I'm clearly not going to need it, and dab on some red lipstick.

Despite my jitters, I have confidence in my menu. It had taken two weeks to come up with it, searching through old cookbooks for inspiration, remembering childhood recipes, experimenting with taste combinations that bring me joy. Each dish feels deeply personal, even though I can't fully express why. I created them without thinking too hard about it, letting my memory of food, knowledge of taste combinations, and basic skills guide me. It was worth it. I had to figure out who I was and tell my story through the food I made. It's all there in this menu. All of what means the most to me. Whether it works, I don't know. But I'm about to find out.

Macon

The morning after Delilah told me her dreams, she woke up with a wide smile and said, "I want to cook." That was that. She disappeared into the kitchen and began to whip up dishes that made my knees weak and my mouth water. My diet went out the window; production orders be damned. I'd rather spend my days as her willing taste tester.

She's become a woman fueled by a creative drive that lights her up. She cooks; I eat; we make love. Over and over. For two weeks. I don't fully believe in karma, but somewhere, at some point, I must have done something right.

Now I have a chance to return the favor for the woman who's become my everything. But first, there's something I have to do for both of us. I pull out my phone and find Sam's number.

> Saint to Sam Baker: I was set to hate you. But I can't anymore because you brought Delilah back into my life.
>
> I'm not going to forgive you for the watch; I'm not that magnanimous. But I'm no longer going to look for you. Stay gone if that's your wish. Or come back and ease your family's worries.
>
> Either way, you and I are done. Pax, Saint.

I have no idea if Samantha will get the texts. I'm not certain I care. But officially letting Sam go releases something in me as well. I feel lighter. I want that lightness for Delilah, too, and remind myself to tell her about the texts. Right now, she's downstairs cooking and giving her staff instructions.

The doorbell rings just as I'm sliding a shirt on. I hustle to the door, buttoning my shirt as I go. Kelly is waiting on the other side. "Ronan, good to see you."

"Hey, Saint." He steps into the hall. "You're looking better. Well, for an overgrown mountain."

I top him by five inches, and he likes to give me shit for it. "Thanks, pretty boy."

I've known Ronan for years. He has several restaurants, all of them with monthlong wait lists and endless accolades. His singular talent is identifying top chef talent and creating restaurants that perfectly highlight that chef's food. A partnership with Ronan is like finding a golden ticket.

I'm nervous. I never get nervous anymore. At least, not when it comes to my career. After the first year working, I finally realized things either happen, or they don't. No use worrying over shit you can't control. But this is for Delilah. I know how much this means to her, and I cannot control one single thing about this dinner. I want Ronan to see the genius in her cooking. But if he can't, then he's a dumb ass, and we'll find someone else. And then I'll kick Ronan's ass.

With that in mind, I lead Ronan into the living room, where North and his date are waiting to join us for dinner. Then I head to the kitchen.

Delilah is giving some instructions to her staff. I was intending to offer a few words of encouragement; I'm temporarily struck mute by the sight of her.

Half-bent over the counter, she's wearing a tan dress that hugs every delectable curve. Her ass is a thing of beauty. I want to run my hand over it, give that peachy butt a firm slap. It would jiggle so nicely. And she'd probably kick my ass. Then again, maybe she'd be into some light spanking. I want to know this. I need to concentrate.

"Hey," I say, coming up to stand alongside her. "You doing all right?"

She brushes a lock of hair back behind her ear. "I got this."

"I know you do." I bend down to kiss her cheek and feel the tension in her.

Delilah grabs hold of my forearm. "Macon . . ." She pauses, hesitating, then takes a breath. "Thank you for this."

I'm not certain that's what she really wanted to say, but I'm not going to push it. "There's nothing to thank." Caressing the curve of her cheek, I give her a smile of encouragement. "He's going to love you."

My throat closes on the words, emotion throwing me off for a second. But she doesn't notice. Bracing her shoulders, she walks with me to meet our guests.

I shouldn't have worried. Delilah handles Ronan with a cool confidence that totally belies the case of nerves she showed me. I try to keep track of the conversation, but then one of Delilah's former catering waitstaff brings out a round of drinks and a tray of little spheres the size of a large marble.

"Gin blackberry bramble and peanut brittle spheres," Delilah tells us.

I take a sip of the drink. Instantly, I'm back in the South on a summer's day, eating plump blackberries straight from the bush. The peanut brittle sphere melts in my mouth, reminding me of the cookies Delilah's mom used to make for us, more savory than sweet. It's such a strong childhood moment that I swear I can practically feel the sun on my back.

After our drinks, she has us sit, and our first course arrives.

"Oysters topped with watermelon-and-habanero *brunoise*," the server says, setting a plate before me. It's a little work of art.

"The menu tonight," Delilah tells us, "is a take on what I'm thinking about offering. It's a compilation of the things I love and hold dear.

However, I'd be creating dishes based on the best produce available for the week."

"As long as you don't call it farm to table," Ronan says. "That catchphrase has died a swift death."

She smiles easily. "I'll leave you to come up with the new catchphrase. For me, a dish is only as good as its ingredients. It's my job to start with the best and make them shine in a way that you never expected."

He's charmed. Of course he is; she's brilliant. "That's the trick, isn't it?"

"It's no trick, Mr. Kelly. It's love. Love of food and the desire to show people how much they can love it too."

They start to talk business, but again I'm distracted by Delilah's food. With the oysters, I'm at the shore, swimming in the heat of the day. She serves us baby cream biscuits and smoked peach butter that taste exactly like those we'd eat around her mother's table during a Sunday dinner, only better, tweaked in a way that makes me want to taste it again and again. Buttermilk *panna cotta* with spot prawns and spring vegetables pulls me right into lazy picnics in Delilah's backyard, when we'd gorge on plump peas, sweet tomatoes, crisp cucumbers. The tender shrimp and tart buttermilk—all of this is our childhood on a plate.

I never wanted to look too closely at that time, but it's slapping me right in the face. Oddly, it doesn't hurt. Not this version. It feels fragile and rare, like I should be protecting it, like I should be proud of where we come from and who we are.

And then the menu changes on me. The servers bring out what Delilah says is butter-poached cod with potato galette and shellfish emulsion dotted with petals of mango and peach. It is the clean taste of the sea; it is buttery velvet along my tongue, bright bursts of juicy fruit. Underneath it all is a crisp, airy version of what is essentially a gourmet tater tot.

The taste is erotic. Heat and lust wash over me in a wave that has my balls clenching and my cock stiffening. I can't figure out why. Then it hits me like a kick to the chest. This dish is us. Frantic kissing on the beach, eating juicy mangos at the market, peaches and tater tots. She's created us. A compilation of all she holds dear.

A laugh bursts out of me, and everyone glances my way.

North looks at me like I'm nuts. Delilah quirks a brow but doesn't say a word. I have no idea what was said while I was lost in her food. Hell.

"Sorry. Spontaneous laughter." I clear my throat, feeling like a grade A ass. "I do that when I'm enjoying my food."

The silence is deafening. Ronan smothers a laugh with a cough. Delilah's eyes narrow just the tiniest bit. I stare back, all innocence. But in my head, I'm thinking about what she's done. And all that lust and need rise up again, hard, needy, but tempered with something I don't want to name just yet. But it is real, and it's demanding.

I don't know what she sees in my eyes, but she shakes her head and laughs lightly. "I'll take that as a compliment."

"You should." I want to kiss her. Right here. Pull her onto the table and taste her mouth, tell her everything. "This is the best meal of my life."

North glances away as though he's fighting not to laugh at me too. But Ronan, who I'm liking more and more, sits back and nods. "I have to agree with Macon. I am honestly stunned here. This menu isn't pretentious or showy, but that's the point. I'm not trying to figure out what I'm eating but simply enjoying every bite and wondering how it is that I never realized how good these simple ingredients were."

She blushes prettily. For him. "Thank you. There's dessert."

With that, they bring out individual pies. Banana cream pie with bitter chocolate. I manage one bite of what is the best pie I've ever had, all lush cream and sweetness, a bite of Delilah incarnate, the intense, hot richness of the chocolate pushing its way almost rudely into all that, just like I did. Sex and salvation on a plate. I can't take it anymore.

My fork hits the plate with a clatter, my breath unsteady. Blood rushes through my ears, and I push back from the table. "Excuse us for a moment." I take hold of Delilah's hand and pull her up with me. "We'll be right back."

Then I get us the hell out of the room before I make a greater fool of myself.

CHAPTER
TWENTY-NINE

Delilah

"Macon," I hiss as soon as we're out of the dining room. "What in the great hell is wrong with you?"

He's been acting strange the entire meal, unfocused and not saying a damn word to anyone. Frankly, it has pissed me off and hurt in ways I wasn't prepared for.

He doesn't answer but tugs me along with brisk steps, forcing me to clatter after him in my high heels. I follow willingly because I'm not about to make a scene. Too bad he's already done that. Another burst of rage hits hot as fire. How dare he act like this now of all times? It was the ultimate bait and switch.

"Are you high?" It's a struggle to keep my voice down. "Seriously, did you take some sort of drug before dinner?"

He stops and backs me into the shadowed alcove at the end of the hall stairs. "I know I'm out of line. I . . ." He runs a hand through his hair hard enough for the dark ends to stick up wildly. "I had to talk . . . I couldn't sit there anymore and not say something . . . fuck."

I realize what a good actor Macon can be. Until now he's appeared so placid, a cool lake with hardly a ripple of emotion showing. He isn't placid now. And he isn't cool and collected. He's weirdly unhinged.

"Okay," I say calmly because now he's freaking me out. "We're alone. Tell me what's wrong."

Macon's dark gaze searches my face. "That meal. You were telling the story of us."

My heart flips within my chest, and I suck in a breath, stunned into silence.

"It was us," he says. "Every bite. It was our childhood. It was you, me. Mangoes in the market, kissing on the beach, banana cream pie . . ." He steps closer, his chin lifting as though he's in for a fight. But there's so much heat and emotion in his eyes that my mouth goes dry. "Tell me I'm wrong."

"I hadn't thought . . ." I trail off, pressing my palm to my overwarm forehead. Yes, I was telling my story through the meal, but he's right; it was about Macon too. About us. Because he is part of my story. Always. My gaze collides with his. "You understood that? Just by tasting?"

His nostrils flare as he gives a short nod. "With every bite. You made me remember. You pulled me into those memories." Macon's head dips, his breath brushing against my lips. "You made me love it."

I don't know what to say. I'm exposed. Utterly. Both to him and to myself.

"Did you mean it?" he asks, peering down at me with tense eyes. "All that emotion you put into the food. Did you mean it?"

But he knows. He tasted it, after all. Good food is evocative. I unknowingly put my heart on my freaking sleeve, and I'm not certain how I feel about that. Being this open is new to me.

"Macon—"

His mouth is on mine, his hands tunneling into my hair. He goes all in, taking my mouth like he owns it. Devouring me just as thoroughly as any meal. And I let him. For all my fears, I feel it too, this desperate need, that maybe I won't get another chance to touch him.

And then it changes, becomes soft and melting. I melt right with it, falling into him. He makes me weak in my knees, in my heart. Maybe I do that to him as well, because he stumbles a bit, his back bumping into the wall, his hands still holding me close.

He pulls away to catch his breath. And I'm the one following, my hand on the column of his neck, my mouth seeking his. I need more. Another taste. The feel of him. With a groan, he dips his head, giving me what I need.

"You're killing me, Tot. I don't know whether I'm coming or going with you." Hot words against my skin. I swallow them down, lick them up. Savor him. And he lets me, pressing his body against mine as if he can't get close enough.

Because he can't. Somehow, it's never enough when it comes to us. There must always be *more*. Another touch. Another taste. Deeper, harder, longer. He is the rich sweet so long denied me. And I am his. I feel it in every touch that lingers, every breath that catches, the hot stroke of his tongue, the greedy movement of his lips along mine.

His grip on me tightens for a second, and then both of his hands slide up to cup my jaw. When he speaks, his voice is rough and earnest, his words flowing over my lips. "I adore you." Another hot, greedy kiss. "I fucking adore you, Delilah Baker. Every. Damn. Inch." Each word punctuated by mouth meeting mouth. "That's what I pulled you out here to say. Because I couldn't take another minute of you not knowing that."

Giddiness bubbles up within me, and I find myself laughing softly as I keep kissing him. "I adore you too, Macon Saint." Because I do. Every bit of him, even the dark corners where he fears to tread.

"Shit," he groans, spinning so I'm pressed to the wall. His thick thigh slips between mine and grinds against my sex. I whimper, and he does it harder, slower.

"Let's go upstairs." I'm panting now, my hands stealing under his shirt to find the hot, smooth skin of his waist.

From down the hall comes the sound of laughter. North says something, and there's another round of laughter. Macon pauses, our lips brushing with each ragged breath. "Fuck. We need to get back."

That I forgot where we are is disconcerting, and I nod but can't seem to make myself move. "Do we have to?" I'm swollen and slick. My breasts ache where they press into the hard wall of his chest.

Macon huffs out a sound that's close to a whimper. "It's your dinner party. Behave, because I'm holding on to a thread here."

With a regretful sigh, I push him away. "Then don't kiss me again. All rational thought flies from my brain when you kiss me."

His eyes crinkle. "That is not an incentive for me to stop kissing you."

"If you do, I'm taking you upstairs." I can't stop myself from tracing the swollen line of his lower lip. He nips my finger, and I yelp even though it doesn't hurt. "Evil man."

Macon laughs, more carefree than I've ever seen him. And it takes my breath. He takes my hand in his and tugs me back toward our guests. "When everyone leaves, I will be."

"Promises, promises." But I know he will deliver. So I follow him willingly, happiness flowing through my veins like sunshine. This is happiness. It's so pure and fragile I feel the need to treat it with the delicacy of soufflé, fearful that the slightest mishandling will deflate the whole thing.

When dinner is over and our guests are leaving, Ronan Kelly pulls me aside and says he'd like to work with me. "We can discuss terms, but you'd be head chef, full creative control with the menu. I'll be responsible for the capital and promotion."

"I have a place in mind," I tell him, trying to hold in the urge to jump around and squeal. I tell him about the location and my idea for it.

"We can go take a look next week," he promises.

And like that, my dreams are all falling into place. I've never been more terrified. Because when you truly want something, it will hurt that much more if it gets taken away.

CHAPTER THIRTY

Delilah

"I want to move." Delicately shaking, slickly sweating, I strain against Macon's bulk. It's no use; he has me pinned to the chair, his cock thick and pulsing deep inside. And not fucking moving.

He grins down at me, a drop of sweat trickling down the side of his flushed face. "Not yet."

Slowly, too damn slowly, he circles his hips, stretching me, making me ache.

"I need to come," I whisper. Whine. Plead. It's all the same. Every inch of me throbs. Pleasure is a tightly drawn bow within, and I need that snap of release.

His grin fades, replaced by intention. "You will. When I'm ready."

"Sadist."

He nips my earlobe. "You love it."

I shudder as that glorious dick of his eases out, making me feel every hard inch, only to slowly push back in. Too fucking slowly. I'm writhing on him, and he loves it. Dark eyes glint as he works me.

Naked in the sun and sprawled on an armchair that barely holds us, he's been fucking me with a steady deliberation designed to drive me out of my mind. And though I'm a pleading, panting mess, I love it too.

God, he's gorgeous. Endless muscle and tan skin beaded with sweat, flush from exertion. His expression is slack, hazy with lust. It sends licks of pleasure along my skin. Panting, I reach up and touch his jaw, trying to draw him near. He complies, dipping his head. Our mouths meet in a lazy, deep kiss, an exchange of air, messy exploration of lips and tongues.

He groans, shivering. Not unaffected. Just so very good at torturing me.

In. Out. Pull. Push.

"Macon," I whisper into his mouth. "Please. Fuck me."

He freezes, and then with another groan, all that power and need breaks free. I can only hold on as he goes hard and deep. The chair scrapes along the floor as he pounds into me. Every thrust impacts my swollen, sensitive sex. Pleasure builds and builds until I'm keening, my eyes closed as though I can somehow hang on to the feeling forever. But it breaks over me in a shimmering wave.

Macon's teeth clamp down on the meaty curve of my neck, not hard but holding me there as his thrusts turn rapid, a greedy chase of his own pleasure. It's so animalistic and unexpected that another orgasm slams into me with unexpected power.

I lose track of myself, of him. My fingers claw at his back, thread through his hair. I'm struggling to get closer, get more. He comes with a great shout, his big strong body straining against mine.

Light headed from release, I go limp with a sigh. Macon lies panting and replete on top of me, but he holds most of his weight on his knees. Our breaths slow, and he stirs enough to press a hot but weak kiss to my neck. "Delilah, I . . ."

The front door flings open, startling us both. North always knocks, and no one else knows the key code. Or so I thought. Until I hear a voice that I know as well as my own. Cold shock and disbelief slam into me as it rings out.

"Helloooo? Saint, babe, you home—oh my God!"

Sam's cry is shrill, horrified, and enough to have Macon and me snapping out of our frozen surprise. I scramble to get up, but I have two hundred pounds of muscled man on me. Macon snarls a curse and reaches for a throw to cover me, even as he's turning to glare over his shoulder at a gaping Sam.

"Get the hell out," he practically shouts.

She doesn't move. Tanned and styled as though she's just come from the salon, my sister stands in the living room entryway, glaring as if this is her house, and I'm some interloper she's found with her man.

"What the hell? You're fucking Delilah?" she shouts at Macon. "Are you serious?"

Given that he's still half on me, blocking my body with his, I feel the surge of anger that punches through Macon. Naked, he rises in one swift move and turns on Sam as I frantically wrap the throw around me.

"Get out." He points to the door. "Now!"

The intensity of his shout makes both Sam and me jump. She blanches, but her gaze travels south, and her lips part.

Oh, hell no.

I finally find my feet and step in front of Macon. I'm not tall enough to cover all of him, but the essential bits are blocked. Sam gaping at Macon's nakedness has made me surprisingly territorial. I have to bite back a snarl of "Mine!"

Macon's hand comes down on my shoulder. For a second, I fear he might tug me behind him, but he gives me a quick comforting squeeze instead.

Sam's eyes narrow in on the gesture, and her lips purse in a tight line of hot-pink gloss. "You're together now?" The shock and disgust at the prospect rings loud and clear.

Macon makes a noise, his hand on my shoulder twitching, and I know he's about to blow again.

"Sam," I say before he can talk. "Focus. You've just walked into Macon's house without invitation. He's asked you to leave."

I swear to all the cooking gods, now she shows up? Now? And like this? I expected a call of warning. A "Hey, I'm back!" text. Not for her to waltz into Macon's house as though she owns it.

Her blonde brow wings up. "Leave? When he's been calling and texting me to come back to him for weeks?" She snorts in amusement. "I'm not leaving."

Behind me, Macon curses. "Did we enter the twilight zone? Tell me this is the fucking twilight zone, because I swear to God that is the only explanation for your utter batshit behavior, Sam."

Sam flushes red, and I know a shouting match is imminent.

"Sam," I say calmly, even though I'm anything but. "Go into the kitchen, and make yourself some coffee. Now."

I use the tone Mama does when she's about to lay down the law. And it works. Sam gives me and Macon one long look of loathing but then lifts her chin and saunters toward the kitchen.

My heart is going like a metronome, slamming too fast against my ribs. I shouldn't be surprised she's here. I asked her to return. But the reality of it and seeing her outraged face when she realized I was with Macon has rattled me so much I've gone oddly numb.

With a sigh, I turn to Macon. Dull red paints his cheeks, and he looks about a second away from blowing. But when I place my palm to his chest, he glances down at me with eyes that are a little lost and worried.

"I didn't ask her to come back," he says. "I texted that I wasn't going to look for her anymore."

"What? When?"

He runs a hand through his damp hair. "Right before dinner with Ronan. I wanted this *thing* with Sam and us to be over. For us to move on." Trepidation darkens his gaze. "I was going to tell you, but I got distracted."

Since I know exactly how he got distracted, I can't exactly blame him. I stroke his sweat-slicked chest, now cool in the open air. "I want that too. Let's get dressed and deal with this."

I'm not looking forward to it at all.

Our clothes are upstairs. We were slowly screwing our way around the house all day—all week, really. Reveling in each other, learning what turns the other on, shutting the world out. Every second of it, I fell deeper, needed him more.

Sam's return feels like a blade slicing through all that. Inside I'm shaking. If Macon's expression is anything to go by, he's just as unsettled. With a short nod and a long glare in the direction of the kitchen, he gently puts his hand on the small of my back and guides me upstairs.

"I can't believe she's back," he grumps, stomping along as if to show his ire.

"I can't believe she has the house code," I mutter. It's nonsensical that I even care, but I'm not thinking clearly. All I can think is that my sister is back, and like a virus she's going to infect everything.

"I didn't think to change it," Macon says, scowling. "It never crossed my mind that she'd have the nerve to waltz into my house. Hell, I thought there was a good chance she'd never come back."

Dread swells up within. I knew she'd return. I knew for a while and didn't tell him. Shit. I need to, but that conversation is too complicated to have with Sam hanging out downstairs. And I'm a chicken. A complete and utter chicken.

"Well, she has." It's all I can say.

"Fucking Sam" is all Macon can say.

Despite the fact that my long-lost scheming, thieving sister has returned and is currently in the kitchen, Macon insists on leading us into the shower. He stays silent as he carefully washes me and then himself. His dark gaze is a mixture of anxiety and anger. I empathize. It's as though we've been pulled out of a dream and don't know what to do with reality.

Clean and dressed, we descend the stairs together, marching along as though gearing up to face a firing squad.

Sam is curled up on the kitchen banquette, a glass of sweet tea in her hand. "Your handiwork, I'm guessing," she says by way of greeting. Glaring at me from over the glass, she takes a slow sip. "Not as good as Mama's, but it will do."

I roll my eyes. If she's going to try to insult me, she'll have to try harder than that. "I'm wounded. Truly."

Macon crosses his arms over his chest. "Cut the shit, Sam, and explain yourself."

The glass lands on the table with a clink. "You're not my man, and you're certainly not my daddy. So don't talk to me as if you are."

He doesn't blink. "You told fucking stalkers where I'd be. And while I sat there in a hospital in part because of *your* actions, you riffled through my stuff, stole my mother's watch, then cut and ran."

Silence rings out. Because what can she say to all that? Not a thing, and we all know it.

Macon's nostrils flare as he stares her down. "Yeah, I'll speak to you however the hell I want."

Sam laughs, a light trill that works like nails on my skin. "I didn't steal it. I was only borrowing the damn thing." The silver bangles on her slim wrist chime as she reaches over and opens her purse to root around in it.

The diamond watch glitters in the sun as she holds it aloft. "See? All better."

Macon's snort is eloquent, but he doesn't move to take it. He merely stares her down as she sets it carefully on the table, then gives him an innocent smile.

"Where have you been, Sam?" My voice is thick and unsteady. I'm so ashamed of her right now I can barely stand being in the room.

"Here and there." She takes another sip of tea. "I had some things I needed to take care of."

"Like pawning my mother's watch?" Macon supplies.

"You see it here, don't you?"

"I'm guessing you had a harder time getting rid of it than you expected," he deadpans.

Sam flicks a lock of golden hair over her shoulder but doesn't answer.

Pinching the bridge of my nose, I pull in my temper. "Enough. Samantha, Macon's right. Cut the shit. I don't know why you're acting like this, but it isn't funny. I expected you to return and apologize, not antagonize him. God, do you have any remorse?"

All pretense of casual, carefree Sam melts away, and she surges to her feet. "You got some nerve, Dee."

"What?" Macon and I both say at the same time with different levels of outrage.

She ignores him. "Acting all high and mighty when you're fucking my boyfriend."

"Your boyfriend?" Macon repeats, incredulous.

But I know exactly what she means. She zeroes in on me. "He was mine. For years! My first man. Mine. That makes him off limits."

"I don't believe this," Macon says, cutting in. "What are you, thirteen? We've been ancient history for a decade."

"Shut up," Sam says, not looking his way. She only has eyes for me. "You're my sister," she cries, tearing up. "My best friend. And you had to go there? With him? I get that he's hot and famous, but you are way out of your depth here, Dee."

A flutter of guilt tickles my conscience because there is a sister code. I've broken it. But I shove that guilt away. On the surface, I am guilty, true. And if it had been any other man, I'd feel ashamed. But our tangled history with Macon makes it more complicated.

"First off, he's not a toy. Shouting 'mine' doesn't make it so. And I've had it with the insults. You want to be upset about this, fine. I can't tell you how to feel, but I can tell you to watch your mouth. You don't get to make me feel like shit anymore."

Sam's eyes narrow to slits. "If the truth hurts, Dee, that's on you."

At my side, Macon makes an aggravated movement like he's going to say something. I touch his wrist, and he stills, holding his tongue.

"It's not just sex. It's serious."

She snorts. "Which only makes it worse. I've told you time and again not to believe a word he says. He's an actor." Finally, she looks at Macon. "And you. What bullshit are you filling her head with?"

Macon cocks his head, his brows lifting high. "Bullshit? What the hell?"

"Sam," I cut in. "You're totally out of line here."

"See? He's trying to turn you against me," Sam says with an air of hysteria.

I swear Macon is going to burst out of his skin. My hand finds his and holds on.

"Macon's right. We aren't kids anymore. We've made our peace and moved on. Perhaps you should too. The only anger he's displayed toward you is entirely justifiable."

She makes a stubborn face and won't meet my gaze.

"Now you show up with this self-righteous territorial act when you should be offering up apologies. To me as well."

At this Sam straightens. "I knew it. What's he been saying? I suppose he told you about prom—"

"Sam," Macon snaps, so fast and angry that I jump.

He's gone pale, his jaw bunching.

Sam ignores him. "He did, didn't he?"

"Prom?" I parrot, my gaze darting between them.

"Sam." Macon takes a step in her direction. "I mean it. Shut. Up."

"That's how he got you to forgive him, isn't it?" She laughs, short and unhinged. "He told you."

"Sam!" Macon's voice carries a hint of desperation.

I hold up a hand. "No, let her talk."

She's tearing up again; Sam always did cry quickly. "Okay, fine. I did it. I thought it would be funny. It was just a stupid joke, a mistake. But he"—she points at Macon—"promised he'd never tell. He lied."

A joke? And then it hits me. The prom. Tater tots in trays. The mocking laughter. Sam staring at me as though she'd seen a ghost. And Macon standing there looking furious, looking horrified. I thought it was guilt. I called him worthless.

It was the final straw in our crumbling relationship and cemented the hate I felt for him.

A joke.

And it was Sam's doing. My sister. Oh, how she cried that night. She told me how sorry she was. I thought she'd meant for Macon's bad deed. But it was her. I've spent my entire life protecting her in any small way I could, and she did that?

Blood rushes from my head and pools at my feet. Dimly, I hear Macon swear. My ears are ringing. Sam stares at me with tears in her eyes and a hopeful expression on her face.

For the first time in my life, I act without thinking. My hand snaps out and connects with Sam's cheek. The slap echoes in the kitchen. My palm tingles as I turn and walk away.

———

Macon

Delilah walks out of the kitchen with quiet dignity, leaving me alone with Sam.

"You selfish little fool. You had to tell her, didn't you?" I want to go to Delilah so badly my heart hurts, but I know my girl needs her space for a moment. Sam needs to be dealt with.

Sam stares in the direction Delilah took, holding a hand to her reddened cheek as though she can't believe Delilah actually slapped her. "You didn't tell her?"

"Why would I? I kept it secret all these years." Something that I hated doing. Especially when I started to fall for Delilah. The truth sat like a brittle stone under my ribs every time Delilah mentioned the incident. "Do you honestly think I agreed to take the fall for your stunt all because I was trying to protect *you*? I did it for her. Because I knew, even back then, that it would devastate Delilah if she learned her own sister humiliated her as a cruel joke."

Sam blanches. "I didn't mean to hurt her."

"Bull. You did it because you were jealous." I'm beginning to think Sam always was. That the only reason she held on to me so tightly when we were children was because she knew it hurt Delilah.

"Why are you here?" I ask Sam when she says nothing. "Why now? And don't give me that shit about borrowing the watch. You knew I was looking for you and wanted it back. So why now?"

Sam lifts her chin in defiance. "I saw a picture of you two at that gala. You had a look on your face. I know that look. You were either screwing her or wanted to."

She isn't wrong there. I had wanted to.

"And so you had to return and ruin any chance of happiness she might have?" I shake my head in disappointment.

Sam's gray eyes ice over. "Despite what you think, Saint, I do love my sister. You never liked her. Hell, you two hated each other. I'm supposed to believe you're what, suddenly in love?"

"You know what I think? You couldn't stand the idea of Delilah and I together. Why is that? And don't give me any crap about being attached to me. We've been over for years."

"You were still my boyfriend. Sisters do not poach old flames."

"Oh, bullshit. You simply hate the idea that Delilah and I might be happy." When she looks away and lifts her chin in defiance, I push on.

"What did you say to her? That I was yours?" I snort in disgust. "Here's a bit of news. I was never yours."

Sam flinches. It's slight, but I see it, and regret pings in my chest.

"Be cruel if you want," she says, flipping her hair in a move I know is self-protective. "I don't care anymore. But don't pretend that we were nothing. We were together practically our whole childhood. No matter how much you deny it, you can't erase that."

The fight goes out of me with a sigh. I feel battered, and the greater half of me is still pulling toward Delilah, wanting to comfort her. Just hold her. Leaning against the counter, I regard the woman who was my partner in pettiness for years.

She's right. We have a history. And not all of it was bad. There were times when we had fun, when she was the only person I could turn to. I both cared for her and loathed her. For better or worse, she was part of me for a long time.

"I don't want to erase it because it's part of my history. You were a friend when I didn't have any. In all honesty, hanging out with you probably saved my life in more ways than one."

Sam's look of surprise is tentative but pleased.

I hold her gaze with my own. "But we brought out an ugliness in each other that was unhealthy and petty. And any nostalgic fondness died when you sold me out, stole the watch, and went into hiding."

To her credit, she flinches. "I'm sorry about that. Truly. I know it was horrible. But I didn't think that woman would hurt you. I thought she was a reporter. Okay, yes, it was stupid. And the watch . . . I was desperate." For a moment, she appears frightened before she retreats under her mask. "But I brought it back. Doesn't that count for something?"

The watch lying on the table sparkles in the sun like a living thing. Seeing it brings a familiar pang of longing for my mother, but it's muted now, a ghost of feeling whispering along my heart. I'm happy to have the watch back, but now that it's returned, I know that it was never about the watch. Not when it came to Delilah.

I'd have just as happily never seen it again if it meant I could keep Delilah in my life.

"Do you know why Delilah got in touch with me?" I ask Sam.

She hesitates for a beat, but then her nose wrinkles, and I know it's out of annoyance. "I got her texts. I know she was smoothing things over for me."

Anger pulls tight along my neck and shoulders. "She was working off your debt, Sam."

"I know." She sighs. "She shouldn't have done that."

If she wasn't a woman and ten times weaker than me, I'd be tempted to wring her neck. As it is, I can barely look at her. "A year's worth of work instead of touring Asia like she'd planned. All so that I wouldn't call the police to report your crime, and your mother could rest easy. And you knew?"

She shakes her head like I'm slow, and she's trying really hard to be patient with me. "Saint, you and I both know you wouldn't have called the police."

The urge to shout pushes at my skin. "Do we?"

"Once Delilah told you about Mama's health and how me being arrested might affect her health, you wouldn't have risked it."

I fucking hate that she's right. When it came down to the wire, I wouldn't have been able to go through with it. The fact that Sam understood this about me before I did really irks. I snort without humor. "You are some piece of work. Delilah has always covered for you, protected you, and in return you shit on her every chance you get. If that's what you call love, you might want to rethink your priorities."

Having nothing more to say, I go to find the woman who taught me what love truly means.

CHAPTER THIRTY-ONE

Macon

Delilah is huddled on her bed. As soon as I walk in, she lifts her head. There are tears in her eyes. I've never seen her cry. It rips into my heart.

"Honey . . ." Crawling onto the bed, I gather her in my arms, half-afraid she'll slap me away. But she doesn't.

With a sob, she curls into me and burrows her face into the crook of my neck. I hold her close, rocking us and murmuring nonsense words into her hair.

"I can't believe it," she says, her voice muffled on my skin. "How could she do that?"

"I don't know." I kiss her head, stroke her back. "I'm sorry. For everything."

"That bitch made me cry," she sobs. "I never cry."

"I know, baby. I know."

Delilah cries harder, and it isn't pretty. It wracks her body and wets the side of my neck. All I can do is cuddle her and wait it out. When she settles, I reach over and grab a tissue.

"Blow."

She obliges, and I use another tissue to wipe her tears. Delilah sits back, leaning on the headboard. Her face is red and swollen. And I love her. I don't know when it truly hit me, but I feel it now with every breath I take. I want to tell her, but it isn't the time. Truth is, I don't know what to do to make it better.

Delilah crumples her tissue and tosses it aside. "All this time, it was Sam who did that stupid prank." Red-rimmed eyes meet mine. "You never said a word. Never defended yourself."

"To what purpose? You hated me and loved Sam. It was better for everyone if you kept on assuming it was me."

She huffs, her blunt nose wrinkling. "You hated me. By all accounts, you could have easily torn me apart by telling on Sam."

Wincing, I take her hand. It lies limp in my grip. "I never truly hated you, Delilah. That night, you walked in wearing that killer dress, and it occurred to me that I'd been an utter fool when it came to you. I wanted to say something that night. Call a truce, apologize, something. But then those fucking tater tots showed up, and it was too late."

Her pink lips wobble, and she shakes her head. "You know what's strange? When I saw you that night, it finally hit me that we were both outsiders there."

Because Delilah is the only one who ever truly saw me for me. I don't want to lose that. I hold her hand a little tighter. "It wasn't our time yet."

Biting her lip, she ducks her head. "Would you have ever told me?"

"Delilah, I'd have taken it to my grave if it meant sparing you pain. The fact that you were able to forgive me despite thinking I'd done that to you was a rare gift. How could I selfishly hurt you just so I could look better in your eyes?"

"Instead I was left thinking my sister was someone I could trust."

My throat clogs, and I clear it. "I'm sorry. I thought I was protecting you."

She laughs bitterly. "And I thought I was protecting Mama and Sam. You called me a martyr for it."

Shit. "I was wrong. Stupid."

Her lips twist in a sad smirk. "You always got so pissed when I tried to defend Sam. You said she wasn't worth it. Now I know why."

My fingers curl into the comforter by her hip. "You weren't wrong to try."

Delilah blows a raspberry and then tilts her head back to blink up at the ceiling. Tears trail down her cheeks. "I was a fool. And you know it."

"There's nothing wrong with trying to help the people you love. That's what I know now."

It's all but a confession, but Delilah doesn't seem to hear it. She's scowling at the door. "I hit her."

"Pretty soundly," I agree. Is it wrong that I silently cheered her? Probably. But I couldn't help feeling proud of her for standing up to Sam.

"I want to hit her again."

She sounds so fierce I have to smile. As if she can't contain her fury, she rises and starts to pace.

"And when she called me . . . not only did she convince me to keep quiet, she infected our relationship again, feeding me doubts, telling me that you were just manipulating me, that you'd always hated me."

Alarm bells begin to clang. I find myself standing too. "What do you mean when she called you?"

Delilah halts and pales, her eyes going wide. For the first time in our lives, she actually looks guilty. She licks her lips quickly. "She called me."

"When?" My ears are beginning to ring. I'm not sure what I'm feeling, but it isn't good.

Her gaze slides away, and she grips the bottom of her shirt. "Before the letters."

Icy-hot prickles explode over my skin as though she slapped me. "All this time we've been together, you've been in contact with Sam?"

My damn heart hurts. I thought we were a unit when it came to the wrongness of what Sam did. And she kept this from me?

Delilah puffs out a breath but then rallies. "It was one phone call."

"One call is enough." I run a shaking hand through my hair and grip the ends. "Jesus. Here I am feeling like a heel because I didn't tell you about Sam's prank. And you talked to her while you were with me? I don't like being lied to either."

"I'm sorry." It's a thin whisper. Because she knows she's in the wrong.

"Why?" I snap. "Why would you keep this from me? After all she'd done?"

"Sam begged me not to—"

"Yeah, I just bet she did." I take a hard step toward her but stop, unable to close the distance. "Did it occur to you that I'd want to know she'd called?"

"It did . . ." She bites her lip. "She said she wouldn't come back if I told you. So I held my tongue. I'm sorry, Macon."

The fact that she's not fighting me ticks me off. I want that spark, a better explanation. I want to be told I'm getting this all wrong, that she didn't put Sam before me. She's known since the letters. A thought hits me, and I rock back on my heels. My skin feels cold as I force the words out.

"When I found you in the kitchen . . ." I swallow thickly, anger rising. "And you tried to pull away from us because you couldn't get past how I'd treated you when we were kids . . ." She winces, not meeting my eyes. "It was because of Sam, wasn't it? What did you say just now? That she made you think I was manipulating you?"

Her eyes squeeze shut for a second. When she opens them, they are overbright and pained. "Yes. It was because of Sam. She played on my insecurities."

I nod, quick and hard. "Right. And instead of talking to me about it and telling me what really happened, you tried to pull away."

It hurts. In ways I wasn't prepared for. I can handle Delilah not telling me about Sam if she thought it would get the brat to return. But this? I rub a hand over my chest.

Her lower lip trembles, but she presses them together before answering. "I'm not perfect. Some things are so ingrained it's hard to break free of them. When Sam said—"

"Sam," I sneer. "Always fucking Sam. She shits all over you, and you still let her lead you around. When are you going to learn?"

Delilah's eyes flash. "You just told me it wasn't wrong to try helping the people you love."

"That's when I thought you were talking about protecting your mother. Not this . . . bullshit. What about me, Delilah? I laid myself open, showed you every dark corner I had. I trusted you with all of me." *With my damn heart.* "And you didn't trust me enough to tell the truth about why you had doubts."

"I'm sorry, Macon." She visibly deflates. And it pisses me off that I want to hug her. I'm too angry right now. I feel like the damn rug has been pulled out from under my feet. How can she understand me so well and not get this?

"When we were kids, all I had was my pride," I say tightly. "I thought protecting my pride was the most important thing in the world. But I grew up and realized that trust meant more. I let you in because I thought I had that—"

"Macon . . ."

"If we can't trust each other with the worst parts of ourselves, what's the point?" I throw my arms wide.

"I do trust you. Aside from Sam, I have never lied to you."

"Unfortunately, that's the lie I'm stuck on."

We stare at each other in silence. And I wait for her to tell me something to make it better. That she loves me, that I won't have to wonder if she'll always put Sam over me. Something.

She doesn't speak. For once in our relationship, she's silent.

I let out a long breath. "This is getting us nowhere. I need to clear my head. I can't do that with you around."

I might as well have slapped her. She visibly recoils. But then she pulls her shoulders back. "All right. I'll just get my things. I can stay with my mother."

Get her things? "You're leaving?"

A little wrinkle forms between her brows. "You said you need space. I'm giving it to you. What did you expect me to do?"

I expected her to leave me alone for a while until I calmed down, not move out. I expected her to fight, not walk away. To pick me—us.

"Besides," she says, walking toward the bedroom door. "There are things that I need to discuss with my sister."

I see red. Admittedly, Sam has become a trigger for me. "You're going with *her*?"

Delilah pauses long enough to catch sight of my expression. "I just found out that my sister was responsible for the worst humiliation of my life. I've hated you for years for something you didn't do. I lied for her and caused you pain. You want space. Yes, Macon, I'm going to talk to my sister."

It's a sucker punch to the gut. "So go, then."

She's looking through me the way she used to, like I'm nothing other than a painful reminder of things best left in the past. Like I'm the enemy. I hate that look. My temper snaps. "What are you waiting for? Go!"

Delilah's chin lifts, and that spark I've been waiting for lights in her eyes. But I see the pain there too. When she speaks, her voice is stiff. "I never wanted to hurt you. I know I lied, but it was only—"

"One more lie between us?"

Delilah blinks once before answering. "Yeah. I guess it was."

She leaves then. And that hurts most of all.

———

Delilah

Everything is crumbling beneath my feet. Sam's confession has taken a jackhammer to my solid foundation. But the fight with Macon was worse. Inside, I'm shaking.

We both lied. We both let each other down in our own ways.

A lie is still a lie. We were supposed to be pushing past all that, starting anew with everything laid out on the table. Yet I kept Sam's call a secret. And he planned to keep the knowledge of the prank secret forever if he had his way.

The thought of him and Sam sharing this knowledge of my worst humiliation turns my stomach. I know he feels much the same about me keeping Sam's call from him.

He's right. If we can't fully trust each other, what's the point?

Tears blur my vision. He kicked me out. That hurt most of all. I'd gotten out of his room as fast as I could so he wouldn't see me fall apart.

Sam isn't in the house. I have no idea where she's gone, and if I'm honest, part of me doesn't care. I told Macon I wanted to talk to my sister—something I know pisses him off—but I'm so disgusted in her, in myself, I don't know what I'd do right now.

I head to my mother's because short of a hotel, I don't have anywhere else to go. A sob breaks free as soon as I leave Macon's property. It's become my home. I know he's angry and wants his space, but leaving him behind feels like a betrayal. Part of me wants to turn around and tell him, "Fuck no, I'm not going anywhere." But I hurt him, and if he wants space, I'll give it to him.

My mother takes me in without question, though I know she can tell I've been crying. Quietly, she hand washes the dishes, affording me a moment of privacy.

I sit at my customary spot at the table, feeling all of twelve years old. I'm half-tempted to ask for peanut butter cookies. But it's soothing here as well, with the familiar sounds of my mother cleaning and the faint scent of lemon Pledge rising from the oak table.

"Well," I say with a wobble in my voice. "Here I am again."

"Now then," she says, setting down the dishrag. "What's this all about?"

"Macon . . ." It's all I can get out before losing it.

When tears well up in my eyes, she gasps and sits by my side to grab my hand with her cool one. "Did he hurt you?" She asks it mildly, but there's a promise in her voice that tells me that she will, in fact, tan Macon's hide if he did.

My smile is wobbly and brief. "No. Not at all. He's been . . ." A revelation. "Wonderful. We started up, and it was wonderful. Perfect. And then Sam showed up."

One silvery-blonde brow lifts delicately. "Sam? Has she finally returned, then? What has that girl gotten herself into this time?"

"Oh, Mama . . ." I press my hands against my hot face. "Everything."

My confession comes in a great purge of words, quickly spilled so I don't have to feel the full impact of them. I tell her everything, starting with the texts and ending with Sam showing up at Macon's house. I keep out the details of exactly how she found Macon and me, but I don't hide my culpability.

When I'm finished, I drop my hands from my eyes and face my mother.

"Well, fuck," she says. I choke out a laugh, and she quirks a brow. "Some things need cursing. And this is one."

"You're right about that." I let out a shuddery breath and attempt to rein in my tears. I'm a damn leaky faucet now. A lifetime of not crying undone in a single night. "Macon was so hurt that I didn't tell him about Sam calling. And he's pissed that I always try to cover for her."

Mama rests her hand on mine. "Delilah, honey, he has a point. Why did you offer to work off her debt? You didn't have to do that."

"He said he'd call the police. If she went to jail . . . your heart . . ."

Her face darkens, thunderclouds gathering in her eyes. "Delilah Ann, are you telling me you thought I am so delicate that I cannot handle my own daughter's bad behavior?"

"Yes?"

That silver brow wings up again. This time it's a warning.

My shoulders sag. "I was afraid. I don't want to lose you or see you upset."

"Honey." Her hand returns to mine. "What's this really about? Why do you really feel this need to protect us?"

"You and Daddy chose me. You didn't have to, but you did." Tears well up again. "How can I not pay you back by trying my best to protect our family?"

"Pay me back . . . ," she repeats faintly before hot color rises to her cheeks, and she hauls me close, her thin arms wrapping around me like steel bands. "Baby girl. No, no. Tell me you don't believe that."

I'm sobbing now, a complete mess. My words come out hot and muffled against her shoulder. "I was such an awkward kid, a real mess most of the time. I wanted you to be proud . . ."

"I *am* proud." She grasps my shoulders and pulls me back to look in my eyes. Hers are filled with tears. "Hear me well, Delilah Ann. You chose *us*. I fully believe that. And the second I set eyes on you, you were my daughter in every way."

"Mama . . ."

She gives me a little shake. "In every way. Do you hear?"

"Yes." I rub at my leaking eyes, feeling drained.

Mama grabs a napkin and hands it to me, but she doesn't let me go. She tucks me against her side and rocks me like she did when I was a girl. "You have a protective streak a mile wide, baby. You always have. There's nothing wrong with that. But don't let Sam take advantage of your loving nature. She won't learn anything that way. Frankly, she's too manipulative by far."

"Mama, she's your daughter."

She shrugs. "I love my girls, but I see you both clearly, faults and all."

"She had a fit when she found out Macon and I were together."

"Do you care?"

I pull away from my mother and sit up, wiping my cheeks. A small defiant smile tickles my lips. "No, not really."

"Good. And she'll get over it." Mama gives my arms a quick squeeze. "She'll have to because I have the suspicion neither you or Macon will get over each other."

I suck in a breath and stare down at the table. "He told me to go. Said he needed to clear his head."

When my mother speaks, her voice is soft and hesitant. "Do you love him?"

Love. My heart gives a great big thump. I have avoided love all of my life. Logically, I shouldn't have. I knew what a happy relationship looked like; my parents' marriage was ideal. And yet whenever I thought of falling in love, I'd feel slightly ill and unsettled. Love is risk. For me, opening myself up to certain risks meant opening myself up to pain.

"You don't have to tell me how you feel about Macon. You have to tell *him*. You fight for everyone you love. Maybe it's time to show Macon that you'll fight for him too."

Fight for Macon. I hadn't thought about our relationship in those terms. Is that what he wanted from me? I remember the look in his eyes when I said I was going. He was shocked. Disappointed, even.

I settle down in the guest bed for the night, and the ache in my heart grows so wide and deep I can barely breathe through it. One thing is certain; Mama was right when she said I'd never get over Macon.

CHAPTER THIRTY-TWO

Macon

The light of the screen flickers over the dark media room. I stare at the footage playing with unseeing eyes. I only came in here to get away. The door opens, spilling light into the darkness. My chest clenches tight, expecting to see Delilah, but disappointment quickly follows as North steps into the room.

"What are you doing?" he asks, taking a seat next to me.

"Watching a movie. Obviously."

"Seems to me like you're brooding."

I snort without enthusiasm. "How'd you guess?"

"You always come in here to brood." He grins when I give him the finger. "Is this a southern thing?"

Rolling my head to the side, I meet his gaze. "Yes. We southern gents brood in dark theaters when the mood so strikes us. Later, I shall be performing all my favorite Tennessee Williams monologues."

North smirks. "Fucking lit majors."

With a grunt, I roll my head back to face the screen. We fall silent. That is, until North ruins it by talking again.

"*About a Boy*? I expected you to be watching some film noir."

"I like this movie." It reminds me of Delilah. Shit. I all but kicked her out of my house. At least that's how she took it. Is it any wonder she fled?

I need to talk to her. I need . . . her.

His mouth opens; then he closes it. "Right."

"I'm in love with Delilah." My confession, blurted out, sounds overloud and makes me wince. I didn't mean to say that, but now that I have, I feel worse. Because if this is love, it isn't the fluffy-clouds, walking-on-air shit they claim it to be. And North is here to witness my misery. Hell. Confiding in people is overrated.

North snorts and shakes his head as though I'm being ridiculous. Truthfully, I feel a bit ridiculous at the moment.

"I'm pretty sure everyone who sees you two together knows that," he says. "I knew you were a goner the second you agreed to her crazy deal."

"I'm that obvious?"

"Don't look so horrified," he says. "I don't think it's obvious to Delilah. And clearly you were blind to it."

"Not anymore."

His blond brow wings up. "You told her?"

"No." I pinch the aching space between my eyes. "I was going to. But then Sam showed up, and it all went to hell." Briefly, I explain, the words just as bitter on the tongue as they were when Delilah and I fought.

"Shit," he says when I finish.

"Pretty much."

He rolls his shoulders, then sits back. "So now what?"

The question is a leaden weight on my chest. "I don't know. Hell, I don't know what I'm doing. I've never . . . fallen."

361

I glance his way, but he shakes his head and chokes out a short laugh. "Don't look at me. I'm the last person who could give you good advice about women."

He frowns at the screen like it's his job.

"You fall for Sam?"

I regret asking because he flinches, his entire body recoiling like he's taken a punch to the gut. But he shrugs lightly. "Fell far enough for it to hurt when I landed. But love?" He looks like he's tasting something foul. "It was never love with Sam. Just . . . blindly stupid. It quickly became clear she was using me as a distraction and a way to fuck you over."

"I was afraid of that," I murmur.

The couch creaks as he turns my way. "You aren't pissed?"

"Yeah, I'm pissed." I glare at the screen. "She shit all over you."

A protracted noise from North has me looking his way. He stares back as though he doesn't understand. "I meant pissed at me," he says.

"Why would I be pissed at you?"

"Because Sam was your high school girlfriend. Hell, Saint, you warned me off her."

"I warned you off her because I knew how she operates and didn't want you getting caught up in her antics."

"You warned me off Delilah too."

My laugh is short and flat. "We both know I did that out of petty jealousy."

"You said it, not me."

We're both quiet for a moment before North speaks again. "I actually came in here for a reason."

"Aside from all this awkward-ass talk of our feelings and women who stomp on them?"

He laughs. "Not that this hasn't been fun." He sobers. "Lisa Brown is dead."

Blood rushes from my head so quickly my hands prickle. Lisa Brown. The woman who ran me off the road and took pictures of the aftermath. In the darkest shadows of my heart, I can admit that she scared the hell out of me. "How?"

"I don't know if you'd call it irony, but she was struck by a car crossing Sunset last week. I only just heard from Martin about it today."

My breath expels with an audible whoosh. She's dead.

The numbness crawls along my fingers, and I flex my hand. "And Michelle Fredericks?" The friend who was with her. "What's going on with her?"

"From what Martin has gathered, Fredericks is heading back to her hometown in Arizona. Apparently that was in the works for a couple of months."

It's over. I close my eyes and take a couple of deep breaths. When I can talk, my words come out in a rasp. "I'm a horrible person, North."

"Why?"

I can't look at him. "Because I'm relieved. A woman is dead, and my first emotion is relief."

"You're human, Saint. She stalked you. You were physically injured. A lot of stalkers never give up. Of course you're going to feel relief when that threat is gone."

"Because she's dead."

North nudges my arm with a fist. His expression is resolute. "I was relieved, too, okay? Not because I wanted her dead. But because it was over. Don't feel guilty for being human, man."

Dully, I nod. I'm tired. All I want to do is curl up around Delilah and sleep. But she's gone. When faced with the notion of actual death, my jealousy and hurt pride becomes meaningless. She made a mistake. I've made far worse ones when it comes to Delilah, and she's forgiven me at every turn.

"Shit," I mutter, resting my face in my palms. "I shouldn't have been so hard on Delilah."

North doesn't say anything. It's gone so quiet that I wonder if he's left the room. But when I lift my head, I find him looking back with a thoughtful expression.

"What?"

He shakes out of whatever fog he was in. "I was just thinking how alike you two were. In the most basic ways, that is. I still like Delilah better."

"As you should."

He stands, stretching out a kink in his back. "You've been given a gift, Macon. Sometimes that's all you need to know."

He heads for the door.

"North?"

He stops and turns back my way.

"Lisa Brown? Did she have any family? Maybe I should . . . I don't know. Should I offer condolences?"

The faint lines around North's eyes deepen as he looks at me. "No family."

"Then it's truly over." I think of Lisa Brown. A woman who, for whatever reason, fixated on me as her one chance of happiness. She died alone in the world. I used to relish my solitude.

I don't want to be alone anymore.

Delilah

I can't sleep. Macon is out there, hurting and upset, and I'm tucked up in a bed. The wrongness of that scrapes against my skin, and I fling the covers back. I can't stay here another second. I get dressed in the dark and grab my purse and keys. But when I wrench the kitchen door open to leave, I come face to face with the last person I expected to see: Sam.

Neither of us says a word as Sam and I retreat into the kitchen. I pour myself a glass of water and take a huge gulp that burns its way down my throat. As much as I want to go to Macon right now, there are things I need to say to my sister.

"That fucking *joke* with the tater tots. Why would you do that to me? You had *everything*: beauty, popularity, a boyfriend. I had none of those things. All I asked for of prom was to have fun. And you took that away from me."

Clearly she wasn't expecting that word vomit, and it takes her a moment to react. She has the grace to duck her head. "I don't know."

"Oh, bullshit. You have a good reason for everything. Because everything in life is a game, right?"

"Because I was jealous!"

The shout hits me like a slap. I gape at her. "Of what? Being a loner? Getting teased by the entire school? Of being plump and plain and overlooked? Which one of those things did you covet, Sam?"

Sam wipes at her eyes. "You think you were plain? You were pretty."

"Oh, for the love of . . . compared to you, I was average at best. Something you made certain to remind me of at every turn."

Sam frowns but then laughs as if I'm deluded. "And yet he never looked at me the way he looked at you. He never talked to me as though he truly wanted to know what I was thinking. He gave you a nickname, not me."

"Macon?" I can't believe this. "He hated me. He was dating *you*."

"He was wasting time with me." Her lips pinch sourly. "And there's a fine line between love and hate. At best I got apathy. You got his attention. God, no one even calls him Macon but you."

Her jealousy is so foreign to me that I can only gape. It takes effort to find my voice. "So this was all about Macon?"

Sam shrugs and hugs her arms to her chest. "No. Not all of it."

"Then what?"

"You were their favorite," she whispers. "Mama and Daddy. They were always so proud of you." Her voice takes on Mama's tone. "Our Delilah got straight As again. Did you taste Delilah's casserole; I declare it's the best in five counties. Delilah is such a special child."

I'm poleaxed. Unable to breathe for a long moment. "They had to say all that. Because I was fucking miserable, and they knew it!"

Her silvery-blue eyes, so like my mother's, flash in outrage. "They said it because they meant it, Dee. You can't be that clueless. They loved you best."

"I wasn't even their child!" My shout comes out of nowhere, hurting my chest, my throat.

"What?" Sam asks, bewildered. "What are you talking about?"

"I'm adopted." It's a ridiculous thing to say, given that she knows this.

Sam swallows hard, then takes a hesitant step closer. Her voice softens. "Do you honestly think they loved you less?"

"Not anymore." My conversation with Mama eased the last strands of those worries. "But back then? It was always on my mind. Oddball Delilah, sticking out like a sore thumb amid the rest of you."

Sam shakes her head. "Hell, Dee. They *picked* you. I was an unexpected arrival; they *had* to love me."

My laugh is unhinged. "I can't believe this. All this time you were jealous of our parents' love for me, and I was jealous of the same?"

In our mother's cheery kitchen, Sam and I stare at each other, and then she starts to snicker. "I guess we were."

We both laugh; it isn't really in amusement. I'm too battered, but it feels good to let it go. Sam finishes with a shaking breath and then sobers. Tentatively, she reaches out, and I accept her hug. She smells of Chanel and cigarettes that I know she still smokes on the sly. "I'm sorry, Dee. So sorry."

"You hurt me." I *still* hurt.

"I'm sorry," she says again. I know she means it. But it doesn't feel like enough.

"And you let Macon take the fall."

Her nose wrinkles. Red faced and teary eyed, she's still beautiful. Still guarded. "He insisted. The night he dumped me, he said he'd do that for me because of all we'd been through together, but he was done with the Baker sisters."

It wasn't exactly what Macon said to me. In Sam's version, Macon was protecting her, not me. This again. The same old manipulations and twisted truths. I pull out of her embrace. "You should have told me."

"I know." Sam worries her bottom lip.

"What's done is done."

She brightens at that. "And hey, I returned and brought the watch back as promised."

Does she want a cookie for doing the right thing? Inside, I grow a bit more numb. She's my sister. But the person she's become is the absolute worst version of her.

She won't meet my eyes. "It was stupid taking the watch. No one would touch it . . ." She trails off with a strangled sound, realizing what she's said.

I stare at her, disappointment so keen that I can't seem to move. She tried to sell the watch. "What's going on with you, Sam? Why did you need that much money?"

The gentle sweep of her jaw lifts. "I just did."

"Three hundred thousand worth? Why?"

When she finally turns my way, her eyes are hard. "I have a bit of a gambling addiction. Sometimes I run low on funds."

She could have knocked me over with a feather. Sam smirks. "You should see your face, Dee. So shocked."

"This isn't funny."

"No," she snaps. "It's not. At any rate, I had a good run and no longer need money."

A good run? My sister is a gambler, and I never noticed. What the hell has she gotten herself into? "Sammy . . ."

"It's my business, so don't go getting all Saint Delilah and try to fix it."

My impulse is to snap back, tell her off. But I'm suddenly weary. I don't want to fight her. I just want to get on with my life in peace. "Don't worry, Sam. I learned my lesson. You fight your own battles now. I'm officially done."

The clock on the wall ticks loud and clear as she stares at me. Some emotion passes over her face—regret or worry, I can't tell—then she pulls in a breath and straightens her shoulders. "I've learned my lesson too. No more stealing for me."

She says it like a joke that I'm expected to laugh at. I can't. It worries me that she's being so glib about her problem. It worries me that despite her claims of this good run, she might still owe someone an ungodly amount of cash. How did she pay it off without using Macon's watch? But I hold my tongue. If I'm going to stick to my word and stay out of her business, I have to start now.

"Delilah," Sam begins after a moment. "This thing with Saint—tell me it isn't serious."

I move to the end of the counter and wipe away a water ring. "I know he was your boyfriend during school. And I wouldn't have gone there with him if it wasn't . . ." I take a deep breath and face her. "Yes, this is serious. I care about him."

Pity fills her eyes. "Oh, Dee, you should know better. Saint isn't capable of love."

"That's not true . . ."

"Did he tell you he loves you?" Her tone implies she already knows he didn't.

I adore you. Every. Damn. Inch.

"We haven't said those words yet . . ."

"And he never will." She walks toward me, that damn pity all over her damn face. "Because he is playing you for a fool. I know you don't believe me, but he did watch you all those years ago. Saint would have loved to get into your pants, if only to have the experience of catching you."

"Why are you like this?" I rasp. "Why are you so hateful to anything good that comes into my life? This goes beyond jealousy. It's cruel."

Sam halts. "I'm trying to help you."

"This isn't help. This is an attempt to tear into my insecurities."

"Dee," she intones as if I'm a child. "If you have those fears, you have to ask yourself why."

"I'm not listening to this anymore."

Sam snags my wrist, and her tears are back. "He used me. For years he used me because he was bored. He'll use you, too, because you're safe and familiar."

She knows me so well. Knows all the soft spots and ways to place a direct hit. She always has. I want to laugh until I howl. Bile fills my mouth. I swallow it back down, and it burns.

Sam stands there, smug but trying her best to look sad. "Think what you want. But ask yourself if you're really willing to risk our relationship on someone as emotionally empty as Macon Saint. The boy who made your life a misery."

When I don't answer, Sam shrugs and turns to grab a glass from the cabinet as if she hasn't just tried to cut my legs out from under me. While she hums and pours herself a glass of white wine from the fridge, I think about Macon. Every word he said. Every word I said. The way he touched me. The tenderness and need in his eyes when he looked at me. The way he laughed with me, held my hand, told me about his pain. The letters he wrote.

He lied. Sam lied. I lied.

Everyone lies sometimes.

Sam keeps humming. A stupid tune.

369

I gather my keys in hand. "Samantha?"

She raises an expectant brow.

"I love you very much."

"I love you too, Dee. I'm glad we got that settled—"

"I love you," I cut in. "But you've been a crap sister. Call me when you decide to grow the fuck up."

I leave her and her ranting protests behind.

———

Macon

She's gone. I pushed her away, and she left. I tell myself she'll come back eventually. It's not as though I'm just going to let her go without any further discussion. I'm not giving up. But I can't control the outcome of everything. Which means I could lose her.

Did I truly have her? Here in the dark, it all feels like a strange dream. Maybe I imagined the whole thing. Maybe I'm still trapped in that wreckage of a car.

"Hell," I say, disgusted at my own drama. I've been reading too many scripts. Rolling onto my side, I try to get comfortable. The sooner I sleep, the sooner I can wake up and see her.

The sound of the front door opening has me sitting up so fast my head spins. The house is too damn big to hear anything. It could be Delilah. Then again, it might not be. I ease out of bed, grab my discarded cane as a weapon, and move toward the bedroom door.

I hear the familiar sound of her footsteps a second before she enters the room. She sees me just as I'm lowering the cane, and she screeches.

"Jesus," she shouts, holding her chest. "You scared the hell out of me."

Heart pounding with released adrenaline, I slump against the wall. "I'm not the one creeping into bedrooms at two in the morning."

Her shadowed face is a picture of indignant outrage. "I'm not creeping; I live here!"

Those words crack the tension that's held my body prisoner for the past few hours.

"You're back," I say. *Don't leave me again. Don't leave.*

Delilah relaxes too. She's barefoot and still wearing the jeans and pink T-shirt she left in. It's too dark to see her properly, but she seems . . . not happy but calm.

"I'm back." There's hesitation in her tone as though she's unsure if she should be here. The fact that she doesn't know is a tragedy. "Is that okay?"

"Okay?" I blow out a breath. "We were in a fight, Delilah. It's going to happen now and then."

A slow smile blooms. "Probably a lot."

I smile too. It feels fragile but good. "Hopefully not too much."

Her teeth snag on her lower lip, and she bites down, eyeing me from under her thick lashes. "But then we can make up?"

God, I want to make up. And then make up some more. Spend the entire week making up.

"Come to bed?" I'm this close to begging.

Delilah walks to the bed, slipping into a band of moonlight that slants through the bank of bedroom windows. But she sits instead of crawling under the covers. "I should have waited until morning and let you sleep."

Fat chance of that.

"But I wanted to talk to you," she goes on.

I don't like the way she's holding herself so stiffly. My guard comes up, and the tension in my neck returns. I sit beside her on the bed. "Delilah, you can say anything to me."

Her teeth snag her lower lip. "I talked things out with Sam."

I'm not sure where she's going with this, but the sadness in her eyes hurts to witness. "You don't sound happy about it."

She makes a face. "Nothing is ever easy when it comes to Sam."

Truer words.

"You all right?" I ask.

"I will be." Which means she isn't now. I can't hold back from taking her hands and holding them between mine.

She threads her fingers through mine. "I'm so sorry I didn't tell you about the call."

"It's okay. I understand why you didn't." Now that I've calmed down and faced a few dark, lonely hours without her, I understand a lot of things.

Her gaze searches my face with a tenderness that I feel along my skin. "But most of all, I'm sorry I didn't tell you exactly why I was feeling vulnerable. I may get things wrong when it comes to you, Macon, but I trust you more than anyone. No one sees me the way you do. It's a gift I never saw coming, but I treasure it with my whole heart."

"Oh, hell, Delilah . . ." I reach for her, gently squeezing the nape of her neck. But she doesn't let me draw her in.

Her hand lands on my chest, not pushing me away but resting there like she needs to feel me as much as I need to feel her. "Let me say this."

When I nod, she seems to steel herself. "I've realized a few things. First, my sister is an asshole."

I choke on a laugh, shocked as hell.

But Delilah doesn't notice; her lips purse in disapproval. "I don't know why she is how she is. We essentially had identical upbringings. And yet she ended up selfish and petty. She finds a person's weakness and exploits it. That she did it to me for so long hurts, and yet I feel sorry for her because she could be so much more—even if I want to punch her in the tit for all that she's done. Despite all that, I still love her. I can't help it. I do, and I always will."

"She's your sister. Of course you will." My thumb sweeps across her cheek. "I'm sorry I tried to make you feel guilty about helping her. I was jealous, and I shouldn't be—"

Delilah touches my chin, instantly making me quiet. "I'm not finished." She takes an unsteady breath. "I realized that when my mother said she would always hold out hope for Sam, it was out of love, not because she had blinders on. I can't protect my mama against Sam's antics because she's always seen them clearly. She simply loves her anyway."

"She sees the good in everyone. I always admired her for that."

Delilah hums in vague agreement. Then she fidgets, smoothing a wrinkle in the covers, tucking a lock of her hair back, looking everywhere but at me. "That brings me to my last point."

"All right," I say because she falls silent.

She blows out a hard breath as if bracing herself. "If Sam had it her way, you and I would be back to square one. I'd hate you forever, and we'd part as enemies. She actually begged me to leave you. She implied our relationship would drive a wedge between her and me that would never heal."

I want to protest. Rant a little myself. But that won't get me anywhere. Even so, my chest is tight and pained as Delilah continues. "She might be right about that wedge."

No, no, no. She can't.

"While she ranted and cried, I stood there and thought about never seeing you again . . ."

"Delilah . . ."

"The utter futility of that . . ." She shakes her head in distraction. "As if I could turn away from you and it not feel like the loss of a limb. It was that moment when I realized, without doubt, that I loved you."

"I . . ." My breath leaves in a whoosh when her words truly hit me. "What?"

Her smile is gentle, shy even. "I love you, Macon Saint. So much."

Lips numb, I stare at her, unable to say a word, much less think. A loud thud is pounding hard and fast, and I realize it's my heart.

"Macon?" Delilah starts to frown, raising her hand to touch my bloodless cheek. I'm cold, I know. Then my breath releases, and heat rushes along my tingling limbs.

"No one has ever said that to me. No one." Not my mother—certainly not my shit father. Not a single person. I've never heard those words directed at me. Until now.

Until her.

Delilah.

Delilah loves me.

Shaking, I tug her close, awkward and bumbling as I crush her against my chest and hold on tight, my nose buried in her hair. "I love you too. I love you too."

With a sigh, she rests against me, her cheek pressed to my heart. "It's been a long road getting here."

"We were always on it, Delilah." I ease my grip, let my hands smooth down the curve of her back. I press my lips to her temple, rest them there, and breathe her in. "Loving you was inevitable. You got under my skin at age eleven and never left."

Smiling, she pulls back enough to look up at me. God, it's all there in her eyes. She really does love me. As if she knows that I can't get over that truth, she cups the back of my neck with warm, kneading fingers. "I'm going to love you, Macon Saint. So long and so hard you're not going to remember what it feels like to be without love."

And that's when it finally happens. The prickling heat building behind my lids turns to a blur and slips over. I don't hide it. It's a relief. "I don't know a lot about love other than what I feel for you. I might make mistakes, but I know this much—you are utterly precious to me. I'll honor you every damn day of my life, if you let me."

I frame her face with my hands as the words come out thick, unsteady, but directly from my heart. "And what's between us, Delilah? It's forever."

EPILOGUE

Delilah

"Look what my mother found in the attic." I hold aloft the battered red leather book in question as Macon enters the trailer dressed in full Arasmus gear.

Good Lord, but the man is sex in leather wearing those clothes. How I did not appreciate the glory that was the Warrior King up until now, I'll never know.

He sets down his ax and is about to unbuckle the leather baldric that holds his sword when his gaze clashes with mine. A slow, sweet smile spreads over his dirt-smudged face. "Stop giving me those sexy eyes, Ms. Delilah."

I recognize that order. I gave it to him once before. Licking my lower lip, I continue to look him over. "Sexy eyes?"

Macon slowly stalks forward, grinning with intent. "Yes, sexy eyes. Making eyes at me like you . . ."

"Want to stick my head between your thighs and slowly suck you until we both come?" I offer.

With a low growl that goes straight to all my happy places, he scoops me up and brings us both back down onto the small couch, this time with me straddling his lap. "Nice trick," I murmur.

He brushes the hair back from my face and kisses me deep and long. "Mmm . . . you taste like honey." His tongue slides over mine in a languid glide. "Speaking of tricks, you were saying something about sucking."

I'm already unlacing his leather pants. He slides free, hot and heavy. All hail the king.

Two orgasms later, we're slumped in a sweaty tangle, and Macon toys with the ends of my fluffed-up hair. From outside comes the occasional shouts or calls from various crew members, but in our trailer it's cozy and quiet.

When Macon had to go back to work, he encouraged me to go on my trip through Asia, that he'd always be there, waiting for me. I was ready to go, but somehow, I found myself on a plane to Iceland, where Macon is filming this season of *Dark Castle*. I no longer wanted to take a trip of a lifetime if he wasn't there to share it with me. So we're going in the fall.

The restaurant, which we're calling Black Delilah, is in the process of being renovated. I Skype with Ronan daily, and we hope to open the following year.

Beneath me, Macon shifts a bit to get more comfortable. But he doesn't let me go. "Did you say something about a book?"

My laugh is weak and lazy. "When you distracted me with your sexy pecs? Yes."

He snorts.

Slowly, I ease off him and pick up the book that ended up on the floor. "It's my childhood diary."

Macon's dark brow quirks high. "Do I want to know?"

Grinning, I crawl back onto his lap and rest my head on his big shoulder. "It's probably just as you suspect. But I read through it now, and all I feel is a happy fondness. Here, take a look."

"You sure?" He's eyeing the diary like it might bite.

"Baby, there is nothing between us now but love. Besides, I added to it, and everything is as it should be."

———

Delilah's Diary

Dear Diary (age 11),
I still do not have a dog. Mama claims I am allergic, and Daddy won't listen to reason. It's a conspirisy conpr It's a sham!
In other news, today I called Macon Saint an ass canal, the most vile and disgusting thing I could think of. I am sorry to say, Mama agreed. Had I known she was behind me, I would have waited until later to call Macon that.
Now my fingers are pruny and smelly because I spent the day polishing all the silver—including old Grandma Belle's holiday service ware. The only justice is that Macon had to polish it too because Mama heard him call me a fuck-munch.
But it's still not fair because Sam—who started the whole thing by blabbing to Macon that Mama's oyster soup gave me diarit diarrhea—got away free as a bird. SHE had a clear view of the den's doorway and shut her big mouth as soon as she saw Mama coming.
I don't know who I hate worse, Sam or Macon.
Sam.
Macon.
Both.
No, definitely Macon.

———

Dear Diary,
Today was the day I planned to enter my first pie in the summer church bake off. I've been waiting forever to be thirteen—the official minimum age for entrants. Mama convinced me to wear the sky-blue eyelet sundress that has been hanging in my closet since spring, and I had to admit that it looked quite pretty on me.

I soon came to regret my decision. Upon seeing me, Macon Saint, shithead and ass face, asked (in a loud voice) if I was smuggling baby bananas under my top. Right in front of Jonas Hardy—Macon knew I had a crush on him. Stupid Sam tells him everything.

Jonas laughed, and Macon started calling me Banana Boobs. And I . . . I got so mad that I threw my beloved Bountiful Banana Cream Pie (oh, why did it have to be banana *cream???) at Macon's fat face. Only the rat turd ducked, and my beautiful pie hit mean old Mrs. Lynch square in the face.*

The humiliation! I am now grounded for the remainder of the summer and banned from entering any pies in any of the church bake offs.

I hate Macon Saint. Hate. Him*!!!*

———

Dear Diary,
Last night, I kissed a boy. First kiss. It was nice. Until it wasn't. All and all, I am greatly disappointed.

I only went to Geoff Martin's birthday party because Mama said it would be rude to ignore the invitation. I didn't feel like telling her that I'd likely been invited because Geoff was desperate for Sam to show up.

As suspected, the party was horrible. We had to play a stupid game called The Shed. Basically, everyone took a numbered paper and, when your number came up, you'd go in the dark garden shed and kiss the person who had the matching number. The idea being you never knew who you kissed until the end of the night when you held up your number and found out who had the same one.

I wanted to throw up. Run. I don't know. Sam called me a chicken, so I stayed.

I never saw the boy's face. All I know is that his breath smelled like peppermint, and his lips were soft and sweet. I was so shocked by the contact, and the way it made my insides warmly flip, that I ran out of the shed as if it were on fire. Like a chicken. And that was that. Surprising, but ultimately a letdown of my own making.

It was no surprise to me, however, when Macon and Sam both revealed they had the number six. Macon has shot up several inches and has become the most sighed over boy in school. Yuck. Every girl except me had wanted to draw his number. I don't know how she did it, but I know Sam cheated to get that number. She was Miss Smug Socks the entire night.

My night got worse. We were about to leave when I found out I kissed Xander Dubois, one of Macon's friends, who winked at me and said I could feel free to slip him the tongue any time I'd like as long as he got to feel my boobs in return. Gross. I went home disappointed, and Sam ended the night as Macon's girlfriend. Lord help us all.

I hate kissing.

Dear Diary, (age 16)
There are far better words than hate. Loathe is one.
Loathing. I love how it rolls off the tongue . . . lah-oo-
thing. Or detest. So nice and crisp. "I detest him." Abhor?
No, that's too light. You can't really get a good sneer with
"abhor." Although it does have a certain snobby quality
about it. "I simply abhor him, dahling."
    I'm hiding out in my room because Macon Saint is
here. He arrived shortly after the school baseball game—a
game he lost when he failed to catch a high ball, result-
ing in Greenfield High taking the lead. Not that I said
anything; I am a lady, after all. Although I <u>may</u> have
complimented the athletic prowess of the Greenfield team.
Sam called me a turncoat—she has to show school loyalty,
she's a cheerleader.
    Anyway, he has been hanging around like a bad
smell ever since. I'd asked if he planned to pay rent here
any time soon, earning a reprimand from Mama, while
Macon got cookies and the best seat in the family room.
Bah. He played it up something good, ever so subtly winc-
ing when he walked back into the kitchen to put his plate
in the dishwasher.
    Mama instantly began to fuss, asking if he'd hurt
himself during the game. Macon laughed it off, insisting
that he was fine and just a little tight from stretching too
much. Oh, but he's a good actor, letting us see just the
tiniest bit of pain in his eyes, letting Mama think he's
trying to hide that wince. Worked like a charm. Now he's
invited to dinner.
    I hate loathe when Macon has dinner with us. The
rat always makes faces at me that no one else ever catches.
Either that, or he's kicking me under the table, or trying

*to squish my toes with his big, stupid foot. Tonight, I'm
going to wear my steel-toed boots that Mama hates and
get him good.*
    —Delilah Ann

———

Dear Diary,
*They say there's a fine line between love and hate. I don't
know if that's true for every situation, but for me? Well,
you be the judge. Because I love Macon Saint. So many
words I have for Macon: love, lust, tenderness, joy, hope,
and love. Always love. Somewhere along the way, he and
I became part of each other. All we needed was to flip the
switch. Are you surprised? Given that this entire book was
dedicated to all things Macon, somehow I doubt anyone
would be. It was always about Macon. And it always
will be.*

———

Delilah's Dinner Menu

- Gin blackberry bramble and peanut brittle spheres
- Oysters topped with watermelon-and-habanero *brunoise*
- Baby cream biscuits and smoked peach butter
- Buttermilk *panna cotta* with spot prawns and spring vegetables
- Cod with potato galette and shellfish emulsion and stone fruit
- Banana cream pie with bitter chocolate

ACKNOWLEDGMENTS

Many thanks to my delightful agent, Kimberly Brower; to the wonderful and hardworking team at Montlake publishing; and a special thank-you to my editor, Lauren Plude. I'm so glad we finally got to work together again. You are a joy.

ABOUT THE AUTHOR

Kristen Callihan is an author because there's nothing else she'd rather be. She is a *New York Times*, *Wall Street Journal*, and *USA Today* bestseller. Her novels have garnered starred reviews from *Publishers Weekly* and *Library Journal*. Her debut book, *Firelight*, received *RT* magazine's Seal of Excellence and was named a best book of the year by *Library Journal*, best book of spring 2012 by *Publishers Weekly*, and best romance book of 2012 by ALA RUSA. When she's not writing, she's reading.